'I'm sorry, but I can't do it, sir.'

'Why not?'

'I told you. My family needs me.'

'What your family needs is good food. They can have that if you come with us. And a better cottage, too.'

Tears filled her eyes. 'But I don't want to leave them. I don't. I'm sorry, sir, but I won't change my mind about that.'

She turned to walk on, but he grasped her arm and pulled her back to stand in front of him. 'A moment if you please. What you want isn't the only thing that matters, Keara. I want my wife to be happy, and you keep her happier than anyone else has been able to. Your mother wants to put food on the table for your sisters every day, to see them growing sturdy and strong. Am I not right?'

She stared at him, unable to frame a word, feeling the strength in the hand that held her. She'd thought him a kind man, but now, seeing the power behind the friendliness, she shivered suddenly.

About Anna Jacobs

Anna Jacobs grew up in Lancashire and emigrated to Australia in 1973, but loves to return to England regularly to visit her family and soak up the history. She has two grown-up daughters and now lives with her husband in a spacious waterfront home. Often as she writes, dolphins frolic outside the window of her study. Inside, the house is crammed with thousands of books.

ANNA JACOBS

A Pennyworth of Sunshine

CORONET BOOKS
Hodder & Stoughton

First published in Great Britain in 2003 by Hodder and Stoughton
A division of Hodder Headline

A Coronet paperback

10

A CIP catalogue record for this title is available from the British Library

ISBN 978 0 340 82136 7

Typeset in Plantin Light by
Phoenix Typesetting, Burley-in-Wharfedale, West Yorkshire

Printed and bound in Great Britain by
CPI Group (UK) Ltd, Croydon, CR0 4YY

Hodder and Stoughton
A division of Hodder Headline
338 Euston Road
London NW1 3BH

With fondest wishes and lots of happy memories to Anne and David Drysdale who have known me since grammar school. (Thank goodness we don't have to wear that uniform ever again!)

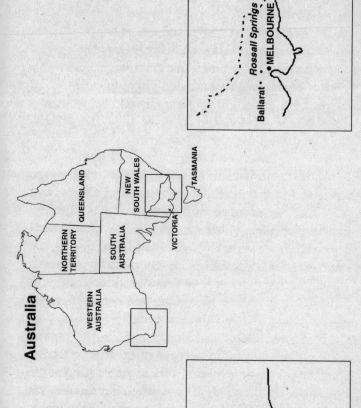

Australia

QUEENSLAND

NORTHERN TERRITORY

WESTERN AUSTRALIA

SOUTH AUSTRALIA

NEW SOUTH WALES

VICTORIA

TASMANIA

Ballarat •
Rossall Springs •
• MELBOURNE

Map by Sas Jacobs

PERTH •
Merinup •
Bunbury •

Towns in Italics are Imaginary

CHAPTER ONE

March 1859

━━━━━◆◆◆━━━━━

Keara Michaels hauled the heavy bucket up from the well and set it on the rim for a moment. Panting from the effort, she scooped up a few mouthfuls of water, then dipped a fold of her skirt into the bucket and used it to wipe her sweaty face. She had been digging last year's potatoes out of their rapidly dwindling mound, which was heavy work for a scrawny, underfed girl of sixteen, but they were all hungry and her mother was too far gone with the baby now to dig.

Her father should be helping more, but he'd gone off to visit his cousins in the next village from where he could just as easily get to his work as stable hand at the big house. He always went away when her mother was near her time and Keara was old enough now to resent this. He'd be back once the baby was born, though, choosing the name and strutting around as if he'd carried the child in his own belly, especially if this one turned out to be the boy he was praying for.

Keara had no illusions about her father, no illusions about anything very much, but she did have a few dreams still: a full stomach, a proper cottage with paved floors, not beaten dirt, and a separate bedroom for the children to sleep in, where they wouldn't hear their parents carrying on. She looked down at her skirt with its tears and ragged hemline and added another small dream: decent clothes to wear.

Father Cornelius said she was being greedy to dream like that and should accept her lowly station in life as the Lord's will. But she couldn't. And she never would! Some folk had so much while she and her family had so little. It just wasn't fair!

She'd like to leave home and get a job, because there was no real work for her in Ballymullan, but her mother wouldn't be able to manage without her. Besides, many people from the nearby villages had gone away to work and had never come back again. Imagine never seeing her sisters Mara and Ismay again! The mere thought of that made Keara shiver. So she got day work here and there, whatever she could – weeding in the fields, helping with the harvest, lending a hand when someone had a new baby, and lately helping with the washing and scrubbing up at the big house.

And when she did earn a few pennies she spent them quickly on food for herself and her mother and sisters, because if she didn't her father would take them from her and spend them on booze. She made it plain whenever she accepted a job that she wasn't going to do it unless the money was paid to her and not her father.

It was one of the many reasons he hated her.

Mara came round the corner just then, hugging the

rag doll their mother had made her and smiling when she saw her sister. She was small for seven, much smaller than Keara or Ismay. Was it any wonder? She'd never eaten well in her whole life, for all Keara's efforts to bring home more food.

Suddenly a scream rang out from the cottage and Keara jerked in shock, nearly knocking the wooden bucket back into the well. Her mother only screamed like that when she was having a baby. The rest of the time her mother was so quiet you'd hardly know she was there.

Not yet! Keara prayed. *Please, God, not yet. I'll be good. I'll say a hundred Hail Marys, but don't let the baby come yet.* She'd wanted to clean up the cottage before her next brother or sister was born and get the wrapping cloths washed and aired on the line. 'Go and find Ismay! Quick!' she told Mara and when the child ran off, picked up the bucket. Heedless of how the water sloshed and splashed over her bare, muddy feet, Keara began to lug it towards the house.

Inside she found her mother doubled up on the straw mattress in the corner, hands clutching the belly that jutted out so far from her thin body, face twisted into a mask of pain.

'Is it coming now, Mam?' Keara dumped the bucket hastily near the door.

Her mother nodded without opening her eyes. 'Aye, it is that. An' just as quickly as they allus do, thank God. Fetch Mrs Raney, will you, love?' She groaned and rolled into a tight ball.

Ismay came rushing into the cottage. 'Is it—?'

'Go and fetch the midwife,' Keara said. 'And take Mara with you. I'll stay with Mam.'

Ismay nodded and left quickly. At eleven she was old enough to help protect their little sister from the worst a life like theirs had to offer, their father's kicks and blows and their mother's painful childbirths. Two babies had been born dead since Mara, poor white little things that had come early. Her father had buried them at night in a corner of the churchyard. Her mother had wept for days. There had been a brother after Keara, too, but he'd died just after his first birthday, and another sister after Ismay, but she'd only lived a few short weeks.

Her mother groaned. 'Eh, I'll be glad to be shut of this one. I've 'ad such a belly-warch for t'past few days.'

Keara had seen her rubbing her swollen stomach several times lately and muttering to herself. The pains must be really bad because her mam only spoke with such a strong Lancashire accent when she was upset. The rest of the time Betsy spoke softly, trying to imitate the way the villagers talked, doing her best to fit in as she had for all the years since Mick Michaels had brought his pregnant young wife back with him to this small Irish village. The folk of Ballymullan were kind enough to her, but she wasn't one of them.

'Hold on to my hand, Mam,' Keara urged, but Betsy was beyond hearing, grunting with the pain as she started to bear down. The baby would soon be born, the girl guessed. She only hoped Mrs Raney would come quickly.

When she heard footsteps, she groaned in relief, but

looked up to see only Ismay standing in the doorway.

'Mrs Raney's out at her daughter's. They'll send her when she gets back.' She hesitated. 'Will I stay and help?'

'No, you're too young.' Keara knew her mother didn't want the younger girls seeing her like this. She didn't want any of them there, but there was no help for it this time. 'Best if you take Mara away till it's over.'

She went to stand for a minute by the door, watching her sisters trail off down the lane, with Ismay holding Mara by the hand and Mara still dangling the rag doll from the other. It was like looking at younger versions of herself. Everyone commented on how alike the three of them were, with their father's dark, curly hair and the Michaels eyes. Oh, you could never mistake those eyes, folk said, such a bright blue and framed in long, dark lashes.

With a sigh Keara went back inside and began to get the cloths out.

Betsy looked up between pains. 'Will Mrs Raney – be long?'

'She's out, Mam. They'll send her over as soon as she gets back.'

'Nooo! The baby's coming now.'

The last one had come fast, as well as early, but it had been born dead. Keara had cradled its limp little blue-white body in her hands and wept over it.

She knelt by the mattress. 'I was with you last time, Mam, so I know what to do.'

'Eh, lass, you're too young for all this.'

Keara forced a smile. 'I'm all you've got, so.'

For the next few minutes, Betsy alternately screamed and groaned, then was delivered suddenly of the baby. She lay back panting. 'What is it?'

'A girl.' Working efficiently, remembering what Mrs Raney had done last time, Keara knelt to pick up the baby and smack her sharply on the backside.

'Is she all right? I can't hear her crying.'

'She's not breathing, Mam.'

'Smack her again.'

'She's – not made right, Mam.'

'Show me.' Betsy stared at the still little body with its over-large head, touched the face gently with one hand, then closed her eyes wearily. 'Tie off the birth cord, then wrap the poor thing up.'

When Mrs Raney came hurrying down the lane, she praised what Keara had done and set about tidying the mother up, frowning at how weak poor Betsy still was. 'You shouldn't let him use you any more,' she whispered. 'You can't go on like this.'

'How can I stop him?' Betsy asked, tears welling anew in her eyes.

'I'd kick him where it hurts if it were me,' Mrs Raney said bluntly. But she knew even as she spoke that Betsy Michaels would never be able to prevent her husband doing what he wanted because she was a gentle soul. As for Mick, he might be a fine figure of a man, but handsome is as handsome does, Mrs Raney always thought, and he was a selfish devil, as well as unkind and a bad provider.

She caught him on his way home later that day and

told him to his face that if he didn't leave his wife alone, he'd be raising his children without Betsy's help.

'What would you be knowin' about such things?' he sneered. 'You're not a doctor.'

'I had the divvil's job stopping the bleeding today. Have ye seen how pale she is?'

He walked on without a word and would have ignored her warning completely had a widow from Dublin not come to live in the next village the following week, a woman past childbearing who missed having a man in her bed and made it plain how attracted she was to Mick.

The next day Diarmid O'Neal, the estate manager, sent down five shillings from Mr Mullane to help with the expenses. Since he had married his new, rich wife the landowner had started this custom and the villagers blessed him for it.

'It's little enough,' Theo Mullane had told Diarmid. 'Half a guinea for a live child, five shillings for a dead one.'

'It's a big help for them, though your father must be turning in his grave.' Old Mr Mullane had been tight-fisted where his tenants were concerned, but had spent lavishly on himself, wasting the family fortunes so that his son had had to marry an heiress.

Theo lived in Lancashire most of the time now, because his wife Lavinia didn't like Ireland, but he came over regularly to visit Ballymullan, occasionally bringing her with him.

No one liked the landowner's wife who was plump and well-fed and even so always looked miserable. How you could be miserable with a full belly, a fine house and beautiful clothes, they didn't understand.

Keara kept watch for the money, intercepting the lad bringing the five shillings then hiding it quickly before her da got back from work.

Not even a sound thrashing could persuade her to hand it over to him because she knew exactly what he'd do with it: go down to Benny Noonan's shebeen, which was an open secret in the village, and treat his friends to as many drinks as the money would buy. Lords of Poteen, Mrs Raney called them with a sniff of disgust.

'Give that money to your da, love,' Betsy whispered from her bed as the beating continued.

But Keara would tell him nothing, just continued to wail loudly every time her da hit her since that usually made him stop more quickly.

'Ye're an ungrateful little bitch,' he said at last, shoving her across the room. 'That's what happens when a man's wife only gives him daughters.' He ate half the potatoes Keara had cooked then went out to drown his sorrows with his friends.

Only then did Ismay bring Mara back inside. 'Did he leave anything for us?'

'He ate half of them, the greedy pig.'

The two sisters looked at each other in dismay, then down at the bowl of boiled potatoes. Keara carefully divided up what was left and took one plate across to her mother.

Betsy pushed it aside. 'You have them, love. I'm not hungry.'

'You need to eat, Mam, or you won't get better. If you don't eat yours, I won't eat mine.'

When they'd finished their meagre meal, the three girls went to bed, cuddling up under the ragged blankets as Keara told them a story. After Ismay and Mara fell asleep, she lay awake for a time, hunger cramping in her stomach, wishing she could find proper work, wishing her father would look after his family better.

He didn't come back that night. She heard her mother weeping quietly, but didn't say anything. Her mother only wept when she thought no one else would see or hear her.

Keara only wept, or pretended to weep, when her father slapped her, because weeping didn't get you anywhere.

Mick Michaels returned home for his breakfast, raging at them when there was nothing to eat. He slapped out at Keara as he passed her. 'I'll be having that money out of you tonight,' he snapped, then slammed out of the cottage.

Only when he was safely at work did Keara go to the top end of their potato field and dig up the coins. She hurried to the village store and consulted the shopkeeper Arla Lynch about how best to use the windfall. After much serious discussion they decided on a loaf and some cheese, half of which Keara would come back for the next day, because Da was very partial to cheese and was inclined to eat the lot if he found any.

With the money that was left Keara bought some flour, because they could use it to eke out the potatoes. Since her father neglected their small field, it never produced quite enough for the family's needs. The girl's mouth watered at the mere thought of potato cakes made with part flour, part mashed potato, then cooked till crispy on the griddle. They'd be best eaten hot with butter, but the Michaels family didn't see much butter. They'd had it occasionally, though, and Keara could think of nothing nicer.

'That one has a wise head on her shoulders,' Mrs Lynch said to the next customer.

'She'll be needin' it in that family,' the other woman said sourly. 'Mick only gets wilder as he gets older and that poor little wife of his has never been able to manage him. Have you heard about that widow giving him the glad eye?'

'Sure, who hasn't? And did you see the bruises on that girl's face and arms today?'

'I did, I did. He's hitting *her* now as well as the mother.'

They both shook their heads and made tutting noises, but Arla could not get the memory of the child's gaunt face out of her mind. Keara was so thin she reminded Arla of her own daughter, Shealagh, who had died in the great potato famine, oh, it must be ten years ago now. Shealagh had caught the fever and simply faded away. Since that dreadful time, Arla had regularly adopted a village girl as her protégée. She and her husband didn't have much to spare, the good Lord knew, for it was a tiny village and the shop didn't bring in a lot of money, though they did all right with their smallholding because Brian was a hard worker, unlike some. But they could spare enough to help one child at a time in memory of Shealagh.

The priest said it was a blessed act and certainly the doing of it helped ease the maternal ache in Arla's heart as nothing else could, for the famine years had stopped her monthly courses so that she'd never been able to have another child.

The last girl she'd been helping had left the village only the week before to take up a position in service, her body stronger for the good food Arla had given her, able to read and write properly, too. The priest taught the village children their letters in his little afternoon school, but no one did very well because they were more often needed to help out at home, so Brian always had to help their chosen girls improve their skills.

With a nod for a decision taken, Arla went to inform her husband.

'Isn't Keara a bit old?'

'You're never too old to learn.'

'Will we go and tell her tonight, then?' he asked indulgently.

'I'll have a bit of a chat with her meself the next time she comes in.'

For this child was special, Arla just knew it. There was something about Keara's clear gaze and firm chin that said she would not allow life simply to toss her where it would.

*

In their large, comfortable house in Lancashire, Theo Mullane found the bedroom door locked against him when he made his way carefully upstairs after consuming a bottle of wine. Lavinia had threatened to do this if he came to her bed again, but he hadn't believed she'd have the courage to carry out her threat. A soft blancmange of a woman Lavinia, who had brought him a good dowry but little else, not even a child. And stupid with it. He had not realised just how stupid until he'd had to live with her.

He scowled at the door. If his dear wife thought he'd trot meekly off to his own bed, or put up with her threatening him, she was far and out. He smiled grimly as he crashed his strong body against the door. It gave a little and with a laugh he continued banging against it until he had kicked it in.

In the master's bedroom next door the valet, Dick Pearson, heard his mistress begin to scream and beg her maid not to leave her. Fat lot of good that would do the silly bitch!

'Get out of here this minute, Mary, if you value your job!' Theo snapped to the maid once he was inside, and gave her such a dark look she scuttled to the door with a squeak of fear.

He slammed the door after her, though it didn't close properly now, and strode across to the bed. As he stood looking down at his wife, he wondered if this was worth it. But apart from the money, his main reason for marrying had been to get children and he would not be denied his rights.

'You'll not do that again,' he told her, thumping one hand down on a small table for emphasis and precipitating an ornament off it on to the floor with a tinkle of broken china.

Lavinia shrieked, pulled the covers up to her neck and began weeping.

'Shut up!' he roared.

She continued to sob even more loudly and before he knew it he'd slapped her face. He stared down at her, annoyed with himself for losing control like that, but she'd drive a saint to sin, this one would, with her wailing and moaning, her utter selfishness. 'Shut – up!' he repeated, giving her a shake instead.

Lavinia hiccupped to a halt, staring at him in shock. 'Theo, no!' she pleaded, her pale blue eyes welling with tears. 'I hate it.'

'Lavinia, yes!' he mocked, scowling down at her. There were no strong colours to the woman: light hair, neither brown nor blond, pale skin, marked with red now where his hand had hit her, and those small eyes that peered out from between folds of flesh as if terrified of what they saw. 'If you ever try to deny me your bed again,' he said slowly and distinctly, 'I'll have the door removed from your room permanently.'

'You're unkind,' she moaned.

'Faugh! What's unkind about a man sharing his wife's bed? I want sons to my name. Which means getting them on you for you're the only wife I've got, heaven help me.'

'I'm not strong enough yet. It's only a few months since the last miscarriage.'

'The doctor says you've had long enough to recover. Now, since this door is no use at present, we can either do the act here publicly or we can go into my bedroom. Your choice.'

Without a word, every inch of her plump body proclaiming her martyrdom beneath the voluminous and very ugly flannel nightgown she wore, Lavinia led the way next door to his room. There she lay like a dead fish beneath him while he completed the act that would, he prayed, give him a living child this time.

Afterwards she left his bed without a word and he heard her muttering angrily as she washed herself, then the springs of her bed creaked in protest as she climbed into it.

Theo lay awake for a long time, staring into the darkness. He'd been wrong to marry Lavinia Hardwick, but his father had pushed him into it by showing him the disastrous state of their finances. And her father had offered him a ridiculously large dowry – he now knew why – to marry his stupid daughter. So for the sake of keeping Ballymullan Manor he had acquiesced, though only on condition that the dowry be paid to him and not to his father. Which had caused further quarrels and arguments.

But a vigorous man like him needed a warm-blooded woman, not a faded creature who cringed if you so much as brushed against her. And he *must* get an heir or what sense was there in preserving the estate? Besides, he loved children, desperately wanted some of his own. And he wanted legitimate ones, too. No good ever came from begetting bastards and he'd been careful not to plant any in his casual encounters.

In her room Lavinia lay awake for a long time, angry with her husband and wishing, as she had wished ever since the marriage, that her father had let her bring Nancy with her. Nancy had been her nurse, then her maid, and she had felt safe with her. But her father said it was time she stopped depending on that old hag and had pensioned Nancy off.

Which wasn't fair. Nothing was fair. She wept herself to sleep, sobbing loudly till Theo came to the door and roared, 'Shut up!'

When Keara entered the shop the following day, Arla exchanged smiles and nods with her husband. She served the girl, watched her place her meagre purchases in the frayed sacking bag, then folded her arms across her breast and asked, 'Have you a moment? I'd like a bit of a chat with you.'

Keara nodded, surprised by this invitation.

'Good, good. Will you come away into the back, then, and share a pot of tea with me?' She gestured towards the rear of the shop.

Keara stopped in the doorway for a moment to take it all in, awed at this honour because very few people got invited into the Lynches' back room. She had only caught glimpses of it before. It was set up like a little palace, with a stone-flagged floor, a real linen cloth on a table whose carved legs shone with polish, two rocking chairs upholstered in crimson and a proper rug to set your feet on, bought from a shop, with coloured patterns on it. 'Ah, it's a grand room, this is, Mrs Lynch, grand.'

Arla glanced round in satisfaction. 'Well, I do like to keep things nice. Now . . .' She explained her proposal, watching carefully to gauge Keara's reactions (mostly open-mouthed astonishment) and ending with, 'So – are you happy for me and Brian to help you, then?'

Keara stared at her with tears brimming in her eyes, unable to speak for a moment. She knew, the whole village knew, that the Lynches had helped Breda and Colleen and Mona, fed them and taught them things so that they could find good jobs in service. But she had never expected them to choose her as the next girl. She had to swallow hard before she could get the words out past the lump in her throat. 'Oh, Mrs Lynch, I'd be so grateful!'

'You'll eat the food I give you here in the house,' Arla went on. 'No taking it home to share with your family. If I had enough for them as well, I'd feed them, too – sure, I'd feed the whole village if I could.'

Keara blushed. She had indeed been thinking that maybe she could slip the odd morsel out for her sisters.

'I know 'tis hard, but we want to make sure *you* get the benefit.' Arla relented a little at the disappointment on the girl's face. 'But I dare say there may be a scrap or two for Ismay and Mara from time to time.'

'Thank you, Mrs Lynch.'

'Brian will teach you the reading and the writing. I'll teach you your manners and proper housekeeping and a bit about the world.' For Arla had been a maid in Sligo before her marriage and knew the ways of the gentry.

Keara closed her eyes in ecstasy, then opened them to say hoarsely, 'I'll never let you down, Mrs Lynch, I promise. I'll work hard, learn as much as I can.'

'Bless you, don't I know that already.' Arla took off her apron and picked up her bonnet, tying it firmly beneath her chin. 'I'll walk home with you now, shall I, and we'll tell your mammy together.'

But to Keara's horror, Da was at home as well. He'd been kicked and knocked out by a new horse so they'd laid him in a cart and driven him home to recover. She could see at a glance that he was in a foul mood, and plucked at Arla's arm to gain her attention. 'Could you come back another time, Mrs Lynch, when Da's not so – upset? He – he might not like your offer.'

Arla looked at her in surprise. 'Now, why ever should he not?'

Keara hung her head, unable to explain how unreasonable her father could be and how he'd taken against her even worse since she'd kept back the birthing money. He'd been getting at her in every petty way he could since then, enjoying making her life miserable, and didn't she have the bruises to prove it!

Arla led the way into the house, confident of her offer being accepted with a flattering degree of gratitude. She exchanged greetings then spoke her piece.

Glowering, Mick listened and before anyone else could speak, said flatly, 'No. We thank you for the kind thought, Arla, but it'll be better if you find someone else, someone more deserving than this one.'

Keara felt tears rise in her eyes. How could he do this to her? And why? Surely he'd benefit as well when she was able to get work as a proper maid at the big house and earn a steady wage?

Betsy laid one hand on her husband's arm, only to have it tossed off again. 'Mick, don't do this!' she pleaded.

He jumped to his feet, wincing as his head thumped with pain. 'I said no!' he roared. 'Am I the master in my own house or am I not?'

His face was so congested with fury that Arla took an involuntary step backwards, then another.

Keara rushed outside, sobbing loudly. Arla followed, finding no sign of the girl. She walked slowly home, baffled by Mick's reaction.

Inside the cottage he stood and smiled like a big contented cat which had just eaten a bird.

'Why in God's name did you do that?' Betsy asked.

'Because as long as she lives under my roof, that daughter of yours needs to learn to obey me. I *will* be master in my own house!'

Unable to bear the sight of him a minute longer, her eyes blinded with tears, she headed towards the door, ignoring his roar of, 'Come back here this minute, woman!'

Mick was left to enjoy his victory on his own, the bandage not yet pinned in place around his head and already unravelling. 'I'll show them who's master!' he muttered, then sat down suddenly as the room spun.

When he felt a bit better he went round to the lean-to at the back, got out his bottle of poteen and took it inside. Taking a big swig, he sighed in relief. Nothing like a drink to help a man through hard times.

'That learned her, the bitch!' Smiling, he gulped down another mouthful of the fiery spirit.

A little later, when Ismay poked her head round the door, he roared at her to get away out of here.

After he'd emptied the bottle, he fell asleep at the table, his head on his arms.

CHAPTER TWO

Betsy stumbled along blindly until she reached the tiny church, then stopped to catch her breath in the porch. This was the only place she could think of to come, the only place she found any peace and privacy these days. She went inside, crossed herself automatically and sank down in a rear pew.

What was she to do? She couldn't bear the thought of Keara missing out on this opportunity. It might be the only chance her daughter ever had to better herself.

She tried to pray for guidance, but couldn't think of a single word after *Please God, please*, so in the end bowed her head and simply let the tears flow and her heart speak for her. She wished, as she often did, that she had never met Mick Michaels. She had been a maid in the Hardwick household in Lancashire when Mick had come over to work in the stables. He had been sent by old Mr Mullane because his friend Chas Hardwick wanted a groom who was good with horses and Mick was keen to see something of the world.

She'd been pretty in those days and had let Mick

sweep her off her feet. The worst mistake of his life, that, he said openly whenever he was drunk. That was what had driven him to drink.

Well, it was the worst mistake of her life, too, one for which she'd paid dearly ever since. Mr Hardwick had insisted Mick marry their pregnant maidservant and then sent the couple back to the Irish estate, saying he wasn't having a philanderer and a whore working in his household. Harsh words. They'd only been two lonely young people seeking companionship and imagining themselves in love – or at least she had imagined herself in love. All Mick had wanted was her body.

'What's wrong?' a voice asked behind her.

She jumped in shock and jerked round, terrified Mick had come after her. It was Father Cornelius, which was almost as bad. He wasn't like the kindly priest she'd known as a girl in Lancashire. All this man ever did was tell her to obey her husband while at the same time scolding her for not persuading that same husband to come to church more often.

'Tell me what's wrong, Betsy Michaels,' he ordered.

She forgot her nervousness of him in her anguish for her daughter. 'It's Mick. He's ruining our Keara's life out of sheer spite.' When she had finished her tale she let out a long, shuddering sigh and waited for the priest to tell her to accept her husband's wishes in this matter as in all others. But he surprised her for once.

'Let me talk to the Lynches about this, then I'll speak to your husband. 'Tis a fine chance for the girl and wrong he is to deny it to her.'

'Thank you, Father, but it won't make any difference. Once he's set on something, Mick never changes his mind.'

'We'll see about that. Now let us pray together for the Lord's help and then you go home and leave it to me.'

Afterwards he escorted her to the church door and stood watching her walk slowly down the muddy street, noting the weariness in every line of her body. Like many of the women round here Mrs Michaels looked years older than her age, so thin a whisper of wind would have blown her away and with dark rings round her eyes that spoke of constant ill health. Light rain was falling and mud was splashing the bottom of her skirt and the backs of her bare legs as she walked, but she didn't seem to notice it. Unlike the other poorer villagers she never went barefoot, but her shoes were as worn as her clothes, slopping about on her feet and tied with frayed twine.

The following morning the Michaels children got nothing to eat because Mick found the hunk of bread Betsy had set aside for them and ate it all, claiming the need to build up his strength after his accident. He then staggered out grudgingly to dig out some potatoes from the clamp and when he got back from this arduous mission, flung himself down at the table and scowled at his family.

'Can't even give a man a live son, can you?' he flung at Betsy.

She bowed her head and said nothing, knowing it did no good to argue with him.

Balked, he turned to scowl at Ismay and Mara, who were watching him nervously from the corner. 'Get out of here, you two! Doesn't a sick man need a little peace?'

Keara was washing the blood-stained cloths her mother was using and she waited for him to fling some insult at her, but luckily Diarmid popped in just then.

'How are you feeling, lad?'

'Badly,' Mick said at once.

Diarmid looked at the other man's swollen face with its massive bruise. 'You'd better stay home for another day, then.'

'But we need the money,' Mick whined.

'There'll be no money docked from your wages. I saw what happened and you were only doing your job.'

Mick gave a little snigger after the land agent had left. 'Makes a nice change to get paid for doing nothing. That O'Neal is a slave driver, so he is.'

A little later Father Cornelius turned up.

Mick greeted him with a scowl and, 'What do *you* want?'

'To speak to you, my son.'

'Well, I don't want to speak to *you* and I'm no son of yours.'

Betsy gasped in horror at his rudeness.

Father Cornelius ignored it. 'I hear you've been refusing to let your daughter learn from Arla.'

Mick glared at Betsy. 'Who told you that?'

'The whole village knows.' But although Father Cornelius spoke eloquently, he got only abuse from Mick and in the end went away, tight-lipped and wondering whether to write to the landowner to complain about the fellow. It was a terrible thing to see a man letting his family go without food because of the drink.

Seeing the two younger girls down the lane, he stopped to talk to them. 'Are you hungry?'

'Yes, Father.'

He could never bear to see little children with that pinched look on their faces. 'If you come back with me I'll maybe find you a piece of bread.'

Beaming and nudging one another, they followed him to the comfortable little house next to the church.

By afternoon Mick was complaining bitterly that there was nothing to eat in the house.

'Give me the money and I'll go and buy you some food.' For Betsy this was outright defiance, since they both knew he'd spent his last few coins on poteen two nights ago, hence his hangover and carelessness yesterday morning with the horse.

'Ah, go and ask Arla Lynch to give us credit,' he growled. 'Tell her I'll pay her back when I get me wages on Saturday.'

'You offended her yesterday. She'll just laugh in my face.'

'I said, go and ask her!' he roared, giving Betsy a shove that sent her crashing into the door frame, then raising his fist to his eldest daughter when she gave him a black look and ran across to stand between her mother and him. She didn't even attempt to hide her scorn as she helped her mother outside.

'Keara, will you come with me into the village? I need the lean of an arm.'

'Of course I will, Mam. But why don't you stay here and let me go instead?'

'Because he'll say you didn't ask her properly and hit you.'

But he was just as likely to hit her mother these days, Keara thought. He was getting worse. Why did God have to give them a father like that?

Betsy walked along slowly, leaning heavily on her daughter. She'd felt exhausted even before she started, not having really recovered from the birth yet. As they entered the shop she felt so dizzy she sagged against the counter.

Arla stared at her, then held up one finger to signify they should wait a moment and vanished into the back room, returning a couple of minutes later carrying two pieces of bread and butter. With a peremptory, 'Eat that now!' she held them out. As she saw the calculation in Betsy's eyes, she added sharply, 'I'll see you eat them here, though. You're not taking anything home to *him*.'

'But the girls—'

'Will be all the better for having a mother who's not near fainting from starvation. When did ye last eat, Betsy Michaels? Tell me that now.'

Tears of shame and weakness began to run down Betsy's cheeks.

Keara looked at the piece of bread, her mouth

watering, stretched out one hand then pulled it back, glancing at her mother for permission.

Arla had missed nothing of this. 'Ah, eat the bread, will ye now, then send the little ones along to me and I'll give them a piece as well. Just this once, mind! I'm not made of money.'

'But Mick will still be hungry and when he's like that, he . . .' Betsy flushed. It was one thing for everyone to know he thumped her and the children, quite another for her to admit it publicly.

'I'm giving that one nothing, which is exactly what he deserves.' Arla folded her arms and set her lips just so.

Few cared to argue with her in this mood, even her husband. Betsy hesitated for a few seconds longer then picked up the bread and took a small bite, closing her eyes in sheer ecstasy as she chewed it, for it was newly baked. She turned to Keara. 'Eat your butty slowly, love. It'll fill you up better.'

When they returned home, Mick looked at his wife. 'Well?'

'Arla says she doesn't give credit, and told me to tell you that after the way you spoke to her, she's giving nothing to you.'

He thumped her for that, sending her crashing awkwardly to the floor. Mara, who had just come back, began to sob and he yelled at Betsy to quieten that damned brat before storming out.

She lay on the floor for a moment, eyes closed, then pulled herself to her feet, rubbing her cheek. 'Has he gone now?'

Keara, who had dodged out of her father's way to avoid a kick as he passed, watched him make his way across the fields and let out a sigh of relief. 'He's heading for the big house. Will I tell Ismay and Mara to go down to Mrs Lynch's now for their piece?'

'Go with them and see that they're all right. I'll have a bit of a sleep, I think.' Betsy saw how the girl's shoulders were drooping, knew how unhappy she was about losing such a good opportunity and tried to pull herself together. 'Oh, and Keara, love!'

She turned to look back at her mother.

'Bring us back a pennyworth of sunshine as well. I'm that sick of all this rain.'

It was an old saying of Betsy's and when she heard it, Keara knew her mother must be getting better at last. 'Only a pennyworth?'

'That'll do for starters.'

'What'll I carry it in?' This was part of their little joke.

'Cup your hands together and let it fill them. And don't spill any on the way back.'

'All right, Mam.'

Her mother had been saying that for as long as Keara could remember. She loved her dearly, but she'd grown to hate their father. He didn't care about anyone but himself and she could never understand what her mother had ever seen in him.

She wished she really could bring back some warm sunshine. The dampness often made her mother cough and wheeze, and they couldn't afford to warm even their one room properly.

*

The estate manager blinked in shock as his cousin Arla erupted into his office.

'I need your help, Diarmid O'Neal, and I'll not be taking no for an answer.'

He listened in growing irritation to her tale. Mick Michaels was never quite sober these days, though Diarmid had not managed to catch him actually drinking on duty. The trouble was, the man had a way with horses that made him a valuable employee, drunk or sober. If he'd been able to keep his trousers buttoned, Mick could have made something of himself, but he'd come back from England sullen and bitter, and now saved all his affection for the horses and the poteen.

'Mr Mullane is coming to stay in a couple of days' time,' Diarmid said abruptly. 'I'll discuss it with him, but I'm not promising anything.' He could simply order Mick to let the girl go to Arla, but if he did that, Mick would take it out on Keara. Not that the girl had much of a life at the best of times. No, best to leave the matter to Theo. He was one of the few people of whom Mick was afraid.

If Theo Mullane decided something was to happen on the estate, then it happened. Diarmid considered him a friend, but even he wouldn't say no if his employer got a certain look in his eye.

When the priest also came to discuss the matter, huddling like a black crow under his big umbrella, Diarmid gave him the same answer.

'You're sure Mr Mullane will intervene?' Father Cornelius asked.

'Yes, Father. Certain.' Well, he was pretty certain. You could never quite tell with Theo, who was kind at heart but much tried by his foolish wife and then inclined to snap.

In Lancashire the day was stormy and rain was beating against the window panes. At Eastwood House Theo scowled out of the window as he waited for Dick to finish packing his clothes. Dick combined the roles of valet, groom and almost-friend, for the two of them had been lads together at Ballymullan. 'Finished, Dick? Right then, find out if your mistress is ready. I'm going down to collect my letters. The second post should be here by now.'

Dick grimaced. Increasingly his employers were communicating through their personal servants and that didn't make for a comfortable life for him and Mary. 'Yes, sir.'

'Ah, call me Theo. You always did till I got married.'

'Mrs Mullane doesn't like it, sir.'

'To hell with Mrs Mullane!'

'I'd better not, sir.' He grinned suddenly. 'Well, not when she's around, anyway.'

As Theo returned with a fistful of letters, which he was sorting as he walked, Dick cleared his throat. 'Mary's packed the valises, as you instructed, but the mistress is still in bed. I gather she's – um – rather upset.'

Theo sighed. That translated as still weeping and protesting she was too ill to travel. 'Then it's time I paid her a visit.' He banged open the connecting door without knocking, then stood there, hands on hips, watching his wife sob piteously into her pillow – or it would have been piteously had Lavinia not spoiled the effect by peeping sideways to gauge the effect on him.

'You'll find it cold travelling in your nightdress,' he said in a conversational tone.

She stopped sobbing for long enough to ask, 'What do you mean by that?'

'Exactly what I said. We're catching the next train and if you're not dressed when it's time to leave for the station, then you'll have to go as you are.'

The tearfulness changed into anger. 'You wouldn't *dare*!'

'Oh, wouldn't I?' He folded his arms and studied her dispassionately. She was plump and pale because she never did any exercise and refused to lift a finger unless she absolutely had to. And she was absolutely the most stupid woman he'd ever met. For the hundredth time he wondered why he had not realised that when he was courting her.

He knew the answer, really. He hadn't paid much attention to her because he hadn't been attracted to her so much as her money, it being the only way to save his acres. And her family had not allowed him to be alone with her but had surrounded them with people, providing activities and entertainments that suited her and showed her to her best advantage. Or rather, her father had done all that. Her mother had always been ailing and had died just after their marriage. Yes, Mr Hardwick had played his cards very cleverly and Theo had been fooled.

But two years later his father-in-law had been killed in a carriage accident and Lavinia had inherited everything – or rather, her husband had. And there hadn't been nearly as much money as he'd expected, not to mention a surprising number of debts due to Mr Hardwick's mismanagement. Theo sometimes thought he'd have done better to sell his estate and use the money to go out to the colonies, where people said you could make a fortune. But he couldn't imagine Lavinia living that sort of life.

He shook those thoughts aside. What was the use of dwelling on what might have been? She was his wife now and he must make the best of that. Pulling his pocket watch out, he checked it and reiterated, 'We'll be leaving this house in exactly half an hour, whether you're dressed or not. And don't wear one of those damned crinolines for travelling, either, or I'll pull it off you. I never saw such a stupid fashion.'

Lavinia watched him go, her expression sullen. She hated him. And she hated the Irish house, too. It was a tumbledown sort of place and the servants there spoke to you too familiarly, as if they considered themselves as good as you.

Mary seized her opportunity. 'I think we'd better get you dressed, ma'am. You know what the master's like when he decides on something and he looked very determined to me.'

Lavinia heaved herself upright. 'Oh, very well! Find

me some clothes – it doesn't matter what because I'll not survive the journey. And pack some cherry bonbons to give me strength.'

Suppressing a sigh of relief, Mary hurried to carry out her orders.

Lavinia lay for a moment or two longer, but could think of no way of avoiding the trip. Half an hour later she allowed her maid to help her slowly down the stairs.

The front door was open and Theo was standing in the hall, foot tapping in impatience. 'Hurry up, woman! Trains don't wait for anyone.'

Lavinia moved even more slowly, but as she reached the foot of the stairs, he grasped her arm and tugged her forward. Ignoring her squeal of shock and attempt to pull away from him, he force-marched her outside and stuffed her into the carriage with scant regard for her dignity.

At the railway station Theo put his arm under her elbow and made sure she walked quickly towards the train. 'You can ride with Dick today, Mary,' he called over his shoulder as they found their compartment.

'I need her help for the journey,' Lavinia said. 'She *always* rides with us.'

'Well, today she isn't going to. You can sit in a compartment without her help. Move along now, Mary!' He looked at the maid, who bobbed a quick curtsey, handed her mistress a basket and scurried along the platform to join Dick.

Once the train had set off Lavinia picked up the small picnic basket, but Theo took it from her before she could open it. He pulled out the dish of cherry bonbons, a new novel with its pages still uncut, a piece of cake wrapped in a fine linen napkin, and some biscuits wrapped in another napkin, setting them in a row on the seat beside him then studying her dispassionately. 'You're getting fatter by the day and these don't help.' Without another word he opened the window and tossed out the food, napkins and all, before giving her back the basket, which now contained only the book and an empty silver dish.

Apart from one shriek of outrage, followed by a few half-hearted sobs, she didn't say another word until they reached Liverpool, but the looks she threw in his direction were resentful.

When they were shown to their adjoining cabins on the ferry, she slammed her door shut on him and quickly shot the bolt inside.

He waited outside until the maid arrived and was let into her mistress's cabin, then followed. 'There are to be no sweetmeats, cakes or biscuits for your mistress from now on, Mary, except at meal times, and if I catch you disobeying me, you'll be dismissed on the spot. Is that understood?'

She goggled at him, but managed a quick curtsey and a 'Yes, sir'. As the door banged shut behind him she turned to her mistress, who was looking mutinous. 'I'm sorry, ma'am, but I daren't disobey him. For my life I daren't.' She was well paid for the onerous task of looking after Mrs Mullane, who was not the easiest of mistresses, and didn't want to lose the job.

Lavinia gave way to a full-scale fit of hysterics and nothing Mary did would soothe her.

When this had gone on for a minute or two, Theo erupted into the cabin and shook his wife hard. 'If you don't stop that caterwauling, I'll gag you. Don't you care that people can hear you?'

'Why are you so cruel to me?' she sobbed, but more quietly now.

'Because I want a son. Or a daughter. When I have one, I'll be delighted to leave you completely alone. Now, are you going to settle down quietly or must I do something about it?'

She nodded.

When he had left she stared at the door, a vicious expression on her face. *If I ever bore his son, I'd strangle it at birth,* she decided. *One of him is too much for this world.* She had never been so deceived in anyone. She'd thought Theo very handsome when her father proposed him as a husband. He was of just over medium height, good-looking in a careless sort of way, with a strong body and the sort of fresh complexion you get from spending a lot of time outdoors. She'd always preferred dark hair in a man and he had grey-green eyes that could laugh at the world when he was in a good mood.

But appearance aside, he'd been a great disappointment to her. He hob-nobbed with the servants and seemed to care for only two things in the whole world: breeding horses and getting her with child, neither of which interested her. And no one had warned her about what went on in bed or she'd never have agreed to marry him or any man. Without other people to keep the conversation going, they tended to sit silently when they spent an evening alone together. She preferred her female friends with whom she did not have to be continually thinking of things to say. They were always full of the latest gossip and quite content for her just to sit and listen to them.

And this insistence of Theo's on having children . . . as if she wanted any! Children were noisy, dirty creatures and she'd never liked them, even when she'd been a child herself, because they'd teased her and mocked her, calling her stupid. If she hadn't had her nurse Nancy, she'd have been very unhappy as a child.

Mary said nothing, just sat in the corner and waited. It looked like they were in for a rough crossing and soon her mistress would be too ill to trouble anyone. Indeed, Mary was feeling a little queasy herself, but did not have the luxury of giving way to it. Lavinia Mullane still expected to be waited on hand and foot, whatever the crossing was like, and never thought about the difficulties of walking along a heaving deck to empty buckets of slops or bowls of vomit, just insisted on getting rid of such smelly things at once.

Diarmid did not inform Theo Mullane about Mick Michaels' spiteful behaviour towards his daughter until they'd finished discussing the main business of the estate and were sitting sharing a bottle of claret in the little room where the guns were kept.

'Do I need more problems?' Theo asked with a sigh. 'And why should this one matter to me anyway?'

'It was Arla Lynch who found you your present

kitchen maid and trained her up. If it weren't for Arla, we'd have trouble getting decent help. Unless they're born round here, girls don't like to work in such a lonely place, so far away from the nearest town. Besides, it's a fine thing Arla's doing for the girls of the village.'

Diarmid left it at that, staring into his glass and praying that this cause would catch his companion's fancy. When Theo said nothing, he added, 'Ah, go on! Keara's a fine lass and deserves better of life. She's quick-witted, too. Takes after her father not her mother there, though she'd not thank you for saying that. He's a selfish, spiteful bugger, Mick is. Only good for looking after horses and crooking his elbow. It'd be a shame to let him hold her back. She won't get any other chance to make something of herself.'

Theo shrugged. Diarmid was another man with whom he'd played as a lad. He felt comfortable with him as he never did with the land agent at Eastwood House, who couldn't relax in his company and consequently was a great bore. 'Oh, very well! I'll play the bloody philanthropist for you. What exactly do you want me to do? Order Mick to let Arla teach the girl?'

The steward gave him a rueful glance. 'No. If we order him to do it, he'll take it out on her. He already beats his wife and thumps the children – as well as drinking most of what he earns so that they often go hungry. When the girl goes for a maid, her wages could make a big difference to her mother and sisters. The difference between life and death, maybe.'

Theo let out a little growl of anger. Here was he, unable to father a child, and there was one of his employees starving the children he had got so casually.

Diarmid took another sip as he thought it over. 'Could you perhaps – I don't know – be a bit cunning about how you tell him?'

Theo rolled his eyes and poured himself another glass of wine. As he sat there sipping it, a smile twitched at the corners of his mouth. 'Is the fellow back at work now?'

'Yes.'

'Let's stroll down to the stables, then.'

They found Mick mucking out a stall and talking in a low voice to the horse which was tied up outside. When his employer paused nearby, he stopped work to bob his head in respect and eye them warily.

Diarmid spoke first. 'How's that head of yours today, Mick me boy?'

He shrugged. 'Still a bit sore, sir.'

'And how's your family?' Theo asked. 'I was sorry to hear that you and your wife lost the new baby. Here, have a drink to cheer yourself up.'

He tossed sixpence to Mick, who caught it with the ease of long practice, his face brightening.

'And I believe you're to be congratulated on your oldest daughter as well,' Theo went on, patting the neck of the horse.

Mick didn't answer, but stood frowning as he tried to work out what exactly his master meant by this.

'She's a chip off the old block, they tell me. Looks like you and smart with it.'

'Thank you, sir.' Mick's tone was unenthusiastic. 'But I'd rather have had a son. Three of them I've got now, girls, and the new one would have been a female, too.'

Theo breathed deeply. He'd settle for a girl any day. But he controlled his irritation and said gently, 'It'll be a big help when you're getting older, won't it, having a daughter in service? Keara will be able to help you and your wife out when you're past working, keep you out of the poorhouse.'

'She will?' Mick struggled to get his aching head round this idea.

'Yes. Housemaids who don't marry go on earning wages until they're old themselves, then we pension them off. They usually send most of their wages home to their families. Yes, it'll be a big help for you, having a daughter go out as a maid. And when she starts work, it'll be you who'll get her wages.'

Mick's mouth dropped open.

Theo wondered why Diarmid considered the man quick-witted. He seemed particularly stupid today.

'I daresay you weren't thinking straight when Arla came to see you yesterday, because of your head,' Diarmid put in. 'That was a nasty blow you got.'

Mick seized on this excuse. 'You're right there. Sure and wasn't me poor head thumping like a drum. Still is.'

'You'd better nip down to see Arla Lynch tonight, then, and make your peace with her,' Theo said, satisfied the man had taken the bait. 'Diarmid will let you go half an hour early to do it, won't you? Right, then, if you've finished here, bring that new chestnut out, Mick, and let's see how he moves. He sounds to be a bit lively.'

'But he's a fine stepper and we'll soon train him into better manners,' Mick said fondly. He wasn't sure he liked the idea of backing down about Keara, but Mr Mullane was right. He definitely hadn't considered the benefits to himself.

Arla looked up as Mick entered her shop. 'I've got nothing to say to *you*.'

'Ah, Arla, I've come to apologise, so I have. I'd just got kicked on the head the day you came to see us and I wasn't after thinking clearly.' He pressed one hand to his chest and hung his head. 'I hope you'll forgive me if I sounded ungrateful.' He peeped at her from under his long lashes. 'Ah, go on! You'll still take on my girl, won't you?'

She breathed deeply, but her mind was set on having Keara as her next protégée so she nodded. 'I will, then. But you've to stop taking your bad temper out on her. If I see any bruises on that girl, I'll be complaining to my cousin Diarmid.'

'Why should I be hitting her? Won't she be the support of my old age if she goes for a maid, as Mr Mullane himself has just been pointing out to me?'

Arla watched him go, open-mouthed. Mr Theo had taken a hand in this? Then she smiled, guessing she owed this intervention to Diarmid. Three girls she'd helped now, and they'd all got work at the big house first, though Breda and Colleen had moved on now to better places in Sligo and Belfast. Well, that was as it should be. She did her part getting them started, then it was up to them what they made of their chance. If her own daughter had lived, she would have set her on the same path, for there was nothing for these girls in the village.

It suddenly occurred to her that Keara had two sisters and Ismay at least was a bright little thing. Too soon to tell with Mara, who clung to her sisters and said little. She smiled in satisfaction. Plenty of good to be done yet.

Then she realised she was standing there staring down the street like a fool at a fair, tutted and hurried inside. What was she doing out here when she had a shop to run, a goat to feed, and a garden to tend? Not to mention a new shirt to make for her Brian.

CHAPTER THREE

Mark Gibson arrived in London one grey, rainy morning in March and made his way to the office of the shipping line whose advertisements he'd seen in the newspaper several times.

'You've fallen lucky today, young fellow,' the agent told him. 'Very lucky. There's still room on the ship which is sailing for Australia in three days' time – well, it'll sail if the wind is in the right direction, otherwise you'll all sit out there on the water and wait.' He smiled at his own pleasantry then studied Mark's face with a frown. 'Have you been in a fight?'

Mark nodded. No use denying that with his face so bruised and his cracked rib still hurting if he moved unwisely.

'I hope you're not fond of fighting. They don't allow that sort of behaviour on board ship.'

'I was attacked one night coming home from work. If I'd had more experience of fighting, they might not have made such a mess of me.' He'd learned enough as a child to keep bullies at bay, but there was no way one man could hold his own against three hefty Burns brothers all wanting to punish him for getting their sister in trouble.

The agent stared at him thoughtfully, then nodded. 'Well, as long as you understand.' He turned back to the piece of paper on which he was noting details. 'Single, you say?'

'Yes.'

'I'm surprised a strapping young fellow like you isn't married.' Another assessing stare. 'There are some fellows who go out to Australia to escape from their wives, you know.'

Mark stiffened. 'Well, I'm not one of them. I've never been married and I shan't be until I'm in a position to support a family.' Which wasn't quite true. He had been in such a position for a while, but had never found a woman who'd tempted him into the big step of marriage.

'Well, if a good-looking young fellow like you has managed to avoid parson's mousetrap till you're twenty-five, you've not done badly. The ladies can be very determined and most young fellows have been well and truly caught by that age. I know I was.' He sighed and stared into the distance for a minute, then signed the piece of paper. 'You'll have to pass a medical, but you look fit enough to me, apart from the bruises. That'll be twenty pounds, please.'

Having paid his fare, Mark was directed to take the paper to the doctor's office and get it signed, but was allowed to leave his luggage with the agent.

After a cursory examination, the doctor said the

bruises would soon fade and the rib would mend in a few days, then pronounced him fit to travel. He signed the piece of paper and shoved it across the desk to Mark. 'You'll need to take this back to the agent. Have you got anywhere to stay?'

'No. I thought I'd find lodgings for a night or two.'

'We prefer you to stay in the emigrants' depot with the other steerage passengers until it's time to board. It's free. Here. This'll get you in.' The doctor gave him a signed chit.

By the time Mark had finished with the doctor it was four o'clock in the afternoon. Very weary now because he hadn't slept much the night before, and ravenously hungry because he hadn't felt like eating either, he trudged back to hand the paper to the agent, who then directed him to a barn-like building on the corner of a street near the docks. 'They'll be serving the evening meal in an hour or two.' He slapped yet another piece of paper into Mark's hand. 'This is a list of what you'll need for the voyage. Better check you've got it all.'

At the depot the warden studied the pass then let Mark in, rattling off a list of rules as he showed him to a vacant bunk. 'You can put your bags underneath for now, but you'll have to have the luggage for the hold ready to be taken on board by tomorrow afternoon at two o'clock sharp. Most of the other steerage passengers' things went yesterday.'

Mark stood by the bunk looking round. He felt so numb with tiredness that it was a minute or two before the details began to sink in. Two-tier bunks made of rough, unvarnished wood were crammed all round the walls, with barely room to stand between each pair. The only other furniture was a row of wooden tables and benches in the middle of the room. Everywhere he looked there were people: children playing, women chatting in low voices with their heads close together and men standing talking earnestly in groups. A few individuals were lying on their bunks, backs turned to the room or faces covered by an arm.

With a sigh Mark sat down on the lower bunk he had been allotted. As he was wondering what to do with himself, a family group came over to introduce themselves and said they were occupying the bunks nearest to his, so he had to stand up again.

The father, who was a short man with a stern, unsmiling face and sparse grey hair, offered his hand. 'I'm Alex Jenner and this is my wife Nan – my daughter Patience – my son Harry.' The son was taller than his father and looked to be about sixteen. He gave Mark a quick smile, bobbing his head in greeting but saying nothing. Both son and daughter had fine blond hair and were slender in build.

'I'm Mark Gibson.'

'And you're from the North like us by the sound of your voice. Whereabouts?'

'Bilsden.' It was out before he could stop himself.

'I've never been there. We're from Todmorden. Sailing to join my brother and his family in Melbourne, if the Lord preserves us against the perils of the deep.' Mr Jenner heaved a heavy sigh as if he doubted that.

As the bell rang just then for the evening meal, Mark could do no other than sit with the Jenners, though he hadn't taken to the father at all. The man seemed puffed up with his own importance and none of his family so much as dared to interrupt him speaking, let alone disagree with his pronouncements. It was in great contrast to Mark's own family where lively discussions were held every time they gathered, with people interrupting one another and laughing together over the foolishnesses of everyday life. Conversation with Mr Jenner was solemn and he filled it with Biblical quotations and pronouncements based on them, which usually put an end to that topic.

It was Mrs Jenner who asked as they waited for their evening meal which ship's kit Mark had bought.

He stared at her blankly. 'Ship's kit?'

Mr Jenner took over again. 'Eh, haven't you got one yet, lad? Didn't they give you a list of what you'd need?'

'Oh. Yes.' Mark pulled a crumpled piece of paper out of his pocket. He hadn't even looked at it.

His companion took it from him, smoothing it out carefully and tapping it with his forefinger. 'There, see! You have to provide your own bedding, toilet articles and table utensils. They sell them in kits to make it easy.' He hesitated then asked, 'You have some money for that?'

Mark nodded, but couldn't seem to concentrate.

When a bell rang, Mr Jenner excused himself. 'I have to collect the food for this section of the table.'

Mrs Jenner said in her slow, comfortable voice, 'You look exhausted, Mr Gibson. Why don't you let my husband take you to the ship's chandler's tomorrow morning? You'll probably want to buy some extra food

Anna Jacobs

for the voyage as well. I know you young men have hearty appetites.'

'I thought food was provided.'

She laughed comfortably and her daughter smiled in sympathy. The minute the father had left, the rest of the family had relaxed visibly. Mrs Jenner shook her head and pursed her lips. 'They give you what they call a basic weekly allowance of food: salt, meat, flour, oatmeal, suet, rice, raisins and that sort of thing. I don't call it enough.'

'Don't forget the lime juice, Mum,' Patience said. 'They give you lime juice to stop you getting scurvy, Mr Gibson. We've got extra nuts, apples, dried fruit, cheese in wax and lots of pickles. My uncle said in his letter that you get a craving for pickles when you're on a long voyage.'

Mr Jenner returned and the two women fell silent again as he placed the dishes on the table. Before people could start their meal, Mr Jenner stood up and began to say grace in a loud voice. Most people set their knives and forks down and bowed their heads, but a few ignored him and began eating.

The man seemed to go on praying for a long time, Mark thought, when a simple grace would surely have been more appropriate, given the number of children present. 'I hadn't realised I'd need a ship's kit,' he admitted when Mr Jenner finally stopped praying. 'In fact, I think I need a few other things as well. I had to – um – leave in a hurry,' he saw their eyes on him and added hastily, 'due to sad family circumstances.' To his relief they did not pursue the matter.

He served the daughter, then the mother, though Mr Jenner had only served himself and made no effort to help his womenfolk with the heavy dishes.

After a few mouthfuls, the man said, 'I'll take you to the chandler's after breakfast. I'll be glad of a chance to stretch my legs and you'll not know where to go.'

'Um – thank you.' Mark didn't enjoy his company but if he had to have his luggage ready by two o'clock in the afternoon, he needed to get things done quickly.

The meal seemed interminable to Mark, whose head was still aching, and he was glad when he was able to leave the table and return to his bunk. It seemed strange to be sleeping in such crowded and public conditions, so he didn't remove his outer clothing until he was under the covers.

The lamps in the depot were extinguished at nine o'clock and just beforehand the warden came out of his office to call, 'Five minutes, please.'

Alex Jenner got down on his knees, followed by his family, and began to pray loudly. The son looked embarrassed and once or twice squinted round, but the women followed the father's example and kept their eyes closed.

A man came over to pull himself up into the top bunk while this was going on, nodding at Mark and jerking his head in the direction of the Jenners. 'Noisy bugger, isn't he? I keep my distance from fellows like that and you'd be wise to do the same.'

Mark nodded. He was already regretting accepting Mr Jenner's offer to help him choose a ship's kit, but it was too late to do anything about that now. He pulled the coarse grey blanket up higher and tried to settle into sleep. One wall lamp was still burning on a low light near the door, which left the room in near darkness, but it was a long time before quietness reigned in the crowded space. He sighed and wriggled round in a vain attempt to get comfortable on the hard, narrow bed.

As he lay there he felt very alone, more on his own than ever before in his whole life. He had run away and left his family – eight brothers and sisters and their children. Even to think of them made a lump come in his throat and his eyes well with tears. What did they think of him for running away from his responsibilities like that? Well, he knew what his father thought. John Gibson had said it very plainly: 'You're no son of mine.' And his father's condemnation hurt more than anything else.

Mark turned his back to the lighter side of the room and let the tears flow unchecked in the darkness. He had thought about Australia on and off for years because they said it was always warm and sunny there, something you longed for in rainy old Lancashire. Now he was not at all sure he wanted to go.

But it was too late to change his mind. He'd messed up his life and needed to make a new start. It might as well be in Australia, now he'd booked his passage.

Breakfast was as badly prepared and served as the evening meal had been. Mark ate the lumpy porridge because he was hungry and paid a penny extra for a dollop of honey to flavour it. He wondered how much money the warden and his wife were allowed for feeding so many people and how much more they made from extras like the honey. He was quite certain he could arrange the catering better than this. He'd learned his trade well, knew how to cook plain food in large quantities and had been making a good income from his chop house.

Before they could leave the depot, Mark and Mr Jenner had to get the warden's permission and a signed pass.

'It's like being in prison,' Mark said angrily as they walked down the street. 'Who do they think they are, telling me when I can come and go? I'm an Englishman leaving the country of his own free choice, not a felon being transported to the colonies!'

'Nay, they have to make sure no one tries to sneak on board and they have to keep an eye on folk's health. It'd be a bad thing if there was an outbreak of measles or some such thing while we were at sea.'

Mark's anger left him as abruptly as it had flared up. 'I suppose so.'

Mr Jenner stopped walking to grasp his arm and fix him with a burning gaze. 'Look, lad, I don't mean to interfere but I can see you're not happy. I won't ask why unless you want to tell me. But I will ask you this: are you quite sure you're doing the right thing going to Australia?'

'I'm not sure about anything, sir, but I must go somewhere and I used to think about Australia sometimes. It always sounded interesting. And sunny. That's why I chose it.'

'Well, if you're in doubt you can always turn to the Lord and pray for guidance. Do you have a Bible?'

'Er – no.'

'Then you should buy one. You're never alone if you can read the Lord's word.'

Mark made a non-committal sound, but fortunately they arrived at the big ship's chandler's just then and Mr Jenner had to let the subject drop.

The warehouse was enormous and was piled to the ceiling with goods and equipment, much of which was completely strange to Mark. He paid careful attention to what the clerk and Mr Jenner said, checking the quality and calculating the best value to be obtained among the different kits offered. The one he finally chose contained blankets and sheets, water bottle, wash basin, a plate and bowl, a one-pint pannikin for drinking out of, cutlery, plus three pounds of marine soap, writing materials and a blank diary.

'A lot of them write a diary of their voyage,' the sales clerk said. 'It helps pass the time.'

'Yes. Good idea, I suppose.'

'Some of them send their diaries back so that their families will know what's happened to them. Or they make copies for their families.'

'Yes. I see. All right, I'll have that kit.' Mark also purchased some more underclothes, shirts and trousers, for he'd not been able to bring all his own things with him, and finally, remembering Mrs Jenner's advice, he purchased extra foodstuffs for the journey, knowing what a good appetite he normally had.

That made him realise there might be an opportunity to make money here and he smiled wryly at himself. He was Annie Gibson's brother all right, keeping an eye out for any stray chance of profit wherever he went! His half-sister was an incredible woman and he felt bad about letting her down. She had pulled them all out of Salem Street with her business sense, first running a second-hand clothes stall, then opening a dressmaking salon for the richer women of Bilsden. After his mother had died, leaving them in abject poverty from her mismanagement, Annie had taken them and their father to live with her in a house that had seemed like a palace to them all. She had even found him and Luke jobs in the junk yard she and Tom owned, then helped him set up his own business. They all owed so much to her.

He looked at the man serving him and banished thoughts of his family. 'Tell me, do people take any foodstuffs or other goods out to sell in Australia? Or even to sell on board ship?' He could break down a box of raisins into small lots, say a cupful at a time, and probably make at least double the price he'd paid for them.

'Oh, yes, sir. And they take other things besides food. Shoes and hairpins and razors. Small metal items always sell well in Australia, they tell me.'

So Mark laid out more of his capital than he'd expected, rejecting some suggestions but recognising the good sense of others. He couldn't see that Australia would be all that different from Lancashire when it came to everyday necessities. He had to buy a tin trunk to store these additional purchases in.

'You're not short of money, then,' Mr Jenner said as they left the warehouse.

'I have some but not a lot,' Mark said curtly, not liking the calculating look in his companion's eyes.

When they got back to the emigrants' depot, Mr Jenner sat reading his Bible while Mrs Jenner took it upon herself to supervise Mark's packing, with her daughter's help. He had two bags and a trunk now, and needed to put clothes into each one, as well as dividing up the trading goods to fit the space available. When they'd finished, Patience fetched the warden across to check and seal the luggage destined for the hold because certain items like firearms and alcoholic spirits were forbidden.

All the bags then had to be carefully marked with his name and for a few more pence the warden was happy to sell him the use of a small paintbrush and some white paint. One bag would go to the steerage quarters with Mark, as well as the ship's kit and his extra food-stuffs. The second would be brought up from the hold partway through the voyage, so that he could have access to clean clothes, and the third one would be brought up on deck a day or two before their arrival in Australia.

'You should put your smartest clothes in that one, Mr Gibson,' Mrs Jenner advised. 'You'll need to make a good impression on those offering employment.' She hesitated, then asked suddenly, 'My Harry has to go into the single men's quarters. I wonder if you could keep an eye on him, please? It'll be all right for Patience in the single women's quarters, because there's a matron to watch over them, but young men can be a bit wild and my Harry's been strictly brought up. He's not used to rough behaviour. I shall be worried about him on his own.'

Harry, who was sitting on his bunk nearby, gave an embarrassed smile and Mark said easily, 'Of course I'll keep an eye on him and he can look after me, too. I'm going to miss my brothers and sisters.' His voice choked on the last word and he let Mrs Jenner do what she wanted with his things because grief had suddenly over-whelmed him again and he was fighting to hold it in. If only he'd been able to say goodbye to his family prop-erly! His next and closest brother, Luke, knew what he was doing and had helped him carry his things to the station, and by sheer chance his nephew William had been on the same train, but Mark's running away would come as a shock to the others.

At one stage during the evening he felt so low in spirits he again contemplated returning home, but a little thought brought him to the same conclusion he'd reached before: going back to Bilsden would mean marrying Nelly Burns and he could never do that, never, whatever his father said. As a child he'd seen his father's feckless second wife ruin the whole family, mis-managing John Gibson's wages, turning to gin and gradually dragging them down to such dire poverty that they'd had to accept charity to survive. He remembered going hungry many a time.

No one was going to drag him down to such poverty again. *Not even the mother of his unborn child!*

The Gibson curse, he and his brothers called it,

joking about the fact that the men of the family found it all too easy to father children. His own father had nine living children from his three wives.

Well, at least Mark had provided for Nelly and her child financially – and generously – before he left. No one could fault him on that. He'd left his chop house in his brother Tom's hands, so there would be an income for Nelly and the baby – which might or might not be Mark's child.

But his brothers and sisters would fault him for running away, he was sure.

He was ashamed of that himself, but could not stand the thought of living even a month with foolish, spiteful Nelly Burns, let alone a lifetime.

It was a relief when at last the steerage passengers were allowed on board ship. But at the sight of the living conditions Mark was shaken out of his misery, horrified at how closely confined he'd be. The advertisements had said that this was a comfortable modern ship, but he didn't call this 'comfortable'. The single men's quarters were divided into tiny box-like cabins around a central space, with wooden tables and benches bolted to the floor. They were situated two levels below the deck and the air was stuffy. What's more, they would be living in perpetual twilight and always need lamps to find their way around. The flimsy wooden partitions did not reach the low roof to allow for ventilation, so you could not really hold a private conversation, and most of the cabins contained four very narrow bunks with room to stand up between them but not stretch out your arms fully. Blankets were the only doors the cabins had, tied back at present with lengths of cord.

'It's very cramped, isn't it?' Harry said.

An older man poked his head out of the next cabin and grinned at them. 'This is luxury, lads, sheer bloody luxury! Should ha' seen it on one of the older ships when I first went out to Australia. No separate cabins then, just bunks six feet wide with four of us crammed into each. Now that *were* crowded!' He cast a quick glance over his shoulder as another group of young men started to descend the companionway. 'If you two have any sense, you'll grab them upper bunks quick. It's no fun to have someone tossing and turning just a few inches above your head.'

They did as he'd suggested and when they turned round found a fresh-faced young fellow standing in the doorway.

'I'm Ned Leigh, but folk usually call me Ginger and you can guess why.' He indicated his curly red hair with a grin. Bemused, Mark found himself shaking hands with an unshakably cheerful young man of his own age, who did not seem in the least deterred by his reluctance to maintain his part in the conversation.

'Are the bottom bunks free?'

'Yes.'

'I reckon we'll join you two, then. All young fellows together. Over here, Bert!' Mark introduced himself and Harry, forcing a smile, not feeling at all sociable.

'I'm told they put us in messes – groups of eight – for the food. Do you know anything about cooking? We'll be in a right old pickle if anyone leaves that to me.' Ginger let out another high-pitched chuckle.

Mark debated with himself for a moment, then shrugged. 'I used to run an eating house. I know a fair bit.' After all, he didn't want to eat rubbish prepared by someone with no idea how to treat good food.

Ginger gaped at him for a moment, then let out a crow of laughter and clapped Mark on the back. 'Well, looks like we've fallen lucky. You're hereby elected captain of the mess and chief cook.'

'Thank God!' his companion said fervently.

The following day the pilot came on board to guide the *Matilda Mary* down from Greenwich and then they had to wait for a favourable wind to take them south towards Australia.

Everyone was delighted when they were able to set sail the day after, but Mark felt numb as he stood among an excited crowd of passengers to watch the shore of England vanish into the distance. He'd be so far away from everything he knew, and all because of his own stupidity. He'd fancied going to live in a warm, sunny country, but not like this.

The only thing he was certain of now was that he wasn't going to write to his family until he'd made something of himself. It was more than time he got out from Annie's shadow and stood on his own feet anyway.

Keara hummed happily as she walked up to the big house early one morning in April. Spring always made her feel happy and even her mam perked up as soon as the sun shone.

She had been helping out occasionally with the housework at the big house for a while now, but this would be the first time she'd worked there while the family was in residence. She repeated those magic words under her breath – 'the family is in residence' – and smiled at her own accent. Arla had given her lots of good advice and Brian Lynch was teaching her to read and write better.

She was also learning to talk in several ways, because she was a good mimic. Like her father and the villagers she spoke naturally with an Irish accent, but she could imitate her mother's Lancashire accent, and Arla was teaching her to speak in a new way for when she was working at the big house. It was a strange, clipped way of pronouncing words, 'a touch of the English' Arla called it.

Keara stopped walking to say a quick prayer that she would do well and be a credit to everyone who had helped her. Why, even Mr Mullane had spoken out for her to her father last time he came to visit. Fancy a man like him even knowing she existed!

It had rained during the night, so the trees and bushes were still beaded with droplets that glistened in the sunshine. 'Yes, Mr Mullane,' she practised aloud, shaking one branch to see the moisture fall in a silver shower. She bobbed a quick curtsey. 'No, sir.' 'Certainly, ma'am.'

The housekeeper was going to let her make the family's beds today, a fearsome responsibility, because they had to be done just so. But she'd been practising and was sure she could manage. Such a lot of covers they had. They'd be snug in those beds, even in winter, and wouldn't need to huddle together for warmth as she and her sisters did.

The master and his wife turned up in their carriage soon after she'd started on the beds, taking everyone by surprise because they usually stayed overnight at an inn after they'd got off the ferry from England and then took a mid-morning train to Sligo.

'They're here! They've come early!' someone called from the front of the house and there was the sound of feet pattering down the stairs, for they usually all went outside to welcome Mr and Mrs Mullane.

Keara stared at the unfinished bed. What should she do? She decided she'd better finish making this up in case the mistress wanted to lie down. Anyway, who would miss her? She wasn't even a regular maid here.

She tried to work as quickly as possible, but two minutes later, to her dismay, there was the sound of someone sobbing, then footsteps on the front stairs, as well as heavy breathing. The master himself came in, together with Dick Pearson, supporting the mistress between them. The poor lady looked to be in a dreadful state, her eyes all puffy and red. Without being told, Keara whipped back the covers and stepped aside to let them lay Mrs Mullane down.

'Good girl,' the master said, straightening himself up.

The mistress lay where they'd put her, continuing to weep. There was no sign of her maid.

Keara waited a minute, but the master only stood there scowling down at his wife. Keara couldn't bear to see the poor woman suffer like that, so stepped forward and laid one hand on the quivering shoulder. 'There, there, ma'am,' she said as if she were speaking to her little sister after Mara had fallen over. 'Tell me what I can do to help you.'

As the master turned to scowl at her Keara realised she'd spoken out of turn, but before he could say anything the mistress grabbed hold of her arm and clutched it, crying all the harder. So the girl plumped herself down to comfort her mistress in the only way she knew, holding her and rocking her, making shushing noises.

Gradually the wracking sobs lessened and Keara dared to glance sideways at her master for guidance. He was looking thoughtful rather than angry now, thank the Lord, and gave her a quick nod of approval.

Cook arrived then, followed by Theresa the house-maid.

'Who's the new girl?' Theo asked Cook in a low voice.

'Keara Michaels. A good little worker. Arla's helping me train her.'

'She's more than good, she's a damned miracle worker,' he said. 'This is the first time my wife has stopped weeping since we got off the ferry.'

'Did Mary not come with you, sir?'

'Yes.' He shot a quick glance towards his wife, saw she was still being petted and leaned across to whisper, 'Unfortunately the poor woman was knocked overboard in the storm and sank without trace in the rough seas.'

Cook gasped and crossed herself, muttering a quick prayer for Mary's eternal soul, then frowning. 'How could that happen?'

'My dear wife wanted something and sent Mary to find the steward, in spite of the rough weather. It seems that some drunken fool bumped into the girl as he was rushing to vomit over the side and knocked her over- board.' Theo watched the way the new maid was stroking his wife's plump white arm while continuing to make soothing noises, saw how Lavinia was enjoying this attention. 'Can this lass stay and help my wife until we find a new lady's maid for her? She's dealing with her better than anyone else has been able to since the accident.'

'Of course, sir. But Keara's only just starting – she won't know how to do things. And she's not quite seventeen.'

He turned to study the maid he had spoken up for to Mick. She looked younger than her age, very thin, as if she still had some growing to do. She'd have been quite pretty if she'd been better dressed and her hair done properly, but at the moment it was stuffed under a mob cap and strands had escaped to hang down becomingly. 'Her face looks older than sixteen.'

'Well, she's had a hard life. Mick Michaels doesn't get any kinder as he gets older and the mother's always ailing.'

'Mick's good with the horses, though, which is what I employ him for. Look, as long as Keara can keep my wife calm, let her stay here and act as her maid – just temporarily.'

Cook nodded and watched him leave the room, then turned to study the pair on the bed, her brow furrowed. That girl had no idea whatsoever how to behave with the gentry. Fancy stroking the mistress's arm in that familiar way! She bit back a gasp of shock as her newest maid put an arm round the plump shoulders of their mistress and gave her a quick hug, then helped Mrs Mullane sit up and untie her bonnet before smoothing back her tangled hair as if she were a child.

The mistress was acting like a child, too, seemingly enjoying this treatment.

'You'll feel better if we wash your face and brush your hair,' Keara murmured, adding a belated, 'ma'am'.

'Yes. Yes, you're right, child. Send up some hot water, please, Cook.' Lavinia held on tight to the girl's hand, finding her soft touches and caresses a great comfort after hours of her husband's shouting and scolding.

Cook nudged Theresa. 'Come away now and fetch up some hot water for the mistress.'

'Me? That's *her* job!' She pointed to Keara.

'Well, she can't be leaving the mistress to do it, can she? And it won't kill you to help out.'

With a flounce, Theresa accompanied her down the back stairs to the kitchen, where she told Mona the kitchen maid that Keara Michaels was trying to worm her way in with the mistress. But as she got a jug of hot water, she thought about it and shrugged. Rather Keara than her. The girl would be out of favour by tomorrow, the way their mistress blew hot and cold. She was a terrible woman to serve, changing her mind a dozen times a day about what she wanted, and looking down her nose at you. Theresa tittered at that thought. As if you could look down a squashy button of a nose like that! The mistress hadn't been chosen for her looks, that was sure. Or for her good temper. They were always glad when Mrs Mullane went back to Lancashire.

The master was all right, though. Always spoke pleasantly and quite good-looking too.

In his bedroom Theo changed out of his crumpled travelling clothes, thanked Dick for his assistance, then went down for a belated breakfast. After that he'd have to write to Mary's family and tell them what had happened because Lavinia hated writing letters.

When he had finished eating, he went to find Cook in the kitchen. 'How's Mrs Mullane? Has she rung for anything?'

'She's drinking a cup of tea and eating some toast, sir. Didn't I take them up to her meself.' She hesitated then added, 'I have to admit, young Keara's doing well. She doesn't know how to behave with the gentry, so I hope you'll forgive her if she seems a bit –' she hesitated, searching for a word '– forward.'

'She was treating my wife like a little child when I was up there and Mrs Mullane seemed to be enjoying it. But who cares as long as that keeps her calm? Not always easy, as we both know.'

They exchanged glances of understanding then he went back to the small parlour they used when they had no company and sat there alone, feeling depressed. Lavinia had lost a child before full term three times now – poor malformed little creatures. But the third pregnancy had gone on for longer than the others, so he'd begun to hope, the more fool he. The dead foetus had even looked like a real baby. A son. He'd insisted on seeing it.

The doctor said he doubted whether Lavinia would ever carry a baby to term, which was no comfort to a man who needed an heir. No comfort at all.

They had come so close last time – six months. He would give her a further spell of rest then as soon as the doctor gave permission they'd try again, whatever she said. He didn't think he could bear to go through life without a child.

The doctor said that when Lavinia was fully recovered they could try again for a baby, as long as she was looked after carefully, because she was rather delicate. But he had warned Theo to let her have a good long rest first.

CHAPTER FOUR

April 1859

To Mark's surprise the steerage passengers were kept quite busy during the voyage. They had to clean up their own cabins according to a strict system, and the men had to help clean other parts of the ship as well, such as the decks, all according to a roster. And woe betide anyone who didn't do the work properly.

Mark didn't mind because it helped pass the time, but when he was not so engaged, it sometimes seemed as if people wouldn't leave him alone for a second. He was trying to keep a diary but found it hard to put his thoughts and feelings into words, so confined himself mainly to short entries giving their latitude and longitude, how far the ship had sailed in the past twenty-four hours, and such useless information. When he re-read it, it seemed meaningless and he vowed to have nothing more to do with it, but boredom would soon send him back to his painstaking daily entries. He'd rather be doing the accounts and running a business any day!

He refused to join the men's choir, declined to take part in a group that was reading books aloud chapter by chapter, and had trouble with a persistent couple who wanted help teaching both adults and children to read, write and do arithmetic. Why ask him to teach them? What did he care whether other people could read and write or not?

Most difficult of all was avoiding Mr Jenner's attempts to enlist him in his Bible classes, or draw him into the morning prayers he held on deck. The man was a nuisance, always pushing his version of religion down your throat. A lot of people avoided him when they could. The trouble was, Mark had become quite friendly with Harry and enjoyed the company of Patience Jenner as well. She was a gentle, sensitive girl to whom the children on board often gravitated when they were in trouble. And when her father wasn't nearby, listening, she was pleasant to talk to.

Harry grumbled about the daily chores, saying it was women's work to clean and scrub, and so did his father, who had very strong views about that sort of thing. But there was nothing either of them could do about it as the chores were obligatory and the captain was a stickler for having a clean ship, as was the ship's doctor.

Harry lazed around when they were in their quarters and even had to be chivvied into doing his share of their mess duties. 'Isn't it wonderful,' he said one day, 'just to sit and do nothing?'

It was a while before Mark realised that, like Patience, Harry changed abruptly when he was with his family on deck, growing quieter and outwardly obedient to his father's orders. In fact, the whole family jumped when Alex Jenner told them to do something, and Mrs Jenner seemed to regard him with faint apprehension, never contradicting him in any way. Mark couldn't imagine his own father behaving in this dictatorial way or inspiring anyone with apprehension.

But if he wanted to enjoy Patience's company, Mark could not avoid her family. Her soothing voice and sensible comments about shipboard life didn't grate on his nerves like Ginger's stupid jokes or Harry's never-ending complaints about the work they had to do. Sometimes Mark and Patience would simply stand together at the rail, neither of them speaking, staring out over the water in a companionable silence. He was sorry when bad weather kept all the passengers below decks, but to his relief found he was a pretty good sailor and rarely felt more than a passing queasiness.

Patience had not lost her frail look, even though she had more colour in her cheeks now, but she insisted the sea air was doing her good and never complained about her health. She was a poor sailor and suffered greatly during stormy weather, always emerging from confinement below decks looking wan and listless.

She attracted respectful attention from a few young men, though nothing she said or did was in the least flirtatious. But her mother kept her by her side most of the time, apart from allowing her to walk round the decks with Mark or her brother.

One day when Harry was elsewhere Ginger grinned at Mark and said, 'Got a fondness for Miss Jenner, have you?'

'What?'

'She's a pretty little thing, though a bit wishy-washy for my taste. But then, her parents would never let her walk alone with me. They've got their sights set on you, my lad, and you're walking right into their trap.'

'Don't you dare speak about Patience like that! She's not at all calculating. You've got a nasty way of speaking. No wonder they won't let her be alone with you.'

'You take that back!'

'Why should I? It's the truth. Which is more than what you said is.'

The two men glared at one another. Mark had never thought of himself as quarrelsome, but in the end he had to walk away or he'd have thumped his cabin-mate.

That evening Ginger followed him on deck as he went to collect the evening meal for their mess. 'Look, Gibson, I just wanted to say – well, I didn't mean any insult to Miss Jenner, really I didn't. I just felt you and she looked,' he shrugged, 'comfortable together. I can see that it's serious by the way you got upset.'

Mark took a deep breath. 'I'm sorry, too. I shouldn't have fired up like that. I greatly respect and like Pa—Miss Jenner, but I don't intend to start courting *anyone* until I'm established in Melbourne and able to support a wife and family.' On that he was utterly resolved. He'd almost ruined his life over one young woman and didn't intend to take any more risks.

When Mark brought back the food – boiled potatoes and salt pork, followed by suet pudding with currants – the young men all fell upon it with their usual sharp appetite. Afterwards the conversation turned to their hopes for life in the new country. Some of them intended to head straight for the goldfields and waxed eloquent about how a man could make himself a fortune in a short time. Mark had never thought about prospecting for gold, but now, for some strange reason, he felt tempted to give it a try. Harry said wistfully that he wished he could join them, by George he did, but his father wouldn't let him.

Which brought him a lot of teasing about being a 'Daddy's boy' and had him glowering for the rest of the evening.

The following morning Mark didn't seek Patience's company but asked Mr Jenner if he could speak to him. Feeling embarrassed, he said what he had to quickly. 'Someone teased me about courting your daughter, Mr Jenner. I'm not in a position to do that, so if I've raised any expectations, I'm sorry.'

Alex Jenner frowned at him. 'We had indeed thought your intentions serious. You've spent a great deal of time talking to her – courting her, we thought.'

'I'm sorry.'

'Aye, well, I'm sorry, too. You should have been more careful about what you were doing.' He walked away, scowling.

After that relations with the Jenners, except for Harry, were very stiff, confined mainly to a nod and greeting as they passed on deck. Patience looked at him wistfully sometimes, but Mark hardened his heart to that. He had done the right thing by being honest.

But it didn't feel like the right thing and he greatly missed Patience's company.

He found himself spending time with Walter Hudson instead. The older man in the next cabin was returning to Australia after visiting his family in England and was full of tales of the goldfields. He'd financed his trip to England by his finds there and spoke in glowing terms of a miner's life and the opportunities to make your fortune.

'It's nearly all used up now, the gold money,' he said regretfully one day, 'but I had a damned good time while it lasted and I reckon I can always find more gold, whatever they say about them sodding crushing machines taking over.'

'Didn't you save any of the money?'

'No. Why should I? Haven't got a wife to nag me, have I? Don't want to settle down. No, a short life and a merry one, that's my motto. Anyway, I *like* life on the goldfields. You make good pals out there. Fellows who know how to enjoy themselves.'

Mark had never met anyone quite like Walter. In his family, you didn't place such importance on enjoying yourself but worked hard, saved your money and tried to make your way in the world.

Yes, and look where that had led him!

'What are you planning to do when you get to Australia, if you don't mind me asking?' Walter said one evening when they were about a week away from Port Melbourne. 'I thought you were going to open an eating house, but you sound as if you've changed your mind.'

'Yes, well, I thought I'd go out to the goldfields with some of the other lads. Give it a try for a while.'

'Don't.'

Mark eyed him in puzzlement. 'Why not?'

'Them lot know nowt about getting gold. You'd be better off going with someone like me instead, someone as knows all the tricks of the trade.'

'Oh? And why should you show them to me?'

Walter grinned at him. 'Because I need a stake and you need a partner who knows his way round. If you provide the money, I'll show you the ropes. We split anything we find fifty-fifty.'

'What'll you do if I say no?'

'Find some other greenhorn and ask him. But I'd rather have you. You're my first choice, because you've got a bit of sense in your noddle.' He poked Mark's upper arm and laughed. 'Though you need to harden up and build some muscles. You must have led a soft life until now.'

Mark answered obliquely. 'I'm twenty-five. Not a lad any more.'

'I'm nearing fifty. You're still a lad to me.' Walter took a long puff on the clay pipe he smoked only in the evenings to make his tobacco last the journey. 'Think about it. You could do worse, far worse.'

Mark had been dreading leaving the ship and managing on his own in a strange country. And it did make sense to go with someone who knew what he was doing. 'All right. Why not?' he said recklessly. 'But I'll want paying back for the money I put up for the equipment. I shan't charge you interest, though.'

Walter scowled for a moment, then shrugged. 'That's a bit tight-fisted.'

Mark shrugged. 'Take it or leave it.' He wasn't

giving his hard-earned money to a spendthrift like Walter, who might not be able to deliver what he boasted. If they found gold, the money might not matter, but if they didn't he was only risking his share.

Walter clapped him on the shoulder. 'Oh, all right. It won't really matter because we'll make a fortune together, you'll see. I feel lucky, just like I did last time.'

When Mr Mullane told her she could take a couple of hours off that afternoon, Keara stared at him in surprise. 'But the mistress didn't say anything about it.'

'Aye, well, my wife always forgets that her maids have a life and family of their own, not to mention a right to some time off. I'll tell her. You get off now and visit your mother.'

'Thank you very much, sir.'

He watched her walk away. She was appallingly dressed, wearing badly scuffed shoes that looked as if they had once belonged to someone with much bigger feet and a dark dress that also fitted badly, but even so there was something very attractive about her. Strange, that. His wife didn't usually hire young or pretty maids. But Keara Michaels had such a kind heart, she had been completely taken in by his wife's complaining and moaning, and her kindness was balm to Lavinia's selfish soul.

His wife also seemed to enjoy teaching her new maid. They spent hours practising doing her hair or dressing and undressing. The lass knew nothing about looking after a lady and her clothes, but was quick to learn. And when he had asked around, everyone on the estate seemed to have a good word for Keara – except her father. Which made him feel sorry for her. Fancy a father talking so scornfully about his own daughter.

He'd heard Keara and his wife talking and laughing together from his own bedroom. It'd been a while since he'd heard Lavinia laughing. Well, she didn't laugh when she was with him, only when she was with those spiteful, gossiping friends of hers.

Already, with the good food the household ate, Keara's complexion had cleared up, the skin becoming soft and creamy, the cheeks rosy . . . He shook his head in irritation. What was he thinking about? He didn't tamper with his wife's maids because it was foolish to foul your own nest. Perhaps he could find himself a mistress here in Ireland. A man had his needs, and even a *gentleman* had those same needs, contrary to what his wife believed.

Ah, gentleman! The very word was a trap. Theo didn't feel like a gentleman, just a man, and he hated fuss and ceremony, while his bloody wife couldn't even drink a cup of tea without the tray being perfectly set out and the tasks of pouring the tea completed in exactly the right order.

Unaware that she was the object of her master's lustful thoughts, Keara went hurrying down to tell Cook that the master had given her permission to take the afternoon off, then made her way home, happy that her father was busy in the stables and unable to interfere.

As she walked she thought how kind Mr Mullane was! A pleasant smile for everyone, even her, the lowliest of his employees. She'd never thought you could *like* a landowner, but all the servants liked him and she did too now that she knew him a bit better. And he was a good-looking man, all the maids agreed about that. Such thick, dark hair. And kept himself so clean, always having baths and changing his clothes. Her father smelled strongly of the stables, but although Mr Mullane spent a lot of time with his horses, he left his mucky boots at the scullery door and changed his clothes before dinner. They were always changing their clothes, the gentry.

Keara smiled down at herself. She was cleaner too because Cook insisted on the maids washing every single day. Even Arla hadn't insisted on that. But it made your skin feel nice. She hugged the bundle of scraps Cook had given her, delighted to be taking such good food back for her family. She would be sorry when the Mullanes went back to Lancashire because there was a lot of wasted food when they were in residence and her sisters were benefiting greatly from that. Her mother still had very little appetite, though.

She smiled as she walked along, remembering her own ignorance when she arrived at the big house. There were so many things she hadn't known, such as what a perk was, but Theresa had soon explained the strict customs about which servant was entitled to what. Well, as long as they gave her the food scraps, Keara didn't care about what the others got as perks.

Mara looked up as her sister entered the cottage and came running across to greet her, arms outstretched. Keara dropped the bundle of food on the table and gave the child a big hug, lifting her off her feet and spinning her round and round till she was shrieking in delight. Keara sometimes thought she would melt with the love she had for Mara and Ismay, and when she set her little sister down, held her close for a minute without saying anything.

Ismay watched them from the corner, as quiet and self-contained as ever. Keara went across and gave her a quick hug because Ismay didn't like anyone to hold her for long, then turned to walk into her mother's out-stretched arms and rock to and fro in the long but silent cuddle Betsy always gave her.

Only today, for the first time, she realised how sour they all smelled. It made her feel guilty for even noticing. And the cottage smelled, too.

'Eh, it's that good to see you, love.' Her mother smiled at her fondly. 'Have you got the afternoon off?'

'Yes, Mr Mullane said I could come and see you. Look what I've brought.' She spread out the food proudly. 'You'd better eat something now, Mam, before *he* comes back and gobbles it all. Look, there's a nice piece of lean ham. Take that for yourself. And the ham fat'll be lovely for frying up some potatoes, won't it?'

Tears came into Betsy's eyes as she picked up the ham, something they rarely saw. 'Eh, lass, you shouldn't talk about your father like that.' She ate a few mouth-fuls, but as usual displayed little appetite.

'Well, *he* shouldn't take all my wages and spend them on drink.' Cook had told her how her da had been buying drinks for all his friends. 'Did he give you *any* of my money?'

'No, and it's no use fretting about it, love. They do what they want, fellows, an' you won't change your father by shouting at him. That only makes him more stubborn.'

Keara noticed the bruise on her mother's face and touched it gently. 'Why did he hit you this time?'

Betsy lowered her voice. 'Same reason. Because I wouldn't let him . . .' She shrugged and let her voice trail away. Even though the doctor had warned him it would probably kill her to have another baby, Mick still tried to use her body sometimes. Father Cornelius had scolded him about this, so had the doctor, but it made no difference once he was drunk.

'He didn't – force you?'

'No, love. Not this time. And there was no problem from last time. I think the Virgin's looking after me.' Betsy patted her flat stomach.

Her father had forced himself on his wife a few times since the last baby was born, Keara knew. If he killed her mother by getting her with child, she'd never go near him again. She wished sometimes he'd drop dead. She could hardly bear to speak to him, either here or at the big house. And no matter how many penances the priest gave her when she confessed to such thoughts – she'd had to say ten Hail Marys last time, not five! – the thought that they'd be far better off without her father wouldn't go away. Apart from the money Keara could earn, Ismay was twelve now, old enough to earn a bit here and there, and even Mara could have got occasional work in the fields, scaring off the birds or weeding.

She drifted off for a moment into her favourite daydream of them all living together in this cottage without *him*, then felt a hand tugging at hers.

'Can we go for a walk in the woods, please?' Mara smiled up at her pleadingly. 'Mam's always too tired to go, but it's such a lovely day.'

Keara looked at her mother. 'Is it all right? Just for an hour or so.'

'Of course it is, love. It'll do her good to get out. As long as the rain holds off.'

Keara turned to Ismay. 'Do you want to come with us?'

'No. Arla says she'll give me an hour or two's work this afternoon. I've been helping her quite a bit because she's not been well, but you're not to tell anyone that. And I don't let on to Da about how often I work there. He thinks I get paid only in food. I'm saving the pennies she gives me. It's not much but it might help us one day.'

Surprised by these revelations Keara watched as her sister walked off down the lane. Ismay looked as neat and quiet as usual. She was twelve now and growing up fast. Turning back, Keara looked at her mother. 'You're to have a good rest while we're gone, mind.'

'Aye, I'll do that.' Betsy went to the door to see them off. As they got to the end of the garden, she called out suddenly, 'Hey, girls! Don't forget to bring me back my pennyworth of sunshine!'

Keara smiled. 'You always say that.'

'Because I always wish you could do it. We've not had a really sunny day for ages.'

She watched them as they walked away. With Keara so tall and womanly now, they looked more like mother and child than sisters, and they acted it, too. As the sun appeared from behind the clouds Betsy lifted her face, enjoying the warmth on her skin.

She stayed there until the sun went in again, then decided to go and lie down. Tears came into her eyes as she turned back into the cottage. What way was this to live? She'd seen Keara's face as she'd looked round. Little better than animals, they were, and it was all Mick's fault. Diarmid could have found them another cottage, but the rent would have been higher, so Mick had said they were all right as they were. How could he think *this* was all right, with just the one room and the girls growing fast into women? It was a hovel.

The only comfort she had was that she had stayed respectable. Her girls knew how to behave and neither begged nor stole. And although Keara was grown up now, Betsy knew that she was a good girl. She'd had several talks with her about keeping herself pure because she didn't want her daughters making the same mistake as she had and spending the rest of their lives ruing it.

She lay down on the straw mattress she and Mick shared, sighing as she tried to calm her thoughts. But images were running through her mind. Of Keara mostly. Eh, what was going to happen to the lass? Even if she kept herself decent, which was hard enough for a pretty girl, Betsy didn't want to see her marry someone like Mick. She didn't want any of her girls to live like this. She said a quick prayer to the Virgin, begging her intercession for all three daughters and felt better afterwards as she settled to sleep, letting her thoughts drift from one girl to the other.

Ismay was quieter than the other two, less demonstrative, but you couldn't doubt that all three of them loved one another. Betsy was sure they'd watch out for one another if anything happened to her. She liked to watch their dark, curly hair flying in the breeze as they ran for no reason but the joy of it, see their bright blue eyes sparkling with interest at the world around them.

Their father had been like that when she first met him. Eh, Mick had been so set up with himself to have landed a job in Lancashire and got away from the village. And he'd been so angry when they made him marry her and come back to Ballymullan. She'd been a fool to give in to him, but she'd really believed he loved her. And whatever he said, it had ruined her life far more than his. Though you couldn't really regret having a daughter like Keara.

Now, Mick's hair was getting thinner and turning grey, his face was puffy and his eyes were usually bloodshot. His drinking would be the undoing of them all, she knew it. And he was getting bad-tempered, hitting her, hitting the children. She didn't know what to do about that. She got so tired sometimes, as if she had no bones to hold her up, but he still expected her to rush round after him.

Her health was failing, she knew, but she didn't want to die until her children were old enough to manage without her. Keara was old enough to fend for herself now, but Ismay and Mara weren't. What worried Betsy most was the thought of someone putting the younger ones in the poorhouse. It didn't matter how many times the priest or other people in the village assured her that it would never come to that, not on Mr Theo's estate. The poorhouse was an abiding memory from her own childhood and not a pleasant one, either. When her mother had died, they'd put Betsy in that place and she'd not escaped its grim confines until she was old enough to go into service at the age of twelve.

Eh, I'm being silly today, she thought. That's all in the past now. Nothing's going to happen to my children. Mr Theo's a good landlord, not at all like his father. He didn't throw Moira out when her husband died, did he? And he won't throw my girls out if anything happens to me.

She decided she wasn't going to sleep, got up and went to sort through the scraps of food, forcing a few more mouthfuls down to keep her strength up, then just sitting by the table because it seemed too much trouble to go across to the bed and lie down again.

When the two girls came back from their walk, they found their mother asleep, with her head on her arms.

Keara put one finger to her lips and took Mara outside again, giving her something to eat and making it a game to keep very quiet. Before she left she would tell her mother to hide some of the food so that her father didn't gobble it all. He was always begging scraps from Cook and yet he ate more than his share at home. He was a greedy devil.

She was hungry now herself, but she got plenty to

eat at the big house so didn't take anything, enjoying the sight of Mara eating so heartily. But within a few minutes of finishing her food, Mara had woken their mother with her laughter, and anyway Keara knew by the lengthening shadows that it was time to leave. She stood up reluctantly, hugging Mara then turning to her mother. 'Will you walk me to the end of the lane, Mam?'

Arm in arm they walked slowly along, with Mara skipping in front of them.

'Eh, you're a lovely daughter,' her mother told her as they said goodbye, emotion bringing the Lancashire accent more strongly into her voice.

'Eh, you're a luvly mam, too,' Keara teased, mimicking her accent.

'And you're – keeping yourself pure – like I told you?'

'You know I am, Mam. Who is there to go with anyway? Mr Mullane?' She laughed at the mere thought. As if a lovely man like him would look twice at a girl like her.

'That's a good lass.'

'That's a good mam, too.' She left her mother laughing and looking almost pretty for once.

It was hard to live and work in the big house away from them all, but at least she saw them every day or two, and Cook said it'd be more often once the family had gone back to England. Keara really pitied the girls who had to go away from the village to find work. She never wanted to leave.

★

'I think I'll take Keara back to Lancashire with us,' Lavinia said abruptly over dinner that same night. 'She's a good little worker.'

Theo looked across the table, his fork poised close to his mouth, surprised as much by her decisive tone as by what she had said. 'I think that'd be a mistake. She's ignorant of so many things, can't even read and write properly. The other servants will make her life difficult.'

'She won't be working with the other servants most of the time, she'll be with me. And I can teach her, can't I?'

'Lavinia, she's not suitable for a lady's maid. She's too young and untrained.' He looked at his wife's simpler hairstyle and wondered whether that really mattered. Lavinia was looking better than she had for a long time, happier too. She had even lost the unhealthy pallor that came from staying indoors all the time because Keara encouraged her to take short walks to see a bush in flower or a pretty pond, things he would never have expected Lavinia to enjoy. He frowned. Surely all these changes couldn't be due solely to a sixteen-year-old girl's influence?

Lavinia waved one hand impatiently. 'I shall enjoy training her.' Her voice took on a coaxing tone, something rare in their relationship which for several years had been frosty at best, more often openly antagonistic. 'Please, Theo. I *need* Keara. She cheers me up. I haven't felt so well in a long time.'

'I'll think about it.' He decided to watch them carefully when they were together from now on. If it really was because of Keara that Lavinia had cheered up, then he'd definitely take the girl back to England with them. 'Have you asked her if she wants to leave Ireland?'

'*Asked her?* She'll jump at the opportunity to better herself.'

'They don't always.' Diarmid had told him how devoted Keara was to her family and how much they needed her.

'But she *couldn't* refuse! Theo – you won't let her, will you?'

He was surprised by her vehemence and liked her better for her encouragement of the girl. She avoided so many of the duties of the lady of the manor, both here and in Lancashire that he had almost given up urging her to look after their people. 'No, of course not. If I decide to take her, we'll make sure she can't refuse.'

The other side to this was that his wife wanted it so much. Well, he wanted something from her. If Lavinia was grateful enough, feeling happier about life, it might be easier for them both to try for another child.

Keara stared at her mistress in horror, unable to hide her shock. '*Go to England with you?* Oh, I'm sorry, ma'am, but I couldn't be thinking of it. Not at all. My mam wouldn't be able to manage without me.'

Lavinia stared at her in even greater shock. 'You can't mean that, Keara! It'd be such a wonderful opportunity for you to better yourself. And anyway – I need you.' Her voice wobbled as she said that and her pale eyes welled with tears.

Keara's voice softened as she sought for ways to persuade her mistress that it wouldn't work. 'Mrs Mullane, when you get back to your fine house in England, you'll need a maid who knows about clothes and hair and things like that, you know you will. You've had to teach me everything and I'm still so ignorant I can only do simple hairstyles. I'm sure they'd be after laughing at me in England.'

'I'd make sure they didn't.' Besides, it was very soothing to have someone practise brushing and arranging your hair.

'You're very kind, ma'am, but . . .' Keara hesitated, then explained in more detail about the situation at home and how badly her mother needed her here.

Theo stood quietly in the next room, listening shamelessly to the conversation. He'd been watching the two of them for the past few days and had concluded that the girl was indeed responsible for Lavinia's better humour. Strange that one so young could be so capable. And that Lavinia should enjoy teaching her. He pulled a wry face. Well, she wasn't usually better at things than other people. It must be something new for her to feel superior. Those so-called friends of hers in England merely tolerated her, because they were used to her and she was one of them.

As the conversation continued and he heard Keara speak about life in the Michaels' cottage, however, he grew annoyed at the thought of the child's wages being wasted on drink. He hadn't realised quite how bad things were for them when he told Mick that his daughter's wages would be paid to him.

★

The next time Keara went to visit her family, she heard footsteps behind her in the woods and a voice called, 'Wait!'

She turned round, surprised to see her master walking towards her, for he usually rode a horse when he went out. 'Mr Mullane, sir!'

He came up to her, staring at her in a way that made her wonder if her hair was in a mess. He did stare at her sometimes. Other times she could have been invisible for all he noticed her. But you couldn't help noticing him. He was so full of life and energy.

'Have you thought better about coming to Lancashire with us?' he asked abruptly.

Her heart sank and she shook her head. 'I'm sorry, but I can't do it, sir.'

'Why not?'

'I told you. My family needs me.'

'What your family needs is good food. They can have that if you come with us. And a better cottage, too.'

Tears filled her eyes. 'But I don't want to leave them. I don't. I'm sorry, sir, but I won't change my mind about that.'

She turned to walk on, but he grasped her arm and pulled her back to stand in front of him. 'A moment, if you please. What you want isn't the only thing that matters, Keara. I want my wife to be happy, and you keep her happier than anyone else has been able to. Your mother wants to put food on the table for your sisters every day, to see them growing sturdy and strong. Am I not right?'

She stared at him, unable to frame a word, feeling the strength in the hand that held her. She'd thought him a kind man, but now, seeing the power behind the friendliness, she shivered suddenly.

'I'm not asking you now, Keara, I'm telling you. You're coming to England with us and you're going to continue doing whatever it is that keeps my wife content.' As she opened her mouth to refuse, he held up one forefinger to silence her. 'If you don't, your father will be out of a job and your family will be thrown out of that hovel you call home.'

'Ah, sir, you wouldn't! You wouldn't do that, surely?'

'I would, Keara. When I want something, I do whatever's necessary to get it.' And he wanted a child out of his wife more than he wanted anything else in the whole world. 'On the other hand, if you come with me, I'll give your family one of the new cottages – at the same rent.'

Keara quailed at the determination in his eyes. She'd seen cats stalking birds and sometimes the bird would stop trying to escape and remain motionless while the stalker pounced. She felt like that now. Trapped. She couldn't move, couldn't do anything about the sudden dread that he'd planted inside her. Something deep inside her began keening softly, as if it sensed her coming loss.

He released her arm and took a step backwards. 'I'm not giving you any more time to think, I'm telling you straight, Keara Michaels. You're coming to England with us.'

This time she didn't dare protest, only make a whimpering sound in her throat.

He hardened his heart against the pain on her face. He wouldn't throw her family out – of course he wouldn't! – but she was not to know that. 'When you get back from your visit this afternoon, you can tell my wife you've changed your mind. Tell her you couldn't bear to leave her, even though you and I know you're doing it out of love for your family. Is that understood?' When she didn't reply, only looked at him pleadingly, her beautiful blue eyes full of tears, he said again, 'Is – that – understood?'

Keara looked at him in dumb misery. It would kill her mother to lose her home and have to go on the road. Or, worse, go back into the poorhouse. It would ruin Ismay and Mara's lives, too. She couldn't do that to them. And it would make her mother very happy indeed to have a better cottage, she knew that as well. Her mother craved respectability and tried desperately to keep up appearances. When Cook had given Keara some old clothes they'd cleared out of the attic, her mother had been over the moon about them, altering them carefully, walking proudly to Mass on Sundays in her new dress and shoes. Never mind that the shoes didn't fit her properly and hurt her feet, or that the brown material of the dress made her look even paler.

One last look Keara gave him, begging him silently to change his mind, and even thought for a minute that she'd seen shame in his eyes. But she must have been mistaken. All he did was stare at her and say icily, 'Well?'

'I don't have any choice, do I, sir?'

'No. You don't.' He surprised her by adding, 'I'm sorry. But there are other people to think of besides yourself. That's what life's like.'

Keara said nothing. But one day she would find a way to escape from England and come back to be with her sisters. One day, when her mother no longer needed her wages.

When she looked up there was a different expression on his face, one that made her feel – uneasy. Mother of God, he was looking at her as a man looks at a woman! Her mother would have a fit if she saw that.

Then his expression changed again and Keara had to wonder if she'd been imagining the other thing. Yes, of course she had! How could a fine, handsome gentleman like him ever be attracted to a rough village girl like her?

'Goodbye, Keara,' he said abruptly, and turned on his heel.

She watched him go and even though she felt angry about what he was doing to her, she could not help thinking how well he looked, crackling with energy and life. As she continued on her way, she used the back of her hand to wipe away a tear or two. She looked round because every tree, every bush that she passed, seemed more beautiful than ever before, so softly green with the tender look of spring foliage.

What was it like in Lancashire? It couldn't possibly be as beautiful as here in Ballymullan, with the steep hills rising beyond the village, their tops wreathed in cloud as often as not and ah, the softness of the air on a summer evening. She knew every curl and twist of the landscape, every tree, bush and rock. Memories flooded into her mind of the different seasons, of *her* village, of the woods in autumn, the flowers in summer, and more tears flowed.

How would she bear leaving Ireland? It was as much a part of her as her family was.

As she got near home she stopped, taking a few deep breaths and trying to smile. She didn't want to upset her mother, so would have to pretend she was excited about going to England. She could never pretend to be glad at leaving her family, though. Never.

But to her great disappointment, her mother was delighted about her news and insisted it'd be the making of her.

'But I'll have to leave you,' Keara sobbed.

'Eh, you'd be doing that soon anyway, love. Lasses don't stay at home once they reach your age. They either get wed or they go somewhere to find work.' Betsy looked round, for once allowing her dislike of their home to show. 'And if we're to have one of the new cottages, well, I can't think of anything better for your sisters. What sort of place is this? I don't even *want* you to stay here.'

She turned back to Keara and said firmly, 'So we'll not have any more of this nonsense. You be thankful for such a good chance and make the most of it. What you're doing will help all of us.'

But when Keara had gone, Betsy sighed. She would

miss her desperately. It would be like losing a best friend as well as a daughter. She sobbed, then balled one hand up and pressed it to her mouth. She mustn't cry. This was the best thing for Keara, the very best. She must take her comfort from that.

When she got back to the big house that afternoon, Keara did as her employer had ordered and told her mistress she'd changed her mind about going to England.

Mrs Mullane beamed at her. 'Oh, Keara, I'm glad, so very glad!' She saw that the girl was looking sad and added, 'I know you love your family, but it'll mean we're still together. And anyway, no one can have everything they want in this world.' She scowled on this thought as she said, 'You just have to do the best you can.'

After another pause, she added, 'You'll grow to love your new home, I'm sure. Eastwood House is much nicer than this place, much bigger too, and the part of Lancashire where we live is near the moors, which are very pretty. Theo says your mother's from Lancashire. She must have told you about it.'

But although Keara pretended to be happy about the change and encouraged her mistress to tell her about the big house and all its comforts, England was a foreign country and it meant nothing to her.

And already she was finding Mrs Mullane – difficult.

★

Father Cornelius found Keara sobbing her heart out in the little church a few afternoons later. 'What's the matter, child?'

She hiccupped to a halt. 'I don't want to go to England.'

'How can you say that?'

'Because it's true.'

'But think of your family. Think of the difference your wages will make to them. And I hear they're to move to one of the new cottages as well, because of you.'

'But Da will spend the extra money I earn on drink. It's not fair! My mother and sisters will still be hungry.'

Father Cornelius was silent for a moment or two. She was right about that and it was a crying shame. 'Shall I ask Mr Mullane to have your wages paid to Arla instead, then? And to say that only your mother can use them to buy food?'

She blinked at him. 'Could you be doing that, Father?'

'Indeed I could. I'm sure Mr Mullane will agree that it's a good idea. We'll leave you a shilling or two, because you'll need some money, but the rest can come to your mother. Will that make you feel better, child?'

'Yes. Thank you.' It still didn't make up for losing everything she knew and loved, but to know that her mother and sisters were eating decently would be a great comfort.

His voice grew gentler. 'It's a good thing for you as well, you know, taking this position.' He studied her face, flushed now with tears but still pretty, and decided on a word of caution. 'As long as you don't start courting and getting yourself married while you're over there in England.'

Keara let out a scornful bark of laughter that turned into a sob. '*Me? Marry?* I'll never do that, Father. Never in this world! I've seen what marriage does to women and I'm not letting a man ruin *my* life, thank you very much.'

The priest smiled wryly as he watched her walk away, shoulders still slumped and head drooping. He'd heard that vehement denial of any intention to marry before, but most girls got wed all the same. And rightly so. Or there would be no next generation.

His smile faded. He just hoped Keara didn't get into trouble in England, as her father had. And her mother. He'd have a word with her about that and about mortal sin before she left.

CHAPTER FIVE

April–May 1859

A few days later Keara got into the second carriage with Mr Mullane's manservant and sat trying not to weep as it drove them to the station.

'Mr Mullane will be angry if he sees you in tears,' Dick warned. 'He wants you to cheer his wife up.'

'Then he shouldn't be making me leave my family, should he?'

He sighed and thrust an immaculate handkerchief into her hand. 'Wipe your eyes this minute, you silly girl. Have you no pride, to let your feelings show for all the world to see?'

Keara hiccupped to a halt.

'Wipe your eyes!' he repeated more gently. 'We'll be back in a month or two, you know. It's not as if you're going away for ever.'

She did as he'd ordered because you couldn't keep on crying even when your heart was breaking. She'd wept herself to sleep in the servants' attic at the big house last night after saying goodbye to her family. 'Thank you, Mr Pearson.'

'Ah, call me Dick. I'm not one to stand on ceremony.'

She blinked in surprise, then gave him a tiny smile. 'Dick.' Calling him that made her feel more grown-up and important, somehow.

When the carriages drew up at the railway station in Sligo, Dick gave her a nudge. 'Go and see if your mistress wants anything. They're paying you to fuss over her, so go and fuss.' His own relationship with his employer was easy enough. They'd played together as lads and Theo mostly treated him like a friend. His valeting duties were light because Theo wasn't one for fancy clothes and elaborate hairstyles, nor would he wear the full side whiskers or moustache that were so popular these days. He said they were too much trouble and made his face itch. And when, at Lavinia's urging, they'd tried a central parting all the way from the front to the nape of the neck, brushing the side hair out into full clumps, which were all the go, Theo had burst out laughing and said to hell with fashion, he didn't want to look like a tailor's dummy.

Lavinia complained bitterly about her husband's lack of 'gentlemanly style', but other ladies didn't seem to mind and Dick had seen them trying to flirt with Theo at the rare social functions he hosted.

Keara went across and bobbed a curtsey, asking if there was anything she could do for her mistress. Her voice sounded flat, not like it usually did, but she couldn't help that.

Mr Mullane looked at her through narrowed eyes, as if he knew how she was feeling.

Mrs Mullane gave her a smug smile. 'Not at the moment, dear. You stay with Pearson.'

Keara stared round as she walked back to join Dick. She had never been to Sligo before, never seen a railway station, let alone ridden in a train. Arla had explained what trains were like, but that hadn't prepared Keara for the sight of the noisy metal monster puffing out clouds of steam that drew into the station soon afterwards and she cried out in shock, crossing herself and edging closer to Dick.

He grinned. 'It's all right. That's only steam and noise. Just think of it as a big kettle boiling.'

It was like no kettle she'd ever seen.

The station master himself came out to escort the Mullanes to their compartment and when Keara would have followed them, Dick tugged her back. 'Us servants ride second-class. Come on. This way.'

She swallowed hard as they got into the train, trying to hold back her fear and sitting very upright as she waited for something to happen. When the train jerked forward a few inches, she squeaked and clutched the edge of the seat. Then a whistle blew and there were clouds of steam everywhere outside the carriage window. She edged closer to Dick.

'It's not going to hurt you,' he said. 'For heaven's sake, girl, people ride in trains all the time.'

As they moved off, the cloud of white vapour cleared and they began to travel across the countryside so quickly Keara couldn't imagine how the train even stayed on the rails. Which gave her something new to worry about.

But as the journey continued, the rhythmic clack-
ing noise began to soothe her. 'I'm sorry,' she said
suddenly.

Dick raised his head from his book. 'Mmm? What
for?'

'Being such an eejit! About the train.'

'That's all right.' He lowered his eyes to his book
again.

Since he clearly didn't want to chat she watched
through the window as they travelled on, stopping here
and there so that people could get on or off, or, as Dick
informed her at one of the stops, go and relieve themselves in the station waiting rooms. He took her to
the ladies' second-class waiting room at one of the
stops and gave her a quick push when she hesitated
outside it.

'Go on! You'll not last all the way otherwise.'

When she came out again, he wasn't there and for
a minute she almost panicked, then she saw Mr and Mrs
Mullane walking past and knew she hadn't been
deserted. She hurried back to the train to find Dick still
reading his book. She wondered what it was about. She
could read a bit, but not the long words and not whole
books like that. Who would ever want to sit indoors
reading, anyway, when you could be outside in the
open air?

Only – the journey seemed to be taking a long time.
She wasn't used to sitting still doing nothing. She
wished she had something to occupy her other than sad
thoughts about what her mother and sisters might be
doing now.

★

The ferry was just as frightening as the train had been and as the ship pulled away from the dock Keara crossed herself automatically.

'*Don't* do that!' Mrs Mullane snapped.

'Don't do what, ma'am?'

'Cross yourself all the time. We're not Catholics and neither are most of our staff. They'll laugh at you if you act so superstitiously.'

'I'll – try not to, ma'am.' But she hadn't even realised she was doing it, so how she was to stop, she didn't know.

'That's a good girl. And now, I think I'll go and lie down. You can come with me to help. Ships always make me feel sick. I may need a basin quickly.'

Keara did as she was told and watched her mistress lie down on a narrow bed. She had only a hard chair and sat on it staring listlessly out of the porthole of her mistress's cabin as it gradually grew dark. A short distance below her the grey-green water of the Irish Sea was heaving up and down and just to look at it made her feel queasy.

Suddenly Mrs Mullane called out, 'Fetch the bowl! Quickly!' and was very sick.

She vomited several times more, which Dick had also warned Keara would happen, but Mrs Mullane wouldn't let her maid take the bucket away to empty it. Indeed, she seemed absolutely terrified of Keara so much as poking her nose outside the cabin door after the dreadful accident that had killed poor Mary.

It was near dawn when they disembarked in Liverpool and her mistress had already recovered enough to complain about having to wake up at such a ridiculously early hour. Keara, who had not slept a wink on the hard chair, cast scared glances around her as they walked off the ship. Heavens, this was worse than Sligo. She'd never seen so many people in all her life! Who were they all? Where had they come from? And why were they not at home, minding their own business?

Mr Mullane handed his wife into a cab, which he summoned with one twitch of a forefinger. Another signal and a second cab drew up behind it, into which Dick waved Keara while he supervised the loading of the luggage.

'We'll be home before noon,' he told her when they were on board yet another train. 'You'll find Ellerdale very different from Ballymullan.'

'Yes. My mother told me.'

'The town's changed a lot since your mother left, I'm sure. It grows bigger every year. A dirty old place it is nowadays, but you won't be seeing much of it because Eastwood House is out in the country. Theo would hate to live in a town.'

'Do you call the master Theo?' she asked, wide-eyed.

'Not when we're in public, but in private, yes. Didn't the two of us play together as boys?'

He leaned back and closed his eyes with a tired sigh, so Keara didn't say anything else. Every minute was taking her further from her family. And she wouldn't be able to run away if she didn't like it in England because she didn't have the money to pay her fare back to Ballymullan. Even if she'd known how to get there.

At Ellerdale Station Mr Mullane's own carriages were waiting for them and even the one provided for the servants was clean and comfortable. Keara stared out in dismay at the rows of dirty-looking terraced houses that climbed the hillside behind the station and the big chimneys to one side that were belching out black smoke. 'Why is everything so dirty?' she whispered.

'Because of the smoke from the mills, of course,' Dick said.

'What makes all the smoke?'

'The engines that drive the machinery.' But he could see she didn't understand what he was talking about, so he didn't elaborate. The poor lass looked exhausted, but Mrs Mullane would have her running here and there once they'd arrived.

Half an hour later the master's carriage stopped in front of a large, ugly, red-brick house while Keara and Dick were taken round the back. He took her inside to the servants' hall and told her to sit there and wait for Mrs Bertram.

The housekeeper didn't come for a quarter of an hour and she didn't look pleased as she finally took Keara into her office. 'Stand there.' She went to sit behind the desk. 'Now, how old are you?'

'Sixteen, ma'am.'

'Not "ma'am" – Mrs Bertram.'

'Sorry. Mrs Bertram, then.'

'You look older.'

What did you say to that? Keara wondered. 'I'll be seventeen soon, Mrs Bertram.' Could she help how she looked? She didn't understand why the housekeeper seemed so displeased with her.

'Well, I don't know how you wormed your way into the mistress's favour, but you won't find me so easy to charm, I promise you. I could find a dozen maids in Ellerdale who'd know their jobs better than you and not cause me a minute's trouble. There's no good ever comes from a mistress making a pet of a maid, so don't get above yourself.'

Keara kept silent only with difficulty at the injustice of this. As if she'd wanted to come here!

'You haven't got any decent clothes and Mrs Mullane says your family is too poor to provide you with a proper outfit, so we'll have to supply you with one. I'll talk to you about that tomorrow. In the meantime the mistress wants you to help her.' She opened the door and called out, 'Minnie, this is Keara, Mrs Mullane's new maid. Take her upstairs.'

Minnie gaped at Keara then back at the housekeeper.

'Did you hear me, Minnie?'

'Yes, Mrs Bertram. Sorry. Come this way, please, Keara.'

Mrs Mullane greeted her with, 'There you are at last. My poor head is still aching from that *dreadful* journey. I want you to rub it.'

The girl stifled a sigh. Didn't she feel exhausted herself? But she succeeded so well in soothing her mistress that Mrs Mullane was smiling as she went down to join her husband for a stylishly late dinner.

Left behind in the lavishly furnished bedroom, Keara began to tidy up, tears dripping down her cheeks, try as she would to hold them back. After a while she grew angry with herself. What good did it do to weep? She was here now and that was that. She must make the best of it.

She got lost on the way down to the servants' quarters, only to find everyone already seated at the long table eating their supper. Eight people stared at her and when she offered them a tentative smile, no one smiled back.

'You're late,' said Mrs Bertram from the head of the table.

'I'm sorry. I was tidying Mrs Mullane's things.'

'Minnie should have come up for you.' She frowned at the other maid.

'Sorry, Mrs B. I forgot.'

Keara could see Minnie wasn't at all sorry and wondered if she had 'forgotten' on purpose.

Mrs Bertram's voice reminded her where she was. 'Well, sit down and eat your meal quickly now.'

Keara took the empty chair and found that someone had filled a plate with food for her. Good food, too, but she didn't feel hungry. She bent her head for a moment to say grace, then forced herself to eat. The rows of staring faces terrified her. Everything here terrified her. She felt more tears well up and wiped them away surreptitiously, but she could see that Minnie had noticed and was looking scornful.

Afterwards, the master sent Dick down with a message that Mrs Mullane wouldn't need her maid any more, which made Minnie and another woman exchange glances and titter. They took Keara up to the maids' room in the attics, which she would share with four other women, but they made little effort to include her in their conversation and when she brought out the ragged nightgown which was all she owned, Minnie rolled her eyes and nudged the woman next to her, who sniggered and whispered something behind her hand. Then they both tittered.

Keara got into bed, beyond tears now, and lay there wondering how she was going to face living here.

'I hope you're not snivelling again,' said a voice in the darkness. 'You should be grateful for your luck in getting that job. You'll have to teach the rest of us how to win the mistress's favour.'

'Sure, I didn't want to come here at all!'

Minnie just laughed. 'Tell that to the trees! They might believe you, but *we* know better. And however you wormed your way into her good books, you won't stay there. No one ever does. You'll be sorry one day.'

Keara was sorry now, but didn't waste time saying so. She let herself sink into the sleep of exhaustion and didn't stir until Minnie shook her awake in the morning.

After a week of working in the Lancashire house, Keara was in the deepest despair. Those seven days had been the worst – the very worst! – of her whole life. Not only was she homesick for Ireland and her family, but she was ignorant of so many everyday things that the other maids mocked her openly.

One day Minnie sent her to fetch a 'bucket of steam' from the laundry and she went for it without thinking because the soft patter of rain against the window panes had reminded her of home. The laundress laughed so much she nearly choked before telling the girl she'd fallen for an old trick. Red-faced, Keara returned to her duties. It was her birthday today, but she hadn't told anyone. What would they care?

Later that morning she made another foolish mistake and Minnie told the others about it in the servants' hall as they ate their midday meal.

They all laughed so heartily Keara couldn't bear it a second longer and shoved back her chair so hard it crashed to the ground. She ran out of the house, bawling as loudly as a child, ignoring Mrs Bertram's call to come back this minute. Not caring where she was going, she raced across the stable yard in the new shoes that Arla had found for her, but which hurt her feet and had rubbed blisters on her heels. When she saw a man coming towards her, she ran away from him down the path that led into the cool shadiness of the woods, wanting only to be alone. Further down the path she came to a stream and flung herself down on the grassy bank, letting out her unhappiness in a hearty bout of sobbing.

A short time later someone touched her on the shoulder, and thinking one of the other maids had come after her, she jerked away, shouting, 'Leave me alone, will ye!'

'Keara.'

The voice was gentler than usual. She gasped and opened her eyes to see the master squatting on his haunches beside her.

He handed her a handkerchief. 'What's the matter?'

She sat up and tried to stop crying, but couldn't.

Muttering something under his breath, he knelt and pulled her towards him, letting her weep against his chest until the tears stopped flowing. When she was quiet again, except for an occasional breathy sob, he held her at arm's length and repeated, 'Tell me what the matter is, Keara.'

She stared at him mutely as he let go of her and moved to a more comfortable position sitting beside her. He patted the grass and she sat down, wary now.

'Let me guess, then. The other servants are teasing you. Tell me who's the ringleader and I'll see that it stops.'

If she told him anyone's name, things would get worse, not better. She was not too stupid to understand that. 'There's no one special,' she muttered, avoiding his eyes. 'It's – everything. Meself, mainly. I make such stupid mistakes.'

There was silence, then he patted her on the shoulder and said, 'You're probably right not to name anyone. But we can't let this go on.' The girl was too valuable to his wife. 'Come on.' He stood up and reached out one hand to her.

Without thinking she let him pull her to her feet. For a moment or two they stood there looking at one another, still holding hands. Then he muttered something and took a step backwards, so she used his handkerchief to scrub at her eyes again before holding it out to him.

He gave her a wry smile as he waved it away. 'Put it in the laundry when you get back. It's no use to me like that.'

'I'm sorry, sir.'

'That's all right. Now, go back to the house and wash your face. I'll have a word with Mrs Bertram.'

As she started limping back, he called out, 'Wait! What's wrong with your feet?'

'What? Oh, blisters, sir.'

'Show me.'

She lifted her skirt and showed him the back of one ankle.

'The other?' He whistled in sympathy. 'Those must be hurting like hell.'

'It's because the shoes are a bit big for me, but they're all we could get at such short notice.'

'You should have said something and we'd have sent you to get some new ones made to fit.' His voice softened. 'Poor Keara. I don't like to think of anyone being unhappy and in pain under my roof.'

It made her feel warm inside for him to care. He was a kind man and though the other servants had hinted that he was a womaniser, keeping a cottage in the grounds where he'd bring an occasional woman to stay, she didn't believe them.

It was funny, though, she thought as she walked slowly and reluctantly back to the house. He didn't like people being unhappy and could be kind even to a lowly maidservant, but his own wife was one of the unhappiest people she had ever met. Yet he wouldn't leave Mrs Mullane alone at night, just as her father wouldn't leave her mother alone.

Keara was coming to realise that men were all alike and the gentry weren't all that different from ordinary folk like her – something which had never occurred to her before. And if Mr Mullane did have other women, well, she'd bet he was kind to them. Which was more than you could say for her father.

The next day Minnie stopped her on the back stairs and whispered, 'Thanks for not saying it was me who was doing most of the teasing.'

Teasing! Keara thought. It was more than teasing. But she realised this was an attempt to make amends, so she shrugged and said just as quietly, 'I wouldn't be doing something like that.'

'Did you really not want to come here?'

Keara couldn't prevent tears from welling in her eyes and didn't dare trust her voice, so just shook her head.

'I'd give my eye teeth to get a job as lady's maid,' Minnie admitted. 'That's why I was upset.'

'And I'd give my eye teeth to go home.'

'Funny old world, ain't it?' She patted Keara awkwardly on the arm. 'Eh, you daft ha'p'orth! Don't take on. Things will be better from now on. You'll see.'

Keara sighed and wiped her eyes on her apron before continuing on her way. However much better things became, she wouldn't be at home, would she? And she wouldn't be seeing her family.

*

Mark Gibson watched the shore of Australia come into clearer focus as the ship crossed Port Phillip Bay. The land seemed flat and muddy and as they drew closer he could see that the vegetation was a dull, lifeless sort of green. He'd expected sunlight and bright-coloured foliage, with a large city waiting for them like a jewel on the breast of the land. Instead it was drizzling with rain, which added a grey tone to the landscape.

'Not quite what I expected,' he said to Harry.

'No. Looks a miserable sort of place to me, and it'll be still more miserable when I'm living with *him* again.'

'Your father?'

Harry nodded. 'You can't have a minute to yourself with him around and it's pray, pray, pray all the time! I wish I could come to the goldfields with you.'

'You need money for a stake.'

'I'll find it somehow. I'm not staying with *him* much longer.'

Mark didn't comment, but couldn't help thinking how much he wished he could be with his own father.

Walter Hudson joined them at the rail. 'They've put up a lot more buildings since I were last here. It's turning into a fine city, that it is.'

To Mark it didn't look like a fine city at all. From here the buildings appeared low and mean and the countryside looked barren, with low scrubby vegetation and trees twisted by the wind. His spirits sank still further. Why had he panicked and come so far away from his family? He could have gone to London and made a new life there just as easily. He missed them so much, especially Luke.

What if he never saw them again?

When he looked to his left, he saw the Jenner family standing nearby. Patience glanced up and caught his eye. She looked away immediately, but not before he'd seen the hurt on her face. Mr Jenner scowled at him and beckoned his son across to join them. With a sigh, Harry left his friends and went to stand in silence behind his father.

When they got to the wharf, it was a while before they were allowed to leave the ship. They had to watch the luggage being unloaded and dumped wherever there was space while they stood impatiently waiting, crammed together at the rail.

Walter grinned at Mark. 'Keep your eyes open for your things. It'll be a rush to find a cab once we're off the ship.'

Three hours later they'd retrieved their luggage and Walter had somehow found them transport into the city. Mark sat beside his new partner on a cart with just enough room for them, their trunks and bags, and some other goods the driver had come to collect.

Mark was glad Walter seemed to know his way around because it was all utterly bewildering to him. The city was much bigger than it had looked from the water, with some fine modern buildings, but the streets were extremely muddy and already he was beginning to understand why so many men wore high boots.

At one point they passed a place with the doors open wide and people dancing inside. Two men staggered out with gaudily dressed women on their arms.

'They're some of the lucky ones,' Walter said. 'That's Barlow's. A good place to go when you've had a find. I stayed there for two days once, celebrating.' He sighed. 'If there hadn't been a ship nearly ready to sail, I might have stayed there for weeks instead of going back to England. They have some very obliging girls at Barlow's.' He chuckled at the memory. 'You wouldn't like to buy us a drink there tonight, would you?'

'No. I'm a bit tired and we need to find lodgings.'

'I suppose so.'

Mark could hear the disappointment in Walter's voice. The man had some strange ideas about money. If they were lucky and found gold, Mark didn't intend to waste it on whores and boozing. Could a man really win himself a fortune just by digging in the ground? If he couldn't – and he certainly didn't feel optimistic about there being gold nuggets lying around waiting to be picked up, whatever Walter said – he would come back and look for a business opportunity in Melbourne instead. Surely he had learned enough in Lancashire to earn his daily bread here in Australia? People had to eat, wherever they lived in the world.

Patience stood by her trunk, watching Mark Gibson's tall, manly figure disappear into the distance. She sighed. Her father said it was God's will that Mark didn't want to wed her. Even her normally good-tempered mother had been very irritable about it and said she should have tried a little harder to attract him. But Patience had no idea how to set about doing that. She just knew she liked being with Mark better than with anyone else she'd ever met.

Harry liked him too, though he said Mark was a bit of a sobersides and didn't know how to have fun. From the sound of it, Harry had had rather too much fun once he was out of their father's reach. The two of them hadn't been getting on at all well lately. And Harry was wild to go gold prospecting, which further outraged her father who kept talking about 'devil's lures' and the love of money being the root of all evil whenever the subject came up.

She hoped her father and mother would soon find the rest of the luggage. She would be glad when they had a proper house and a life of their own again. She had not really enjoyed being in the single women's quarters. The other girls of her age had been so noisy and all they thought about was catching a husband. It was the main reason half of them had come to Australia, while the other half were like her and had been given no choice because their fathers or some other relative had decided to bring the whole family out here to make a new life.

They were expecting her uncle to meet them and when there was no sign of him, Father began to fret.

Eventually a man came up and asked if he was Mr Jenner.

'Yes. Do you have a message from my brother?'

'Well, not exactly. From his wife. I'm sorry to tell you that your brother died three months ago, just keeled over and died. Pamela says you'll have to make your own way to Melbourne but you can stay with her for a few days till you find somewhere of your own.'

Patience's mother began to sob so the girl put her arm round her shoulders. Harry shoved his hands in his pockets and scowled at the world. Even Father seemed lost for words, for once.

It had all seemed such a bright dream and her uncle had talked so glowingly about the prospects in Australia for an honest man willing to work hard that her father had taken a sudden decision to join him. He'd never had the success he felt he deserved working in a grocer's shop in Todmorden. Now they would have to make their own way in a strange country because they all knew that Aunt Pamela was a weak reed and would be more likely to rely on them than help them settle in.

Nothing was going right, Patience thought. Nothing at all.

It took hours to get all their things and find transport into the city and by that time they were ravenously hungry.

When they got to her uncle's house, it looked very small. Aunt Pamela opened the door and smiled at them somewhat nervously. 'Come in, come in. You must be tired. I have beds ready for you, but I'm afraid you'll all have to share the one room. And you'll have to leave your trunks in the store-room at the back and take out what you need to be going on with because there's no room for them upstairs. I suppose everything will be dirty and you'll want to have a wash-day.' She seemed annoyed at this prospect, though it was only to be expected after such a long voyage, and watched with a frown as Nan and her daughter unpacked some of their clothes and took them upstairs.

When they came down again, Patience's father said, 'I'm deeply sorry the Lord has seen fit to take your husband away from you, sister. I hope your fellow chapel goers have been a support to you in your time of trouble.'

'Well, um, I haven't needed their help. You'd better come and sit down. I have something else to tell you. Come into the front parlour.'

Her aunt seemed very ill at ease and Patience was surprised that they'd been offered no refreshments yet.

A man was waiting in the front room, dressed in what looked like his Sunday best. He looked as uneasy as her aunt.

'This is Ralph. His shop was – *is* next to ours and, well, he and I have got married. He lost his wife last year and it makes good sense to help one another . . .'

Patience's mother gasped and looked towards her husband for the guidance he never failed to provide. Patience kept her eyes downcast but a quick glance sideways revealed that Harry was staring out of the window as if he didn't want to be a part of this scene.

It was a minute or two before her father spoke, and his voice sounded less certain than usual.

'Are things so different here in Australia that people remarry before they've even had time to mourn their loss?' he asked at last.

'They were different for me.' Aunt Pamela moved closer to her new husband.

'Your brother had been acting strangely for a while before he died, I'm afraid,' Ralph said bluntly. 'His mind had been – well, he'd been getting very disoriented. We'd had to restrain him a few times. In the end, it was a merciful release for poor Pamela.'

'And then I needed someone to look after me and help with the shop,' she added. 'I didn't even know you were coming out to Australia. He'd hidden that from me. He could be very cunning towards the end. Some days he'd seem quite normal. Others he'd be – strange. I found your letters only when I was clearing his drawers out and by then it was too late to stop you coming. So you see, things have changed here. There's no work for you in the shop because Ralph has his own brothers there now and, well, that's how things are.'

Alex Jenner had been following this with a deepening frown. 'I don't know what to say. The Lord can move in mysterious ways at times, ways beyond our mortal understanding. But this will be a hard burden to bear. We shall have to pray for guidance.'

Pamela exchanged glances with her new husband that said their belief in the efficacy of prayer was not as strong as her brother-in-law's. 'We've sent the older children to stay with friends so that you'll have somewhere to sleep for a week or two at least. We'll do what we can to help you settle in, but really it's up to you and your son to find employment, Alex, and to make a new life for yourselves here. It's very different from England. Some settle. Some don't.'

From her tone of voice Patience guessed her aunt thought they wouldn't settle, though she couldn't understand why. Her father had been eager to come out here but had been expecting to work with his brother in the shop. Her uncle had even written about his chapel and the godly people who were members of the congregation.

As if he were thinking on the same lines, her father asked, 'What about the chapel? Surely there are people there who will help us?'

'There is no chapel, I'm afraid. It was all in his mind. He didn't even attend church towards the end.'

Patience's father had no reply to that. He was so gloomy that she was glad when they could all go to bed. She lay there in the darkness beside her mother, worrying, hearing her father tossing and turning on a mattress on the floor. Surely he and Harry would soon find jobs? Her mother would look after the house, as usual, but Patience could look for employment, too. There must be something she could do. She was in far better health now.

Yes, they would soon find their feet, she was certain of it. They could not have come all this way only to fail.

CHAPTER SIX

June–August 1859

───────◆◆───────

Within three months of their return to Lancashire, Mr Mullane grew restless and everyone in the house was affected by it.

'He's getting grumpy. He'll be dragging her off to Ireland again soon,' Minnie said to Keara one day. 'And won't she complain and throw a fit then! I don't envy you.'

'What do you mean? Mrs Mullane hasn't said anything to me about them planning a visit to Ireland.'

'If it was up to her they'd never go. It's him who likes it there. He loves them blessed horses a deal more than he loves her, that's for sure. But he never stays anywhere for long. You'd think with all that money he'd be happy – I would be – but he never seems so. Nor does she.'

Two days later Keara found Mrs Mullane in tears and was told they were going back to Ireland for a while. She couldn't help clapping her hands together and beaming at her mistress.

Lavinia stared at her sourly. 'It's all right for you,

you're going home. That place isn't home to me and never will be. This house is so much grander – and it's near my friends.'

She continued to moan and complain until Keara could have shaken her. At first she had thought her mistress hard done by, but she had soon begun to understand how difficult it was for a vigorous man like Mr Mullane to be married to an indolent and stupid woman. Mrs Mullane could be spiteful, too, even when you were doing your best to please her.

Mr Mullane stopped her in the corridor later that day to say, 'You look happy!'

Keara nodded. 'I'm looking forward to seeing my family again.' Nothing mattered as much as that. Nothing in the whole world.

When they arrived at Ballymullan Manor, Keara saw her father in the stable yard and called, 'Da! I'm back.' But all he did was scowl at her and walk away. She followed Dick into the kitchen, feeling like weeping at this public rejection of her.

Cook looked up from stirring a big pan. 'Hello, Keara.' Then she saw the girl's expression. 'What's the matter?'

'It's Da – he wouldn't speak to me, just walked away.'

'Ah, that isn't your fault, girl. Mick gets more bad-tempered with every year that passes. 'Tis only the horses he cares for now – them and the poteen.'

Keara had forgotten how friendly and relaxed the

servants were here at Ballymullan, how different it was to be with people who knew your family and back-ground. 'He's still drinking heavily, then?'

'Oh, yes. Worse than ever. There's a group of fellows making the stuff themselves now. They'll get caught and taken before the magistrate one day, so they will.'

The following afternoon Lavinia Mullane looked at her maid and sighed. 'You'll be no good to me till you've been to see your family. You may take two hours.'

Keara rushed down to the village as soon as she'd finished clearing up her mistress's bedroom, not stop-ping to talk to anyone, just waving as she passed. At first she turned off towards her old home, then someone called out that her family had moved to one of the new cottages and she went back to the main street. When she got to the houses she wasn't even sure which one her family were living in and stood uncertainly in front of the group of four dwellings, feeling like an outsider.

A woman came out of one, saw Keara and called, 'It's the end one.'

It was a fine day and the front door stood open. Keara hesitated for a moment or two with tears in her eyes, watching her mother humming as she prepared some food, then said in a voice thick with emotion, 'I'm back, Mam.'

With a cry of delight, Betsy dropped her knife and went to clip her daughter in her arms, exclaiming at how well she looked. Then she called out, 'Mara! Mara love, your sister's here.'

Another shriek and Mara came running from the

back room. Keara picked up her little sister, hugging and kissing her, swinging her round as she always had done. 'You've put on weight,' she teased, setting her sister down again.

Mara nodded solemnly. 'We get plenty to eat now.'

Keara turned back to her mother. 'It's a lovely place. Three rooms, is it?'

Betsy beamed at her. 'Yes. Come and see.' Proudly she showed off the separate bedrooms and the new bits of furniture Diarmid had sent down to help out.

Although Keara was pleased for her mother, this only emphasised how tied she was to the Mullanes. She sat on a stool, with Mara leaning against her, not quite knowing what to do. 'You look a bit better, Mam.'

'It's the good food. We're all feeling better, love, and it's thanks to you. Look at the roses in Mara's cheeks, and I'd swear Ismay's grown an inch.'

'I saw Da in the stable yard, but he –' she had to gulp back tears before she could continue '– turned away from me.'

'Oh, love, he didn't!'

Keara nodded miserably.

'He's angry about not getting any of your money, but Arla won't give him a farthing and I don't let him bully me about it either. He's not going to stop the children getting enough to eat and that's that.' But even as Betsy spoke a sigh escaped her. 'He's been so surly about it, hardly speaking to me.'

Keara managed to summon up a tremulous smile. What she really wanted was to hear that they missed her so much they couldn't do without her any longer. She'd half-expected her mother to beg her to come back. But that had been silly. 'Well, I'm glad you have this cottage to live in.'

'Eh, you're getting to speak with an English accent,' her mother teased.

'You have to talk proper over there or they laugh at you. Where's Ismay, then?'

'Helping in the shop this morning. Arla's taken her on regular now. Such a kind woman she is.'

After chatting to her mother for a few minutes, Keara took Mara out for a walk and that at least hadn't changed. Her little sister still clung tightly to her hand and told her all her childish secrets.

'Where did that new dress come from?' Keara asked.

'From the big house. Mr O'Neal sent us down some things. The Mammy got a pretty blue dress and Da tried to sell it, but Mr O'Neal got angry at him so he had to give it her back. The Mammy wears it for church on Sundays and she just sits and looks at it sometimes with a smile on her face.'

As Keara walked slowly back to the big house it came to her that she didn't really have a home any more, didn't belong anywhere. Coming back to Ireland hadn't solved any problems, just made her realise she had no choice but to continue working for Mrs Mullane.

Theo strolled out to see the new foals with Diarmid, delighted to be back. He hated the stiff formality of the Lancashire house. As far as he was concerned,

Ballymullan was his home, a place where he could pop into the kitchen to see Cook any time of day and wheedle a snack out of her. Or nip across the garden to chat to Diarmid about anything and everything. Or even go for a stroll with Dick. Funny how comfortable he always felt with him.

'Is Keara Michaels working out all right?' Diarmid asked suddenly.

'Yes. To my surprise, I must admit. My wife has been a lot happier since she started working for us.'

'She's a nice little lass, Keara.'

'Not so little now,' Theo commented dryly. 'She's filled out nicely since she's been eating properly.'

Diarmid shot him a quick glance. 'You haven't . . . you wouldn't . . .'

'You know I don't tamper with my own maids, though I must admit to being tempted. That wild tangled hair gives a man ideas and she has the most beautiful eyes I've ever seen.'

Diarmid was a bit worried by these eulogies. However, there was a line he didn't dare cross in his dealings with Theo, so he held his tongue and changed the subject.

Two weeks later Theo told his wife he wanted to spend a few months at Ballymullan this time and she burst into tears, begging him to let her go home to Lancashire alone.

'You can go back when you're carrying my child and not until.'

Her temper tantrum must have been heard by every living creature in the house. Furious at her lack of self-control, he rang the bell and when Keara came running, gestured to his wife. 'Work your magic, girl. Persuade your mistress that staying here in Ireland will not be the death of her.'

Open-mouthed, Keara watched him leave, wincing as he slammed the bedroom door behind him. Without a second thought, she went to gather Lavinia into her arms and rock her, making shushing noises more suited to a child, because it was the best way to calm her mistress down. She sometimes wondered if anyone had ever cuddled Lavinia Mullane before. Keara's mam had always cuddled her and her sisters, though her father never had, and they had cuddled one another, too. She missed that, hated sleeping in a bed on her own.

An hour later she tiptoed out of the bedroom and went to find Dick. 'Mrs Mullane isn't going down to dinner. Can you tell the master for me, please?' When he nodded, she added, 'And if you could ask Cook to send me up a plate of something, I'd be grateful.' She gave a wry smile. 'I'm hungry, even if she isn't.'

When the bedroom door opened a few minutes later, Mrs Mullane was asleep and Keara didn't even turn round as she whispered, 'Set it on the table. I'll get it in a minute.'

'Set what on the table?'

Keara gasped and jumped to her feet. 'Sorry, sir. I didn't realise it was you.'

Mrs Mullane mumbled something and snuggled down into the pillow.

'How long did it take you to calm her this time?' Theo asked in a low voice.

Keara shrugged. 'Over an hour.'

'Will she be in a state to receive me tonight?'

Keara blushed bright red. Fancy asking her that!

'Well, will she?'

He was clearly amused by her embarrassment, so she raised her chin and stared straight back at him. 'I think it might be better to let her rest tonight, sir.'

'She does too much resting, but I will leave it for tonight. See if you can get her out and about a bit from now on.'

Keara nodded.

When he'd gone, Mrs Mullane rolled on to her back and said, 'Thank you, Keara. My husband's a monster.'

'Sure he's just a man, ma'am. They're all like that, wanting it all the time.'

'Surely not?'

'They are so.'

Mrs Mullane frowned at her. 'How do you know that?'

'We only had the one room in our old cottage so I've seen what my da is like for myself. Though *he* has several children so it's not for wanting them that he keeps doing it, more for the pleasure. And I've heard other women talking, saying the same thing about their men.' She saw that her mistress was wide-eyed with amazement. Had no one ever talked to her about it before?

Lavinia covered her eyes with one arm. 'Well, I don't want a child if that's the way you have to get them. I hate doing it!'

Keara heard the suppressed hysteria in her mistress's voice, but felt she needed frank talk rather than soothing nonsense. 'He'll not stop until you give him a child and all the crying in the world won't change that.'

Lavinia turned her head to stare indignantly across the room. 'Well, what a thing to say!'

Keara didn't bother to reply. It was enough that she'd dropped the idea into her mistress's mind. It was funny, she thought, as she watched the other woman fall asleep again. All the money in the world couldn't buy Mr Mullane the child he longed for, nor could it buy Mrs Mullane freedom from her husband's attentions. Then Keara suddenly realised what this change of plan would mean. She'd be spending several months near her family. A smile crept across her face. She'd be able to see them every day or two. It was an ill wind . . .

A few weeks later, when it seemed as if his wife might be with child, the master stopped visiting her at night. When Lavinia began to be sick in the mornings, he walked round whistling and smiling.

It did Keara's heart good to see his happiness. He was a lovely man. She wished she could marry someone as nice one day. She didn't blame him for spending as little time as possible with his wife though it left her with the task of trying to keep her mistress entertained during the day.

Lavinia remained obstinately bored because she would hardly stir out of her room, and she was often fretful. 'See!' she wept. 'He doesn't care about me, only about getting a child.'

'Tell me again about when you were young,' Keara coaxed. 'I love hearing about that.' Which was a lie. She had listened to the same old tales of Lavinia's childhood and her friends and her old nurse Nancy until she knew them by heart. But her mistress never seemed to tire of repeating them.

However, there was also an underlying tension in the house that was very noticeable, in spite of Mr Mullane's happiness. It was Cook who explained to Keara that Mrs Mullane had lost several previous babies.

'Well, she's not losing this one, if I can help it!' the girl said at once.

'That's in the Lord's hands,' Cook said. 'She hates it when she's carrying a child, you'll see. She'll get grumpier as she grows fatter.'

Which was unfortunately true. It seemed to Keara now as if her mistress was equally divided between hating her husband and hating the stranger sharing her body. She grew very chancy-tempered, taking out a lot of her anger on Keara, even slapping her once or twice.

It had never been easy to deal with her, but now things were much more difficult.

Melbourne surprised Mark. It was a city of great contrasts, with some fine buildings and some appalling shacks within a few hundred yards of one another. The vehicles people used to get around it were called 'jingles', two-wheeled and pulled by one horse, with wooden seats and a square canopy supposed to protect

you from the weather, but they didn't do it very success-
fully and the first time he rode in one he thought he was
going to be shaken to pieces.

Walter roared with laughter at his expression.
'You'll get used to riding in 'em, Mark lad. You'll have
to. There's nowt else for folk like us.'

'I'd like to see more of the city even so. Why don't
we spend a few days here before we leave for the goldfields?'

Walter's smile changed into a scowl. 'You can see
the city later, after you've made yourself a fortune. We
need to head off as soon as we can or others will get
there before us. You don't find gold by sitting and
talking about it.'

It surprised Mark how Walter seemed to think that
people were conspiring to get to the goldfields before
them, but he didn't think it worth arguing about.

That evening Walter took him to Canvas City,
where those who'd found gold came to have a good
time, but Mark was horrified at how some of the men
were throwing their money around, buying anything
which took their fancy, brandishing bottles of expensive
champagne as if they were water, acquiring mistresses
or marrying their whores, and shouting rounds of
drinks for new friends who were, Mark was sure, more
interested in their money and largesse than their friendship.

When he said as much, Walter looked at him sourly.
'A man's entitled to enjoy hisself when he's worked so
hard. You'll change your tune after you've broke your
back on the diggings for a few months.'

After that he went out in the evenings on his own to 'see a few old friends as have their noses to the ground'. He inevitably came back the worse for wear, which made their landlady frown.

In the daytime, however, Walter bustled them here and there to some purpose. They each had to buy a Miner's Right, paying twenty shillings a year for the privilege of digging for gold.

'Better than the old days,' Walter admitted grudgingly. 'Had to pay three pound a month for a licence at one time.' He gave Mark one of his evil grins. 'Well, you did if the damned troopers caught you.'

His tales of the early gold diggings painted a vivid picture of what sounded to Mark to be a rather lawless life and he began to worry about whether things had changed much when Walter insisted they buy revolvers to protect themselves. Mark had never even held a gun before, let alone fired one, but Walter took him to some parkland to practise. Mark didn't do badly, though he was sure he couldn't shoot at another human being.

Under Walter's guidance Mark also bought himself some red Crimean shirts, moleskin trousers and a cabbage tree hat – a straw hat with a wide brim to protect him from the sun. It was made from the leaves of the cabbage tree palm, Walter said, but it looked just like fine straw to Mark. The sturdy garments and high boots he was now wearing were very different from the town clothes he'd brought to Australia with him, most of which he intended to leave in Melbourne.

They also bought digging implements, blankets, a

small tent and cooking utensils. These included pots to heat water for what Walter called 'pint-pot tea' and pannikins from which to drink it.

'You've never known what it's like to be thirsty till you've worked in the Australian sun,' Walter said. 'And there's nothin' as good as pint-pot tea. Nothing in the world. You'll not put milk in your tea again once you've got used to it without.'

Mark arranged to leave a trunk and bag at the lodging house where they were staying, agreeing to pay the owner, who seemed an honest man, a small weekly sum to have them stored safely in the attic. He still had some trade goods, but didn't want to risk taking them with him. How could he possibly protect his possessions at the same time as panning for gold? So he packed into a sturdy new metal trunk such items as might be considered necessary in his new life, or which he might easily be able to sell, and bought a money belt which he wore from then on.

When they had everything they needed, they paid for a ride out to the new diggings on a big bullock wagon that was delivering food and other essentials to the gold miners. That cost them five pounds each, which Mark thought a ridiculously high price for such an uncomfortable ride.

Walter shrugged. 'We won't be able to carry our things if we walk, so we don't have a choice.' He hesitated, looking sideways at Mark before adding, 'You'll have to lend me the money for my fare, though. I've just about run out now.'

Mark hadn't realised the other man was that short

of money. Why had he been spending so much on drinking then? 'What would you have done if you hadn't met me?'

'Found some other greenhorn as wanted to go after the gold and got him to help me.' Walter clapped Mark on the shoulder. 'Ah, we'll soon make enough money for me to pay you back. And with me to show you how to go on, you won't make the stupid mistakes most newcomers do, so I'll more than earn my way.'

'I'd better keep an accounting of what you owe me, then.' Mark pulled out the small notebook and pencil he always carried with him.

'Write it down, do you mean?'

'Yes.'

'Don't you bloody trust me?'

'I just think it's better if we agree on the amount each time. I'll write it down and you can initial it, so there can be no arguing.' He met the older man's eyes squarely.

After a minute Walter looked away and spat on the ground. 'Suit your bloody self.'

Mark had written down the cost of each item they had purchased. He now divided everything by two and added the money he was lending Walter. This was eating a big hole in his reserves and for what? A vague chance that they'd make a rich find?

And did he even trust his partner? he wondered as they climbed up on the wagon which was pulled by ten bullocks, harnessed in pairs. He trusted Walter's knowledge of how to prospect for gold, but he did not, he decided, trust the older man in other ways. Which probably meant he shouldn't have gone into business with him.

Only it was too late to worry about that now. With several cracks of the whip the driver urged his beasts into motion and the wagon rumbled forward.

And anyway, there was something rather exciting about going after gold. You couldn't do that in a Lancashire mill town. It was a big adventure.

The journey from Melbourne to the diggings was punctuated by the sound of the driver calling to his team of animals. Sometimes the calls grew louder and more profane, and the driver would crack his whip sharply as he urged the great creatures onwards through particularly bad patches where mud sucked at the wheels. In hollows it sometimes reached right up to the axles and Mark grew used to jumping on and off the vehicle to lighten the load, used to the mud even, because it was everywhere in this new life.

He could make no sense of the landscape, which was alien to him, and it irked him that he didn't know the names of the plants. Walter clearly considered him mad for asking. Even the road didn't behave like an English road, for it didn't lead straight ahead but sometimes split into several rutted tracks and he had no idea how the driver knew which one to take.

When he asked, the man laughed. 'I'm just trying to avoid the muddy hollows, young fellow. The side tracks will all join up into one again as soon as we get to better ground.'

The first night Mark tasted the pint-pot tea Walter had praised so loudly and often. Each man's pot was filled with water and set on the fire. When the water boiled, a pinch of tea was added, then the resulting liquid poured into a pint pannikin with a handle. After the day's travelling it was indeed wonderfully refreshing and Mark quickly developed a taste for it.

As they got further away from Melbourne, they passed some abandoned diggings. There was only a haphazard collection of holes in the ground left now, with heaps of spoil tossed around as if at a giant's whim and blackened places where camp fires might once have burned. Flaps of torn canvas were still attached to one triangular arrangement of poles that must have been a tent, and these were flapping in the breeze, the only thing moving, which added to the eerie effect of the place.

'Where did everyone go?' Mark asked Walter.

'Who knows? When they stop finding gold in one place, they move to another. It happens quickly sometimes. That's part of the excitement. Who'd want to stay in the same place for more than a few months? Not me.'

But from the driver Mark heard a different tale; that in most places the surface gold was being panned out and though there was still gold to be found, it was getting too deep for men to mine on their own and they were starting to need better equipment and crushing machines to extract it from the ore. Walter continued to pooh-pooh that, however, and said there would always be gold lying around if you had the wit to look for it. You just had to go further afield nowadays, that was all.

And sometimes you had to dig a bit of a tunnel, yes, but you didn't need a fancy machine to do that.

As they got closer to the new goldfield at Jarandyne, Walter's eyes began to gleam and a feverish excitement radiated from him. Mark caught some of his eagerness as he listened to constant talk of the early days. Though he'd heard most of his companion's tales before, the driver had others to add and his sounded more credible to Mark.

'There it is,' the driver said suddenly, pointing one grimy forefinger.

The diggings at Jarandyne spread out before them in a dark ochre stain on the landscape, eating away at the green of trees and fields. As they drew closer they could see men toiling like mud-encrusted ants, paying no heed to the newcomers or even to one another in their feverish search for gold.

The driver stopped outside a tent which had the words 'General Store' painted on the canvas wall. 'This is it.'

Walter had already jumped off. 'You unload our stuff and stay here with it, Mark lad, while I take a quick look around. I've a nose for gold. I'll send someone to fetch you when I find a place that looks likely for our claim.'

And he was off before Mark could even frame a protest.

It was three hours before a boy came up, asked if he was Mr Gibson, and added simply, 'Mr Hudson sent me to fetch you. Said you'd give me a shillin'.'

'When you've taken me to him and not before.'

Mark stared at the pile of equipment. How did Walter think he could carry all that? 'We'll need a handcart.'

'I know a fellow as has one. It'll cost you to borrow it, though.' The boy ran off and returned with an old man pushing a rickety handcart, which cost Mark five shillings for an hour's hire. He complained that this was sheer robbery and the old man sniggered. 'You can't move your things without me, so you got no choice. I make more from this handcart than I ever made looking for gold, young fellow, and with less effort, too.'

Which made Mark wonder if his earlier idea of supplying food to the miners hadn't been a better one.

During the days that followed, he laboured dog-gedly alongside Walter on their claim. His first efforts at panning sent water and gravel all over his feet and made his partner curse him for a fumble-fingered fool. Walter soon decided that they needed a rocker cradle in which to wash the ore, so they stopped searching for long enough to build one. Then, of course, that gave them the regular chore of fetching water from the nearby stream to wash the muck they'd dug up.

After a week or two Mark's muscles stopped hurting so much and he no longer fell asleep over his evening meal. He was even beginning to make sense of what they were doing and to recognise the specks of gold that resulted occasionally from their labours.

The first week they were rewarded by a minute amount of light-coloured gold dust, which didn't cover their costs but which had Walter whooping for joy.

'I told you there was gold round here, lad,' he said again and again. 'I can smell it.'

By the third week they were earning enough to pay their way, but not enough for Walter to pay back what he owed. Mark continued to make notes in his little book every day, to Walter's intense annoyance. He was now recording the amount of gold retrieved and the amount of money it had brought them.

'You'll not care about making them chicken tracks across the paper when we strike it big,' Walter would say as they sat by the camp fire after dark with Mark squinting at his notebook in the light of the flames.

'It's a good habit to keep note of what's happening when it comes to making your living.'

'I'm still alive, aren't I? So I must have been making a good enough living all these years.'

And Walter would laugh, get out a bottle of grog and take a big pull. Somehow he always had enough money to buy that. The fiery spirit made Mark choke when he tried it and it didn't taste particularly pleasant, either, so he stuck to his pint-pot tea.

What pleased him most about his present life was not the gold but that he was fitter and stronger than he had ever been, his body lean but with muscles honed by hard physical labour. It had upset him how easily the Burns brothers had beaten him up. No one was going to do that to him again if he could help it.

He avoided the fights that blew up regularly on the diggings, fights in which some men joined for the sheer hell of it. He also kept a careful watch on their tent and equipment, once catching a man poking around inside the tent.

'Get out!' he roared.

The man sauntered out so slowly that Mark ended up shoving him hard. He stumbled and fell, then stood up, fists clenched. Still angry, Mark stepped forward, raising his own fists and feeling a surge of confidence in his growing ability to defend himself. 'Just try it.'

For a moment there was a stand-off, then the man let his fists drop, shrugged and limped away.

Mark watched him go, then, as he heard someone moving behind him, swung round quickly in case he was being attacked from the rear.

Walter stood grinning at him. 'That poor old sod hurt his leg last month and can't keep up with the work any more. You should have give him summat 'stead of chasin' him off like that.'

'What? Pay a man who was trying to rob us?'

'Well, he didn't rob us, did he? I been down on my luck a few times an' I know how he feels.'

'I'll never know how it feels to rob someone,' Mark said coldly. 'It's wrong to steal.'

'You'd soon find out if you was hungry enough.' Walter sauntered off, heading for the grog tent no doubt.

Mark was starting to feel wary about his partner, glad he'd bought himself a money belt, uncomfortable as it was when it got wet. He even wore it in bed at night.

Patience stared in dismay round the small room her father had rented and exchanged horrified glances with Harry. How could they all live here? She glimpsed her mother's eyes and saw that they were filled with tears, too. Somehow that stiffened her spine, so that she managed to say quite cheerfully, 'It'll be nice to have our own home again, won't it, Mum?'

'Home?' Her mother gave a harsh laugh, then caught her husband's disapproving look and bit back further words. 'I need to buy food. Can you let me have some money, Alex?'

'I'll come with you. We must get to know the neighbourhood.' He turned to his children. 'You two can start unpacking.'

Patience didn't say that it was not much use unpacking when there was only one small chest of drawers between the four of them.

As soon as their mother and father had gone, Harry picked up his own bag. 'I'm leaving,' he said abruptly.

'Leaving?' She was bewildered. 'Are you going for a job somewhere?'

He looked at her pityingly. 'I'm leaving home – permanently. There are jobs everywhere with so many men having gone to the goldfields. I'll soon earn enough for a stake and then I'll follow them. But if I stay here, Father will take all my earnings and I'll never get a chance to do anything exciting.' He turned towards the door.

Patience grabbed his arm. 'Harry, you can't!'

'I have to.' He hesitated. 'I'm sorry to leave you alone with him. If you see a chance, you should get out, too. Find yourself a live-in job. He's getting worse. I hate him and his stupid canting ways.'

He walked out then and when she followed him to

the front door, she noticed that he didn't look back.

With tears in her eyes she went back inside and set about putting some of their underwear in the three drawers, which were soon full. The rest of their clothes would have to stay in the bags and trunks, though they were clean now, at least, after a series of washing days that had had her aunt scowling and complaining. She tried to push the trunks against the wall, but wasn't strong enough. She'd have to wait and get her father to help her.

It seemed a long time before her parents returned, carrying two string bags of shopping.

'Where's Harry?' her father asked at once.

She felt her stomach lurch with nervousness. 'He's gone.'

'What do you mean by that?'

'He's run away from home.'

Alex stood still but his face had that red angry look to it. 'And you didn't try to stop him?'

'How could I? He's stronger than me.'

Nan sat down on the bed, weeping quietly. She looked at her daughter. 'He'll come back. Don't you think Harry will come back, Patience?'

'I don't know.' She didn't think so. Not if he had any other choice. And if she found a way of leaving, she'd take it too. Her father had always been strict but now he'd turned into a tyrant, making all their lives and wishes subservient to his, and making them thoroughly miserable in the process.

When a week had passed, an uncomfortable week during which her father alternately berated Patience and the absent Harry, he said one night after they'd eaten. 'He won't be allowed back!'

No need to say who 'he' was.

Nan could not hold back a sob.

'If he does try to come back, I shall not accept him into this family again because he has betrayed my trust. He's no longer a son of mine!' Getting out the big Bible and the ink bottle, he opened the book at the page where the family names were inscribed.

'No!' Nan pleaded. 'Alex, you can't do this.'

'Be quiet, woman.'

'Don't do it!'

He struck out at her, something he had never done before. For a moment there was complete silence in the room, then she stood up, rubbing her reddened cheek, and went to lie down on the bed with her back to the room.

Patience stood up and her father snarled, 'Stay where you are. I intend you to witness this so that you know what will happen to you if you ever try to leave home without my permission.'

With a flourish he dipped his pen into the ink and ceremoniously struck out Harry's name.

Patience said nothing. What did a few lines on paper mean? She knew if she saw Harry again she'd definitely speak to him. He was still her brother, whatever her father said or did. Her only reason for staying at home now was her mother whom she loved dearly. She could not just abandon her and knew Nan wouldn't leave her husband.

The following day her father came home from his

new job in a grocery shop, smiling. 'The Lord has already provided me with a job and now there is a chance of work as a daily nursemaid for you nearby, Patience. We won't be staying here for long, though, just until I find a suitable chapel to attend, but you needn't tell your employer that. I prefer to live close to my place of worship. When we're settled, you'll both be able to make friends from among the congregation and we'll all be much happier.'

Patience tried to keep her expression calm. Finding a suitable chapel seemed to have become the main focus of her father's life – almost more important to him than putting bread on the table or renting a proper house. He had, she sometimes felt, moved beyond reason about his faith. She didn't, couldn't, share his excesses and it upset her when the other people who had lodgings in the house laughed openly at him – and at them too.

A few days later he found a small chapel which called itself The Lord's House, to which he took them on Sunday, even though it was a long walk and tired Patience. He had already spoken to the minister, he said, and found him a godly man.

Patience didn't like the chapel at all. It didn't belong to any sect she'd ever heard of and the service was even longer than the one back in England had been. As for the minister, he ranted at them from the pulpit in a loud, ugly voice, calling them sinners and demanding that they repent. He went on and on until some members of the congregation were moaning and begging to be saved.

Patience knew she wasn't a sinner and her mother wasn't, either.

When her father joined in with the shouts of 'Hallelujah', eyes filled with a wild light, her heart sank. The minister, Elisha Medbury, had a cruel face and never mentioned God's love, only sin and repentance. In England Patience had loved the Sunday services and the feeling of warmth and respect between members of the congregation. She hated this place instinctively and Mr Medbury terrified her.

When they got home, her father was much more cheerful. 'Now we can look for a proper house to rent. In fact, Mr Medbury knows of one close to the chapel and he's taking me to see it tomorrow after work.'

'I'd like to come and look at it, too, Alex,' Nan said. 'After all, you won't know what I need in a kitchen and – and things like that.'

'As head of the household, it's for me to decide where we live. We don't want you getting foolish ideas into your heads like my sister-in-law. I've failed with Harry, who may or may not return to the Lord's grace but shall never return to this family. I'm not going to fail with you and my daughter.'

Patience's heart sank still further.

Her mother spent most of the following day weeping.

She wept still more when she saw the mean little house her husband had rented whose only advantage, as far as she could see, was that it was a mere one street away from the chapel. It had a long, narrow back garden, overgrown with weeds, and was only two yards away from the street at the front, so that dust blew in constantly and people walking past stared through the window at them.

Lavinia tried very hard to persuade her husband to return to Lancashire. 'I don't want my baby born here,' she kept repeating, getting so agitated about it that in the end Theo gave in.

As a consequence, for the following six months Keara had no chance to see her family and that upset her greatly. With the occasional grudging help of her mistress, she improved her writing skills enough to write short letters and learned to address them properly. But she had to beg stamps from her mistress because she could rarely get into Ellerdale to buy them. She was trying to save her share of her wages money 'just in case', but always seemed to have things she needed so had only a few shillings put by.

Not nearly enough to get back to Ballymullan if anything went wrong.

'He's a good-looking fellow, the master, isn't he?' Minnie whispered one day. The two maids were turning out Mrs Mullane's bedroom and had paused for a rest near the window after pummelling the feather bed into shape.

Keara nodded, her eyes following their master through the window as he walked over a field outside. 'My da says he's the best rider he's ever known.' And Mick didn't often praise other men's ways with horses.

Minnie sighed and stayed where she was for a

minute or two longer, then clicked her tongue in annoyance. 'Well, he's not for the likes of us, is he? Come on, let's get that bed finished.'

Keara forced herself to turn away from the window, hoping Minnie hadn't noticed her blushing. She found herself dreaming of Mr Mullane sometimes, lovely dreams where they walked down the lanes near Ballymullan or sat by the river. You couldn't help your dreams, could you? And the one last night had been so lovely . . .

Lavinia was brought to bed at eight months, for no reason that anyone could tell. As the pains ripped through her she screamed and refused to do as the doctor and the expensive midwife told her, thrashing around in the bed instead like a huge, stranded sea beast as she begged someone to stop the pain.

Even Keara could not get her to do what was necessary. They had to bring her husband in to make her even pay attention to what her attendants were telling her and Keara, watching from the side of the room, was amazed at how well he handled his wife.

The infant that was eventually born never breathed and reminded Keara of the dead ones her mother had produced. But her mother had been too weary to care deeply while Theo's face was so filled with pain it made Keara's eyes fill with tears of sympathy for him.

'Give him to me,' he said.

She watched as he held out his arms for his dead son.

'Best leave it to the midwife,' the doctor advised.

'I want to hold him,' Theo insisted.

The tears blurred Keara's vision and overflowed as she watched him cradle the child's tiny body to his chest. For all his faults, the man did not deserve this pain. And she knew more about his faults now: the occasional woman kept in that cottage on the estate, his sudden absences, normally after a worse than usual quarrel with his wife. Only Dick knew where he went then and he wasn't telling. But Theo Mullane's faults were more than balanced by his innate kindness and she kept finding herself staring at him, liking the way his dark hair curved over his forehead or he strode across a field like a prince, head up, breathing deeply. And to see him on a horse was to see a man totally happy with himself and his world, a man many women turned to watch, not only her but the other maids and even ladies visiting her mistress.

Then Lavinia roused herself to ask for her child and they had to tell her it was dead, which brought on a storm of weeping. It was Keara she wanted to comfort her, not her husband.

When a door slammed, Keara looked round and saw the midwife holding the dead child again, mouth pressed tight in a line of disapproval. There was no sign of the master.

Who would comfort him? Keara wondered.

In the end the doctor gave Mrs Mullane laudanum to quieten her and when she was sleeping peacefully, Keara went down and asked the housekeeper's permission to go out for a walk in the grounds.

'Yes, you go and get a breath of fresh air, Keara love. It's been a long, hard day for you. Do you want something to eat first?'

'When I get back, if that's all right.'

'I'll tell Cook.'

The night air smelled sweet and cool after the stifling heat of Mrs Mullane's bedroom, though Keara found it took a while to get the smells of childbirth out of her nostrils. She wandered down to the stream where she had once wept out her pain and homesickness, remembering how soft the grassy bank had been. If she could just sit quietly for a while . . .

But she found her master there before her, standing staring into the darkness on the other side of the water, his face like an iron mask in the moonlight, rigid and frozen with pain.

When Keara would have backed away, he said, 'Don't go.'

She stood there uncertainly, not knowing what to say or do.

'How is she?'

'Sleeping now, sir. The doctor's given her something.'

'Perhaps I should have asked for something too. Is there anything you can give a man who longs for a child and has just seen his dead son's face?' His voice broke and he made a strangled sound, covering his face with one arm.

She took one hesitant step towards him then ran the rest of the way, folding him in her arms as she had so often done with his wife and letting him sob against her, for she could never stand aside when someone was in pain, whether it was imagined or real. But unlike his wife's petulant weeping fits, this pain was all too real. The sounds he made, the suppressed agony in every jerk of his tense body, brought more tears to Keara's eyes and when he buckled at the knees and pulled her down to the ground, she went with him, still holding him close.

The harsh weeping died down eventually, but he didn't move away from her. There was nothing threatening about the way he lay with his head in her lap, only an anguished soul's need for human warmth and comfort. So she stroked his hair, murmuring meaningless words as she would have done to Mara or Ismay.

At last he gave a great sigh and sat up again. 'No other servant would have dared offer me comfort this night, Keara Michaels.'

'Sure, they'd all have done anything they could for you. And there's Dick. He cares about you.'

'The others would have crept away and I don't think *I* could have let anyone else see my grief, not even Dick.' He looked sideways, his grey-green eyes darkened by the shadows around them. 'There's something special about you, Keara.'

'No, no, sir. I'm just an ignorant country girl.' She edged a short distance away from him, not wanting him to think she had intended to offer anything else but comfort that night. But she didn't get up and leave because she knew that her mere presence was a comfort to him.

He noticed her inch away and wished she had been

brought up less strictly. He would not repay her kindness tonight by offering her that kind of attention, but one day it seemed inevitable they'd share a bed. Something deep within him knew that because something just as deeply elemental in her responded to him. You could always tell when a woman was interested and he had seen her eyes lingering upon him more than once. As his eyes had lingered on her pretty fresh face and firm young body.

'You'll not speak of this to anyone,' he said to break the silence. It was a statement, not an order. He was already certain of her silence.

'Of course not, sir.'

As she waited for him to speak again, Keara watched the water rippling past, reflecting the moonlight in fractured patterns of brightness that tugged your eyes hither and thither.

'Do you think I'm mad, wanting a son so much?'

'Doesn't every man want a son? Even my da. He has three girls, but he thinks nothing of us.'

Theo laid one hand on her shoulder. 'Well, he ought to be proud of a daughter like you. I'd sell my soul for a son *or* a daughter.' The hand tightened for a moment then he pulled it away abruptly. 'Thank you, Keara. Get back to the house now. I think I'll sit on here for a while.'

She stole a glance sideways, relieved to see that his expression was calmer, the agony replaced by a deep sadness. She wished there were a Catholic church nearby where she could pray for him to get the child he wanted. You felt your prayers had more chance of being answered if you spoke them in God's own house. But there wasn't a Catholic church and she had not pressed for permission to go to one, contenting herself with attending the village church with the other servants because she hadn't her mother's unquestioning belief in the rightness of everything Father Cornelius said.

How could it be a sin to enter another sort of church? They were all worshipping the same god, weren't they? Besides, she loved to sit in the small stone church on Sundays, watching the play of light through its stained glass windows and listening to the choir. She looked forward to that outing all week.

Coming to England had changed her. She didn't know whether that was good or bad, only that she thought differently. She felt the master's gaze upon her and glanced sideways, her breath catching in her throat as she saw how sad he still looked. Well, she had done all she could to comfort him, all anyone could. Getting to her feet, she smoothed down her skirt. 'Good night to you, then, sir.'

'Good night, Keara.'

Theo turned his head to watch her go and when she stopped once to look back at him, he raised his hand in farewell and she raised hers before walking away into the shadows with that free and easy stride that was so characteristic of her.

Christ, but he wanted her!

CHAPTER SEVEN

August 1860 – January 1861

The following year in August, as a long muddy winter edged its way towards spring, Mark succumbed to the temptation to write to his family in Lancashire. He tore up his first effort because he'd poured out his heart in it and sounded like a complaining fool. If he was lonely it was his own fault. If he wished he'd never come to Australia, well, that was his own fault, too. In the end he decided not to tell them the whole truth, just reassure them that he was in good health.

It took him several attempts to write the letter. In it, he spoke of 'friends', though he hadn't made any real friends. He wrote that there was plenty of work in Australia, but said nothing about his life on the diggings. And he used the address of the lodging house in Melbourne where his things were still languishing in the attic. The Parkers were as near friends as he'd made since his arrival, simple folk, happy to make a little extra money by letting him store his trunk and bag in the attic and far more concerned about their children and grandchildren than anything else.

He was not getting on well with Walter these days, though they'd established a work routine that brought them in some money and had even allowed Walter to pay off a quarter of his debt – with much grumbling.

Mark had made a couple of short visits to Melbourne to get supplies, staying with the Parkers each time. Unlike Walter who thought only of the next meal, he insisted on buying flour by the sack, not to mention larger amounts of sugar and tea than other miners, then storing them in a second tin trunk he'd bought cheaply from a disillusioned man selling up and going back to Sydney. He also bought tins of sardines, bacon, cheese, salt beef and jam. It was much cheaper to bring these back to the diggings himself than buy them there. To get to and fro he hired himself out as an extra guard on one of the big carts, and instead of pay had his own supplies carted free.

Walter shrugged when he saw the extra food, as if it wasn't worthwhile bothering to bring it back. When he tried to help himself to some one day, he found the trunk locked and Mark told him he would have to pay for anything used from these stores. The two had a furious row that nearly ended in a fight, after which they each saw to their own meals. Walter paid little attention to what he ate and grew very thin, going drinking every night with 'friends' who seemed to change from one week to the next.

Mark found the trips to Melbourne a bit of a relief. He was getting tired of chasing after what he now considered to be fool's gold and had given up believing that he and Walter would strike it rich. However, he had learned a lot from this new life and knew himself to be stronger both mentally and physically for the experience. He had even saved money, some of which was kept in Melbourne. But this definitely wasn't what he wanted to do for much longer.

The second time he got back from Melbourne he found Walter about to decamp for a new goldfield where he was sure they'd do much better. He had sold their claim, packed all their belongings and loaded them on a cart belonging to a fellow he'd spent a lot of time with recently. In fact, if Mark hadn't returned then it was obvious his so-called partner would have set off without him, taking all their equipment.

They had another raging quarrel over this.

'You had no right to sell the claim without consulting me!' Mark shouted.

Walter shrugged. 'You've got to seize the moment. I told you it were stupid to go back to Melbourne. You won't find gold there, only shopkeepers wanting to take it off you.' He waved one hand in a dismissive gesture. 'This place is never going to amount to much – the gold's petering out already – so when I heard about this new place I didn't waste no time. I was leaving you a message, wasn't I? I don't know what you're complaining about.'

'But—'

'Look, if you want to split up, say so.'

'You still owe me money.'

Walter's expression turned sour. 'All listed in your bloody notebook! A man should be able to trust his partner's word, not have to write everything down.

You're a soddin' shopkeeper at heart, you are, not a miner. That's why you keep bringing stuff back to sell.'

'I make good money from that.'

'And miss chances to strike it rich.'

Mark bit back more angry words. Maybe he should cut his losses, give up on the money Walter owed him and share out their remaining possessions. But something made him hold on. Why should he lose so much of his hard-earned stake? In silence he transferred the supplies he'd brought from Melbourne to the cart belonging to Walter's friend Mac, on which other men were also travelling, taking it in turns to ride or walk in order to spare the horses, two worn-out creatures who looked ready to expire at any minute.

When the others got drunk at the first little inn, a roadside shanty selling grog of a questionable nature, Mark didn't join them. Where, he wondered as he watched them drink themselves insensible, had Walter got the money to pay for this booze? Had his partner found more gold than he'd admitted while Mark had been in Melbourne?

The next diggings were further north. The group of men travelling together worried Mark because it included some of the more disreputable or violent types from Jarandyne. He knew they mocked him behind his back for not drinking with them, but although he enjoyed the occasional beer he didn't intend to lose control of himself in such company. And he not only slept each night with his revolver to hand, but made sure they all knew it.

To Walter's delight, they were among the early

arrivals at the new site which was near a tiny settlement called Wardleworth Hill.

Again Mark let Walter pick out the claim, but be made sure they went to register ownership together. They worked in silence as they staked out their territory and erected the tent, doing things by habit now, not needing to talk.

When they didn't find much gold for a week or two, Mark refused point-blank to advance Walter any more money. He could have made a good living in his old trade by setting up the equivalent of a chop house here and seriously contemplated doing so.

The irony of that made him smile. And continue to consider it. But soon the claim was starting to bring them more gold, so he put off his decision.

The only redeeming feature about Wardleworth Hill was their neighbours on the next claim, a father and his teenage son with whom Mark became friends. Ross Campbell was a large man with a gentle smile and manner. The son was a young giant, barely out of boyhood but already six foot tall. No one was likely to try to take advantage of these two and Mark felt safer for having them nearby because Walter looked at him sometimes as if he hated him, and he certainly didn't trust his partner.

But they were so used to one another's ways that they continued to work reasonably well together, as long as they didn't try to hold a conversation.

Mark found it a lonely life and mentally set a limit on how long he was prepared to stay there. If the gold petered out again, he was leaving, debt or no debt.

*

Theo found it harder to start visiting his wife's bed again this time and she was delighted to be left alone, but after a few months he steeled himself to continue trying for a child, asking Keara one day if it would be convenient for him to visit his wife that night.

She nodded and stared down, avoiding his eyes. She knew this would upset her mistress, but it was not her place to say anything and he wouldn't listen if she did. Theo was a stubborn man, too stubborn for his own good, but she couldn't help feeling sorry for him, married to a wife like that.

Theo gave a short laugh as the silence continued. 'You don't have to tell me that Lavinia won't welcome my attentions, but it's the only way I know of to get a child and she's the only wife I've got. We were so close to success last time. . .'

When Keara passed on the message, Lavinia looked at her in dismay. 'No! Oh, no! I can't face it. Not again.'

'All women have to face it,' Keara said bluntly, knowing sympathy would only make her mistress worse.

'If he were a gentleman he'd not force himself on me.'

Keara didn't argue with that. What was a gentleman? This man's father had let his tenants starve during the potato famine, offering them only the help he was legally obliged to. Yet he had been respected by the neighbouring gentry. At least Theo Mullane treated his tenants generously. That made him a much better man, in Keara's opinion.

But he was still appearing regularly in her dreams

and that worried her. She had never even seen a man as attractive as him and couldn't understand why her mistress made such a fuss about him lying with her. If Keara had been married to him, she would have wanted to be with him. She'd seen courting couples in Ballymullan holding hands, kissing, smiling at the mere sight of one another. The thought made her sigh. She wanted the same thing. Didn't every girl? No wonder Father Cornelius had warned her. Animals looked for mates and people had the same instinct.

Only she couldn't even think of courting or marriage because she was tied to this selfish woman for as long as her family needed it. Her mistress was different from other women, childlike in many ways, and shouldn't have married at all, Keara had come to believe. And although Mrs Mullane had brought her husband the money he had needed – for all the servants knew about that – it didn't seem to have made either of them happy. *He* was restless, sometimes irritable for no reason, spending as little time as he could with his wife. *She* was just plain stupid as well as selfish. Keara found it easier to treat her mistress like a child, brushing her hair for her, speaking soothingly and finding simple tasks to keep her occupied.

These activities didn't keep Keara's mind occupied, though, and she sometimes thought she would go mad from boredom and frustration.

That night, when it was time for the evening meal, Lavinia refused to put on a dinner gown, let alone join her husband. She didn't want a tray brought to her room, and she didn't want Keara to stay with her, either.

Theo walked in just as Keara was leaving, his expression grim. 'Playing the martyr again, are we, Lavinia?'

His wife sobbed and held a handkerchief to her eyes.

He gestured to Keara to leave and she heard the words, 'Let's get it over with, then,' as she left.

Weeping was no way to touch his heart, she thought as she closed the bedroom door behind her. And since her mistress's tears came so easily, you soon learned not to place any value on them.

Keara went down to the servants' hall and told Cook that their employers' meal might be delayed a little, since the master had just gone in to see her mistress.

'Ah. Starting that again, are we? Poor lady.'

'Poor master, too,' Keara retorted. 'He's not asking for something he's not entitled to, and it's not as if he beats her.'

'I never thought to hear *you* taking his side.'

'I try not to take either side,' Keara said with a sigh, going to her place at the table. She didn't know what had made her speak out on his behalf.

The servants' meal ended and still the mistress's bell didn't ring. Nor did the bell from the dining room. They were all listening for them, couldn't help it. There was no hiding what went on when you shared a house, especially with a mistress who sobbed out her woes and complaints so loudly.

When Mrs Mullane's bell rang at last Keara sighed and stood up, aware that all eyes were upon her.

The master's bell rang almost immediately afterwards and Dick followed her out.

'I don't envy you, lass,' he said abruptly as they made their way up the back stairs. 'Have you ever thought of finding yourself another job?'

'I can't. My family needs the money I earn. My father works in the stables at Ballymullan and their house is a tied cottage. What choice do I have?'

'Mr Theo wouldn't take it out on them.'

'He threatened to throw them out when I said I didn't want to come to England.'

Dick paused on the landing, staring at her, then shook his head. 'He wouldn't have done it.'

'He said he would and I believed him. I think he'd do anything to get a child. And since I'm sometimes the only one who can calm her down, I don't think he would let me go, even now. Though I've surely earned it.'

She sighed and looked so troubled that Dick clasped her hand for a minute. Theo fancies you too much to let you go more likely, he thought, but didn't tell her that. He wasn't quite sure whether she realised it or not. Sometimes he thought she did, other times she seemed unaware of Theo's attraction to her.

When they reached the landing Keara took a deep breath and pushed open the door to her mistress's bedroom. Inside she was greeted by the usual sobbing and tears, but also this time by threats that Lavinia would get her own back on her husband one day.

'I'll make him sorry for treating me like this.'

'He's only treating you as other men do their wives.'

'Hold your tongue, you impertinent creature! What

do you know about anything? Go and fetch me some
warm water. I wish to take a bath.'

In the next room Dick found his master standing by the
window. 'Can I help you, sir?'

'I only wish you could, but no one can change my
wife into a pleasant, accommodating woman, can they?'
Theo tried to laugh, but produced only a scrape of
sound in his throat. 'It's a good thing I'm a lusty man.'

Dick stood waiting, wondering if his master would
go down to the cottage in the woods as he sometimes
did after visiting his wife's bedroom. A lively young
woman called Susan was currently living there. It
occurred to Dick, not for the first time, that none of
these young women had produced a child, but he didn't
dare raise that with Theo. Was it intentional or was his
friend and employer incapable of fathering a living
child?

But all Theo said was, 'Fetch me up some bread and
cheese, will you? And a bottle of brandy – two glasses if
you've a mind to join me for a few drinks.'

So it was going to be like that, was it? Dick thought.
Theo must be in black despair, something that didn't
happen often, for he was not usually a drinking man.

When he returned, Theo looked at him and said,
'You're a good friend, Dick.'

'Not quite a friend, sir.'

'Well, as near as I get to one.'

'You should socialise more with the neighbours and
make friends with people of your own class over here.'

'What class am I? An Irishman – for which they scorn me – and a man who married for money, which they also scorn. They'd like me better if I were a self-made man, but I'm not. I'm a countryman and proud of it. I care about horses, not mills and making money.' He looked at Dick with anguish on his face. 'I only married her to save Ballymullan, but it wasn't worth it. I should have sold the old place and shipped out to Australia or America.'

He looked around him with an expression of loathing. 'This damned mausoleum costs a fortune to maintain. Old Hardwick's money wasn't nearly as much as folk think and is still trickling away under her extravagances.'

Dick made a soothing noise in his throat.

'If I can just get a child out of my wife, I'll sell this place and leave her. She won't want the child, but I will. I'll buy her a house in Ellerdale because she hates Ireland.' He took a deep shuddering breath. 'And because I'll go mad if I have to spend the rest of my life with her.'

Dick couldn't hide his surprise. 'Is that really what you intend to do? Leave her?'

Theo stared down into his glass, swirling the amber liquid round and round with a gentle rhythmic motion. 'Maybe. I've been thinking about it seriously.'

'What about that maid of hers? Keara's pining for her family. If you sell up here, you should take her back with you, at least.'

Theo smiled grimly. 'She'll have to pine for the moment – till after my child is born anyway. She's a lovely girl, though, as healthy and normal as Lavinia is unwholesome. Perhaps one day . . .' He broke off and went back to swirling the brandy.

Dick was shocked. 'Keara's a respectable lass. It'd be a great shame to spoil her just for your pleasure.'

'But she feels something for me, I know she does. And I for her.' Theo stared into the fire, remembering how Keara had comforted him when the baby was born dead, and said almost to himself, 'When the time is ripe, I'll do something about that. And I'll treat her well – in every way. I'd never hurt her.'

Dick knew better than to comment further, but he didn't approve. Theo could have almost any woman he wanted, because he was attractive and kind as well as rich. Why did he have to pick on this one? Unlike some of the other maids, Keara Michaels hadn't a flirtatious bone in her body.

Though she did look at Theo sometimes, Dick had noticed that too. Well, all the young maids did, but Keara was different from those women Theo brought to the cottage, somehow. It'd be wrong to take her there, to make a whore of her.

One searing hot afternoon in January 1861, Mark dug up a few shovelfuls of dirt and stared at it in loathing. He was sick of this. He dumped them in the cradle with a thud and began to rock it too violently so that some pieces fell off.

'Steady on!' Walter said. 'You'll only have to pick 'em up again.'

With a sigh Mark rocked more gently while his companion tipped the contents of the bailer over the mess of rocks and earth inside. As the water washed away the mud he thought he saw something shining in one corner and stopped rocking to examine it more carefully, tossing aside some bigger pieces of stone to get to it.

Walter moved closer. 'What's up?'

'I thought I saw . . .' Mark pointed to something shining in one corner. 'Isn't that—'

His partner made a strangled sound in his throat, then said hoarsely, 'Don't say owt. Not a bloody word. If that's what I think it is, we've hit it rich.' He raised his voice to say scornfully, 'Fool's gold. You should be able to recognise it by now, lad.' Then he lowered his voice again. 'Shovel in some more mud to hide that thing, quick! It's nearly dinner time. We'll get the nugget out when no one's looking.'

In the tent Walter pulled the nugget out of his shirt where he'd hidden it and sat down on his bed, holding the heavy, irregular lump in his hands and brushing away the mud with a gentle fingertip. 'Fetch a bucket of water.'

Mark did this, then let down the tent flaps to hide what they were doing.

Carefully Walter washed the object, his breath rasping in his throat as it was revealed to be a nugget shaped roughly like a heart. He hefted it in his hands. 'I'd say it weighs – oh, two or three hundred ounces, perhaps more. What do you reckon?' He passed it to Mark, who nodded agreement.

'Don't tell anyone,' Walter warned again.

'I'd have thought you'd want to celebrate?'

'I'm not fool enough to let on about this in a new goldfield where the damned bank only sends someone to buy the gold once a week. We could get our heads stove in for this little beauty while we're waiting for them buggers to come and buy it. Anyway, I reckon we'll get more for it if we take it to Melbourne to sell.' He spat on his fingertip and rubbed it across the rough surface of the nugget, stroking the streak of shining metal that was exposed. 'I'm going to call her the Little Beauty.'

'Let me hold her again.'

Walter watched as Mark also hefted the irregularly shaped chunk of gold, but snatched it back again almost immediately with a jealous glance. 'I'll look after it.'

Mark shook his head and took the nugget quickly before Walter realised what he was doing. 'Not if you're going to the booze tent tonight, you won't. I'll stay here with my revolver handy and keep it safe. In the meantime we'd better lock it in my trunk and get back to work or folk will wonder what's wrong.'

Their eyes met and for a moment what sparked there contained the potential for another quarrel, a fight even. Mark held his breath as the silence lengthened because Walter's moods had been increasingly volatile of late.

'All right then. But I'll only have a couple of drinks tonight, so don't think of running off with it. I'd find you, wherever you went.'

'I'd not try to rob you and you know it.' But something told Mark that his partner was not to be similarly trusted and would make off with their find if he possibly could, so he resolved to sleep with the nugget under his pillow and not give it to Walter when he returned.

Only after he had eaten a scratch meal and lain on his bed for a while did it begin to sink in that they had won a small fortune by their efforts. Well, it seemed like a fortune to him. If Walter's estimate of the nugget's weight was correct, they'd get about nine hundred pounds for it, which was more than enough for Walter to pay back his debts and have money left over to waste. Mark would use his share to set himself up comfortably in business.

Relief suddenly made him feel shaky. He had grown to hate this rough life, not because of the discomforts but because of the underlying violence that was always simmering ready to erupt. It might be more peaceful on a bigger site where there were several troopers stationed permanently, though he doubted it, but on these small diggings fights or even riots could erupt in a minute. With only one trooper in residence, it was a miracle no one had been killed as yet and Mark always kept his revolver loaded and within easy reach.

That evening Walter returned early from the booze tent, almost sober for once. 'Let's have another look,' he said as soon as he'd lowered the tent flaps and lit a candle.

With a sigh, Mark heaved himself up on one elbow and pulled the nugget out from under his pillow. When Walter tried to keep it, he took it back. 'I'm younger and stronger than you so I'll look after it. A thief would find it harder to take it away from me.'

Walter glared at him, hesitated, then shrugged.

In the middle of the night Mark heard his companion get up and mumble, 'Going out for a piss.'

When he returned, Mark was just dozing off to sleep. In such a small space their beds were inevitably close together so he thought nothing of it when a foot trod on the edge of his blanket. 'Watch where you're putting your . . .' he began, then the world exploded into pain as something hit him over the head.

He tried to roll out of the way of the second blow but couldn't move fast enough. As he was opening his mouth to cry out for help, something crashed down on his head again and he could feel himself sliding helplessly down, down into a pain-filled darkness.

Mark woke to the sound of flies buzzing close to his ears. At first he didn't know where he was and found it difficult to move or even open his eyes. When he tried, pain stabbed through him and he moaned, lying very still. After a while he managed to half-open his eyes and realised he was lying on the ground inside the tent with sunlight filtering through the canvas. Outside he could hear the normal sounds of voices calling to one another, water splashing, cradles creaking and shovels turning over the dirt.

Where was Walter? What had happened?

As his eyes began to focus better Mark realised that his trunk lid was gaping open and its contents were scattered across the tent. Beneath him was a tangle of bedding. His head throbbed so painfully every time he moved that it was difficult for him to think properly.

Then it all came back to him and anger gave him the strength to push himself into a sitting position. His shirt was unbuttoned and when he fumbled for his money belt he found nothing.

He groaned at the thought of losing all he had worked so hard for. Sitting up made nausea threaten, so he laid his arms on the bed and rested his head on them until his stomach settled down.

He wasn't sure how long passed but eventually he managed to crawl on top of the bed, ignoring the pieces of paper and clothing scattered there. He had intended to call for help but felt so muzzy-headed he closed his eyes – just for a moment.

When he woke again, the sounds outside had taken on the lazier rhythm of the hottest part of the day and he had a raging thirst. The bucket of clean water had been overturned and half the things from the tent were missing.

As was Walter.

No doubt the nugget was missing too!

As he dragged himself to his feet, Mark wondered vaguely why they hadn't killed him. Or perhaps in the darkness they had thought him dead.

Only stubbornness kept him upright as he staggered towards the tent flaps, weaving about like a drunkard even over that short distance. As he pushed his way outside, sunlight hit him like a sledgehammer and pain beat through his head, so that he could not hold back a groan. 'Help!' he called out. 'Someone help me.'

Ross, who had the next claim, looked up from

beside the stream, gaped, then put down his bailer and came running up the slope. 'What the hell's happened to you, Mark lad? Your face is covered in blood.'

'Last night – Walter – he knocked me unconscious. Robbed me.'

'You sure of that, mate?'

'Yes. We found a big nugget yesterday. Several hundred ounces, he said.'

Ross whistled in surprise. 'And he's made off with it?'

'Yes.' His throat was rasping and sore. 'Have you any drinking water?'

'Yeah. I'll get you some.' He guided Mark to the rough seat outside his own tent and brought a full pannikin, which his neighbour gulped down. Obligingly, he refilled it, by which time word had spread and twenty or more men were gathered round Mark, arguing about what they should do. Someone began to push through them and the trooper appeared.

'What's going on here?' A babble of responses made him roar, 'Shut up!' He looked at Mark. 'Someone's hit you a corker. You must have a hard head to be still alive. What happened? I didn't hear any fighting last night.'

Mark explained again.

'Oh, hell, all we need is more men rushing here to look for gold!' Laboriously the trooper wrote down what had happened, then put away the stub of pencil. 'Can't see us finding the bugger. He'll be miles away by now. And I can't go chasing after him myself, though I'll send word out. If you leave the diggings, Mr Gibson, let me know where you're going – just in case we catch up with him.' He didn't sound hopeful.

And suddenly Mark had had enough. He desperately wanted to go somewhere with proper streets and houses, where the nights weren't punctuated by shouts and fighting. He wanted to live a normal life again, with clean clothes and regular meals. And he was going to. He heaved himself to his feet, swaying as he fought the pain and tried to keep his balance.

Ross came and supported him. 'Better sit down for a bit, lad. You're in no fit state to go anywhere yet. Do you want to stay with us tonight?'

'No, thanks. If I don't sleep in my tent, I'll lose the few things I've got left.'

'Aye, you're right there. But call out if you need us.'

By late afternoon Mark had recovered enough to start sorting through his remaining possessions. Although Walter had taken his money belt, the revolver was still there, hidden by the tangle of bedclothes Mark had been lying on. It was still loaded. He grimaced as he hefted it and aimed it at the nearest tent pole. A fat lot of good it had done him. Still, he would keep it to hand and also set a trip wire across the tent entrance. No one was going to surprise him again.

Most of the food was still there in his second tin trunk, as well as his clothing. The mining tools were still scattered around their claim. Presumably Walter had thought he'd have no more need of them now he had the nugget. It puzzled Mark that there were bits of white paper everywhere, few of them bigger than his thumb nail. He picked one up and then another. The second one had figures written on it and he suddenly realised what it was from – his pocket notebook. It had been torn to shreds and the pieces scattered. He gave a wry smile. How his former partner had hated that list of debts!

And now Walter would never pay the money back.

Mark felt bitter that all his hard work had been for nothing. How was he even to get back to Melbourne without a penny to his name?

A shadow moving across the ground made Mark grab the frying pan and turn to defend himself.

'Hey in there!' a voice called from just outside the tent entrance.

'Who is it? What do you want?'

'I wondered if you wanted to sell your claim?'

'I might. Come in.'

A stranger lifted the tent flap and stood looking round. 'He made a mess, didn't he, your partner? Rotten sod. I hate thieves.'

Mark made a noise he hoped signified agreement. He couldn't even think of Walter without feeling sick with anger and disgust, not only at his former partner, but at himself for letting himself be robbed so easily.

'They said you found a big nugget on your claim, but you're leaving because of what happened. I'll buy the claim off you, if you like.'

And then it came to Mark what he could do to get some money at least. Relief made him feel shaky. 'I'm going to hold an auction tomorrow morning, selling the claim and everything I have left, tools and all that stuff. You can bid with the others.'

'You sure you don't want to sell today? Save you a lot of trouble.'

'I want the highest price I can get.' Needed it desperately.

'What time?'

'Ten in the morning.'

'Right.' The man shrugged and left.

Mark slept badly, jerking awake at the slightest sound and feeling for the revolver.

In the morning, he got Ross to keep an eye on his tent while he spread word of what he intended to do. Then, grim-faced, he laid out most of his remaining possessions in the sun. Even as he was doing it men came up and offered to buy this or that, and if he thought the price fair, he agreed.

He sighed in relief as he put away the first money he received. His head was still throbbing and he'd been shocked at the sight of his face in the tiny shaving mirror: swollen eye, bruising down one side, cuts and abrasions. His hair was still matted with blood where one of the blows had landed, but he hadn't had time to deal with that yet and anyway it was too sore to wash properly.

By midday he'd sold the claim and most of the bits and pieces he no longer needed. That left him with the trunk of food. Ironic, really. Back to his old trade. He went to see Ross and beg space inside his neighbour's tent. He wanted to stay on a bit longer and get the maximum benefit from the sale of his food stores, but the man who'd bought his tent had paid extra to take it away immediately. 'In return for space in your tent, I'll provide your evening meals free till I go, Ross,' he offered.

They shook hands.

The next evening Mark fed ten other men on a simple meat stew and damper, as well as his temporary hosts. Word spread and within the week he'd used up his food supplies and made a decent profit on that expenditure at least.

Now at last he could leave. And he was never, ever going to set foot on a goldfield again.

He bargained for a place as an extra guard on a wagon going back to Melbourne to fetch supplies for the camp shop. The last wagon had been held up and robbed, so they were glad to get an extra man for the price of the ride.

After saying goodbye to Ross and his son, Mark left the camp without looking back.

In a new holster attached to his belt he was carrying the revolver, loaded and ready to use. He would never be quite so trusting again. And if anyone tried to hold up this cart, they'd have him to deal with.

He doubted anyone would try, though. Not after last time. Everyone said such villains usually moved on to new ground after a hold-up. They weren't stupid enough to try it twice in the same place.

CHAPTER EIGHT

February 1861

Keara was beginning to get a little worried. Often when she met her employer about the house, he would stop and stare at her with what she could only think of as a hungry expression. Occasionally he would stop her to ask how she was. Mostly he just stared.

She wished desperately that she hadn't comforted him that time because it had drawn his attention to her and that could only lead to trouble. But he looked so unhappy most of the time that her heart still went out to him.

'How are you today, Keara?' he would ask sometimes.

'I'm well, sir, thank you,' she would answer, eyes downcast, hands folded on her apron. She didn't want him to think she was encouraging his attentions.

His replies were equally simple. 'Yes, you look well' or 'I'm glad to hear that'.

But the looks he gave her were quite different from the words and they continued to make her shiver and feel – strange, unlike herself.

On her days off she would go for walks in the grounds if the weather permitted, avoiding the area near *that cottage*, of course. Sometimes she would manage to get into town if there was a chance of a ride in one of the farm carts. The drivers, whom she knew by sight, were older family men, respectful towards the maids at the big house, and she felt at ease with them, interested to hear about their families and doings. She shared her small bits of news with them, but it wasn't often Arla wrote and the letters were disappointingly brief. Still, it was something just to know her mother and sisters were all right and she kept all the letters in a bundle, re-reading them to cheer herself up.

Times were getting harder in Lancashire. Dick had explained to her that there was a war between the northern and southern states in America which was cutting off the supply of cotton and causing many mills to close down or go on short time. A cotton famine, they were calling it, nearly as bad for working folk as the potato famine had been in Ireland.

The first time she saw a group of children standing listlessly on a street corner in the town, looking thin and hungry, Keara walked past with tears in her eyes for it brought back memories of her own childhood. After that she found herself using the small amount of money she received from her wages to buy them food because she just couldn't stand seeing barefoot children with that gaunt, famished look on their faces.

'You'll never have anything for yourself if you go on like that,' Minnie said one day, after watching her buy a loaf in town and tear it up to share among a group of thin, ragged children.

'What do I need money for?' Keara asked lightly. 'Don't I get all my meals and my clothes bought for me?' She looked at the children who were eating their pieces of bread as rapidly as possible and staying near her to prevent others from snatching them.

'Everyone needs something saved against a rainy day,' Minnie said darkly.

Keara knew this was sensible advice, but still couldn't bear to see those hungry faces without doing what she could to help the children.

She went back one day to the news that Mr Mullane was planning another visit to Ireland. It didn't matter that this made her mistress even more peevish than usual, didn't matter how the master looked at Keara. All that mattered was that she would see her mother and sisters again. The mere thought of it filled her with joy and brought her an angry scolding from her mistress for mooning around and 'grinning like an ape'.

'You're happy to be going back to Ireland?' Mr Mullane asked the following day.

She risked looking him in the eye. 'You know I am. I hate being away from my family.' She even wondered if she'd caught a look of shame on his face as she said it.

As the big wagon rumbled slowly towards Melbourne, a shot rang out and the guard sitting next to the driver yelped and clutched his shoulder. Mark, who was sitting in the rear, hidden by some boxes, pulled out his revolver but stayed very still, his expression grim. If he kept his presence a secret he stood more chance of doing something about this attack, and by hell, he wasn't letting anyone steal from him again without a fight.

A voice called, 'Stop now and you won't get hurt!'

As another shot zipped close to the driver's face, Mark saw him nod and hold up one hand to signify he wouldn't cause any trouble. Lowering the hand slowly, he reined in the ten ponderous beasts drawing the huge wagon.

As they came to a halt, three men holding guns and with scarves hiding their lower faces stepped out from behind some trees.

Mark peered between the boxes, his view of the bushrangers partly blocked by the canvas hood of the cart. He still didn't reveal his presence because he felt hot anger rising in him at the thought of these scoundrels taking what little money he had managed to scrape together out of the wreck of his life. He had never felt so overwhelmed by anger, not even after Walter had stolen the nugget.

'Go round and check the rear, see what they're carrying,' the one who seemed to be the leader called, and a man began walking round the wagon, his shadow travelling across the canvas hood as he moved.

'I'm going to shoot that man,' Mark murmured, speaking so quietly he could only be heard by the driver and guard. 'Be ready to jump for cover! It's our only chance.'

There was a low growl of assent. They all knew that bushrangers often shot their victims so that no one could identify them.

Moving very quietly, Mark lifted his revolver and held it ready, sighting along it. The man moving along the side of the wagon joked with his companions that he hoped there was enough money this time to make it worth their trouble.

Anger still flaring hotly, Mark aimed at the open part of the canvas hood at the rear. As soon as the man came into sight, he fired without warning, knowing he'd only have this one chance to turn the tables.

Even before the other bushrangers fired again, the two men on the driving seat were diving over the back of the bench.

As the man at the rear clutched his chest and crumpled to the ground, Mark swung round and fired blindly towards the front. Shots were exchanged, one splintering the wooden planks of the driver's seat. The driver had by now snatched up his rifle, which had been lying behind the seat, and loosed off a shot which hit one man in the arm.

The bushrangers yelled for their companion to join them and fled. The driver fired again, catching the second man full in the back, so that he fell sprawling to the ground.

Mark turned round to check the man he had shot but he hadn't stirred since he'd fallen. He willed the fellow to get to his feet or at least groan, but the bushranger didn't move. Mark's breath caught in his throat.

He hadn't – surely he hadn't killed him?

The only man not badly injured vanished among the trees and a minute later they heard the sound of a horse galloping away.

In the silence that followed the three men in the wagon stayed where they were, lying perfectly still.

'What happened to your fellow?' the driver asked.

'He hasn't moved.' As Mark looked again, he saw the great bloody mess where the man's chest should have been and suddenly felt very faint and distant.

He *had* killed him!

'Has the third bugger gone or do you think it was a trick?' the driver asked, still keeping hidden.

'I think we've driven the bastards off,' the guard replied, groaning as he moved incautiously. 'And I'd be grateful if one of you would tie this damned wound up before I bleed to death.'

'You did well, Gibson!' the driver called. 'I owe you a drink for this and . . . What's up?'

For Mark had scrabbled off the rear of the cart. He went to vomit by the side of the road, then stood there shaking with reaction. He had killed a man! He knew the man would have killed him without blinking, but it didn't make any difference. Bile roiled in his stomach and he heaved again.

It was a while before he straightened up, feeling shaky still and shivery, in spite of the hot summer sun beating down on them. He walked slowly across to the others on legs that seemed to be made of cotton wool.

'First time you've killed someone?' the driver asked in a sympathetic tone.

Mark nodded.

'I've killed three now, all buggers who were trying to rob me on the road. You get used to it and you know you'd do it again, though I'd rather not.' He clapped the younger man on the shoulder. 'You had no choice, lad. You've nothing to blame yourself for. You saved all our lives.'

'What—' Mark swallowed hard as the words stuck in his throat and had to force them out. 'What are we going to do now?'

'Pile the bodies on the back of the wagon and hand 'em over to the next magistrate.' He grinned. 'It's all right. We'll do that. You're as pale as a bloody funeral lily.'

'Their horses may still be around,' the assistant driver said suddenly. 'Might as well take them with us. You go and look behind them trees, Gibson, while we pick these two up. But keep your weapon handy.'

Still feeling as if everything were unreal, Mark left them to their bloody task, checked his revolver and went off, holding it ready in his hand. There were indeed two horses tethered in the shade next to a small campsite. There was also a very bad smell coming from some-where nearby. Puzzled, he moved behind some trees to find that the smell came from a body lying tumbled at the bottom of a dry gully. It had clearly been there for a few days.

He stared down at it in shock as he recognised the man. Walter Hudson. His former partner. So it hadn't done him much good to steal the gold.

Shuddering, Mark went back to untie the two horses and lead them to the wagon. He wasn't going any closer to the decomposing body. Couldn't face it.

'There's a dead man back there,' he told his companions. 'But the body's not in a state to be moved anywhere. It's my former partner, the one who stole the nugget from me. He's been dead for a few days, I reckon. Someone must have killed him and stolen the nugget.'

'Serve the sod right,' said the driver, emphasising his words by spitting to one side. 'Can't abide folk as rob their mates. Never could. Come on then, tie them horses to the back of the cart and let's get going.'

The magistrate in the next small town praised Mark's alertness, only kept them with him for long enough to make and sign statements as to what had happened, then sent them on their way to Melbourne with the bushrangers' horses as their reward.

'I doubt we'll catch the other fellow,' he said as he saw them out. 'But at least you rid us of two of the scum. Well done, lads.'

'I know where we can sell the horses,' the driver said. 'Nice little bonus, that.'

Within minutes he was talking about his wife and children, laughing over their antics.

Mark didn't join in. Everything had begun to seem very unreal to him. In fact his whole time in Australia so far had been unreal. He should have stuck to what he was good at and not been foolish enough to go after gold. And he would do just that from now on.

★

At Ballymullan Keara went running down the lane as
soon as she was given time off, her bonnet coming loose
and hanging by its ribbons. She could feel her hair
streaming behind her as she ran, but was too full of
happiness at the thought of seeing her mother and
sisters again to care.

It was one of those days when you seemed to feel
that spring wasn't far away, though it was still cold.
Only she didn't feel the chill in her warm clothes and
well-fitting shoes.

But the reunion was not as joyful as she'd expected
because her mother was looking ill again. Betsy made
light of it – when had she ever bothered about herself?
– but Keara was shocked at how thin her mother was
and how little colour there was in her face.

When it was time to go back, Ismay offered to walk
to the big house with her and when Mara would have
joined them, told her rather sharply to stay with their
mother. The two young women stopped once they were
out of sight of the cottage.

'She's getting worse, isn't she?' Keara asked, her
voice coming out choked with tears. As Ismay nodded,
she reached out to hug her sister and the two of them
stood there for a moment, holding one another and
rocking slightly.

'I worry about her,' Ismay admitted. 'Even Da's
noticed and he doesn't pester her any more. I bring food
home for her but she hardly touches it. She was so bad
a few weeks ago that I thought . . .' She swallowed hard,

then said, 'But she got better. She keeps saying she's got a few years left in her yet if she's careful.'

'And do you – think that's true?'

'I didn't till she got better this time. Now I don't know. I just take each day as it comes. Only she doesn't want us to worry you with it, so don't say anything.'

They walked in silence for a bit, then Keara asked, 'How's it going with Arla?'

Ismay smiled. 'Oh, it's lovely working for her and Brian. I can read and write so much better now. It keeps me going, being with them does. And I think sometimes: they've had hard times but they've come through them. That gives me the courage to go on, somehow.'

Keara stopped walking again. 'Ought I to stop working for Mrs Mullane? Come home? Look after Mam?'

Without even hesitating, Ismay shook her head. 'No. It's your money that gets us the food and the house. She loves that house, you know. It's made her very happy to live there.'

'I know. She tells me every time I see her.'

'So you're doing what you can. No need to change things.'

Keara stood at the gate watching her sister hurry back towards the village. She might be doing what she could but it didn't feel like enough. She wanted to be with her family, wanted it so very much. It was getting harder and harder to stay patient with her mistress's selfish ways.

*

A week later Theo came into his wife's bedroom, smiling and waving a letter. 'My cousin Caley and his wife are coming to stay for a few days.'

'Coming here?' Lavinia asked.

'Didn't I just say so?'

'But this house is so small and it's in a terrible state. It's not fit for visitors.'

'Caley won't mind that. He and Noreen are going to live in Australia and they want to say a proper goodbye. I shall miss them. He's my favourite cousin.'

She stared at him as if she hadn't understood what he'd told her. 'Why would they go to live in Australia? They have a nice house in Sligo.'

'Because they don't have a nice income to go with it.' He could see that that meant little to Lavinia. She never seemed to understand about getting money, only spending it. He should have been firmer with her when they first married, stopped her being so extravagant. But he hadn't. And now he was trying not to cause any further disagreements between them, trying to keep her as happy as he could. It was hard because they were too different even to hold a proper conversation.

It was a lonely life sometimes. Thank heavens for Dick!

Keara was standing by the window, trying not to intrude on their conversation, but could not help noticing Mr Mullane controlling his impatience only with a visible effort.

'They're going to Australia, Lavinia, because they

want a better life for their sons,' he said when she still looked puzzled.

Which made Keara wonder what Australia was like if you could be so certain of making a better life there.

'They'll be arriving tomorrow afternoon, but the boys will be staying on with Noreen's aunt, so it'll be just Caley and Noreen this time.'

'You should have gone to say goodbye to them in Sligo, Theo. Can't you put them off? I really don't want to—'

His mouth tightened into a grim line as his patience slipped. '*I* want them to come here. And what are you making all this fuss about? You said you liked Noreen last time you met her.'

Lavinia shrugged. 'It'll be such a lot of trouble.'

His voice grew even sharper. 'Not for you, it won't. You never lift a finger these days.'

'Why should I? What are servants for if not to do the work?'

'Well, then, understand clearly that I shall be very angry indeed if you don't make my cousins welcome.'

She pulled a face but said nothing.

When he'd gone, Keara looked at her mistress who had gone to hold her hands out to a fire that did little more than take the chill and dampness off the huge room. 'Will I go and tell Cook about the visitors, ma'am?'

Lavinia didn't even look up. 'I suppose you'd better.'

But Mr Mullane was already down in the kitchen making Cook laugh. He was a different man away from his wife, while Mrs Mullane only came to any semblance of life when she was gossiping with her old friends in Lancashire. Women almost as silly as herself, Keara thought, from what she'd seen as she helped serve them.

How much longer would she have to put up with this woman?

Caley Gallagher and his vivacious wife arrived late the following morning in a ramshackle carriage piled with luggage. Theo went to open the door to them himself, then he and his cousin exchanged hugs and slapped one another on the back while Noreen pecked the air above Lavinia's cheek and said that her hostess was looking well.

'Can we be staying for a week or two, Theo?' Caley asked in his booming voice. 'We sold the house suddenly, and for a decent price too, but the new owner wanted to move in right away so we've had to get out.'

'Aren't we the poor homeless creatures?' Noreen tried to look unhappy but failed completely.

Caley put his arm round his wife's shoulders and smacked a kiss on her cheek, then looked across at Theo. 'The boys will be all right with Noreen's aunt, but they haven't room there for all of us because her mother's living with them now.'

'Stay as long as you like,' Theo said. 'Come into the parlour and make yourselves comfortable.' As Lavinia trailed into the house with their guests, he turned to Keara. 'Would you ask Cook to send us in some refreshments, please?'

'Yes, sir.'

He returned to sit opposite his cousins. 'When does your ship sail?'

'Not for another few weeks.'

'What made you think of going to Australia?'

'The thought of the sunshine,' Noreen said promptly. 'If we have to be poor, I'd prefer to be poor in a place where it doesn't rain all the time.'

'And the thought of buying our own land,' Caley added quietly. 'You know I've always wanted that. Somewhere to raise horses.'

'Yes, I know,' Theo said softly. Caley's father had been the youngest of Theo's mother's three brothers, and there'd been nothing much left for him. Theo's mother had inherited Ballymullan from a godmother and her older brother had inherited the main estate on the other side of Sligo. But he was dead now and the son made little attempt to keep in touch with the rest of the family.

Theo's father had been a disaster for Ballymullan, running the estate down so that Theo had nearly lost it. Sometimes he wished he had. Marriage to Lavinia was a heavy price to pay for keeping it.

Knowing Cook was busy, Keara not only helped prepare the trays but carried in the refreshments as well. Theo and his cousins were talking and laughing, but her mistress was simply sitting there and when she saw her maid, looked annoyed.

'What were you doing serving us, Keara?' Lavinia demanded when she went up to change for dinner.

'Cook was busy so I was helping out, ma'am.'

'Well, don't do that again! You're *my* maid and you're here to look after me – and only me.'

Keara kept her irritation at the unreasonableness of this pushed down inside her.

'And what's more,' that whining voice went on, 'while we have visitors, you are not to go off to see your family in the afternoons. I may need you at any time to help me change my clothes. One has to keep up appearances, even in Ireland.'

'But, Mrs Mullane—'

Her mistress's voice suddenly rose to a shriek and she hit Keara across the face, something she had never done before. 'Don't answer me back! I'm very lenient with you, but if that leads to your taking advantage of my kindness to loll around with your family every afternoon when I need you myself – and I'd have thought you'd have more consideration after all I've done for you – not to mention messing around gossiping with the other servants, then there's going to be trouble.'

Keara could only gape at this unfair attack on her. She rubbed her cheek, feeling aggrieved. She didn't deserve that.

The door opened and Theo came in. 'Can you please keep your voice down, Lavinia? You can be heard all over the house.'

Spots of red bloomed suddenly in his wife's cheeks. 'I shall speak how I choose. I do not intend to creep around like a ghost in my own home just because you've decided to fill the house with your disreputable relatives.'

Theo gestured to Keara to leave, then noticed the red marks on her cheek. 'Just a minute.' He turned to his wife. 'Did you hit Keara just now?'

'She deserved it.'

He drew in breath with an angry hiss. 'Keara, I apologise on my wife's behalf. You won't be subject to such unfair actions again, I promise you.'

'Thank you, sir.' Outside, she hesitated then lingered on the landing to listen to what they were discussing. She didn't usually do that but this might affect her.

'If you hit Keara again, I'll hit you twice as hard.' When his wife said nothing, Theo repeated sharply. 'Did you hear me?'

'Yes.'

'And you're not to stop that girl from visiting her family in the afternoons, Lavinia.'

'I need her here. She has no right to leave me to manage on my own.'

'She has every right to a holiday. All the servants do. She's more than earned it, the way she runs round after you all the time.'

Lavinia began to weep, great gasping sobs. 'If you want me to bear you a child, you should pay more attention to *my* needs and not scold me all the time. Why are you taking a servant's part against me?'

From outside Keara could picture the scene all too well. Any minute now her mistress would go into full-blown hysterics and he would storm out. Then the bell would ring for her. But this time she wouldn't answer it. She would go and see her family, as Mr Mullane had told her to.

He said something Keara couldn't hear and her mistress screeched, '*How dare you?* I was on my own for *hours* yesterday afternoon. What do we pay her for, if not to be with me?'

'I'm not going to argue. Come and join our guests.'

'I'm not feeling well and I shan't be down to dinner, either.'

'You'll be down to dinner if I have to carry you myself.'

'Oh, you like forcing women to do your will, don't you? You're a brute, Theo Mullane, and no gentleman.'

'Well, let me tell you, woman . . .'

As Keara turned to leave a voice next to her asked quietly, 'Does this happen often?'

She could feel her face flame with embarrassment at being caught eavesdropping. 'Sometimes.'

Noreen Gallagher smiled sympathetically at her. 'Don't look so upset. I'd be listening in, too, if I were that woman's maid. She must lead you a terrible dance.'

Keara couldn't think what to say except, 'I'm sorry, ma'am.'

'Don't be. We've known Lavinia for a while now. We don't let her foolish ways worry us.'

She was smiling so warmly, Keara seized the opportunity to ask, 'Where is Australia, ma'am? Is life there really so much better than here?'

'So they say. The weather is much warmer, that's for sure. It's often sunny, they tell me.'

'It'd be a fine place to live then. My mother's always

wishing for a bit of sunshine.' With a sigh she went on her way to visit her family, knowing that whatever Mr Mullane said, her mistress would take it out on her when she got back.

But it would be worth it to see them.

CHAPTER NINE

February 1861 – June 1862

When he got back to Melbourne, Mark went to stay with the Parkers again, thankful that he'd left some of his money with them. He'd have to be careful, but he still had enough to start a business.

He spent a few days walking round, wondering if he'd like to live here and, if so, in which suburb. It felt strange to be choosing where you lived, not just staying in the place where you'd been born and grown up. He stopped to wait for a horse and cart to pass, raising his face to the sun, and realised suddenly that he didn't miss smoky, rainy Bilsden – it was only the people he missed, his family. Had his father forgiven him yet? He dared to hope so. His father was a true Christian, unlike Alex Jenner who was a nasty bigot. Yes, surely his father would have forgiven him.

Although there were some fine streets in the centre of the city lined by elegant shops and one or two imposing banks, behind them lay noisome alleys and narrow roads where filth was allowed to accumulate. Even on some of the more important streets there were open gutters at the side and mud lay thick on the unpaved roadway, causing huge difficulties for pedestrians, especially the ladies with their long skirts. Mark grinned as he stood watching. He had never seen such a fine display of ladies' ankles and calves as skirt hems were lifted to keep them out of the mud.

He went round the food suppliers, not impressed with what he found. He disliked the way carcasses were hung outside butchers' shops, the target of flies and dust and who knew what else? When he went round the back of one or two, driven by professional curiosity, he found that cattle were actually slaughtered on the premises. Wrinkling his nose at the smell, he began to wonder where you would buy good, fresh meat if you lived here.

It occurred to him suddenly that this was what Bilsden might have been like if they hadn't had a doctor like Jeremy Lewis who cared deeply about civic cleanliness, a doctor who had warned people many years previously of the consequences of not paying attention to drainage and clean water. His sister Annie's second husband Frederick, an enlightened mill-owner, had listened to the doctor and had often pushed the town council into doing what was necessary. Mark had taken all that for granted because he'd not travelled round England much, except for a couple of visits to London. Now he fully understood the reasons behind all Jeremy's fuss.

After much consideration and many hours of walking around the suburbs, he decided he didn't want to live in Melbourne or bring up a family there so eventually took a stage coach out of town. One of the country towns in the colony of Victoria might suit him better, perhaps. When the coach stopped at a small town called Rossall Springs, two hours' drive away from the city along the Ballarat road, he got off simply because he liked the look of the place.

He wandered into the general store with its sign saying, 'Proprietor S. Grove' and initiated a conversation with the owner, who told him Rossall Springs had had its own small gold rush which had fizzled out a few years ago.

'I've seen deserted diggings in other places,' Mark said, interested. 'Why has your town continued to prosper, do you think?'

'Because the land around here is fertile and there's a ready market for the farmers' produce in Melbourne.' Samuel Grove gestured widely with one arm. 'We are growing into a regional centre and as we're on the road to Bendigo, there's traffic passing through every day, bringing us extra business. There are three hundred people living permanently in the town now and as many again in the farms round about.'

It seemed a small number to Mark and he'd have called a place like that a village not a town, but his companion seemed proud of it. 'I'm grateful for the information. I wonder, could I leave my luggage here while I look round Rossall? I'm considering starting up a business here, you see.'

'Oh? And may I ask what sort of business?'

'I used to run an eating house in England and thought I might do so again here.'

Samuel beamed at him. 'That sounds an excellent idea. People passing through have nowhere to buy a decent meal and quite a few folk come into town on market days. There are also a lot of single men around who'd be glad of somewhere that provided them with cooked meals. We really do need more women in the colonies.'

Mark set off, walking slowly and observing not only the buildings but the people. They seemed friendly towards one another and there was no feeling of latent violence, as there had been on the diggings. It was very unlike an English town, though, consisting mainly of a central street which rose slightly at one end, curving round so that the street running off it to the left formed a Y-shape. There were a few short back streets, winding haphazardly as if to accommodate the houses, rather than having houses set along them.

Within an hour or two he had not only walked all the streets but had got into conversation with several people. Someone had had the sense to arrange a place to dump refuse outside the town limits – his nose led him to that – so the town itself was cleaner than most. They got their water from the springs after which the town was named and these were situated at the opposite end from the rubbish dump. The man who showed the springs to Mark was proud of how the town council had protected these from being polluted by animals drinking there or people passing through leaving refuse to rot into the water. The council had built a strong fence round them and now piped the clean spring water to houses at a small charge.

Mark returned to the main street and studied it again, with a serious eye to business prospects now. If he couldn't find premises on this street, it'd be no use trying to open an eating house. Again, things seemed to have been built very haphazardly. Some houses were close to the street, others set back with neat gardens. The buildings themselves were mainly made of wooden boards, with tin roofs and picket fences.

There were only two buildings higher than one storey, the church at one end and a bank at the other. A sign outside the church showed it was used by two or three denominations and, again, had been built by community effort. That augured well, Mark thought. The bank was a raw new building of red brick with an imposing façade It amused him that no one had made any attempt to beautify the sides and the plain brick-work there was roughly finished, as if waiting for other buildings to be attached to it.

As Mr Grove had told him, there was no other eating house in town, though the hotel at one end advertised 'Meals and rooms'. But when he went inside and asked for a meal, the owner told him they only served food in the evening and seemed from his tone to think even that was an unwelcome effort. The other drinking house was more of a grog shop and when Mark poked his head inside it smelled of ale and pipe smoke, while the smell of urine came strongly from the rear. And no, they didn't do meals.

He went back to the general store to discuss the matter in more detail. 'I like it here,' he said. 'I think it would be a good place to live.'

Upon hearing this Mr Grove swelled with importance and identified himself as the Mayor. After shouting for someone called Sally to 'Take over here, quick!' he led Mark into the rear parlour, indicated a chair and began to interrogate him about his intentions and financial situation.

With Samuel's enthusiastic help, Mark ended up renting a small house right in the centre of town whose owners had built another one in a quieter street. He declined to consider purchasing it until he'd seen whether his business prospered, but took out a first option to buy. He could not, in any case, have afforded the place yet.

It was enormously satisfying to make plans to settle down and live a normal life. He found himself whistling as he walked.

Only two weeks later he opened his eating house, having made a quick trip to Melbourne for equipment in Mr Grove's cart which went there every week for supplies. When he came back, he stood in the street and looked up at the new maroon and cream sign above his door: EATING HOUSE, Proprietor M. Gibson.

This was a far better way to earn a living than digging for gold.

He hired a woman to help with both cooking and serving, but had to train Ginny in his ways. No one raised in the same house as his sister Annie and his stepmother Kathy could bear the thought of dirt and disorder near food. He'd always kept his kitchens and store cupboards clean back at his chop house in Bilsden and intended to do the same here.

The customers who drifted in at noon on the first day were a rough crowd and men only, which worried him. He made them pay for their food in advance, which caused a few grumbles, but promised to refund the money if they had any complaints after they'd eaten the set meal.

When he returned with their heaped plates, he found that two of them had started to quarrel and were yelling at one another. The bigger one was threatening to 'paste you good and proper if you don't shut up', and slammed his fist down on the table with such force that his spoon skittered off it and across the wooden floor.

Furious, Mark put down the plates on another table, went straight across to them and shouted at them to stop. He had to push between them to get their full attention. 'Any fighting and you're out – permanently. And you won't be let back in again.'

The bigger man, of whom everyone seemed wary, laughed in his face.

Furious, Mark grabbed the man's shirt so quickly he took him by surprise and yanked him away from the table, sending the stool he was sitting on crashing to the floor. 'This is an eating house *not* a sly grog shanty. A *respectable* eating house, what's more.'

Although the man struggled, Mark shook him hard to emphasise his point, glad now of the muscles he'd built up on the goldfields. 'If you want to brawl, you can go and do it elsewhere. If you're determined to fight, come outside and I'll show you I mean what I say.'

The man shook him off and squared up to him.

The room grew very quiet as they stood facing one another, but Mark didn't flinch. They'd have to beat him senseless to stop him protecting his new business.

'Good stew, this,' said a calm voice from the other side of the room. 'Best I've tasted for a long time. Pity to waste it.'

The man who had a moment ago been arguing with Mark's opponent looked at his steaming plate and sat down, spooning up some stew and eating it with relish. 'Damn' right it's good. Aw, sit down and eat, Ratty! We'll sort it all out later.'

Ratty watched as his friend shovelled more meat into his mouth, made appreciative noises and dunked his bread in the gravy. Licking his lips, he took a step towards the table then turned to scowl at Mark. 'I'm only backing off because I'm hungry.' He picked up his stool and plonked himself down on it again.

'The rules won't change and I'll never back off from those who try to upset my business,' Mark said, loudly and clearly, then delivered the two plates to the waiting customers and went to stand at the side of the eating room, arms folded, staying there until Ratty and his companion had gobbled down their food and left.

As the man who'd made the remark that had eased the tension got up and made his way towards the door, Mark intercepted him. 'Thanks for your help.'

'That's all right. Shame to waste good food. I'll be back. So will Ratty, I should think.'

Mark soon had farmers supplying him regularly with fresh meat and vegetables. They were pleased not to have to send all their produce into Melbourne and he was pleased to be able to buy locally. He salted down the meat he couldn't use immediately so that there was never a question of disguising tainted produce.

Still, no women came to eat there, so he asked Mrs Grove's advice about why ladies and families did not patronise his establishment, then set up a second room at the side with a sign saying 'Ladies' and families' room'. Thereafter that room was always full on market days as well, and was used by female travellers when the coaches stopped to change horses.

There was not enough custom in such a small town to make him rich but there was enough for him to make a decent living and he soon settled into his old routines.

But still the nightmares came about the man he had killed. He was beginning to wonder if they'd ever go away.

In April 1862 Mark received a response to his letter to his family. It was a battered package which had been forwarded from Melbourne by the Parkers. When he opened it, he found a photograph of his father and his stepmother Kathy holding a small child on their knees. It could only be Mark's. It affected him so much he was hard put to hold back the tears, and when a customer came into the eating house, he put the photograph and letter hurriedly aside in his small sitting room at the rear, not daring to look at them again until he could do so in private.

It seemed a very long day.

When he had locked the door behind Ginny and extinguished the last wall lamp in the kitchen, he went through to his tiny sitting room and pulled out the package, staring at the photograph and tracing John Gibson's face with one fingertip, swallowing hard against tears. To receive this must mean that his father had forgiven him. Surely it must?

Then he read the letter.

His father and Kathy were well, so were all his brothers and sisters, but Frederick Hallam was dead.

Mark felt very sad to hear that, not only because he had liked and respected Frederick, but because his sister Annie had loved her second husband deeply.

And Nelly was dead as well!

He couldn't believe that and had to read the paragraph three times before he could take it in. Guilt washed through him as he read how she had been forced into marriage by her father, then pined and faded after bearing Mark's child. His fault. All his fault. The Gibson curse! He bowed his head and did not even try to hold back the tears.

Then he went back to the letter, reading that his daughter was called Faith and was being brought up by his father and Kathy rather than the Burns family. Thank heavens for that! He wondered what Faith had been like as a baby. He could see for himself that she was now a pretty little girl, with dark hair and a broad smile. She reminded him of Nelly; of himself as well. He went to find the small mirror he used for shaving and studied his own face, then the photograph. Yes, she was definitely his child. You couldn't doubt that. He had wondered, given the fact that Nelly had definitely not been a virgin, whether someone else had fathered her baby. It had been one of the many reasons he'd refused to marry her, though of course he hadn't said that to anyone.

It was a week before he wrote back and in his letter he talked vaguely of one day returning to England to visit them and asked if they needed more money for Faith or whether his eating house was still providing for her. It would be a long time before he could even think of returning, though he could hope – and give them hope for a visit, too. But he would write regularly from now on.

What he wanted, he gradually came to realise over the next few weeks, was to marry and start a family of his own. The young women of Rossall were showing great interest in such an eligible young man, but he was not drawn to any of them. He only wished he were.

But his body kept letting him know that he wasn't born to be celibate and this was causing him some very restless nights.

Keara was sorry when the Gallaghers left Ballymullan. She had managed to have a few chats with Noreen Gallagher and find out more about Australia. It sounded wonderful and as a series of rainy days set in, she found herself longing for some sunshine and fine weather like they had there.

Mr Mullane, who had been in a good humour during his cousins' visit, grew irritable after they left and spent a lot of time out in the stables or away from home.

Mrs Mullane had been nothing but irritable since they'd come here, but she now made Keara's life utterly miserable, seeming to take delight in being spiteful: messing up the room her maid had just tidied, spilling things on purpose, wanting something fetching and then wanting it taken back again without so much as touching it.

Theo noticed and watched in concern as Keara, who was usually in blooming health, began to look drawn and tired. He knew she was worried about her mother because Diarmid had told him that Betsy Michaels wasn't well. Should he intervene, say something to his wife? Perhaps not. This petty behaviour had only begun after his previous attempt to help the girl.

He tried taking his wife out for drives so that Keara could go and visit her family without recriminations, but this was not a success. Lavinia sat shivering in the carriage, complaining that there was nothing to see or do and that it was always cold and rainy in Ireland.

'It rains just as much in Lancashire, dammit, woman!' he exclaimed in frustration. 'That's why they spin cotton there.'

'But Lancashire is *home* to me,' she said, her lower lip pouting like a child's. 'This place isn't and never will be.'

Some nights he could not bear to go near her, then the next day he'd see a group of children while he was out and the longing would rise up in him again to have one of his own. It didn't matter whether it was a son or daughter, as long as it was his.

He saw Keara sometimes in the village with one or the other of her sisters and when she was there she looked happier. It turned the knife in the wound that a drunkard like Mick Michaels could sire such lovely children while he couldn't even get one.

For Keara the visits to the village were a mixed blessing. Her mother looked so frail, but they had to pretend Betsy was just temporarily ill because she kept insisting she would be all right once the weather grew warmer. You couldn't tell someone you loved that they didn't look as if they would ever get better. Not if you loved them as much as Keara and her sisters loved their mother. Not when Betsy was refusing to admit that she was failing.

Keara spent several sleepless nights worrying about her family and wondering whether she should definitely give notice and stay in Ireland with her sisters. She was worried sick at the thought of returning to Lancashire and leaving her mother.

What if she never saw her again?

When Mark realised he needed some more cooking implements and crockery, he decided to go into Melbourne to choose them and spend a few days there. Ginny was now experienced enough to manage the eating house with her sister Cissy's help while he was away.

He wrote to ask the Parkers if they had a room for him and when they wrote back to say they could always squeeze an old friend in, he took the new coach that ran into the city three times a week. Things were changing quickly, growing more civilised, with more people moving into the town and surrounding countryside. Unfortunately it would be a while before a railway reached Rossall Springs, if it ever did. Mark very much missed the modern comfort of travelling by rail.

People said proudly that Melbourne was the fastest-growing city in Australia, and indeed, it seemed to be more crowded every time he visited it. The main streets were filled with carriages containing well-dressed folk and as he walked along Collins Street, Mark remembered reading somewhere that Melburnians were boasting nowadays about being only a few months behind the London and Paris fashions. He stared at people's clothes and thought some of the women very elegant with their full skirts buoyed up by crinolines. And surely the headwear had changed as well? You couldn't have several sisters, one of them a woman who owned a dressmaking salon, without learning to notice ladies' clothing.

He looked down at himself and grimaced. Shabby. No other word for it. Time for some new clothes as well as kitchen equipment. But not city clothes. He didn't want to live in a big city. And should he grow a moustache? Many of the men were wearing facial hair. No. He was old-fashioned, no doubt, but he liked the feeling of being clean-shaven. When he'd had to grow a beard on the diggings it had felt itchy and he'd vowed never to do so again.

There were more fine buildings being erected in the city and he stopped outside one new bank to marvel at its elaborate marble façade. A little way along from it on the other side was an insurance office, equally splendid in its architecture. And the flash houses of Bourke Street to which Walter had tried to introduce him – as if he'd ever consort with whores! – seemed to have vanished, or more likely moved elsewhere.

As he was turning a corner, he bumped into a woman and stepped back, sweeping his hat off and apologising. Then he realised it was Patience Jenner, who was not only shabbily dressed but looking gaunt and unhappy. He stopped dead, not knowing what to say to her.

She gasped and flattened one hand against her chest as if to contain her shock. 'Mark Gibson!'

He pulled her hastily out of the way of a man who was ploughing through the crowds with little regard for others, and the softness of her body against his made something inside him soften too. 'Do you have time to walk a little, Patience? I'd love to hear how you are – and all your family, too, of course. I've wondered sometimes what happened to you.'

She clutched her shopping basket to her as if she needed its protection, then glanced at a clock on the wall above the entrance to one of the larger shops. 'I'm supposed to go straight home. Mother's not well today and I have the housework to do. But . . .' She hesitated before adding in a breathless rush of words, 'I would like to hear what you've been doing with yourself. Perhaps just a few minutes.'

He offered her his arm and they walked slowly along, turning into a quieter side street, soon oblivious to their surroundings as they chatted and exchanged news. He felt as comfortable with her as he had on the ship.

'You look to be in good health, Mr Gibson.' She glanced sideways, her eyes lingering on his face for a moment.

'I am.' He wished he could say the same about her. She looked even more fragile than before and downright unhappy.

'Did you do well on the goldfields, then?'

'Almost. But my partner stole what we'd gained. After that I decided I'd had enough. It was a very rough life. Violent.'

'Harry went to the goldfields.'

'Which one?'

'I don't know. He ran away soon after we got here and we never heard from him again.' She sighed.

Mark didn't try to offer her false comfort. 'It's a hard life out there and most men don't make a fortune. He'll be back one day, no doubt.'

'My father has disowned him.'

'Ah.'

'And life isn't easy here, either.'

There was a sharpness in her voice that he'd never heard before and her obvious unhappiness upset him. He watched as she opened her mouth to say something else, then closed it again with a tiny shake of her head. 'Tell me what's wrong, Patience,' he urged. 'I'm an old friend, after all, and I can see you're unhappy about something.'

She bowed her head and continued walking.

After a minute the words began pouring out, as if held back for too long. 'Father has grown very fanatical and – and he makes our lives difficult because of it. Worst of all, he's now pressing me to marry a member of the congregation whom he calls a friend.' She shuddered.

'You don't like the man?'

'I hate him! He's cruel. His wife died last year and he has four children already. He wants a housekeeper and stepmother more than a wife. And besides, he's almost as old as my father and just as fanatical.' Her voice broke on a sob. 'Life with him would be dreadful.'

'Can you not say no?'

She looked up at him, despair in every line of her face. 'I have done. Over and over again. You don't know my father. He'd wear down a stone. Every time I refuse, he forces me to my knees and prays for me, on and on, for hours sometimes.'

As they walked on, she said dully, 'I think we'd better go back. I shall be in enough trouble as it is for being late.'

'Should I come to call on your family?'

She shook her head. 'I don't think you'd be made welcome. We only associate with people from the chapel now.'

'I can't leave you unhappy like this.' He felt so easy with her that he suddenly saw the solution to his loneliness and her unhappiness. As they walked on, he took a deep breath and asked, 'Would you consider marrying me instead?' It seemed to him that helping her would make up for the way he had treated Nelly, even atone a little for the man he had killed which had preyed on his mind ever since.

She was so shocked she stopped walking to gape at him. 'But you . . . I . . .' Then she flushed and said frankly, 'Oh, Mark, if only I could. But – I can't help being surprised that you've asked me.'

'I was attracted to you on the ship, Patience, and I think you were attracted to me, but it wasn't the right time then so I drew back. Now – well, it is the right time. I have my own business and I'm in a position to support a wife, not richly but decently. I think myself very lucky to have found you again because I like you best of any woman I've met.'

She looked up at him, her eyes wide and wondering. 'Do you really?'

'Yes. I always did feel comfortable with you.'

'Like an old shoe?' she teased.

'More like an old friend. Shall I come back with you and ask your father's permission?'

Tears filled her eyes. 'He'd refuse. He's absolutely set on my marrying his friend and regards everyone outside the congregation as godless.'

Mark took hold of her hand and smiled down at her. 'But would *you* marry me if you could?'

She nodded, flushing but meeting his eyes steadily.

'How old are you now?'

'Twenty-one, almost twenty-two.'

'Then you don't need your father's permission to marry, do you?'

The sadness vanished from her eyes to be replaced by hope. 'No. No, I don't. Oh, Mark, could we?'

'Yes, we could. You wouldn't mind living in the country, would you?' Thinking she might be worried about his financial situation, he explained about his eating house and where he lived, watching as she tilted her head slightly to one side, something he remembered her doing on the ship when she was listening intently. She could be so pretty, but instead she was dressed in sombre, unflattering garments and wore her unhappiness like a cloak.

'How could we manage it?' she asked, glancing over her shoulder as if terrified of being overheard, though they were standing together at the corner of a quiet side street with very few people about.

'Tell me where you live and how to get a message to you. I'll make all the arrangements and let you know when.' After they had exchanged addresses, he watched her walk away. She turned at the corner to wave and smile at him.

It felt right to marry her, very right indeed. He had been so lonely since he'd come to Australia. This wasn't a great love, such as Annie had felt for Frederick, but it was a warm, happy feeling and that was more than enough for him.

Besides, he didn't deserve a love such as Annie had found, not after the way he'd treated Nelly.

Three mornings later, just before dawn, Patience got up and listened carefully to make sure her father hadn't risen yet. She went along to the kitchen at the rear to start the fire and begin the day's preparations as she usually did, putting the bundle of clothes she'd got ready the night before on a chair.

She set the fire alight in the kitchen grate because she wanted it to sound like a normal morning so that he'd stay in bed a while longer, waiting for the kitchen to warm up. She went outside to use the privy, after which she intended to leave. But when she opened the door of the tiny outhouse, she saw her father standing at the kitchen door, arms folded, scowling at her across the back garden.

Her heart gave a great thump and then began to pound in terror. He could not have missed seeing the bundle of clothes in the kitchen, and knowing him he'd have opened it. He had to know and control everything, it seemed, even down to the trimmings on her dress.

'Come here at once and explain yourself, daughter!' he thundered when she didn't move.

She ran instead for the rear gate and as she passed through it, pushed frantically at the tools stacked next to it.

As she fled down the back lane, she heard the clatter of them falling, followed by a sharp exclamation from her father, then he yelled at her to come back this minute.

But the tools had held him up long enough for her to get out of sight and fear gave her the strength to run as she had never run before. She didn't stop until she was several streets away, and even then only paused briefly in her headlong flight, chest heaving and breath wheezing into her lungs. She glanced behind, listening in case he was following her. But although two men across the road were staring at her in surprise, there were no sounds of pursuit. She set off again, intending to walk quickly so as to attract less attention, but fear set her off running once again. It wasn't until she'd turned three more corners that she felt able to slow down to a fast walk, and that mainly because she was breathless and had a stitch in her side.

She knew Mark's address and it wasn't hard to find the Parkers' house, which was quite near the city centre. When a woman with a kindly face opened the door, Patience gasped, 'I'm Mark's fiancée.' She let out a long, shuddering exhalation of relief as the woman closed the front door behind her.

When Mark came hurrying to join her in the small parlour at the front of the house, she ran to him, sobbing. Only when she was safe in his arms did she truly believe she had escaped and that her father could not drag her back.

CHAPTER TEN

June– November 1863

On their next visit to Ballymullan, Keara went off to visit her family as soon as she could. She stopped in the doorway, her heart sinking at the sight of her mother who seemed to have grown more insubstantial than ever. She had been hoping that Betsy's health had improved; in the letters no one had said anything about her getting worse.

Terror sliced through Keara. No, not yet, she begged. Please, God, don't take her away from us yet.

'Are you all right, Mam?' she asked as they sat drinking a cup of tea together. Ismay was helping Arla in the shop and Mara, her mother explained proudly, was at the new village school which Mr Mullane had helped set up.

'Oh, I'm not as strong as I was, I will admit that, but I manage, dear. I *am* getting older, after all. Mara's a big help to me now. She runs all my little errands.' Betsy looked round with a smile. 'And this cottage is so much more convenient. Please God, I've a few years left in me yet to be with you all.'

But to Keara her mother looked as if she was clinging to life by the merest thread. Even making a cup of tea brought sweat to her pallid forehead. However, Betsy was clearly determined to pretend everything was all right, so Keara didn't say anything. If her mother was fooling herself, perhaps it made things easier for her sisters.

Later, Keara went into the village and Arla let Ismay come out to speak to her for a few minutes. The two sisters hugged one another then Keara said bluntly, 'Mam looks worse.'

Ismay hugged her arms across her chest and nodded. 'She is. She was all right for a bit after your last visit, then she started failing. But she begged Arla and me not to say anything when we wrote to you, kept insisting she always gets better again. Only there's no hiding it this time, is there? Mam gets out of breath if she so much as walks across the room. Mara and I have to do most of the work about the house now and *he* still expects food to be waiting for him when he gets back. *He* never lifts a finger to help anyone but himself, even now.'

When Keara didn't say anything, just stared blindly into the distance, Ismay added, 'Diarmid sent the doctor down to see Mam, but he said there was nothing he could do.' She brushed away a tear. 'He didn't think she'd last past Christmas.'

'*No!*' Keara stared at her in horror. 'Does she know that?'

'Of course not. Da does, but he won't believe it. He says she's just pretending to be worse than she is to get out of doing the work. How can he say that when you can see how she—' Ismay's mouth wobbled for a minute, then she took a deep breath and forced herself to go on. 'Arla hasn't been well, either, though she never complains. She gets a pain in her belly, a bad one.'

'Arla?'

'Yes.'

'But what'll happen to you and Mara if . . . if Mam . . .'

Ismay shook her head. 'I don't know. I can't sleep at night for the worry of it. *He* won't be much use to us, that's for sure.'

Keara gave her sister a quick hug. 'If anything happens, I'll leave Mrs Mullane and we'll all three live together.'

'You'd do that?'

'Of course I would, Ismay. I'm twenty-one now, old enough to look after you both, and . . . Ah, what are you crying for? Come here, come here.' They hugged one another again.

'Because I thought – I thought you wouldn't care,' Ismay wept into her shoulder, 'that you'd stay in your fine job and – and just leave me to manage with *him*. And I didn't think I could.'

'I'd never do that. I didn't want to leave you all in the first place, you know that.'

The two sisters gave each other watery smiles as they wiped their eyes.

'Walk with me down the lane a bit,' Keara said. As they strolled along, she tried to work out how it might be if the worst happened. 'I think we'd have to move to a town, but if you could get a job as well as me, we could maybe rent a room and earn enough to keep the three of us. Da won't care about us. He'll only care that there'll be no one to look after him.'

'He'll find another woman. They seem to like him, even now when he's losing his hair.' After another hesitation she added, 'Me an' Mara have never even been to a town, though. I'd be a bit frightened.'

'Ah, they're big, dirty places, sure, but there's a lot more work there and people still live in houses and do all the usual things. Nothing to be afraid of.' Keara smiled at Ismay. 'We could live somewhere in Ireland, Sligo perhaps, or even go to Lancashire, which isn't too bad once you get used to it. No, that's no good. They're getting short of work there just now. But they say there are plenty of jobs in the south of England. Oh, there are lots of places we could go to.'

She forced a laugh, trying to sound more confident than she felt. 'There'd be no use us looking for work here in Ballymullan, though, and anyway, I don't think I'd want to stay here.' She'd prefer to get right away from Mrs Mullane – and Mr Mullane. Since the day he'd stopped his wife hitting her she had felt a warmth whenever she looked at him, to think he would protect her like that, care about her . . . She had been to confess that to Father Cornelius, but the penances hadn't made the feelings go away – or the confusion they caused inside her.

Ismay gave her another shaky smile and hug as they parted. 'You've taken a load off my mind, Keara.'

But for all her brave words, anxiety about her

mother set a chill fear in Keara's heart that wouldn't be dismissed. She'd better start saving her shillings from now on and not spend them on the poor hungry children. She and her sisters might need them, might be hungry themselves if they had to find work and a new place to live.

A short time later, against all the odds since she'd hardly seen anything of her husband in bed for several months, Lavinia again became pregnant. She was very angry about it, mostly with her husband, but the anger spilled over on to everyone around her – even her maid. And even though she no longer hit Keara, she continued to make her life miserable.

As always, she pleaded with her husband to let her go home to Lancashire and once he was certain that she really was carrying his child, Theo took her there by easy stages, lapped in luxury.

Keara seriously considered giving notice and staying with her family, but Betsy told her not to be so silly and insisted she keep her position, getting so agitated that Keara promised.

When they got back to Lancashire she was caught up, as ever, in the snare of her own compassion. She could not help thinking of the poor baby and how much the master wanted it, so she rubbed her mistress's back when it ached and helped her when she suffered from morning sickness.

But every day she worried about her mother and sisters, too, longing for a letter from home, a letter which never came. Surely Arla was well enough to write now? And surely Father Cornelius would have let her know if anything had happened to her mother? Or was likely to happen.

Only when Theo had to go away for a day or two did Lavinia become calmer, saying bitterly that the mere sight of him was enough to upset her. 'He knows I nearly died last time, but still he must have a child. He'd be happy if I died bearing it, then he could marry some brood mare of a woman and sire a whole dynasty of children with his foul temper and ruttish ways.'

When Theo returned home, Lavinia immediately got agitated again and he called in the doctor. 'She's acting so irrationally. Screeches and cowers away if I so much as walk into a room.'

The doctor pursed his lips. 'It happens sometimes that the state of being with child unsettles the female mind. They are easily overthrown and she has always been – um – prone to nervous agitation.' He cleared his throat, wondering how to make what seemed to him an obvious suggestion.

Theo said it for him, not meaning to be taken seriously. 'Perhaps I should go away until after she's given birth, then?'

'Ahem. Well, it might be the best thing for all concerned – given the circumstances.'

Theo stared at him. 'You really mean it?'

'Yes. 'Fraid so, old fellow.'

After a heavy silence, Theo said, 'Then I'll go to our estate in Ireland.'

But that didn't please Lavinia, either. 'It will take

you too long to come back from Ireland if – if you're needed. I want you with me when the child is born.'

It took a superhuman effort not to demand what the hell she expected him to do with himself for six months, since he was to be banished from his home and yet mustn't go too far away. 'I'll find somewhere else to go, then.'

'Somewhere near a railway station where we can send a telegram if we need you.' She sobbed delicately into a handkerchief, dabbed her eyes, then reached for a Fry's chocolate cream stick which she declared took the edge off her nausea and of which she demanded a constant supply.

'I'll give it my consideration.'

In the end he came to the conclusion that the best thing he could do was leave her in peace.

When he'd gone, Lavinia's tears dried up as if by magic and she smiled with such satisfaction that Keara, watching, realised she had done this on purpose to get rid of him. She felt sickened by her mistress's spiteful manipulation. After the child was born, Keara decided suddenly, she would leave whatever. She simply could not bear this kind of life for much longer. Surely she would be able to get another position as a maid in Ireland? And surely Mr Mullane would give her good references, even if his wife refused?

Theo made plans for a long stay in London, where there must be enough happening to keep a man entertained, but within two weeks of arriving in the capital he was nearly going mad with boredom. He was a man meant for the country, not the town. He liked horses and riding, the pleasure of striding across his own acres, while concerts, theatres and polite tittle-tattle bored him senseless.

However, a chance meeting with Lord Keynsor, a noted horse breeder with whom he was slightly acquainted, led to an invitation to visit his lordship's estate in Leicestershire. And when Theo confessed one evening that he'd been told to stay away from his pregnant wife by her doctor, Keynsor let out a great shout of laughter and invited him to stay as long as he liked.

But although he enjoyed his host's company, Theo would rather have been in Ireland and the months seemed to pass very slowly. He spent a lot of time riding across the countryside, trying to plan what he would do after he returned to his wife.

If the child survived, it would be quite easy. He would bring it up in Ireland. If it didn't survive, he knew he couldn't face bedding Lavinia again. He would just leave her and to hell with what people said. She'd be better off without him, though he doubted she had it in her to be happy. He did, though, and it would be bliss not to live with her.

And as for children, well, he'd always tried to avoid getting them outside marriage, but maybe now he'd have to do that. If he could. If the fault for those poor dead babies didn't reside in him.

That thought kept him awake many a dark night.

By June of that same year Patience was certain she was pregnant. She told Mark about it during the first of the winter storms as rain and strong winds battered the houses of Rossall Springs.

'You're sure?' he asked, though he had begun to suspect it already, of course.

'Yes. I've been talking to Mrs Grove about,' she flushed delicately, 'the symptoms and she's sure I must be with child. Are you pleased?'

'Yes. Yes, of course I am.' He pulled her to him and gave her a hug and a kiss, trying to hide his feelings, for he could not help remembering that he had made another young woman pregnant and she had died because of it. No, that couldn't happen to Patience, who was well loved and cared for.

As time passed she remained quietly delighted by the thought of the coming child, though she wasn't well, experiencing a great deal of nausea which nothing seemed to abate. Mark wished desperately that Rossall Springs had a doctor, and talked of taking his wife into Melbourne to consult one but she refused point-blank.

'I don't want to go anywhere near my father again,' she insisted every time he raised the matter.

But Alex Jenner came to them the following month, arriving on the stage coach and entering the eating house with a martial light in his eyes.

At the mere sight of him, Patience gasped and ran for Mark who was working in the kitchen. To her dismay her father followed her.

'Be sure your sins will find you out!' he thundered.

Mark put one arm round his trembling young wife. 'Patience has committed no sins, Mr Jenner.'

'Am I to believe the fornicator who paid false court

to my daughter on the ship and has now enticed her away from home and family, stealing her from the man she was to marry?'

Ginny was watching them, her eyes wide with fascinated horror, and the customers were craning their necks. Mark went across to close the door to the eating room. 'You'd better come through into our living quarters, Mr Jenner. But I'd be grateful if you'd keep your voice down. We have a business to run.'

'Why should I keep quiet? I am here to redeem a sinner.'

Mark raised his own voice and shouted, 'Because if you don't, I'll throw you out of my house!'

Alex Jenner scowled at him and breathed deeply, then folded his arms. 'I'm here to take my daughter back with me, so that she may redeem herself in the eyes of the Lord and—'

'A wife's place is surely by her husband's side, not her father's.'

Mr Jenner looked suspiciously from one to the other. 'Show me your marriage lines!'

Grim-faced, Mark took out the enamelled box that contained all their papers and passed him their marriage lines. 'See. Patience and I were married before we even left Melbourne.'

Alex scanned the papers and shoved them back at Mark before turning to scowl at his daughter. 'This doesn't change the fact that you disobeyed me, daughter.'

She was white and shaking and even before Mark

could get across the room to her, she gasped and slid to the floor in a faint.

'If your ranting has harmed our child, I'll punch you senseless, father-in-law or not,' Mark threw at their visitor, lifting Patience up and laying her on the sofa, then kneeling beside her patting her hand.

Alex came to stand beside him and say in a low voice, 'You are not the husband I'd have chosen for her.'

'I'm the husband *she* chose and that's all that matters to me.'

Patience sighed and her eyes fluttered open. As she clutched Mark's hand, her father began to pray aloud for them and their unborn child.

'Shall I ask him to leave?' Mark whispered.

She hesitated, then whispered, 'Not yet. I'd like to hear how my mother is – and whether they've heard from Harry.'

Her father said, 'Amen,' loudly and stared down at them before declaring, 'I have decided to forgive you, for your mother's sake.'

'Thank you, Father.'

Mark was upset by how nervous his wife had suddenly become and how pale she still was. He didn't intend to invite his father-in-law to stay if Alex was going to upset her. But he could do no other than to ask, 'Can we offer you some refreshment?'

Alex nodded. 'And a place to sleep, I hope? I have no way of returning to Melbourne until tomorrow's coach. Or must I seek a room at the inn?'

'You'll have to sleep on the sofa,' Mark said. 'We haven't got a spare bedroom.'

Patience squeezed his hand gratefully.

The day passed slowly and Mark was sure his father-in-law made Patience weep several times, though she tried to hide that from him. But he could feel how tense she was and see how her hands shook as she did anything for her father, who seemed to expect her to wait on him hand and foot.

'Well, at least you're a hard-working man,' Alex said as Mark snatched a few minutes to eat an evening meal with them. 'I can respect that, but why is my daughter not working by your side?'

'Because she's not been well. And because there is no need for her to take risks, given that she's with child.'

'I can see she has a soft, pampered life with you. Beware, lest the devil take advantage of her idle hours.'

'I'm sure her upbringing will protect her from that. How is your son?'

'I have no son. The one who was born to my wife has gone over to the devil, so I have cast him out.'

Mark breathed slowly and counted up to twenty.

It seemed a very long time until they could seek their bed. As they lay in the darkness, Mark whispered, 'Even if he is your father, I shall be glad to see the back of him. I wonder what his purpose was in coming here?'

He found out the following morning.

'I am seeking a new home and occupation,' Alex said abruptly over breakfast. 'I am not satisfied with my present employment. The owner of the shop is an ungodly man.'

Patience spilled the milk she was pouring, muttered something incoherent and fled to the kitchen.

'I see you have employment for a stranger here,' Alex went on. 'It would be more appropriate to offer it to a member of your family.'

'Are you talking about yourself?'

Alex nodded. 'I am an honest worker, I believe, and capable of learning what is necessary. The work cannot be difficult if a woman can manage it. And my wife misses her daughter greatly. Besides, I shall be able to spread the Lord's word in new fields if I come here.'

Mark looked beyond him to his wife, standing in the doorway with her hand pressed against her mouth and sheer terror in her eyes. 'I'm afraid that wouldn't be appropriate,' he said firmly. 'I'm sure you're honest and hard-working, but I wouldn't feel comfortable working with you and there certainly isn't room for you to live in this house. Besides, the job is better suited to a woman.'

'Honour thy father and mother . . .' Alex began.

'While I shall always offer you politeness, with due respect, Mr Jenner, you are not *my* father, and to be frank I'm certain we should not get on well enough to deal together in a business. There is no place for you here.'

Alex glared at him. 'Do you deny me access to my daughter?'

'I will not employ you in my business and I would prefer that you didn't come to visit us again, but I'm sure Patience will be happy to write to you and your wife regularly. You are still at the same address, I take it?'

After much deep breathing and visible mental struggle, Alex bit back further arguments and accepted some food for the journey back. 'You will let us know when the child arrives? And you will be sure to have it baptised properly?'

'Of course.'

When Mark went back home after seeing his father-in-law on the coach to Melbourne, he found Patience weeping. He gathered her in his arms and soothed her till the tears stopped, then said sombrely, 'Your father, my dear, is nothing but a ranting hypocrite.'

'And a bully. He frightens me and always has done. But he's got so much worse since our arrival in Australia. I pity my mother and wish I could see her. And how will I ever find Harry if my father won't deal with him?' She started weeping again.

Mark had no answer to that.

From then on letters arrived from the Jenners at the beginning of every month, letters which always made Patience tearful and sad.

It worried Mark greatly that his wife continued to be unwell, her eyes seeming large and luminous in a face that grew thinner and paler by the month.

Mrs Grove, usually a source of good advice, could think of nothing to help her and whispered that dear Patience was not a strong woman; should perhaps not bear too many children.

Mark was in full agreement and had already decided he would try his hardest not to give her any more after this one. There were ways. One experience like this would be more than enough for him. And one child.

Two, he corrected himself mentally. He had another daughter in England about whom he had not yet told Patience. He kept meaning to, but the moment never seemed opportune.

He wished he could at least meet little Faith. But he'd have to save hard if he ever hoped to return to England to visit his family. At the moment all that mattered was Patience, keeping her happy and as well as possible.

Caley and Noreen Gallagher found Western Australia very much to their liking, but it took them a while to find a property to buy, given their limited finances, so they rented a small house on the outskirts of the capital and Caley began to ride out to inspect places that were being offered for sale.

'I want somewhere that's at least partly cleared,' he said ruefully. 'I am not, and I never shall be, the sort of person to grub up trees and build his own house.'

Noreen gurgled with laughter at the mere idea. 'I agree with you absolutely, darling.' She looked round their tiny cottage and her smile faded. 'I wish we could find a maid, though.'

'So do half the other ladies in Perth.'

'Well, at least I've proved a good cook, if an indifferent laundress. And you can't really blame young women for seizing the chance to marry rather than remaining in service, can you?'

In the end they found a suitable property near Bunbury, a small town about a hundred miles south of the capital. The house seemed large after the tiny cottage and there were several paddocks already cleared and suitable for stock.

Caley sent a letter to Theo, asking to have his horses sent out, to which Theo agreed in his reply.

'Now we can settle into breeding them,' he said with relish. 'The ones I've bought here aren't too bad, but with better blood introduced into the stock, we'll soon make a name for ourselves.' He re-read Theo's letter then tossed it to Noreen.

'Theo sounds utterly miserable,' she said as she folded it up. 'Why on earth did he marry that foolish woman?'

'Money.'

They looked at one another.

'It wouldn't have done for me,' she said with a smile, holding out one hand to him.

He went to take her in his arms and kiss her, then held her close. 'Me neither, my darling. And I'm very, very glad indeed to have moved to a larger house where the boys sleep further away from us.'

She chuckled. 'Me, too.'

Within a week of Theo leaving, Lavinia began making changes at Eastwood House. 'The mail is to be brought directly to me and no one is to touch it until I've sorted it out,' she ordered. She had found out that the cottage in the grounds was empty, but wanted to check whether her husband had a mistress elsewhere. What was he doing with all her father's money after all if not spending it on some other woman? He was always so mean about *her* buying things.

She became an expert at steaming open letters and this kept her occupied for hours. Since even her maid was excluded from her room while she was doing it, it also afforded Keara some much-needed respite from her mistress's constant demands.

To Lavinia's disappointment she found no sign of Theo having mistresses elsewhere, let alone corresponding with them or spending money lavishly on them. In fact, he received nothing but boring business letters which she didn't understand and the accounts showed much less money than she had expected. She sealed the letters up and sent them on to him, sure he wouldn't even look to see if they'd been tampered with. He was too trusting about small things.

A month after he had left, however, she found a letter for Keara among the mail and stared at it thoughtfully. This was an educated hand, not the usual scrawls from Arla Lynch. Who was the girl corresponding with? Without hesitation, she steamed that letter open as well.

Father Cornelius regretted to inform Keara that her father had been killed when a new stallion threw him. He had broken his neck and died instantly. Her mother was asking for her. He was sure Mr Mullane would give her leave to return for a week or two to comfort her bereaved parent.

Lavinia crumpled the letter up in her hand and threw it into the heart of the fire, laughing as she watched it burn. Who did this country priest think he was, asking a woman in her condition to do without the services of her personal maid?

She made no mention of Mr Michaels' death and was particularly affectionate towards Keara for the rest of the week.

Theo heard about Mick Michaels being killed but Diarmid had written to him to say Father Cornelius had contacted Keara and asked if she could go back to Ballymullan for a week or two. He meant to check that Lavinia had allowed this, but an exciting invitation to visit another horse stud put it completely out of his mind.

Two weeks after the first letter, the priest sent another one, expressing his sadness that Keara had not seen fit to return, or even reply, and regretting to inform her that her mother had died in her sleep two days previously.

> *There is now the question of what is to happen to your two sisters. Arla is also unwell and would like to see you, but if you didn't come for your mother, I don't suppose you will for your old friend, either.*
>
> *A cousin of Arla's has taken over the shop, so there is no further employment there for Ismay. And Mara, of course, is rather young at eleven to earn her living.*
>
> *I'm writing to your employer to ask if he has any suggestions about providing for your sisters, but Ismay tells me you're prepared to leave your present employment and find a daily job, so that*

you can all make a home together, so I'm sure some-
thing can be worked out.

'What?' screeched Lavinia, then clapped a hand
to her mouth. She didn't want anyone coming near
her until she'd decided what to do about this threat to
her own comfort. Remembering suddenly that the
priest had said he was going to write to Theo, she sorted
through the rest of the letters and found another one
addressed to her husband in the same Italianate hand.

She steamed that one open as well and found a
request to send Keara back to Ballymullan to support
her sisters in their time of bereavement and to find a way
to look after them from now onwards.

She didn't burn these letters as she had the first one
for Keara, because she was a little afraid of doing that
to Theo's letters, but she locked them carefully away
in her writing desk as she tried to decide what to do.
Under no circumstances whatsoever would she consent
to giving up the maid who suited her so well. If she could
keep Theo in ignorance, she could take her time and
work out what to do about this annoying situation. No
good came from rushing at things.

It was another week before she managed to work
out a plan that satisfied her and that was thanks to one
of her friends mentioning they had helped some of their
operatives from the mill to join relatives in Australia,
since they were still short of work in the town because
of the cotton famine.

Australia. Lavinia knew that was a long way away.
It took at least three months to get there, Noreen had

said, or for a letter to come back. 'How did you manage that?' she asked casually. 'We have a few people on the Irish estate who might be better off there. They have such large families, these Irish peasants.'

'There are various relief schemes, my dear, run by the different religious denominations. One has only to supply the money then they make the rest of the arrangements.'

'I see.'

The following day, Lavinia wrote to Father Cornelius.

> *My husband has asked me to deal with this matter, since Keara is very distressed and I can be of more comfort to her than he can. She would not even consider leaving my employment since I am with child and am particularly in need of her services at this trying time. Indeed, the doctor is sure that without her calming influence I would stand no chance of carrying the child to term. I have, as you know, lost others.*

Lavinia chewed the end of the pen and considered her next paragraph very carefully.

> *It seems best for all concerned that the two Michaels girls make a new life for themselves without Keara, and since my husband's cousins were so enthusiastic about the opportunities for advancement to be found in Australia, we have decided to send Ismay and Mara out there.*

I believe the church has various schemes for sending orphans to Australia to work as maids and I am enclosing fifty pounds, which should be sufficient for this purpose, plus an extra twenty pounds for you to use as you see fit to help the poor of the parish. If more is needed for the Michaels girls' expenses, kindly let me know.

Keara has been such an excellent maid that we are happy to help her family in this way, and are sure it will be the making of the two girls, who will have opportunities in Australia they could never meet in Ballymullan.

Yours faithfully,
Lavinia Mullane

She signed the letter with a flourish, read it through and nodded in satisfaction.

Father Cornelius was horrified when he read it. He could not believe that even Theo Mullane would do such a heartless thing, though of course the baby his wife was carrying did make things a little difficult. Everyone knew how desperately the landowner wanted a child, but even so, the priest would not have expected Keara to agree to this arrangement.

He went to pray for guidance, then made his way to the cottage where Ismay and Mara were still living, waiting for their sister's reply.

Mara came skipping down the path to greet him. 'Have you heard from Keara, Father?'

He nodded.

Inside the house he took the chair they offered and sat down heavily.

'Well?' Ismay asked when he didn't speak. 'What did she say?'

'She's spoken to her employers and,' it was hard to say it because it seemed such a heartless decision, 'they all feel it best that you two make a new start in Australia.'

Ismay stared at him in shock. 'I don't believe you.'

'Your sister wishes to stay with her mistress, who is expecting a child and needs her greatly.'

'I still don't believe you. Show me the letter!'

He passed it to her.

She read it slowly and carefully aloud, her finger tracing the lines. She had to ask his help with some of the longer words and when she had finished sat staring down at it before looking at him. 'This isn't from Keara.'

'No. But it's from her mistress, who has taken the matter in hand. You're very lucky to have important people like the Mullanes caring about your welfare, my dear.'

'Getting rid of us, you mean.'

Mara tugged at her sister's arm. 'I don't want to go away. I want Keara. Why isn't she coming?' She began to sob.

Ismay put an arm round her and scowled at the priest. 'We'll not be going to this Australia place and you can tell Mrs Mullane that.'

'What will you do instead?'

She bit her lip. 'I'll think of something.'

'Do you have any money?'

She flushed. She'd spent the last of her small savings that very morning on food. 'We'll *walk* to England if we have to. We need to see Keara, talk to *her*.'

'If you set off walking you'll be taken up as beggars, let alone Mara is too young and will likely fall ill on the road.'

'We're *not* letting them send us to Australia,' Ismay repeated. 'And what's more, I don't believe Keara wants that. We arranged what to do if Mam died last time she was here. It's Mrs Mullane who wants to get rid of us, not Keara.'

He could not persuade her differently, so left her to 'think things over' and made his way wearily back to his church to pray for guidance.

When he'd gone, Ismay turned to Mara. 'We'll go and see Diarmid O'Neal. He'll help us, I'm sure.'

But Diarmid had also received a letter from Lavinia and was torn two ways. He didn't approve of parting the two girls from their sister, let alone sending them to the other side of the world, but if he did anything to upset Lavinia and she lost the child, Theo would be furious.

He tried to explain this to Ismay, but she wouldn't listen to him, only kept repeating, 'We have to see Keara. I won't believe she wants to send us away until I hear it from her own lips.'

'You can't see Keara. Mrs Mullane needs her.'

'*We* need her, too.'

'Her mistress's need is greater.'

'How can it be? We're her sisters and our whole lives depend on what she does.'

'Ismay, there is nothing I can do. The decision has been made.'

When they'd gone he wrote to Theo, asking him if there wasn't another way of helping the girls, explaining how upset they were at the mere thought of going to Australia. In the meantime he gave them work up at the big house and provided food.

The answer was again from Lavinia Mullane, not Theo.

How can you listen to two ignorant girls who don't know what is or is not right? Theo truly believes this is for their own good and even their sister is pleased for them. Kindly continue with the plan to send them to Australia.

Use force, if necessary, but make sure they're on the next available ship. No good will come from delaying matters, only more worry. Once they're under way, they'll soon settle down and accept what has been decided by their betters.

I shall not rest easy until I hear from you that this has been done.

It was the last line that convinced him. He went to see the two girls again.

Ismay and Mara wept and pleaded with him, then, when he wouldn't change his mind about obeying orders, they ran away.

When they didn't turn up to work at the big house, Cook sent him word and he went down to the cottage. There was no one there and the girls' clothes were missing.

'We'll have to go after them,' he told Father Cornelius.

'I suppose so. Is there nothing else we can do for them other than send them to the Antipodes?'

'And risk that stupid woman losing her child? I daren't do it. Besides, the Gallaghers went out there of their own free will, so it can't be a bad place to live. I'll have the carriage harnessed and we'll go after them. You'll come with me, won't you?'

'I suppose so.'

They found the two sisters easily enough because people had noticed them. They caught up with them a few villages away, Mara already looking tired and grubby. When Diarmid confronted them, Ismay refused point-blank to return voluntarily and began to scream and kick when they tried to make her get into the carriage, which brought people running to see what was the matter.

Father Cornelius had to ask the constable of that parish to help take them back forcibly and although the girls protested that they were being kidnapped, of course the constable believed the priest.

On the way back Diarmid tried again to talk sense into Ismay. 'You're only fifteen, girl. Let others with more experience guide you. This is being done to help you and give you a chance to make a far better life for yourselves.'

She stared back at him from a face that was to haunt his dreams for some time, so ravaged by sadness was it. 'It's not a better life if we have to go so far away. We'll never see our sister again if we do that.'

Mara clung to her, sobbing loudly and repeating, 'I want Keara. Where's Keara?'

Diarmid wished he knew. He was amazed she hadn't made an effort at least to come and say goodbye to her sisters, or to write even if Mrs Mullane was too ill to leave. Though the woman didn't sound ill in her letters. But Keara certainly was not too ill to write and she hadn't even sent a message of comfort to her sisters.

'Well, you're going, whether you want to or not,' he said at last, seeing no way out of obeying his orders. 'We can't do anything to upset Mrs Mullane when she's in this delicate condition.'

Ismay stopped weeping then, to stare at him, red-eyed. 'You can pretend to yourself that this is for our own good, but the truth is they're doing it to get rid of us. And you should be ashamed of helping them.'

He felt it prudent to lock them in the attic that night. And he slept badly, worrying about what he was doing.

The following day when he let them out, Ismay was sullen. 'I hate Keara. And I hate you, Diarmid O'Neal. Most of all, I hate Mr and Mrs Mullane. I hope nothing goes right for them from now on.'

'Shut your mouth, girl. Don't you know it's wicked to ill-wish someone?'

'It's even more wicked to send us away to Australia.' She folded her arms and stared at him stubbornly, looking suddenly very much like her elder sister, though she had always been thinner and less confident.

He sighed. 'I'll be taking you to Dublin myself and putting you in the hands of the good Sisters of St Martha and St Zita. They'll send you to Australia as Keara wishes and they'll make the necessary arrangements to help you find work once you're there.'

But they had to drag the two weeping, screaming girls out of the house and push them into the carriage the next day. And the other servants stood around muttering that it wasn't right.

It was the same at the railway station. People stared at them and Ismay called out for help, saying they were being kidnapped.

But the sight of the priest helping restrain them made onlookers turn away and the two girls were not strong enough to prevent the men from dragging them on to the train.

At any other time, Ismay would have been fascinated by the journey, for it was the first time she'd ever travelled by rail. Today she saw everything through a blur of tears and all she was conscious of was Mara's hand clutching hers tightly, her little sister's tear-stained face and the fact that Keara had betrayed them.

She spat defiance at the Sisters who met them at the station, but they were used to recalcitrant girls and these were not the first to be sent out forcibly. Ismay could do nothing against two sturdy nuns, especially when Diarmid went ahead carrying Mara.

In the convent the two sisters were outfitted for the long voyage to Australia then locked in their room. Ismay blistered her fingers cutting up their clothes with the little scissors from the new sewing kit, but more were found for her.

Even at the docks they were given no chance to escape.

'You're not the first girls to fight against going to Australia under the orphans scheme and you won't be the last,' one of the Sisters escorting them said in exasperation. 'It won't make any difference. You might as well make the best of it.'

She watched them manhandled aboard and sighed. None of the other girls had kept up the struggle for so long. She sent up a brief prayer these two would be happy in their new life, then turned her thoughts firmly back to her next duties.

Once the ship was under way, Ismay and Mara were let out of the tiny cabin where they'd been confined and escorted up on deck. The other orphan girls, easily recognisable by their dark uniforms, were taking the air and getting some exercise under the care of Sister Bernadette and Sister Catherine. They were a subdued group and several of them looked as if they had been weeping.

'I hope you two will settle down now and stop being so silly,' Sister Bernadette said, looking at them warily.

'We have no choice,' Ismay replied. She put her arm round Mara's shoulders and refused to let herself weep again. *I'll never forgive Keara for this, never,* she vowed later as she stood by the rail, looking across the vast expanse of water.

From then on she was polite to the nuns and pleasant to the other girls. All she could do now was make the long voyage as easy for her little sister as possible. There was a lot to learn, both about life on board ship and about what to expect in Australia, wherever that was, and they would both do better if they made friends with the others and showed themselves clean and hard-working.

But whenever the nun who was escorting the group chided Ismay for continuing to say they had been kidnapped and forced to come on the ship, she looked the older woman in the eyes and said flatly, 'We both know that that's exactly what happened.'

Sister Bernadette shook her head. 'I had thought you were reconciled to your new life, child.'

'I never shall be *reconciled*. But I don't intend to cause trouble. Mara and I must make the best of this now. And please, I'd like to join the reading class. We both would.'

One day, however, she'd find Keara again and tell her to her face that she was no sister of theirs. Ismay held that thought close in her heart and for some reason it gave her courage to continue and look after Mara. At least she had one sister, still.

Some weeks after he'd sent the two Michaels sisters to Australia, Diarmid at last received a letter directly from his employer. Theo was writing from Leicestershire to tell him to expect two new yearlings which he had bought from a friend of Lord Keynsor, with whom he'd been staying for the past few months. He would be grateful if Diarmid could let him know directly that the two horses had arrived safely. He could be contacted at the above address.

Diarmid sat staring at the letter in shock. Theo hadn't been in Lancashire for several months? And his employer hadn't even asked about Mara and Ismay, which was very unlike him for he always took a personal interest in schemes to help his tenants.

Lavinia Mullane had said Theo had told her to arrange matters. *But what if Theo hadn't done that? What if he didn't even know the two girls had been sent away?*

Diarmid went searching for her letters and found them. Yes, this one said, 'Theo told me'. Was it possible . . . ? Could this mean that Lavinia had acted without her husband's authority? Did he have any idea of what his wife had done?

When the two yearlings arrived, Diarmid wrote to tell Theo, adding that he'd carried out his instructions to send the two Michaels girls to Australia under the aegis of the good Sisters of St Martha and St Zita.

He received a letter by return of post asking what the hell he was talking about.

Then Diarmid was certain his suspicions had been correct. Grim-faced, he wrote to explain in great detail how he'd been instructed to send the two girls overseas, how Ismay and Mara had tried to run away, how they'd been calling for their sister right until the last minute.

He said he'd believed he was acting on Theo's orders for the good of Mrs Mullane and the unborn child, or he would not have done it.

With his letter, he enclosed the communications he'd received from Mrs Mullane, not commenting on them because their contents spoke for themselves.

He ended:

It's too late now to bring Mara and Ismay back, Theo. They'll be halfway to Australia. I wash my hands of the whole business and leave your conscience to dictate what you do next.

CHAPTER ELEVEN

November 1863

———◆◆◆———

Theo read Diarmid's letter in disbelief. '*No!*'

He didn't realise he'd spoken aloud until his host looked across the room and asked, 'Something wrong, old chap?'

'Yes.'

'Anything I can do to help?'

Theo shook his head and jerked to his feet, scattering the letter's enclosures. He picked them up, fighting to contain his anger. 'I think I'll just . . .' He walked out quickly, needing to be alone.

In his bedroom Dick was putting some clean clothes away.

'Leave it! I—' Again Theo couldn't finish the sentence, could only make a gesture of dismissal. He felt himself to be choking with rage.

When he was alone, he laid the crumpled mass of papers on the desk and re-read the letter from Diarmid, then slowly went through the ones his wife had written. After he'd finished he groaned aloud and pushed them aside. Resting his elbows on the desk, he supported his forehead with one hand and closed his eyes. It was hard to believe that Lavinia could be so ruthless, and clever too – Lavinia of all people! Except that the evidence of what she'd done was there in front of him, spelled out in her round, childish script.

His first impulse was to go straight back to Lancashire and confront her with the letters. Then he realised that if he did, she would throw a fit of hysterics and – oh, hell, that might lead to her losing the child.

Besides, Diarmid was right. There was little that could be done. Well, not quickly anyway. They might never even find those two girls again because they'd been sent to Melbourne which was now a big city. Even if they survived the rigours of the trip, they might succumb to a dozen different ailments. People did every day and he'd guess the colonies would be dangerous in ways Ireland wasn't. Especially for two young girls without protectors. He kept coming back to that thought, clinging like a prickly burr to his brain.

With a sigh, he turned to his other letters, which he'd crumpled up in his agitation. His cousin Caley had written to say that he and Noreen had bought a farm south of Perth and were enjoying living in a warm climate. People who went out to Australia with enough money to buy land could make a good living, he said, and he had every hope of providing properly for his children's future now. And could Theo please send out his horses. By the time they arrived he would have his stud properly organised.

Well, at least someone sounded happy.

Realising suddenly that there was someone in

Australia who might be able to help, Theo went down to the library, relieved not to meet anyone on the way. He found an atlas and studied the map of Australia, then consulted a world almanac. It was a huge country, about thirty times as big as the United Kingdom according to the book. The girls were going to one side, to Melbourne in the colony of Victoria, and Caley was at the other. There were two thousand miles between those places.

The hope of being able to do something to help them faded and guilt weighed heavily on him as he made his way back to his bedroom.

When Dick came in later to help him dress for dinner, Theo shook his head. 'I'm not going down. I can't face food just now.'

'Bad news, sir?'

He nodded. 'I'll tell you later. Please present my apologies to Lord Keynsor and say I'll see him tomorrow. There's a problem at home and I have to – decide what to do.'

'Is there anything at all I can do to help? I could bring up some brandy, perhaps.'

Theo shook his head. The last thing he wanted was to get drunk. He looked up to see Dick watching him in concern. 'Just bring me up a sandwich of some sort and then leave me to think. I'll see you in the morning.'

He went to sit by the fire, staring blindly into it. He was rather too fond of women's bodies and undoubtedly selfish – he admitted that to himself with a wry grimace – but he would never, ever have sent two defenceless children to the other side of the world as Lavinia had. Some things just – stuck in your gullet.

He lay awake for most of that night, alternately racked by guilt and seething with fury at what his wife had done.

How was he to tell Keara – Keara of all people, who had comforted him in his hour of need! – that her parents were dead and no one had bothered to tell her, and that the sisters she loved so dearly had been sent away to Australia? No, not *sent*, nothing as gentle as that, put forcibly on a ship and imprisoned there until it had sailed. He'd seen her walking with the younger child, Mara, many a time. They had always looked so happy and comfortable together.

And it was shocking that Keara hadn't been able to say a final farewell to her mother, either. That would hurt her for as long as she lived.

How could Lavinia have done it?

He was vaguely surprised when dawn began chasing the darkness from the room with grey light. Getting up, he went to stare out of the window at the misty landscape, pressing his aching head against the cool glass for a moment or two. Though it didn't really help the anger that was still simmering there. Or the shame and disgust.

He went back to sit on the edge of the bed and face the unpalatable truth he had been trying to avoid all night. There was absolutely nothing he could do at the moment to help Keara, so he was going to try to protect his unborn child before he even told her. It was selfish and he was not proud of himself, but he'd make it up to her later – somehow. For a start, as soon as the child was born he'd get Keara away from Lavinia. He knew she had had more than enough of his damned wife.

At that thought, he sucked in a long breath. Maybe now he could consult his own desires? Keara would have a far better life as his mistress than as a maid and they could send for her sisters, bring them back to England and put the younger one in the charge of some decent woman, find a position for the older one.

If the girls hadn't perished on the way there.

And if they could find them again.

No, of course they'd find them. The Sisters would keep records and even if the girls had moved on from their first places of employment, he could if necessary send someone out to Australia with enough money to discover what had happened to them.

One thing was certain: he was going back to Lancashire immediately to keep an eye on Lavinia. The birth was only a month or so away and if his presence upset her, so be it. It was a risk he would have to take. He didn't want her doing anything else so irresponsible and heartless. He didn't want her hurting Keara again in any way at all.

He would write to Diarmid from there instructing him never to obey instructions from Mrs Mullane again without first checking. He couldn't write yet, though, not until he had stopped feeling so furious with Lavinia.

How could Diarmid have ever thought he'd sanction something as cruel as that? Had he grown so selfish? Hell, he didn't know. He didn't feel he knew anything at the moment, only that there were going to be major changes in his life after the child was born.

★

Lavinia looked up as they heard the sound of a carriage coming up the drive. 'See who that is, Keara.'

The maid went to look out of the window. 'It's the master, ma'am.'

'What!' Lavinia pushed her swollen body up and waddled across to stare out of the window. 'I told him to stay away until I sent for him. How dare he come back?' She looked with satisfaction at the door connecting her room with Theo's. At least he wouldn't be able to walk in on her any more now that she'd had strong bolts fitted. 'Go and tell him I don't want to see him. I shall lock the bedroom door once you're gone and only open it when I hear your voice outside promising me he isn't with you.'

'But—'

'*Do as you're told!*'

Reluctantly Keara went downstairs, passing Dick on his way up the back stairs. He stopped to greet her and say, 'Looks like we're here to stay for a while. How is she?'

'The same as ever.' Keara grimaced. 'No, worse than ever. She's led everyone a right royal dance with her whims and demands.'

'You're looking weary.'

'I am weary. I'm only staying on for the sake of the child.' And for Theo Mullane, who had wept in her arms once after losing another.

Dick lowered his voice. 'He's really upset about something she's done. Have you any idea what it might be?'

Keara shook her head and went on her way. The master was in the hall, talking to the housekeeper. She hesitated near the servants' door but when he saw her, he beckoned her across.

'Mrs Mullane sent me to tell you she feels – indisposed – unable to see anyone today.'

'Good. Because I definitely don't want to see her.'

He smiled at her, though, and she saw the housekeeper glance quickly at them and frown. Feeling embarrassed by the warmth in his eyes, Keara bobbed a curtsey and left as quickly as she could, but was sure she could feel his eyes upon her. When she risked a glance back as she went out through the servants' door, she found she was right and he was still staring at her with a warm smile on his face.

What had got into him?

If he thought she was going to join his collection of mistresses, he could think again. Not that he'd asked her to. But the way he looked at her sometimes . . . She couldn't help sighing. He was such a lovely man, there was no one like him, but he was as far above her as the moon and she had to be sensible about this. Ha! Sensible, when she still kept dreaming about him. Only how could you stop yourself from dreaming? And anyway, dreams hurt no one but yourself.

Her mother would be heartbroken if she did anything wrong, was always saying that she herself had paid dearly for her lapse from grace and she didn't want to see any of her daughters lose their respectability because it was the only thing a poor girl could bring to a husband.

But as the days passed and the other maids also started commenting on the way their employer kept watching her, Keara began to grow even more worried.

One morning the housekeeper stopped her to say, 'I hope you're not encouraging the master, Keara.'

She didn't pretend not to understand. 'No, ma'am. Definitely not. I wish he'd stop looking at me. I do so.'

The housekeeper studied her face. 'I believe you. If you have any trouble with him, come and see me. I'll help you move away, if necessary. I know you're a good girl and I can always get you a job elsewhere.'

Keara sighed in relief. 'Oh, Mrs Bertram, that makes me feel much better. I've so little money, you see. I've been sending it all to my family. I couldn't afford to leave, even if I wanted to.'

But she didn't want to leave now, heaven help her! Theo's coming back after being away so long had shaken all her good intentions.

Lavinia stayed in her bedroom. She and her husband didn't meet, communicating by notes and verbal messages until she was brought to bed one evening in early December. She made the same fuss as always, screaming and moaning, refusing to do what was necessary.

Keara, who had seen her own mother, frail as she was, stifle her cries and work with her body to help birth the child, was disgusted by this and relieved when the master came in to help, as he had before. With his assistance Lavinia was persuaded to do what was necessary.

As she pushed and screamed and groaned, he stayed by her side, controlling his own anxiety and loathing of her, giving her the support and direction she needed.

But when the baby was born, just before two o'clock in the morning, he let go of his wife's hand immediately and went to the end of the bed.

'It's a boy, sir,' said the midwife.

A faint cry came from the bundle in her arms.

The child was alive, then. Theo closed his eyes in sheer relief, then opened them to ask, 'How is he?'

'Why is nobody helping *me*?' Lavinia wailed.

The doctor ignored her and went to examine the infant. He was silent for a moment, then looked up at Theo. 'Frail, but normal.'

'*Frail?* How frail? Will he live?'

Keara could hear the choking fear in her master's voice and something softened within her.

'The infant has a reasonable chance of survival, more than that I cannot promise,' the doctor said. 'He will, after all, have the very best of attention.'

Lavinia began to sob loudly.

Theo didn't even turn round, just snapped, 'See to her, someone.'

The midwife tidied up her patient then Keara helped her straighten the bedcovers and set the furniture to rights. She made soothing noises as she gave her mistress a drink of water and tucked her in, but tried to hear what the small group at the other side of the room were saying.

'It would be better if your wife fed the infant herself, for a while at least,' the doctor continued in a low voice. 'The birth mother's milk seems to help in these cases.'

'Then that's what she'll do.'

'*I will not!*' Lavinia's voice rang out loudly. 'I have no intention of doing such a disgusting thing.'

Theo looked at her coldly. 'You'll do it if we have to tie you down each time.'

She stared at him open-mouthed, then hurled an ornament at him from the bedside table which Keara had just pushed back into place.

As it smashed into the far wall, Theo went round the side of the bed and leaned over his wife. 'Stop that at once or I'll slap your stupid face.'

She opened her mouth, registered his implacable expression, then shut it again.

He looked at the doctor and nurse. 'She's a fool, my dear wife, but cunning with it, so I'd better move in with her until we're sure the baby's going to survive.'

He turned back to Lavinia to add in a low but angry voice, 'Believe me, you'll obey the doctor in every way – unless you *want* to go through all this again?'

She shrank back from the look in his eyes, her own wide with shock at the expression on his face, and made no further protests.

Keara had never seen a man so icily determined on anything. But when she looked at the frail child making little mewing noises in the midwife's arms as he was brought in to feed, she couldn't really blame him. What sort of a woman would refuse to give her own child its best chance of life?

As soon as this first dangerous month was over,

Keara intended to leave. Her heart filled with joy every time she thought of going home, seeing her mother again and being with her sisters. That was what had kept her going through these difficult months. Though she was really worried about not hearing from them.

Somehow she didn't think Theo Mullane would try to prevent her from leaving now. He knew what his wife was like, how difficult it had been for Keara all these years. And he had changed over the past few years, she could see that. Grown gentler and kinder with everyone. Except his wife. Sad to say, gentleness didn't work with Lavinia.

Yes, Keara could be patient now, sure that within a month or so she would be going home to her family.

Two weeks later the doctor and midwife pronounced it possible to try a wet nurse and the baby was removed from his mother's room. With him went his father, to Keara's intense relief. Theo had said nothing, had not attempted to touch her, but his eyes had often lingered on her and even his wife had noticed that and grown increasingly sharp with her maid.

'If you've been creeping into my husband's bed . . .' she said one morning.

'I haven't. I'm not like that and you know it.'

'Don't be impertinent, girl!'

Keara had said nothing, just kept her gaze steady.

Eventually, her mistress said huffily, 'Well, see that you don't encourage him in *any* way.'

Two mornings later, after breakfast in the servants'

hall, Dick told Keara that Mr Mullane wanted to see her in the library. She looked at him and admitted, 'I don't want to be alone with him.'

'You don't have much choice, lass. He's still master here.'

'Do you know what he wants?'

'No.'

In the library Theo was sitting in the brown leather armchair near the fire. He gestured to her to take a seat on the sofa opposite and she sat down, arranging her skirt modestly, lowering her eyes to avoid his and clasping her hands in her lap.

'I have something to tell you, Keara, but before I do, let me assure you that I didn't know about this myself until it was too late to do anything. Your sisters—'

Terror slashed through her and she looked up quickly. 'They're all right?'

He hesitated, finding this as difficult as he had expected. 'As far as we know. They've – there's no gentle way to tell you – they've been sent to Australia.'

She was so surprised by this she couldn't speak for a moment or two.

'There's worse, I'm afraid. Your mother and father died a few months ago. Lavinia didn't pass on the letter from your priest telling you.'

'My mother's – dead?' Keara couldn't hold back the tears, couldn't bear the thought that she'd never see her gentle mother again. '*No! Oh, no!*'

He stood up and moved towards her but when she shrank away from him, went back to sit opposite her again.

It took her a while to win the struggle to control her voice. 'I don't understand about Mara and Ismay. Why should they have been sent to Australia?'

'Because my wife arranged it. There are some nuns who run a scheme for sending out Irish orphan girls as servants and – well, Lavinia arranged for Ismay and Mara to go.'

'And they went?'

'Not willingly, I'm afraid.'

She was too shocked to weep, too shocked to do anything but try to take this in. After a moment or two she said slowly, 'They must think I knew about it. They must hate me.'

She could not hold back the sobs any longer then and when he came across to take her in his arms, she let him, weeping against him, sobbing so long and desperately that in the end he feared for her reason and said, 'Shhh. Shhh, now, Keara. This doesn't help.'

It was still several minutes before she could stop and then she sat in absolute silence beside him, one hand pressed against her mouth as if to hold back further outpourings of grief. He waited for her to speak.

When she eventually lowered her hand, she said in husky, broken tones, 'I don't understand why Mrs Mullane went to such lengths. Mara's so young, too young to go into service.'

'My wife has paid the Sisters to look after her until she's old enough and I'm sure they'll educate her.' Only after he'd said the words did he realise how unsure he was of everything.

He felt guilty. He could have made enquiries while waiting for his son to be born – and he hadn't.

After another short silence she said, 'I must follow them to Australia. Find them. Tell them I didn't know. Bring them home to Ireland again.' She looked at him pleadingly. 'I have no money. Will you help me?'

'Yes, I will help you. I'll give you your wages and whatever else is needed, but you can't go rushing off to Australia until we know exactly where your sisters are. Ismay will have been found an employer and may not be as easy to trace as Mara, you see.'

This brought fresh horror to Keara's face. 'You mean – they'll have been separated?'

'I think it's likely.' Inevitable. But there was no need to emphasise that.

She bent her head and groaned, rocking slightly in her pain.

He ached for her.

Once she looked up and said in a whisper, 'To think I'll never see Mam again. Never.'

More tears flowed at that thought, he could see them dripping down her face and on to the dark material of her gown. He stretched out his hand towards her, then pulled it back. Better not touch her. At the moment they had to sort out the practicalities. 'You'll not want to continue as my wife's maid now, I'm sure.'

'I don't ever want to see her again.'

'Neither do I, but unfortunately she and I are joined in holy matrimony until death do us part.'

Keara gave him a pitying glance and for a moment their eyes met.

'Will you let me find you somewhere to live temporarily, just until we can sort things out?'

She nodded.

He stood up. 'Go and pack your things, then. I'll take you to the cottage in the grounds.'

She looked up. 'Not the one where—'

'It isn't occupied at the moment.' It hadn't been occupied for months, but he'd told Dick a couple of days ago to have it made ready for Keara. She'd be comfortable there and safe from Lavinia's further spite. His dear wife had always ignored its existence and since she didn't take much exercise, probably didn't even know exactly where it was.

Keara walked slowly up to the attics and began piling her clothes on the bed, tossing them out of her drawers with no thought for tidiness, just speed.

Minnie came rushing in. 'There you are! The mistress has been ringing for you for ages. She's in a right old state.'

'Good.'

Only then did Minnie become aware of the clothes. 'What are you doing?'

'Leaving.'

'He's never sacked you?'

'No. But he's helping me get away from *her*.'

Minnie grinned. 'Well, he's had his eye on you for a while, hasn't he? We've all noticed. I suppose he was waiting for the baby to be born before he did anything. They say he's very generous to his mistresses.'

Keara rounded on her, eyes flashing with anger. 'Well, you've all noticed wrong. I'm not going to be anyone's mistress. He's been kind to me, that's all. My parents have died and . . .' She could not continue, but put one hand across her mouth to hold the tears back.

Minnie's expression changed and her voice became gentler. 'I'm sorry. I didn't know.'

'Neither did I. *She's* known for months, though, but didn't bother to tell me because it wasn't convenient for me to go back. Not even for the funerals!' Keara saw the shock on Minnie's face and drew in a wobbly breath. 'Could you help me bring my trunk down?' She didn't want to wait for anyone else to do that.

'Yes, of course.' When they had hauled it into the maids' quarters, Minnie moved towards the door, then hesitated. 'What shall I tell Mrs Mullane?'

'I think the master will tell her what she needs to know.'

'Thank goodness for that!'

Keara packed the trunk with feverish haste, longing to be out of this house. By the time Dick and one of the gardeners came to carry it downstairs, she had her outdoor things on.

'Master says to go out the front way,' one of them said.

What did she care which way she left this house? She was never coming back, that was the only thing that mattered.

As she walked down the main staircase and passed the first floor she heard the sound of hysterics from the direction of Mrs Mullane's bedroom and paused for a moment. Good!

Mr Mullane was waiting in the hall to escort her out to the waiting carriage. He didn't comment on the shrieks still coming from upstairs and neither did Keara. From now on someone else could deal with that.

She didn't even want to see her former mistress and tell her to her face how cruel she had been. What good would it do? It wouldn't bring back Ismay and Mara.

And besides, Lavinia Mullane could only see her own viewpoint. She simply didn't understand other people's needs.

Theo handed Keara into the carriage himself and stood looking into it. 'Dick will see you settled into the cottage. If you need anything, just ask him.'

She nodded and after a slight hesitation he stepped back and gestured to the other man to get in, raising his hand as they drove off.

Dick watched her, saying nothing because what could you say in such circumstances? When Theo had told him what had happened, he had been horrified at the cruelty of it all. Keara's face was ravaged by grief and she seemed hardly aware of his presence, staring down blindly at her tightly clasped hands during the short journey.

When the carriage stopped she didn't even seem to notice and he had to give her a nudge to make her move. 'I'm sorry for what's happened, Keara,' he ventured as he helped her down.

She stared at him as if she didn't understand the words, so he abandoned the attempt to offer comfort and led the way inside before coming back to help the coachman carry in her things.

'Got her at last, has he?' the coachman joked as they lifted the trunk off the back of the carriage.

Dick glared at him. 'It's not like that! She's heard some shocking news – some of it caused by the mistress – and the master needed to get her out of the house. This place just happened to be empty. You *know* Keara isn't a flighty piece.'

The coachman shrugged. 'We're all human. But whatever you say.'

He was clearly unconvinced so Dick abandoned the attempt to explain, knowing nothing would stop the talk. 'Go back to the house and ask Cook to send some food over. I'll ride back with you when you've brought it. Looks like the rain is setting in.'

He went into the cottage to find Keara standing by the fire, still with that dreadful fixed stare. He took one of her hands, finding it icy cold. 'Is there anything I can do, lass?'

Slowly she turned towards him. 'No. But Mr Mullane says he'll help me go after them. However far away Australia is, I have to find them.' Her face crumpled with anguish. 'I can't *bear* them to think I wanted them sent away.'

Dick wasn't so sure Theo would let her go, but he didn't say that. 'They're bringing you over some food.'

She gave a choking half-laugh that turned into a

sob. 'I can't eat anything. I just want to be quiet and think.'

'Mr Mullane says he'll come and see you later, but no one else will disturb you. He's got to make arrangements for the baby first.' And for his wife. He'd admitted to Dick that he didn't trust her an inch. 'Do you want me to show you round?'

Keara shook her head and wandered across to stare out of the window.

When the hamper of food arrived, Dick carried it into the cottage himself. He told Keara it was in the kitchen and urged her to eat something, if only to keep up her strength. Her nod was totally indifferent.

As they drove back, he could not get her unhappiness out of his mind. And what those two young girls were going through, thinking themselves abandoned by their sister, he dreaded to contemplate. He had a cousin the same age as Ismay, a giddy piece but with a heart of gold. What if someone had treated her like that? He'd want to kill them, that's what.

It was a few minutes before Keara realised that Dick had left. She sighed with relief because she needed to be alone more than anything else. Standing up, she wandered round the cottage. This was where Mr Mullane brought his mistresses. It was small but beautifully furnished, with two bedrooms upstairs, two rooms, a kitchen and scullery downstairs. Even the privy was conveniently close to the back door. Her family would have thought it an absolute palace.

Her family!

Grief made her feel she was choking and she leaned her head against the door frame of the main bedroom for a moment, moaning in her throat as she tried to control her feelings. But an animal sound burst from her, would not be held back, then another, and she flung herself on the bed, weeping loudly.

CHAPTER TWELVE

November–December 1863

———◆◆———

Patience's baby was born in November, three weeks early, with the help of Jane Putter, the most experienced woman in Rossall Springs for birthing babies. It was a healthy little girl and when he held her Mark felt joy wash through him in a great warm tide. His daughter!

Jane cleared everything up and went to lie down on the bed they'd provided for her in the sitting room, since she'd promised to stay the night.

Mark got ready to join his wife in bed while Patience lay watching him. She looked white and exhausted, but had a faint smile on her face.

'Are you pleased?' she asked suddenly, in a thread of a voice. 'You don't mind – that it isn't a boy?'

'Of course I don't mind. She's beautiful.'

'I'd like to call her Amy, if that's all right with you? I know we agreed on Annie, but I think she ought to have her own name, not your sister's.'

'Whatever you want, my darling. I love you.'

'I love you too. So happy.' She sighed and closed her eyes. 'Tired, though.'

He watched her fall asleep and went for one final look at the baby who was sleeping peacefully in the cradle, taking little snuffling breaths that made him smile fondly. Before getting into bed, he left a night light burning in a saucer of water on the chest of drawers.

Two hours later he was woken by Patience whimpering beside him.

He laid one hand on her shoulder. 'What is it, love?'

'I feel – wet. Down there. Fetch – Jane.'

He flung the covers back and hurriedly lit a candle, gasping as he turned to see a red stain spreading from her side of the bed. He pushed the covers further back to find a big pool of blood.

Rushing next door, he roused Jane, who clasped one hand to her breast and whispered, 'Please God, no!'

She went to stand by the bed and threw him an anguished glance. 'If only there was a doctor here.'

He followed her instructions and together they tried to stem the bleeding, raising the foot of the mattress, pressing hard on Patience's abdomen, but still the tide of red trickled steadily out of her thin body.

By this time she was unconscious.

Jane turned to Mark and shook her head, not needing to put into words what he already knew. He knelt by the bed and held his wife's hand, his eyes so blurred with tears that only the midwife's touch on his shoulder made him realise Patience had stopped breathing as quietly as she had lived.

Jane bent her head in prayer, then covered the dead woman's face. 'It happens like that sometimes. Something tears inside them, I think, and –' She shook her head sadly. 'Well, there's nothing we can do. It's a hard world for women, it is that.'

He could not think for a minute, could only stand there, but a cry from the cradle in the corner made him look round. 'The baby? How are we to feed her?'

Jane pursed her lips. 'Well, there's no one in town to act as wet nurse except . . .' She hesitated. 'There's an aboriginal woman who lost her child two days ago. Kalaya, she's called. Kalaya Johnson. Nice name, isn't it, for a heathen? Her husband's half-white. She's a decent enough sort and clean. The husband works for Mr Tidbill, looking after the stock. You could pay her to feed your baby and look after it. If you don't object to her, that is?'

He was still lost in grief, staring at his dead wife's face. 'Why should I object to her? You said she's decent and clean.'

Jane's voice was exasperated. 'I've just been telling you, she's a native.'

'I don't think that matters, given the circumstances, do you?'

'Well, I've always found her a good sort, but there's some as don't like 'em,' Jane replied. 'I'll lay out your wife then go and see Kalaya as soon as it's light.'

He nodded and later, when she'd gone, he sat beside Patience and said his farewells, wishing he'd loved her more, wishing he hadn't done this to her. After a minute or two the baby began to cry so he picked Amy up, cradling her against him. She moved her head blindly from side to side, searching for her mother's breast, and that made him start sobbing.

One thing was certain, he vowed, as he rocked his little daughter in a vain attempt to soothe her: he was never going to marry again, never again be responsible for a young woman's untimely death. Two women he'd killed now. Two!

In the morning Jane came back alone.

'Won't Mrs Johnson help us?' he asked, terrified for this scrap of a child in his arms.

'She'll feed the baby and look after it, but she won't come here to do it. They have different beliefs and customs to us. Don't like to come into a house where there's been a death until it's been purified. She says you can take the baby and its things across to her, and she'll feed it and look after it for ten shillings a week. I'm sure you can trust her and the house is very clean, I promise you.'

He nodded, then looked round, feeling helpless. 'What must I take?'

Jane patted his shoulder. 'I'll pack the baby's things in the cradle and you can carry it while I take her in my arms. What are you going to call her, by the way?'

'Amy. It was Patience's choice.'

'I always liked that name.'

It upset him to leave his wife's body lying there alone, but he had to think of the baby now. Patience herself would want that.

The Johnsons lived in a very small house at the edge of town. When Jane knocked on the door, the husband opened it.

'Sorry for your loss,' he said awkwardly to Mark.

'I'm sorry for yours as well, Mr Johnson.'

The man looked surprised as he held the door open for them.

'No need to call him "Mr Johnson",' Jane whispered to Mark. 'Everyone calls him Billy.'

A woman walked forward from inside the room, tall and thin with beautiful brown eyes, a wide, generous mouth and a gentle expression on her face.

When she held out her arms, Jane gave the baby to her.

'What's she called?'

'Amy.'

Mrs Johnson studied the baby's face, repeated her name once or twice, then took out her breast and offered it to the child. Within seconds Amy was sucking energetically and making gurgling noises of satisfaction.

Mark ought to have been embarrassed, but somehow he wasn't. He stood there watching in deep gratitude as this stranger offered his daughter a chance of life. 'Thank you,' he said huskily. 'I can't thank you enough. If I can ever help you in any way, you have only to ask, Mrs Johnson.'

She gave him a gentle smile then went to sit in a rocking chair, murmuring to the child she held.

Mark turned to her husband and held out his hand. 'Thank you as well, Mr Johnson.'

They buried Patience the following day and Mark was touched by how many of the townsfolk made the effort to attend the funeral. He also saw Kalaya Johnson standing at the back of the mourners, carrying Amy, and felt remorse sear through him. *He* should have thought of bringing his daughter, but had been too wrapped up in his own grief – and guilt.

He wanted to beckon the nurse and child forward, but knew that would offend his neighbours so didn't. His eyes were drawn to the two of them several times, though, and it gave him courage to think that his daughter was there, sharing this moment with her mother, at least. He would tell her about it when she grew up.

When it was all over he stayed by the grave for a long time, head bent, lost in regrets. Eventually someone touched his arm and he looked up to see Mrs Johnson. Without speaking she held the baby out to him and he took his daughter in his arms, glad of the comfort of her warm little body. He wanted to weep again but held the unmanly tears back.

They walked back into the town together and as they drew near the eating house, Kalaya held out her arms again for the child. 'You need to work now. Come and visit Amy any time.'

'Would you and your family like some food?' he asked. 'I can send some across to you. As a gift. To thank you.' Because Amy was happy with her nurse, he could see that already.

'If you like,' she said.

'I eat what's left after the customers have gone.'

She smiled. 'Anything would be fine.'

'How many children do you have?'

'Three.' She glanced down at the sleeping child. 'And this one, for a short time.'

He watched her walk away, again admiring her graceful gait.

A woman passing by stopped to say, 'Such a pity she's the only one who can help you with your daughter, Mr Gibson.'

He turned on her, feeling anger rise in him. 'On the contrary. Mrs Johnson is doing a wonderful job and I couldn't have asked for a better wet nurse for Amy.'

'Oh, well, if you think so.' She hurried off, glancing over her shoulder at him, disapproval clear on her face.

He hadn't even thought about the position of Aborigines in Rossall before. They had just been there, at the edge of white folk's life. Now, knowing how well Kalaya Johnson was looking after his daughter, he was beginning to realise how difficult things must be for them. He would never think of them in the same way again, though, and he'd make sure that Amy knew she owed her life to Kalaya.

When he got home he checked that Ginny and her sister could manage in the kitchen then went to sit in the small parlour, feeling very despondent. It wouldn't look right to work in the eating house today, but he wished he could.

After a while he remembered that he would need to write to the Jenners to tell them that their daughter had died and they had a granddaughter. It wasn't a task he relished, but he got out the writing materials and mixed up some ink.

He hoped the Jenners wouldn't feel it necessary to come and visit the grave. He never wanted to see Patience's father again.

★

Theo informed the servants that they were not to let his wife near the baby, on pain of instant dismissal, then went to see Lavinia.

She was lying on the bed but when she saw him bounced to her feet again. 'Where's Keara?'

'Gone.'

'What do you mean?'

'I told her what you'd done. How you'd sent her sisters away. You've hurt her badly. Thanks to you, she never even got a chance to say farewell to her dying mother.'

'These people don't have the same feelings as we do,' she said scornfully. 'Offer to double her wages and she'll soon come back.'

'You're wrong.'

'But I *need* her. She's the only one who knows my ways.'

'She's the only one with so kind a heart she can pity a monster like you.' He bit back further recriminations. What was the use? She wouldn't understand, seemed to have little sense of right and wrong.

Her face was ugly with hatred. 'Now you've got your son, you don't care what happens to me.'

'You're right, I don't. If this infant doesn't live, you'll be quite safe from me in future because I shall never touch you again. You sicken me. In fact, I intend to move permanently back to Ireland.' He looked round the overheated, fussy room. 'I'm going to sell this house, but I'll buy you another in Ellerdale itself and make you an allowance, then you can live your life as you choose.'

'I choose to stay here.'

'No.'

'But it's my *home*. And what will everyone think if you move out and I have to live in a smaller place?' After a minute's struggle against her anger she pleaded, 'For heaven's sake, Theo, can we not be civilised about this?'

'If by civilised you mean continue to share a house, then no. I'm going back to Ireland and I've no intention of frittering away my money running a huge place like this for just one person. Your father didn't leave nearly as much as we expected, you know. In fact, you'll have to curtail some of your extravagances from now on. I'll make you as generous an allowance as I can, but there'll be no more if you spend it all.'

'Theo, I—'

He left without speaking and she plumped down on the bed, anger keeping her warm even when the fire died down. It didn't occur to her to tend it or pick up her clothes, which she dropped where she was standing when she took them off.

She could guess where he'd taken Keara, Lavinia thought resentfully – where he took all his women. Well, she wasn't going to put up with it. Not this time. Not any more. But she needed help to do something about it. She went across to the table and scribbled a note, then rang the bell.

There was only one person who would be able to look after her properly now and she was sure Theo wouldn't prevent her from bringing that person back into her life.

When Minnie appeared, looking apprehensive, Lavinia forced a smile to her face. 'I'm not going to bite you, girl. I want this note delivered – at once! They must take it by carriage, then bring back the person it's addressed to. After you've seen to that, come back and help me dress. Oh, and while you're downstairs, find out what the master is doing, would you?'

Minnie came back to report that the under-coachman would take the note and the master had left the house on foot.

'Good. Now help me get dressed. I'm tired of staying in this room.'

Although Minnie got her ears boxed for her clumsiness with her mistress's hair, she felt she'd got through the ordeal better than she had expected. She lent her mistress an arm down the stairs and left her in the small parlour, going into the kitchen to say with a shudder, 'I don't know how Keara put up with her. She wants you to dress her, as if she's a baby.'

Mrs Bertram recommended her not to gossip about her betters and sent her upstairs again to straighten the mistress's room.

'I don't have to keep on maiding her, do I?' Minnie wailed. 'Can't someone else do that?'

'No, they can't. I'll speak to her in the morning about hiring a new girl, though.' Mrs Bertram paused. 'Who did she say she was expecting?'

'She didn't.'

Over two hours later the carriage came back and the under-coachman helped a woman out. She was very upright but must have been at least seventy, dressed in black with her white hair pulled back into a severe bun beneath an old-fashioned bonnet that half-covered her face. She looked up at the house and smiled, but the coachman shivered as he watched her and told Minnie afterwards he'd rather have anyone else's frown than that one's smile.

Ignoring the rain the woman made her way to the house and walked up the steps. When Minnie opened the door she walked straight inside without a word and the maid had to jump hastily aside to let her pass.

'Where's Mrs Mullane?' the newcomer asked.

'May I have your name, ma'am?'

'No, you may not. Just take me to her.'

The parlour door opened and Lavinia appeared in the hall. 'Nancy! Oh, Nancy, you came!'

The old woman walked across to her. 'I said you'd need me again one day, my girl, didn't I?'

The door shut on them and Minnie went scurrying off to the kitchen to report what had happened. 'She's not gentry, but she's not one of us, either. And there's something about her that makes me shiver.'

'Don't exaggerate!' Mrs Bertram snapped.

'You wait and see. And what's more, she called Mrs Mullane "my girl" and the mistress didn't object. You'll understand when you see her.'

In the parlour Lavinia burst into tears, upon which the old woman tapped her lightly across the cheek.

'You've fallen into silly ways again, I see, girl. How many times have I told you that tears are a weakness?'

Lavinia gulped and stared at her former nurse, wondering whether she'd done the right thing in sending for her because Nancy always took charge and made her do as she was told. But she knew she couldn't manage on her own – she never had been able to – so she'd just have to put up with that.

Nancy studied her. 'I haven't changed my ways, you know. So if you don't want me telling you the truth and helping you behave sensibly, you'd better call that coachman of yours and order him to take me home again.'

Lavinia thought of life without Keara, without anyone, and shook her head. 'No, Nancy, please stay. I really do need you. I've no one else. No one loves me and—'

'Stop pitying yourself and send for some tea. I'm parched. Then you can tell me what you've been up to. I hear you've borne him a son at last.'

'Yes. He's got what he wants now.'

The old woman closed her eyes for a moment, then shook her head. 'No, he hasn't. There's death still hanging over this house. I can feel it.'

'Well, I'm sure I don't care. He won't let me go near the child. Anyway, I'll not be having any more because he says he can't bear to touch me again, though I'll believe that when I see it. And – oh, Nancy, he wants us to separate and he's going to sell this house and buy me one in town and what'll people think?'

'You always were a fool. I told you to be nice to him, make him fond of you, but no, you have to play the temperamental heiress.' The old woman paused at a knock on the door and called, 'Come in! Put the tea things down over there.' Her voice lost its sharpness. 'Pour me a cup, Lavinia dear. You can tell me the rest while I drink it, then we'll read the leaves together.'

Lavinia swallowed hard. The tea leaves didn't always tell you what you wanted to know and sometimes what they said frightened her. So did Nancy. But at least now she had someone devoted to her, someone well able to support her against Theo, or anyone else for that matter.

She poured the tea and settled back in her chair. Actually, Nancy would make a far more formidable ally than Keara ever had. She should have brought her old nurse back years ago.

'Sit up and don't slump!' Nancy snapped. 'And one of those cakes is more than enough.'

With a pout, Lavinia put the second cake back.

'Well, go on, tell me everything . . .'

Theo left the house on foot, glad to be away from the atmosphere of strain and hysteria. It wasn't until he was halfway to the cottage that he realised it was raining and he hadn't even put on an overcoat. By the time he got there, he was soaked. But he could not have borne to go back.

As he knocked on the door the rain eased and the sun began to shine fitfully, though there were more dark clouds in the distance. He hesitated, looking up towards the front bedroom. Should he disturb her in her grief or not? But the temptation to see her, to check that she was recovering and didn't hold a grudge against him for what his wife had done was too great. And besides, he was shivering now.

When he tried the door he found it unlocked. She would have to learn to be more careful. He didn't want to risk anyone breaking in and attacking her in this isolated spot.

'Keara?' he called as he stepped straight into the small parlour. But there was no response.

Feeling chilled to the marrow, he moved across the room to the fire and thrust some pieces of wood from the basket into the dull red glow at its heart. As flames crackled into life he held his hands out to them.

When it was burning brightly, he went to the foot of the stairs and called her name again. 'Keara! Are you there?' This time there was the sound of bed springs and then footsteps crossing the floor above.

As the bedroom door opened, he called, 'It's only me!' and moved back into the parlour to wait for her.

She hesitated in the doorway, looking rumpled, her eyes swollen from weeping.

He wanted to rush across and fold her in his arms, but of course he couldn't. 'I was worried about you.' He couldn't help shivering.

She looked at him, really looked at him this time, her eyes widening in surprise. 'You're wet through! Didn't you have a coat, sir?'

'I forgot it. I was too worried about you – wanted to see that you were all right.'

She came into the room and moved towards the fire, holding out her hands to its warmth.

'How are you? Really.'

She made a tiny movement with her shoulders and hands that might have been a shrug and her eyes filled with tears again. 'I keep thinking of my mother, that I shall never see her again, and of my sisters believing I didn't want them, that I sent them away. And it *hurts*!' Great fat tears rolled down her cheeks.

With no other thought than to comfort, he put his arms round her and she collapsed against him, her body racked by sobs. 'Ah, Keara, don't!' He kissed her cheek, then her swollen eyelids, and when she clung to him he pulled her close again, murmuring inarticulate words of comfort as he cradled her against him.

As he moved to the sofa she clung to him still as if he were her only hope in a hostile world and they sat there without speaking, offering the simple comfort of one body holding another close. When he tried to move away, worried about how he was reacting to her, she made a soft noise of protest, so he continued to hold her.

He didn't set out to seduce her, but without thinking he dropped a kiss on her flushed forehead. She looked up at him in puzzlement then gave a sob and nestled even closer, continuing to respond to his gentle kisses. He could no more have stopped himself than he could have flown to the moon.

Sure that she was still a virgin and not wanting to force her, he took his time. Though he'd had many women, most of them skilled in the arts of love, this time love-making felt as if it were new to him, too – as if it truly were making love not lust between them. A last shred of conscience even made him hold her at arm's length and ask, 'Keara, are you sure about this?'

'I don't want to be alone,' she whispered against his cheek. 'I've been alone for so long. Don't stop holding me, please.' And she pressed against him, kissing him again, which silenced any further words. He didn't try to stop again. Couldn't.

How they found themselves on the rug he didn't know, but as he brought their love-making towards a conclusion the whole room seemed filled with warmth and light. More than the fire. More than the closeness. It was as if this was a very special moment and the glow came as much from that as from the leaping flames.

He too was glad he wasn't alone, glad that Keara was more than just a body in his arms. He realised with a shock that he cared about her, as he had never cared about his other mistresses – or his wife.

When it was over, he pulled her close and lay there with a chill draught on his back as she sighed into sleep against him.

'You were worth waiting for,' he murmured and managed to pull some of their clothes behind him to cut out the damned draught. But the fire was dying down and he was getting cold, so he lifted her into his arms and carried her upstairs.

She murmured something but didn't waken. He went down to fetch a lamp and when he saw by its light how wan she was, how reddened her eyes, he felt guilt sear through him for taking advantage of her need for comfort. Only he *had* comforted her, he knew.

And for her part she had made him feel cleansed after the years of doing his duty with Lavinia.

He joined her in the bed, soon sleeping as soundly as she did.

An exclamation brought him instantly awake and in the grey light of dawn he saw her staring at him in shock.

'Don't look at me like that, Keara.'

'But you . . . we . . .'

'You were a willing partner in last night's loving. I didn't force you.'

She flushed and didn't know what to say, where to look. She had a hazy memory of lying with him, feeling close and warm and loved, of never wanting that feeling to stop. Only he couldn't love her. She had been attracted to him for a long time, but he was still her employer.

And she was a fallen woman now. *What would her mother have said?*

He pulled her towards him and when she protested and struggled half-heartedly, he kissed her again, stifling her murmurs and shushing her, sure that she would soon melt into his arms as she had done the night before.

But this time she didn't. Indeed, she fought so fiercely he let go of her and moved back to lie propped on one arm on the edge of the bed, saying in amusement, 'Isn't it a little late for these maidenly scruples, my dear girl?'

'I must have been mad last night.' She blushed as

his eyes lingered on her naked breasts and pulled the sheet hastily up to her chin.

'If so, I hope you stay mad, because you make a delightful bed partner.'

'It wasn't fair of you to take advantage of my distress, sir,' she said with something of her old spirit.

He laughed softly. '*Sir?* How can you call me sir when your body and mine have been as one? My name is Theo from now on, Keara.'

'Not to me it isn't. I may have been mad last night, but I shan't forget myself again.'

'Shall you not?'

She looked round. 'Where are my clothes, sir?'

'I told you: I don't answer to "sir" any more.'

She glared at him. 'Theo, then! *Theo!* Where are my clothes, *Theo?*'

'Downstairs with mine.'

She bit her lip and looked at him doubtfully, then tugged at the sheet. 'Let me take this.'

He tugged back, smiling. 'It seems a shame to cover up that beautiful body.'

'How can you treat me like this?' she cried.

'I've been wanting to treat you like this for years and don't tell me you haven't been attracted to me, because I won't believe you. You held me in your arms once when I was distressed. I did the same for you last night. What it led to was inevitable between us one day.'

She could see that he had no regrets for what he had done, but she did. 'It's a mortal sin!' she burst out.

'Oh, dear.'

'Don't you even care about that?'

'Not really. I only believe in this world and this life, I'm afraid. Though for all my faults, I try not to hurt anyone.'

'Well, I care about sin and I want to get dressed now, *sir*. And I shan't be staying here another night, if this is the price I have to pay.'

His amusement vanished. 'How can you say that? You know it wasn't like that. As if I'd threaten you like that!'

'I don't know what to think,' she muttered. 'Let me get dressed.'

He waved one hand. 'Go ahead. Your clothes are downstairs. Just a few steps will bring you to them.' But he kept hold of the sheet.

Another blush flooded her face with scarlet and she looked at the door, then back at him. 'You're not being fair.'

'Why should I be, with you here in bed with me, deliciously naked? I'm not made of stone, you know.'

She let out a squeak of dismay at the look in his eyes and tried to leap from the bed, but by the time she had freed herself from the covers, he had caught her and pulled her towards him.

'Don't!' she pleaded. 'Don't do this. Please.'

He sighed and stopped touching her. He could never force this woman against her will. She was not his wife, owed him no duty. 'Then we'd better discuss what we're going to do.' He looked at her flushed, embarrassed face. 'Oh, hell, wrap the sheet round you and let's go and find something to eat. I'm absolutely ravenous. But we do need to talk.'

She didn't want to talk, still felt numb and bewildered, but she did as he'd ordered, turning away as he got out of bed and wrapped a blanket round himself. As she followed him down the stairs, she kept every inch of herself covered but still didn't feel safe because being close to him made some feeling she didn't understand whisper through her body. And she knew he hadn't forced her. It had been as much her fault as his.

She took her clothes back upstairs to dress, edging past him as if he might attack her at any moment. He let her go without protesting.

In the parlour he struggled into his trousers and left the shirt loose over them before going into the kitchen to light the fire. God, it was cold! By the time she came downstairs again, he had the fire burning brightly in the kitchen range. He waved a hand towards the hamper on the table. 'Find out what they've sent us to eat, will you?'

She unpacked the food in silence, feeling diminished by the way he was treating her now. First a whore, then a servant.

'I don't think it's a sin for us to love one another,' he said softly.

She said nothing, but couldn't help wondering what he meant by 'love'. Was it just the bed play or could it be something more? There was no one else left to care about her now.

'Keara?'

She avoided his eyes.

He saw a tear trickling down the soft skin of her cheek and felt even more guilty. 'Don't weep, my dear. We'll work something out. Please eat something.'

She looked down at the plate and pushed it away. The food would have choked her, she was sure.

'Eat!' he repeated in a sharper tone.

She took a piece of bread and began to crumble it on the plate, seeking for something to divert his attention from herself. 'How is the baby?'

'Richard was well when I left last night and I need to get back soon to check that he's still all right. But I'm not leaving until I'm sure you're not going to run away.'

She had already considered that and rejected it. 'Where would I go? And how would I get anywhere? I don't have any money.'

He pulled a few coins out of his pocket, then hesitated and looked at her, not used to treading so carefully with anyone. 'This isn't payment for what we did. I care too much about you to treat you like that. I just thought you might feel better if you had a guinea or two. But don't try to use it to run away from me because I'd come after you and find you, I promise.'

When she made no attempt to take the money from him, he went to stack it on the high mantelpiece. As he turned back, he said, 'I give you my solemn promise, Keara, that I'll help you to trace your sisters. I feel very angry about what my wife has done to you – and to them.'

And suddenly she was sobbing again, making no protest as he went to gather her in his arms and hold her till she'd stopped.

'Will you give me the money to go after them?' she

asked when she had calmed down. 'I have some wages owing. Surely it'll be enough?'

'When we've traced them, I'll have them brought back here. I'm not letting you go wandering the world. What good would it do them for you to put yourself in danger?'

When she looked pleadingly at him, he added, 'Besides, I care too much about you.'

She froze and stared at him in shock. This time she could not ignore the word. 'Care?'

'Yes. Don't you care about me, just a little?'

But she wasn't ready to admit that, and anyway what was the use of loving someone so far above her in status? The feelings she had for him had already led her into sin. From now on she must control herself better. The sin mustn't happen again. But even as she told herself that, a pang went through her as she remembered the wonderful closeness.

'You'll be here when I get back later today? Promise me that, at least, Keara.'

After a slight hesitation, she nodded. To escape from him would take time and careful planning, but she *was* going after her sisters, whatever he said or did.

He looked down with a rueful smile at the crumpled state of his clothes. 'I'd better get back, then. See how things are.'

'Yes, sir.'

'My name is Theo.'

But she wouldn't give him his name. Didn't dare.

When he'd gone she heated some water and washed

herself from head to toe, then knelt down to pray for forgiveness. Only she kept remembering Theo's kisses and that made her falter as she prayed. She needed Father Cornelius to set her straight.

Oh, she didn't know what she needed!

She wandered into the kitchen, eating something now because she would need all her strength of mind and body to achieve her purpose. She was sorry she'd have to deceive Theo because in his own way he'd been kind to her. And – he did seem to care for her a little. But this definitely couldn't go on. Besides, he'd soon weary of her, as they said he always did of his mistresses, and then where would she be?

No, she didn't dare rely on him, only on herself. She would do it, though. She would get to Australia and find her sisters – or die trying.

CHAPTER THIRTEEN

December 1863 – January 1864

———◆◆◆———

To Mark's dismay, the Jenners turned up in Rossall Springs within a week of him sending the letter to say that Patience had died in childbirth. Mr Jenner wore a triumphant expression on his face, but Mrs Jenner looked as if she'd been weeping.

'We wish to see our daughter's grave,' Alex announced at the top of his voice.

Since he was standing in the middle of the eating house and ignoring the curious customers completely, Mark ushered the two of them quickly through to the small parlour at the rear. What was wrong with the man that he couldn't behave in a quieter, more normal way?

'This house needs a woman's touch,' Alex said at once, looking round at the untidy room, which was in sad need of a dusting. He looked back at Mark and his voice had a pronounced sneer to it as he stated, 'You *need* us now.'

Mark began to understand what his father-in-law wanted and his whole being rebelled against it, but he said nothing. Perhaps it wasn't as bad as he feared.

Surely the man didn't intend to profit from the death of his only daughter?

'How is the baby?' Nan asked, after a quick glance from one man to the other. 'Can I see her, please?'

'She's at the wet nurse's house. I'll take you over there once the midday customers have left.'

'You care too much about earthly things, Mark Gibson. The child is more important than your customers.'

'Alex, don't,' Nan begged.

But her husband shook off her hand. 'If the spirit moves me to say something then I shall do so. The Lord is not mocked. Patience broke his commandment: *Honour thy father and mother*. She was punished for that.'

Mark felt sick with disgust at this attitude, but sorry for Mrs Jenner who was fighting against tears. He tried to change the subject. 'I'll fetch you something to eat, shall I?'

'I'll come and get it,' Nan said at once, taking off her ugly black hat and plain mantle.

Alex sat down in Mark's own armchair, waiting for his wife to serve him.

'He doesn't mean to sound so – so harsh,' Nan said in a low voice once they were outside. 'He hasn't been well,' she glanced quickly over her shoulder, 'and I fear he has grown rather inflexible.'

'That must be difficult for you,' Mark said gently. He had no quarrel with this poor faded creature, who looked years older than she had on the ship, but he was quite determined not to let a joyless bigot like Alex

Jenner play any part in bringing Amy up. 'I'll need to finish here before I can take you to see Amy.' He smiled at the mere thought of his chubby little daughter. 'She's a lovely baby. Very good and doesn't cry much.'

'Her mother was the same.' Mrs Jenner took the tray through to the back room without saying anything else, but her expression was sad.

Mark returned to his work. When the lunchtime customers had finished, he ate a plate of mutton pie and mashed potatoes without tasting a mouthful, then returned to his in-laws.

Already Nan had tidied up the room, but Alex was sitting staring moodily into the empty fireplace, seeming not even to notice the heat of the summer's day, though his wife had opened a window.

She looked up as Mark came in. 'Can we go and see the baby now?'

'Yes, of course. Perhaps you'd like to stay here, Mr Jenner. You look tired,' Mark said, but without any hope of being attended to.

'I must see the child.' He stood up. 'You've had her christened?'

'Not yet. There hasn't been time.'

Alex breathed in deeply. 'Then she is still steeped in original sin.'

'Sin!' Mark stared at him in irritation. 'Of what sin can a tiny baby possibly be guilty?'

'Her mother's sins, of course.'

The man was mad, Mark decided, and wished he need not take him anywhere near Amy, but felt he could not in all decency refuse to let them see their only grandchild. As he led the way along the street, he watched the dust rise around their feet, glad when neither of his companions made any effort to speak.

At the Johnsons' tiny house he stopped. 'If you'll wait here, I'll check that it's convenient for us to visit Amy.'

One of the children opened the door and stared up at him shyly.

'Is your mother in?'

A voice called, 'Come in, Mr Gibson!'

'I have my wife's mother and father with me. Is it all right if they come and see the child?'

'Yes, of course. I've just finished feeding and changing her.'

He stood back to let Mrs Jenner precede him, then followed her inside. 'Here she is.'

Kalaya stood holding the baby and smiling at them.

'You have delivered *my* grandchild into the hands of a heathen?' thundered Alex, reaching out as if to snatch the baby from her nurse.

Mark moved quickly to stand between his father-in-law and the young woman who had been so kind to them. 'If you aren't quiet *this minute* then I must ask you to leave. I won't allow such discourtesy to Mrs Johnson.'

'She's a godless heathen, a savage!'

As Kalaya stood frozen, a hurt expression on her face, Mark pushed the old man outside.

Nan didn't move. She stared at the baby who seemed plump and well cared for. A quick glance round showed her only a clean room and a young woman whose person was equally tidy. 'I'm sorry, Mrs Johnson,' she said. 'My husband can be unreasonable sometimes. May I hold my granddaughter?'

Kalaya nodded, encased now in a shell of distant dignity.

Nan took the child and studied her eagerly. 'She's so like her mother was as a baby and yet she has her father's eyes. I pray she'll have a happier life than my poor daughter did, though.' The shouting continued outside and with a sigh she handed the baby back. 'I must go to my husband. I'm sorry for what he said to you.'

Kalaya nodded, saying nothing, but with pity in her eyes now. She moved across to look out of the window. Mark Gibson was forcing the other man to return to the main street and he was gesticulating and shouting, trying to get back to her house. She was used to people despising her because of the colour of her skin, but things were not too bad in Rossall. More often than not the white people here simply ignored her, though every now and then some of them spoke about her to one another as if she couldn't understand what they were saying.

But this old man was worse than any of them, spraying hatred around him along with his cruel words.

She looked down at the child. 'Your father will have to keep that man away from you if he wants you to have a happy life, little one.' She began to sing one of the songs her own mother had used to get babies to sleep.

Mark didn't return until the following day. 'They've gone back to Melbourne,' he said. 'I'm so sorry for what that bigoted man said to you, Mrs Johnson.'

'The grandmother wasn't rude to me. She's a very unhappy woman, though. The old man is filled with anger and hatred.' Kalaya hesitated then dared to say, 'It wouldn't be good for the little one to be in his charge.'

Mark nodded. During a mostly sleepless night he'd come to that conclusion himself.

For a month Keara stayed at the cottage, spending Christmas on her own, feeling sad and lonely as well as guilty. Theo had brought her a book, *Lady Audley's Secret*, which she couldn't read because the words were too long and the characters too alien to her, magazines which she could read in parts, and a jar of brandied fruit. She had never eaten anything half as delicious and greedily ate the whole jar, then drank the juice. That sent her stumbling up to bed with a spinning head and she woke in the morning with a slight headache, but at least she'd slept.

Inevitably she found herself in bed with Theo again, not because he forced her but because he was kind and thoughtful. The very sight of him striding up the garden path set her heart racing. The warmth in his eyes, the loving glances, all seemed to conspire to break down her resistance.

He brought her more presents: a bottle of perfume, clothes. More clothes than she knew what to do with, some of them far too fine for her. They made her feel like a kept woman and she wept when he'd left.

'We're going away,' he said abruptly one day in late January.

'Oh?'

'Just to London for a few days. You need a change and so do I. I'll enjoy showing you a wider world than this.'

'The only place I want to go is Australia, and you know that, Theo.'

'Well, I have news about that. The Order of St Martha and St Zita is the one which sent your sisters to Australia. It has a convent in Melbourne as well as three houses in Ireland and regularly sends girls out to Australia to work as maids.' He handed her a letter. 'See. This is the address in Melbourne. I've already written asking for information about your sisters, explaining that I want to bring them back and will pay whatever that costs. So we can do nothing until we receive their reply. In the meantime we'll go to London together for a few days.'

She studied the letter, memorising the address, then folded the paper and handed it back to him before looking him directly in the eyes and saying, 'I'd rather stay here. I don't want to be seen in public with you, Theo.'

'Well, I'll be proud to be seen in public with the woman I love.'

'You don't love me!'

'I do, Keara.' He'd realised that last night as he lay in his bed at Eastwood House wishing she were sharing it with him.

She shook her head stubbornly. 'If you truly loved me, you'd help me to go to Australia. I don't like being your mistress, you know I don't.' Her voice broke on a sob.

'I've never forced you and I never would.'

'That makes it worse. I'm knowingly committing a sin!'

'Why do you continue to do it, then?'

'Because I'm weak and because you're – you.' And because she could not help loving him, too, though she wasn't going to admit that to him.

That day he didn't take her to bed, just sat and talked to her, clasping her hand in his firm one, dropping it to gesticulate then picking it up again – once to press a very gentle kiss into the palm.

When he'd left she thought that perhaps he did love her a little, in his own way. But it made no difference. There could be no future for two people from such different backgrounds. She might have learned to speak better but she was still an ignorant Irish girl who couldn't even read properly and he was a gentleman.

She flicked through the newspaper he had brought, feeling restless and frustrated, stopping suddenly at one page because she'd seen the word Australia, a word which seemed seared into her brain. She spelled her way through an advertisement which told how much it cost to travel there. Twenty pounds! How would she ever find that much money?

But she cut out the advertisement and hid it in the drawer under her clothes. It seemed like an omen, a promise that one day she would be able to follow her sisters.

Even if that meant leaving Theo.

He stood looking down at his son. Richard wasn't a vigorous baby. He kicked his limbs half-heartedly, had to be coaxed to feed and slept badly, often waking to cry, a thin wailing sound that made Theo shiver to hear it.

'You're sure he'll be all right?' he asked the doctor who came every few days to check the infant.

'One is never sure of anything with babies, Mr Mullane, but I see no present reason to worry. He's got through the first few weeks, which are always the most dangerous, and he's gaining weight, if slowly, which is a good sign.'

'I need to go to London for a few days. I'll leave you my address and would ask you to call here every day while I'm away. Send me a telegram if anything goes wrong and I'll return immediately.'

'Very well.'

Theo stayed in the nursery and when the maid cleared her throat and looked at him anxiously, he asked, 'Is anything wrong?'

'Not exactly. It's your wife's new maid, Nancy . . . is she allowed to see Richard, sir?'

He frowned. He didn't like Nancy whom he'd met before he married Lavinia, and indeed his wife had seemed glad enough to get away from her former nanny at first. Now, the woman had regained her old hold over Lavinia. Only now he didn't care. 'Has Nancy been coming here?'

'Yes, sir. Every evening. Says your wife wants news of him.'

Theo stood thinking for a moment, then shrugged. 'I can't imagine Nancy would do him any harm. Just don't let her take him away and always stay with her while she's here.'

In fact, he met Nancy in the corridor as he left and stopped to ask, 'Why have you been coming to see Richard? Don't expect me to believe that Lavinia cares about him. She cares about no one except herself.'

Nancy looked at him assessingly. 'I wondered how he was. I like babies.'

'He's not thriving as we'd wish – as you must realise.'

'Not thriving at all.'

'What do you mean?'

Her eyes were pitying. 'No one can do the impossible, however much they love a child, Theo Mullane.'

He was shaken by her words, which had a fateful ring to them, and angry with her for voicing his own darkest fears.

To his relief, she inclined her head and walked away before the anger burst forth. He didn't want her to leave because although she looked like a witch and acted like one sometimes, since she'd come Lavinia had started behaving much more reasonably. For that relief he was more than willing to put up with the old woman's fey ways and strange moods.

But Nancy was wrong about Richard. She had to be!

'We'll go to London tomorrow,' he told Keara abruptly that evening.

'You meant it, then?'

'Of course I did.' He scowled round. 'I'm sick of meeting you in this place, but I daren't return to Ireland because it'd take too long to get back from there if – if I were needed.' And anyway, Keara had friends in Ballymullan, friends who might help her to leave him. Not to mention Father Cornelius, who would not mince his words about their immorality.

Theo drew her towards him and kissed her, feeling his worries and unhappiness slide away as he caressed her clean, sweet-smelling skin. What was it about Keara Michaels that made it feel so right?

With a sigh she rested her head against him and they simply stood there, holding one another. He had never acted like this with other women, had always kept a barrier of joviality between himself and them. With Keara he didn't have to pretend about anything.

He knew she didn't believe he loved her, and the feeling had surprised him, too, but time would show he meant it. Time and the way he treated her.

Early the following morning he visited Richard, who had had a good night and was smiling at the world, then got ready to leave. When he arrived at the cottage and saw how plainly Keara was dressed, he insisted she change into the fine new clothes he'd bought for her, threatening to put them on her himself if she didn't.

As he'd expected, that threat made her scurry up the stairs.

'Now I feel even more like your whore!' she said when she came down, standing there dressed in silk and lace, with the first crinoline she had ever owned swaying with her every movement. As she looked down she couldn't help noticing her hands. They were reddened with housework and washing, nothing like a lady's. And she found the clothes confining because she had to wear a stiff corset under them and take short steps to keep the crinoline from bouncing too much and showing her legs and petticoats.

'Don't speak like that about yourself, my darling. I think you look beautiful.'

She walked across the room and back. 'It feels strange.' She gestured down at the great bell of a skirt.

He came forward and held out a small object – a wedding ring. 'Put this on as well, Keara.'

She put her hands behind her back, backing away from him. 'No! I don't have the right to wear it!'

'Don't be foolish. It would look strange for the woman who is supposed to be my wife not to be wearing a wedding ring when we stay at a London hotel.' As she still made no effort to take it from him, he took her left hand and pushed the ring on to her third finger.

She looked down at it, wishing for a moment it were real, then telling herself not to be stupid. It seemed to burn into her flesh.

They sat quietly as the train headed south, but with so many exciting things to see and do, she could not resist asking questions about the places they were passing through. By the time they arrived she was bubbling with excitement at what she had seen already and the thought of visiting the London sights. Why, she might even see Queen Victoria herself! Even the fact that there was one of the new Smith's bookstalls on the London station made her exclaim and marvel.

Only when they got to the hotel did her former constraint return. She stood in the foyer next to Dick with downcast eyes while Theo booked their rooms and explained that his wife's maid had fallen ill.

'He's fond of you in his own way, you know,' Theo's manservant murmured.

Keara stared at him in surprise because he didn't usually interfere and, indeed, was famous in the servants' hall for keeping his feelings to himself. 'Perhaps. For the time being. But what *I* want most is to go and find my sisters, and he won't let me do that.'

'He'll find some way to bring them back, I'm sure.'

'And by that time he'll have found himself another mistress, too, so he might as well let me go to Australia myself. I'll see them so much sooner if I do.' All the servants knew how short a stay most of the women made in the cottage and Keara kept reminding herself of this.

'I think you'll last longer than most, if that's any consolation.'

'And *I* think I should never have let this start.'

He smiled gently. 'Could you have stopped it? You've always had an eye for him.'

She opened her mouth to deny it but couldn't lie to him.

Theo came across just then and held out his arm. Keara took it and let him lead her upstairs to an opulent suite which she inspected in silence.

'It's all very – grand,' she said at length.

'Don't you like it?'

'I don't like being here with you, flaunting myself in clothes like these, wearing a ring to which I don't have a right!' She flapped her left hand at him.

'Ah, Keara, let's just enjoy ourselves for a few days, shall we?'

She doubted she could forget her sisters so easily. There wasn't a day when she hadn't wept for what had happened to them. As Dick came into the room with the luggage she moved away and went to stare out of the window while he unpacked Theo's things. After the two men had left she unpacked her own, touching the beautiful materials and the lace on the under-clothing. In other circumstances she would have loved it all. But now, the garments seemed like badges of shame.

She turned as Theo came back in.

'I like seeing you properly dressed,' he said with one of his melting smiles. 'Wear the blue for dinner. It matches your eyes – well, nearly matches them. It hasn't their brilliance. You must have the most beautiful eyes in the . . . What's the matter? What have I said?'

'I've got the Michaels eyes. My sisters' eyes are just the same.' She began to sob.

He came and held her close, patting her back and making soothing noises.

She had seen the irritation on his face, quickly

though he'd banished the expression. A sudden fear of him withdrawing his help made her pull herself together and try to take an interest in his plans for showing her London.

What good did weeping do anyway?

Two days later Keara decided she must have eaten something that disagreed with her. She felt so nauseous she remained in bed, with Theo hovering beside her.

'We'll send for a doctor,' he said.

'I'll be all right by tomorrow, I'm sure. I'm rarely ill. It must be the rich food.'

'We're taking no chances.'

'Theo, please! I just want to be left alone for a while. It's nothing, I promise you.' She'd have wondered if she was carrying his child only she hadn't missed her monthly courses yet, so couldn't possibly be having morning sickness – and anyway, they both knew he didn't father children that easily. None of the other women who'd lived in the cottage had got pregnant – though he said he'd taken care that they shouldn't because he didn't want any illegitimate brats. She'd been surprised by that. But then he was contradictory in other ways: kind and yet selfish, generous with money and yet careful about small things like wasting candles. He'd take some knowing, that man. She only wished . . .

There was a knock on the door of their room and he went to open it. A pageboy was carrying a silver platter with an envelope on it.

'Telegram for you, Mr Mullane.' He offered it to Theo.

'Thank you.' He shut the door and ripped it open, exclaiming in dismay as he read the message. 'Richard's ill! I have to go back.' He looked at Keara. 'Are you well enough to travel?'

She realised immediately that this might be a chance to get away from him, perhaps her only chance for he always watched her like a hawk. She shook her head, pressing a handkerchief to her mouth as if still nauseous. 'No. I don't think that would be wise at all.'

He stood frowning down at her. 'I'm not leaving you alone in London. I'm sorry, my dear, but you'll have to come. I daren't risk delaying. Get dressed quickly while I go down to the foyer and find out the times of trains. I'm sure I saw a *Bradshaw* on the shelf behind the reception desk.'

The minute he was gone she decided to carry out one part of her escape plan, at least. She slipped out of bed and felt for the money pouch he carried in his suitcase, almost weeping with frustration when she could not at first locate it. As she pulled it out, she let out a great shuddering sigh of relief. She had never thought anyone could need so much money, but Theo always had a wallet full of notes and coins in his jacket pocket as well as this reserve supply, and seemed to think nothing of it. He was so upset about his son she doubted he'd count the money for a while, by which time she hoped to be on her way to Australia.

She sighed. She would miss him, though. Not the luxury he had brought into her life, but him, the man she loved, the one who held her close in the night and kissed away her tears.

When she looked at the contents of the pouch, she couldn't help feeling bitter. If she'd had even a few coins like these when she was younger, she could have bought food for her mother and sisters, even taken them away from Ballymullan – or stayed there herself and not had to act as maid to Lavinia Mullane. Her mother might even be alive still.

She pushed that thought aside as well. No time for regrets now. The pouch had to be back in place before Theo returned. She had already worked out how much money the Mullanes owed her in unpaid wages and quickly counted out notes and coins to that value, telling herself it wasn't really stealing, but feeling guilty nonetheless.

Just then she heard footsteps in the corridor and Theo's voice. She could not move for terror. He was going to come in and find her stealing from him!

Fumbling in her haste, she spilled a few coins, hearing them chink on the polished wooden floor at the edges of the room and hoping he couldn't hear it from outside the door.

As she began picking them up, he put the key in the door and she bit back a groan. Too late!

But then someone spoke to him and the key didn't turn. Quickly she shoved the pouch back where she had found it, closed the suitcase and pushed it back into place, then flung herself towards her clothes. Dragging off the nightgown she began to pull on her petticoats and was tying the waist strings as the key turned in the lock and the door opened. She kept her back to the door, not wanting to face him, afraid that it might show in her face that she was a thief.

Another sin committed!

'There's a train in half an hour,' he announced. 'Hurry up, so that I can bring Dick in to pack my things.'

She flung on the skirt and bodice anyhow. 'Bring him in now. I'm fit to be seen.'

'Come here, let me help you with that.'

His hands were gentle on her back as he buttoned up the tight bodice.

She almost flung herself into his arms and confessed, but Dick came into the room just then and she took a deep breath, telling herself she must think of her sisters.

Within minutes they had left the hotel. It was, Keara thought wearily, like living with a whirlwind. When Theo Mullane decided to do something, heaven help anyone who tried to stop him.

And she still felt nauseous, though she tried to hide it from him.

It couldn't mean *that*, could it?

When Theo arrived home, having dropped Keara and her luggage at the cottage, he saw the doctor's vehicle at the door and his heart gave a lurch. He shoved some money for the cab into Dick's hands with a curt, 'See to the luggage, will you?' and leaped out before the carriage had even stopped.

The doctor came out of the library as Theo turned towards the stairs. 'I need to speak to you before you go up, Mr Mullane.'

Theo swallowed hard and followed him back into the library. 'How is he?'

'Not well at all. A heavy cold.'

Theo frowned. 'A cold? Is that so serious you had to call me back?'

'For Richard it is. He isn't in any danger at the moment, but I thought you'd prefer to come home just in case he took a turn for the worse.'

'Yes, you're right. Of course you are. And I'm very grateful to you.'

The doctor hesitated, then said, 'You owe a great deal to your wife's maid as well. She took a spirit lamp into the baby's room, draped sheets around his cot and boiled water so that the cot was filled with steam to help him breathe. She's a very capable nurse.'

Theo nodded, only really interested in seeing his son. 'I'll go up and see him.'

He found Nancy sitting by the bed.

She put one finger to her lips and jerked her head in the direction of the nursemaid's adjoining bedroom. 'She's been awake most of the night with him.'

'I believe I owe you my thanks.'

She nodded. 'We saved him this time, but it was touch and go. I doubt he's strong enough to survive another crisis.'

They stared at one another.

'I told you once not to marry Lavinia,' she continued in her dry old voice. 'You and she don't suit, either in temperament or in physical make-up. But you *will* get a child one day, Theo Mullane, I promise you that.' She half-closed her eyes. 'I can see your little daughter very clearly. And she will be healthy.' She smiled as if watching some scene. 'A little minx, in fact.'

He felt a shiver run down his spine at the strange light in her eyes, and for a moment he believed her then grew annoyed at himself. 'Save your fortune telling for those more credulous than me. Though I do thank you for your care of Richard.'

She shrugged as she sat down again by the cradle.

'Is there anything I can do?' he asked after a minute of watching his son's face. 'Anything at all?'

'Not now. He'll be with you for a while longer.'

He went across and bent to kiss the child, then walked out again, leaving the house without speaking to the servants and seeking refuge in the woods. He didn't want to see anyone, not even Keara. He just wanted to walk off some of the pain. Was it really only a few weeks since his son had been born? Richard seemed a part of him now, such an important part.

Nancy couldn't be right. Surely no one could predict the future? But she'd seemed utterly certain of what she had said. He remembered his son's flushed little face and weak crying. Terror flooded through him. What would he do if he lost this child?

He wished Nancy had not returned, didn't keep setting such thoughts in his mind. Even the doctor refused to speak with any certainty of the baby surviving. But Nancy had offered him the hope of a daughter, at least. Dare he believe in that? And whose daughter? Keara's face seemed to hover in front of him. Ah, but he'd like a child with her.

His thoughts in a tangle, he stayed for a long time staring into the stream without seeing a thing, and was so chilled by the time he returned to the house that Dick scolded him for not looking after himself.

'Maybe you should go and visit Keara?' he suggested.

Theo shook his head. 'No. Not tonight.' He didn't want to see anyone, needed to come to terms with the possibility that his son might not live or the loss would destroy him.

Dear God, why?

Alone at the cottage Keara unpacked her fine new clothes and also decided to go for a walk in the woods. She had spent so much time indoors lately she felt stifled.

She walked for a good hour, keeping away from the house. She saw people in the distance but met no one, which was what she wanted. The peace of the woods on this still, mild day in January was balm to her soul. Even like this, without leaves, she thought the trees beautiful. Soon they would start making fat buds then spring would burst forth in a haze of palest green.

Would she still be here then? Still here and living in sin?

She didn't know, not now she had some money. Theo had told her the world was shaped like a ball and Australia was right on the other side of it, so far away that it would take at least three months for a ship to carry a letter there and as long again for a reply to come back. It was hard even to imagine distances like that.

But it would only take three months for her to get there and that would be a much quicker way of contacting her sisters. She *had to* escape from Theo and from the spell he seemed to have cast over her. Had to. Or she would be betraying everything her mother had done for her.

As she walked back towards the cottage, chilled now and hungry, she saw a figure approaching, an old woman. She would have walked past her with a nod, but the woman stopped and held out one arm to bar her way.

'You're Keara Michaels, aren't you?'

'If you know, why do you ask?'

'I ask because I'm Lavinia's new maid.' She choked with rusty laughter. 'Old maid, too. I was her nursemaid once.'

Keara drew back.

'She's wronged you, I know, but she doesn't understand. She's a strange one, should never have married but stayed with me instead. No one can look after her as I can.' She studied Keara's face. 'Yes, she's wronged you deeply and you're very sad.'

'Will you let me pass, please?'

'In a minute, lass. Will you invite me to come and drink a cup of tea with you one day, then read the tea leaves? I can sometimes see the future.'

Keara knew that Father Cornelius would have told her to stay away from a woman like this, but was tempted by the thought of finding out if she would be reunited with her sisters. 'You can do that? Read the future?'

'Sometimes. What do you want to know?'

'If I'll get to Australia. If I'll see my sisters again.'

'I may be able to tell you that.'

'All right. Come and visit me.'

Nancy nodded. 'I'll wait until Mr Mullane's gone into town then walk across to your cottage.' Without any word of farewell she walked away.

Keara watched her go and shivered as an icy wind began to tease the edges of her clothing. The sky was looking heavy with clouds and the air seemed to be getting colder by the minute. She wouldn't be surprised if it started snowing. Well, that wouldn't make much difference to her. She was a prisoner here whatever the weather, held fast by a net of hope that Theo would find her sisters for her – and by the lack of anywhere else to turn.

As she walked back, she could not stop thinking about Lavinia's maid. Such a strange woman. Keara began to feel worried about agreeing to see her again. How could she trust someone so close to Lavinia? And there was something about the old woman that made you feel uncomfortable, that planted a sense of unease in you.

As if she really could see the future.

As if she even understood what you were thinking.

The first snowflakes were falling as Keara reached the cottage, but that wasn't what made her shiver.

★

'Well, did you see her?' Lavinia asked when her maid returned.

'I did, my chickie, I did.'

'And what do you think of her?'

'I think she's a nice enough lass.'

'Ha! If she were really nice, she'd be here with me still.'

'Then I wouldn't be here. I prefer it this way.'

Lavinia bit her lip. She had forgotten how Nancy always twisted your words, how she could never fool the old woman about anything or get the better of her. But on the other hand, Nancy looked after her just as well as Keara had and was helping her make plans for the future, talking of houses and making it seem a good idea to leave this place and live separately from Theo. She always had been able to cheer Lavinia up.

'There is one thing,' Nancy said abruptly. 'Keara's carrying his child.'

'*What?*'

'You heard me.'

'She can't be! He's only known her a short time. She's fooling him. It's someone else's.'

'I doubt it. She's not the cheating sort. The thing is, do you want her to stay here and give him a fine healthy child, or do you want to send her away before he finds out?'

Lavinia leaned forward eagerly. 'You can do that? Send her away?'

'Yes. She wants to go to Australia, to chase after those sisters of hers that you sent there.'

'Let her go.'

'She can't do it without our help, so you'll have to give me some money.'

'As much as you need.'

But when Nancy went over to take tea with Keara two days later, she didn't even get into the cottage.

'I've thought better of it.' The girl stood squarely in the doorway and made no attempt to invite her visitor in.

'Why?'

'Because reading tea leaves is the devil's work and I'm committing enough sins. Besides, I don't trust you. Why should you help me when you're working for *her*.' Keara slammed the door quickly before the other woman could say anything else.

Nancy sighed and walked away. It would have made things easier if she could have won Keara Michaels' trust.

When she got back to the house, she went to join Lavinia in her private parlour.

'Well? You weren't gone long. Did you speak to her?'

'She's changed her mind. Won't have anything to do with me.'

Lavinia's face creased as if she was about to cry.

'No tears!' Nancy said sharply.

'But you said you'd send her away.'

'And so I will, my chickie. But I'll have to send for our Fred now and do it by force.'

Lavinia's expression was gleeful. 'Good. Serves her right.' In fact, this way was much more satisfying. Let the girl suffer. She deserved it!

Richard recovered fully from his cold and even put on a little weight again so Theo went into Manchester to see a property broker about selling his estate, anxious to be done with Lavinia and move himself and his son to the peace and beauty of Ireland.

As soon as Mr Mullane had left for Manchester, Nancy sent a message to her nephew Fred and his friend, who had been waiting in a nearby village. They drove a hired carriage to the other side of the estate and made their way quietly through the woods, taking the path Fred's aunt had shown him the previous day. When they got to the cottage, they found Nancy waiting for them out of sight among the trees.

'You come with me to the door, our Fred. Your friend can wait nearby till we've got inside,' she said in her abrupt way. 'And remember, you're not to hurt her.'

When Keara opened the door, she frowned to see Nancy there again. 'I haven't changed my mind. I'm not having anything to do with you.'

As she tried to close the door, Fred moved from one side where he'd been hiding, shoved it open and grabbed her.

Keara tried to fend him off, but he was a strong man and even as she was struggling, another man came running up and helped drag her inside. 'What are you doing?' she cried to Nancy.

'Sending you to Australia,' the old woman said. 'It's where you want to go, after all.'

'I don't believe you.'

'I don't tell lies. And stop fighting us. Do you want to hurt the child you're carrying?'

Keara stilled, staring at her in shock. 'How do you know?'

'I can always tell. It's a gift I have.' She turned to her nephew. 'Tie her up while we get things ready. The less time she has to spend drugged the better.' She got out a small blue bottle and set it on the table, saw the terror on Keara's face and said curtly, 'It's only laudanum. Won't hurt you or the baby.' Then she walked upstairs, leaving the two men to keep an eye on their prisoner.

'Please don't do this to me,' Keara begged, but they didn't even turn their heads to look at her.

One man made himself at home, brewing a pot of strong tea and drinking a mug of it with great relish. Neither man so much as looked at her, whatever she said, so in the end she stopped pleading with them. But she couldn't help feeling afraid and kept hoping Theo would come back early. Nothing happened except the sound of footsteps moving to and fro upstairs. What was the old woman doing up there?

When Nancy came down she was carrying Keara's travelling bag. She too ignored the young woman, saying to the two men, 'There's a trunk upstairs. Go and fetch it down.' She went to the table and measured out a dose from the bottle, putting it into a small blue glass.

Keara felt her fear turn to sheer terror that had her

heart pounding in her chest. Were they going to poison her now? Kill her?

Nancy looked at her as if she knew what she was thinking. 'I told you: it's not poison, just laudanum to put you to sleep. This would all have been much easier if you'd listened to me in the first place.'

'Theo will be furious with you. He'll come after me.'

Nancy smiled. 'He won't know what's happened to you. And he'll be too busy with his son. Does he know about your child?'

Keara didn't answer.

'I can see from your face he doesn't. Why haven't you told him about it?

'I wasn't sure yet.'

'No, that's not the reason. You guessed he'd never let you go if he knew. But you *want* to go after your sisters. Will you swallow this for me?'

'No!'

She beckoned her nephew. 'Come and hold her for me, Fred.'

Keara squirmed and struggled, but to no avail. When Nancy pinched her nostrils together, she tried not to open her mouth but in the end had to gasp in some air. The liquid slid down her throat and although she choked and coughed, Fred held her until Nancy was sure it would stay down.

'You'll soon be asleep and when you wake up you'll be on your way to Australia. Let that thought comfort you. It's what you want, after all.' Nancy stared at her for a moment longer, then turned to the table. 'Is there any tea left in that pot, lads? I'm that thirsty.'

Incredulous at their indifference, Keara watched her sit down and pour herself a cup. As the room began to waver and blur around her, the fear dulled a little, but she still wondered if it really were laudanum or if she had been poisoned and was dying.

She had never felt so helpless in her whole life. Her last thought was of Theo.

Two days later Lavinia looked up as Nancy came back into the bedroom. 'Well, is there any news?'

'Yes. She's on her way now. And you can't get much further away than Australia. We fell lucky with that ship leaving just when we needed it. Which shows this was meant to be. When our Fred booked her passage he told them she'd be late boarding, and when they took her there they pretended she was drunk. He greased a few palms and got her on board without having to see the doctor. Some folk'll do owt if you pay them well enough.'

'And Theo won't know what's happened to her?'

'Not unless you tell him.'

Lavinia scowled. 'I'll never do that. He'll not even know he has another child – but I will.' She tittered, then her expression turned sulky again. 'He never speaks to me these days, won't even share meals with me, let alone go out with me. I might as well not exist. And if I go out on my own, people stare.'

'Well, let them stare, chickie. I've heard about a house that's for sale in the town, just right for you and me. Not too big, but elegant. If you live there you'll have lots of things to see and do, and you'll be able to see your friends every day, or pop out and go shopping any time you want. If you tell the right story about this, how your husband has abandoned you and sold your own home from under you, people will be very sympathetic towards you.'

A smile wreathed Lavinia's plump face. 'They will, won't they?'

Soon she was talking eagerly of how they'd furnish their house, what they'd do with themselves.

Nancy encouraged her and gave no more thought to Keara. She'd done what she had to and now she must look after the girl she had raised, the girl who had never quite grown into a woman.

The Hardwicks had been wrong to take Lavinia away from her, but it was too late now to worry about that.

When Theo came home from Manchester, he ate a quick meal then went up to change his clothes. 'I'm going to see Keara,' he told Dick. 'Don't wait up for me.' He walked through the woods feeling his heart lift at the thought of being with her again. It was like this every time. She had quickly become so important to him that he could not now imagine life without her. He didn't want just to use her body, but to be with her, make her happy. He had the idea, fanciful though it seemed, that his love for her would be the making of him.

When he got to the cottage, he saw the door

swinging to and fro in the breeze, which made him feel suddenly afraid. Why had she left it open on such a cold day? He rushed inside calling, 'Keara! Keara, where are you?'

There was no answer, no sense of her presence even, and the whole house felt icy, as if the door had been open for some time. He quickly searched the two downstairs rooms, seeing several cups sitting dirty on the table and wondering who could have been visiting her. Upstairs he found her bedroom in chaos, with some of her richer clothes lying in a heap at the side of the room, while all her simpler clothes and underclothing were gone.

On a sudden thought he rushed up the narrow stairs to the attic, but there was no sign of her trunk or travelling bag. He clattered down again, looking for a note, walking from room to room now, forcing himself to take the time to check carefully. Surely she'd left him a note?

But she hadn't.

There was only one place she could have gone: Australia. How had she found the money for that? Or made the booking? He'd have sworn she never left the cottage except to walk in the woods.

Did she have friends in town who'd helped her? She'd never even hinted at any.

In the kitchen he searched yet again, unable to believe she wouldn't at least have left him a farewell note. When he found the pile of money on the mantelpiece, he stared at it in chill dismay. Surely she wouldn't have left without all her money?

He hesitated for a moment longer, then, terrified for

her safety, set off running back to the big house. He didn't believe she'd have taken her own life. She wouldn't do that. For a Catholic, that was an even worse sin than becoming his mistress.

But where had she gone? And who with? Wherever it was, he'd find her. He'd send men out to look. It didn't matter what it cost him, he'd find her again and bring her back.

He couldn't live without her. Wouldn't even try.

CHAPTER FOURTEEN

January 1864

On a hot day in January two men got off the stage coach from Melbourne at Rossall Springs. The older one was dressed in black, with his hat pulled well down. The younger one was dressed in dusty brown, had a rather blank expression on his face and was carrying a small travelling bag. They took a room at the hotel and stayed in it until dusk when they went out for a stroll round the town.

The following morning they left their bag at the livery stables, which was also the depot where the stage coach stopped, showing their tickets to Melbourne.

'We're just going to stretch our legs, but we'll be back before the coach gets here,' the older man said. As they walked off down the street, he said, 'You remember what to do, Joseph?'

'Yes, Mr Jenner.' The younger one walked beside him, his eyes vacant and lacklustre.

'I'll take the child and you will tell the woman not to follow us or you'll hit her.'

'But I couldn't hit her,' Joseph protested, as he had done several times that morning. 'Dad says I haven't to hit people.'

'You don't have to hit her, just say you will.'

'My dad won't like that.'

Alex breathed deeply and prayed for patience. Joseph was very strong in body, but the Lord had not given him many wits. 'She won't know that. You're big enough to frighten anyone. So do as I say and pretend you're going to hit her. Just pretend. All right?'

'Pretend.' Joseph nodded, but he looked unhappy and a bit bewildered.

'You remember the way back to the livery stable?'

He looked uncertain.

'You have to come back to where the horses are.'

Joseph's face lit up. 'I like horses.'

'Yes. So afterwards, come and find the horses. I'll be waiting for you.'

Joseph nodded again, but continued to look worried.

When they got to the Johnsons' house, Alex led the way inside without bothering to knock.

Kalaya looked up in shock as two men erupted into her home, recognising the older one at once. 'What do you want?'

'Shut up!' Alex slapped her viciously across the face then turned to snatch the baby from its cradle. He walked out again without even looking at her.

She moved instinctively to protect her own children, who were now cowering in a corner, eyes wide with terror.

The younger man followed him to the door and at a whispered order said, 'If you try to follow us, I'll – I'll hit you.'

Kalaya froze. It was a long time since a white man had threatened violence and she knew better than to fight back, especially against one as huge as this young man. But she was terrified for the poor baby and couldn't understand what the wild-eyed grandfather wanted with Amy.

The minute the younger man had left the house, she dashed to the front door and shot the bolt. Through the window she watched him hurry off down the dusty street after the older one.

Once they had both turned the corner, she shouted to the children, 'Stay here!' and dashed out of the house. She ran as fast as she could towards the eating house, taking the back way, terrified of meeting the men again. Whites didn't care if black people got hurt – well, most of them didn't. But Mark had been kind to her and she loved the baby. How could you not? Babies didn't care what colour your skin was.

Where was that man taking Amy? And why?

He wouldn't hurt her, would he?

When Kalaya burst into the kitchen, out of breath and sobbing, Mark dropped his chopping knife and rushed across to her. 'What's the matter?'

'The old man, the crazy one . . . he came back with another man and took Amy . . . knocked me aside and snatched her out of the cradle. The younger one threatened to hit me if I followed . . . I waited till they were out of sight and ran here the back way.'

'Where did they go?'

'Towards the main street.'

'Go home, Kalaya. I'll deal with this. Ginny, you get on with the cooking.'

She watched them go open-mouthed, then shook her head and carried on cutting up the meat.

Mark arrived in the main street just in time to see the stage coach for Melbourne disappearing into the distance. He ran across to the livery stable and found out that two men and a baby had indeed boarded the stage coach.

'They've stolen my child,' he said. 'I need a horse, quickly.'

The clerk, an elderly man who sometimes came to the eating house for meals, stood gaping at him. 'Stolen your child?'

'Yes. Hurry, will you?'

'All the horses are out, Mr Gibson. There's only the stage-coach horses and they're exhausted.'

'You must have something! They've taken my child!'

'There isn't a fresh horse in the place.'

Mark looked round and saw a gig outside with a man sitting in the driving seat. He ran across to him and again explained what had happened.

'The old devil! Let me just tell my wife and we'll go after them.' The man jumped down and vanished into the shop, coming out almost immediately while two women came to watch them leave from the shop doorway.

'You be careful, Tommy!' called one.

Mark tried to contain his impatience as Tommy urged the horse to start moving.

Only when they had vanished from sight did the clerk from the livery stables regain his wits. He rushed outside and began yelling for someone to fetch the constable. As people gathered round him, clamouring to be told what had happened, two young men looked at one another and went for their horses, galloping off after the gig, eager for a bit of excitement.

By this time the stage coach was out of sight and even the dust of its passage had died down. Mark sat and fidgeted beside Tommy as they jogged along behind the elderly mare.

'I'm sorry. Bessie's getting on and can't go any faster. But we'll catch up with them, don't you worry.'

Mark nodded, his eyes on the road ahead, worried sick about his baby daughter.

The poor horse laboured up the hills and kept trying to slow down into an ambling gait. The two young men caught up with them and fell in behind, joking and laughing. Mark wondered whether to ask them to go ahead and stop the stage coach, but caught a glimpse of it in the distance just then. 'There it is!' he called.

'Haroo!' yelled one young man.

'Shut up, you silly fool,' Tommy snapped. 'This isn't a game. There's a baby been stolen. And we don't want to upset the driver and make him think we're bushrangers, do we? If they go galloping off, my poor old Bess will never catch up with them again. You can see how tired she's getting.'

Gradually, so slowly that Mark felt he could run more quickly, they drew nearer to the lumbering stage coach. When the guard picked up his rifle and turned to sight it at them, Mark stood up and yelled, 'It's only me!' For a moment nothing happened, then the driver turned round, recognised him and reined in.

Even before the gig came to a halt, Mark jumped down and tore open the coach door.

Alex Jenner was already on his feet at the other side of the vehicle, with Amy in his arms. The leather curtain of the window was rolled up because of the heat and he held her little body towards the gap. 'If you try to take her from me, I'll dash her brains out. Better dead than raised by a heathen-lover like you.'

The burly younger man who had accompanied him was cowering in the opposite corner, whimpering, one arm raised protectively to cover his face as if he were expecting someone to hit him. The other passengers stayed motionless in their seats, goggling, their eyes going from one man to another.

Amy began to squall loudly and to jerk about.

For a moment Mark couldn't think what to do, then he saw the guard approaching the window behind Alex. 'You'd kill an innocent child?' he demanded, trying to keep the old man's attention focused on him not the guard.

'She's the fruit of sin and I'm taking her to salvation.' Again Alex held Amy out towards the window then growled under his breath as he saw the guard standing a couple of paces away from him.

Mark hesitated to move, terrified that something might happen to his daughter.

Alex muttered something to the young man who was with him and the latter opened the other coach door. The guard directly outside hesitated.

'Get back or she dies!' Alex held the baby up by her feet, which made her start wailing loudly in terror. There were soft sounds of dismay from the other passengers and he laughed at this.

Suddenly the younger man's face crumpled and he began sobbing and mumbling, 'Don't kill her! Don't kill her!'

'Shut up, you fool!'

An elderly lady who was sitting nearest to Alex used his momentary lapse of attention to snatch Amy. He yelled loudly and began to rain down blows on her as he tried to grab the baby. She turned her back to shield the child and the guard darted forward to the door. He tried to haul a yelling, protesting Alex Jenner through it.

'Someone help me!' he called as Alex fought with maniacal strength.

Mark rushed to his aid and together they got him out and away from the baby.

'You were with him,' another passenger said accusingly to the young man, who was still cowering and moaning in his corner. 'Get out this minute! And don't dare try to help your friend.'

Joseph got out on the opposite side to the struggle, protesting, 'Not my friend. Dad says I have to do as Mr Jenner says, but he's *not* my friend.'

The old lady cuddled the wailing baby and watched through the window as the guard and Mark subdued Alex, who was still struggling and shouting at the top of his voice. In the end they managed to tie his arms and legs with some rope the driver threw down to them. The guard stood up, panting and dusty, looked at Mark and tapped his forehead.

The old lady leaned out of the window and said it openly. 'He's raving mad.' She looked down at the baby, who had stopped sobbing and was looking for food. 'Well, you're a bonny little babby, aren't you? What did the nasty man do to you, eh?'

Mark went to the door of the coach. 'Thank you for saving my daughter, ma'am.'

'Why did he take her?'

'He's her grandfather. My wife died and now he wants the child.'

She looked out of the coach window at the man still writhing on the ground. 'He should be locked away.'

'I'm beginning to believe so.' Mark held out his arms and watched as she dropped a kiss on the baby's forehead before handing Amy over.

The young men who had followed them from town, but who had been conspicuously absent when it came to a struggle, promised to stay with Mr Jenner until the constable came.

'Untie me at once,' Alex yelled.

'Don't untie him, whatever he says,' Mark warned grimly.

'We won't,' one of them said, stepping back hastily to avoid Alex's flailing feet.

He wriggled round on the ground and called to his erstwhile companion, 'Joseph, come and set me free this minute!'

'Don't you dare untie him!' Mark shouted.

The young man took a step forward, hesitated and looked at the men warily.

'He's a big brute, but he doesn't seem violent,' one of the young men said. 'Why don't you take him back to town with you, then he can't help the old man?'

'There isn't room in the gig,' the driver said at once. 'My Bessie's exhausted. She's not pulling that big chap as well.'

'We'll have to keep an eye on him for you, then. You! Go and sit under that tree.'

Joseph looked from one to the other and shambled away, flopping down in a heap in the shade, muttering, '*Not* my friend.'

Mark held Amy close while Tommy drove them back into town. The baby seemed to have forgotten her fright, though there were still traces of tears on her face. He would never forget it and still kept seeing Alex holding her up by the feet. Even the memory of that made him shudder. 'I can't thank you enough for your help,' he said as the mare ambled towards town.

Tommy shrugged and grinned. 'Wife'll be glad to get the news early. Loves a gossip, my Lucy does.'

On the way into town they met Constable Snebble riding out to see what was going on and stopped to explain exactly what had happened.

'Send a cart out to bring him back,' he said, sighing. 'Don't care whose cart it is, but send one. I'll go and see what the fellow has to say for himself and then bring the two of them back to town. Last thing I needed today was trouble.' With another aggrieved sigh he rode on.

By the time the constable got there, Alex was much calmer and when untied spoke politely and at length about a grandfather's natural distaste at seeing his only grandchild being brought up by a native when Amy's grandmother would love to look after her.

Constable Snebble rubbed his chin, not liking to agree with a prisoner but fully sharing the old man's sentiments about natives. Though the Johnsons were better than most. Knew their place and lived quietly.

After they got back to town, Alex continued to speak moderately and to worry about his granddaughter being brought up by 'a woman like that'. Knowing that many of the townsfolk were in sympathy with this viewpoint, Constable Snebble suggested that Mark shouldn't press charges.

'But he tried to kidnap her!'

'There's some sympathy in town for his reasons. It'll only stir up trouble. Not be good for your business.'

Mark stared at him in frustration, disgusted that a man supposed to uphold the law could want to take this easy way out.

'It's best that way,' Constable Snebble coaxed. 'Look, I'll give him a stern warning not to do such a thing again and send him back to Melbourne.'

'I'm not happy with this.'

'It's for the best.'

'Do what you think, then.' Mark was furious. How could people talk of Kalaya so scornfully? She was an excellent mother, a gentle person who had never done anyone any harm. And she was, in his opinion, far saner than Alex Jenner. 'But I want to be there when you warn him.' He didn't even trust Snebble to do that properly.

As the constable read him a stern warning and Mark stood glowering, Alex bowed his head and pretended to listen but inside he was jubilant. Afterwards he agreed to be locked up in his hotel room until the next coach left for Melbourne the following day. He smiled at his son-in-law as he was shown out and said quietly as he passed, 'But I shall come back soon to visit my granddaughter. Perhaps I'll bring my wife next time. She's very eager to hold the child in her arms again.'

He might be smiling but there was such a chill light in his eyes that Mark shivered. At that moment he realised he'd have to leave Rossall Springs and go somewhere the Jenners could never find him if he was to keep his daughter safe from this lunatic.

He carried Amy to Kalaya's for a feed, then took her home with him. 'I can't put you in danger again, Mrs Johnson. I'll keep her with me, except for feeds, until they've left town, then bring her back to stay with you, if that's all right?'

She looked at him with sympathy. 'He's got bad thoughts, that old man. Hard for you, eh?'

'Yes. Very. I hope he didn't hurt you?'

'A bruise or two. That's nothing.'

He clasped her hand in both of his. 'You were wonderful. But as soon as Amy's old enough to manage without your help, I'll have to leave Rossall.'

She nodded and sadness came over her face. 'Sometimes it's better to leave than to stay and live in danger.'

He guessed then that she and her husband had faced hostility on their own account and had also chosen to move on. 'I wouldn't leave if it were just me, but I don't want Amy to live in danger.'

Her eyes went to her own children. 'We felt the same once. And at least in this town no one attacks us or ill-treats us as long as we live quietly and soberly.'

'How do you stand it?'

'What choice do we have?' She looked down at Amy. 'She won't have to face the problems my children will.'

'She also won't have a mother to protect and love her, as yours do.'

'I can love them, yes, but I can't do much to protect them from—' She shrugged and gestured towards the town.

He walked slowly back to his home and business, wondering if anyone in Rossall would like to buy it, feeling adrift again as he had on the ship coming to Australia. Would he never be able to settle anywhere in peace?

That night he sat and earnestly considered whether he should go back to England. Poor Nelly was dead and he'd be quite safe from Alex Jenner in Bilsden, with his family all around him. Then he grimaced and shook his head. No. He wasn't sure when the change had taken place, but he'd grown used to Australia, loved the sunshine and the big wide sky, the fact that parrots flew around wild, whole flocks of them, and even in winter it didn't snow except in the mountains. And anyway, he didn't want to go running back with his tail between his legs.

But – he faced it squarely, having heard the same thing from other migrants – if he stayed here, he would pay for that choice for the rest of his life by being cut off from the brothers and sisters he loved. And from his father.

It wouldn't be easy either way.

And if anything happened to his father before Mark saw him again and received John Gibson's forgiveness in person, it would break his heart. But he had abandoned one daughter, he wasn't going to abandon the other. If he had to be mother and father to Amy, he would.

When Dick got back after three days spent searching for Keara, Theo took one look at his expression and led the way into the library, slamming the door shut on the rest of the household. 'What took you so long and where is she? Couldn't you find her?' His voice cracked on the words.

'I think she's on her way to Australia. I made enquiries at the shipping office in London, but no ship had sailed from there during the past week. They said one had left Liverpool, so I went there.' Dick hesitated.

'And?'

'I believe Keara sailed on the *Silver Princess* the day after she left here.'

'You believe? You're not sure?'

'The agent assured me that there had been no last-minute passengers, let alone a Keara Michaels. But I felt he was lying, so I asked around, bought a few drinks for a fellow who seemed to know everyone and he introduced me to one of the dockside workers who'd been loading last-minute luggage and supplies on the *Silver Princess*. It seems a woman was carried on board a few hours before the ship left and her luggage with her. She was unconscious and smelled very strongly of gin. He said she had dark hair but he couldn't see her face. Two men carried her to the ship and they seemed to be drunk as well. They kept telling everyone they'd all been having a farewell party.'

'Keara doesn't drink.' Theo thumped the flat of his hand down on the arm of his chair. 'And if she was unconscious, it means she didn't go willingly. But who would have had a reason to get rid of her?'

Dick shook his head. The only one he could think of was Theo's wife, but it wasn't his place to say that. 'It was too late to go after her, but the ship *was* going to Australia, which is where she wanted to go.'

Theo stared at his friend with sheer misery in his eyes. 'I don't understand what's happened, but if Lavinia has had a hand in it, I'll—' He broke off, unable to wait a minute longer to find out, rushing from the room, leaving the door open behind him.

Dick stood watching him in amazement. He had never seen Theo behave like this about a woman, especially a decent young girl who didn't really want to be anyone's mistress however fond she was of Theo, and no one could doubt her feelings for him. Even the way she looked at him betrayed her love. In Dick's opinion, sending her to Australia was the best solution to the dilemma because Keara had been fretting about her sisters.

Upstairs, Theo burst into his wife's bedroom just as Nancy was getting her undressed.

Lavinia screamed and started throwing things the minute she saw him, but he dodged the hail of items from her dressing table and grabbed hold of her. 'Stop this! I don't want to get into your bed, you stupid bitch, I just want to know about Keara.'

She stilled, open-mouthed. 'You ask *me* about your mistress? How should I know anything about her? I never want to see that ungrateful wretch again.'

'Did you have her kidnapped? Send her away to Australia?'

'Why would I send her away? I don't want *you* back in my bed. As far as I'm concerned, you and your whore are welcome to each other.'

He let go of her, stepping back. 'My apologies for disturbing you.' At the door he turned. 'You can be quite sure I shan't be trying to get back into your bed again.' Then he looked across at the maid. It could only be her, then.

Nancy gazed steadily back at him, head slightly tilted, looking like a crow in her rusty black gown.

'I'd like to speak to you after you've put your mistress to bed, Nancy.' He turned on his heel and went back downstairs, fidgeting about, waiting.

'Don't tell him she's expecting his child. Promise

me you won't tell him that.' Lavinia said as soon as the door closed behind him. She loved the thought of him not knowing.

'I won't tell him.' It wouldn't make any difference in the long run, anyway.

That seemed to satisfy Lavinia, who returned to her main anxiety. 'He won't want to come back into my bed, will he? And if he does try, you won't let him, will you?'

'No, chickie. He'll never pester you again.' She watched as Lavinia stood up and stretched her arms to have the dressing gown taken from them, then walked slowly across to the bed. The bluish tinge around her nursling's lips was more pronounced now and Nancy knew Lavinia's health was more precarious than anyone realised. The young woman she'd brought into the world, and whom she loved more than anyone or anything else, could perhaps live for a few years but not much longer – or she could die the next day.

Dick was waiting for Theo in the library, pacing up and down, worried about him. 'Did you find anything out?'

'Only that my wife knows nothing. I've asked Nancy to come down and speak to me. It can only be her.' With a groan, he sat down and leaned his head against the chair back. After a minute or two, he asked, 'What must Keara be thinking?'

There was a knock on the door and when he called out, Nancy came in, looking perfectly composed.

Dick turned to leave.

'Stay!' Theo ordered.

Nancy looked from one to the other. 'Half-brothers,' she said suddenly. 'Didn't you ever realise?'

Theo looked at her in shock, then across at Dick. Why had he not seen it before? They were of similar height and colouring, though Dick was a bit thinner and not quite as tall. To his surprise, the other man was grinning. 'Did you know?'

Dick nodded. 'Yes. My mother told me a few years ago.'

'Why did you never say?'

'What difference would it have made?'

'A lot.' Then he swung round to face Nancy. 'If you're trying to distract me, you won't succeed. I want to know what you did with Keara.'

'Can I sit down while we talk? I've had a hard day.'

He waved her towards a chair and watched as she settled down and stared into the fire.

'Keara?' he prompted.

She sighed. 'I sent her where she wanted to go, Australia. That's where her destiny lies. Yours, too.'

'Don't be stupid. I've no intention of going out to Australia. It's Ireland I'll be moving back to when we sell this place.'

She smiled and gave a half-shrug. 'Whatever you say, sir.'

'Is that the only reason?' he asked in bewilderment. 'You sent Keara away because you read her future in the tea leaves or some such nonsense?'

'I didn't need the leaves. It was strong in her, the desire to find her sisters. But her being there was upsetting Lavinia. You shouldn't keep mistresses so close to the house.' She raised her eyes to meet his. 'My main reason was to right the wrong Lavinia did those two girls. But good will come of it, you'll see.'

'So Keara was drugged and put on the *Silver Princess*?'

She nodded. 'Only laudanum. And she wasn't hurt in any way.'

'I don't think I'll ever forgive you for that, Nancy.' Theo waved one hand in dismissal. If his wife weren't so dependent on the old woman, he'd send Nancy packing this very night.

She hesitated, then laid something on the table. 'This is her money. I'm not a thief.'

When the door closed behind her, Theo picked up the purse and tipped it out on the small table beside him. 'Oh, hell! She'll arrive there penniless. How is she going to look for her sisters without money? My family has done nothing but harm her.' He glanced across at Dick and the knowledge of their relationship made him admit, 'If it weren't for Richard, I'd go after her and bring them all back. I love her, Dick. After years of Lavinia, she was – wonderful.'

'But she wasn't happy as your mistress,' the other man said quietly. 'That always worried me –' he hesitated, then added '– sir.'

'No! Don't call me sir again. Never again. My name's Theo, as you well know.'

Dick inclined his head. He'd promised his mother not to tell Theo, but was glad someone else had.

Theo stared down at the pattern on the rug, feeling guilty – a guilt he'd been refusing to acknowledge for weeks. Even if he went after Keara, which was what he really wanted to do, he still couldn't offer her marriage and the respectability she both craved and deserved. He realised Dick had spoken and looked up. 'Sorry. What did you say?'

'I asked if you wanted to send someone after her to Australia? If so, I'll go.'

Theo took a long, shaky breath, then shook his head. 'Not unless I hear she's in trouble. I think all I can do now for her is let her go.'

'There's just one other thing you ought to know before you decide.'

'Yes?'

'That ship was going to Western Australia, which is on the other side of the continent from where her sisters were sent. It's getting on for two thousand miles away from the colony of Victoria.'

Theo groaned aloud. 'Do you think Nancy did this on purpose?'

Dick considered it briefly, then shook his head. 'No. She's not an educated woman. She probably didn't realise.'

'What the hell am I going to do? I can't just leave Keara stranded there. She has no money.'

'You could send some out to your cousin Caley and ask him to pass it on to her. The Gallaghers went to Western Australia too, didn't they?'

Theo stared at him. 'I'm a fool! I hadn't even thought of them.' Had only been able to think of Keara, alone and frightened. 'I could do that, though, couldn't I?' he said slowly. 'It's the only thing I can think of to do for her now.' And he felt like weeping from the frustration of it.

Nothing would fill the great hole she'd leave in his life, even after such a short time. And he had lost his taste for other women since he'd been with Keara, hadn't seen a single one whom he considered even vaguely attractive. He smiled wryly to himself. He was turning into the faithful sort, could have been happy with Keara and her alone. The smile faded. Only it wasn't possible.

His son needed him here.

CHAPTER FIFTEEN

January–May 1864

Keara tried to open her eyes and sit up, but her body would not obey her and all she could do was lie there and wait for the muzzy grey cloud to lift from her brain. Had she been ill? Where was she? The bed she was lying on was narrow and hard, and the room seemed to be swaying around her.

'She's coming to,' a voice said nearby. 'Shall I fetch Matron?'

'Not yet. The poor lass will be a while yet before she can speak properly.'

'Poor lass, my foot! She must have drunk a gallon of gin. I never saw anyone take so long to get over a party. I don't know what they're doing, putting a drunkard in with the rest of us.'

'I'm not sure she is a drunkard. Her clothes smelled of gin but her breath smells of something else, something sweetish.' The woman clicked her fingers suddenly. 'I know what it is! Laudanum. My mother-in-law used it.'

'Maggie Brett, do you always think the best of

people? You even think Matron's all right when she's an absolute ogre. And anyway, you saw this creature come on board with your own eyes. The sailors had to carry her down here and she *reeked* of gin.'

'We'll see.'

After some careful breaths Keara forced her eyes open and stared around. Her head was aching and she was parched with thirst. 'Water,' she croaked.

'Got it here, love. Have a sip or two. No, no more for a minute. Let that settle in your stomach first. We don't want you being sick, do we? I'm Maggie, by the way. What's your first name?'

'Keara.'

'Right, then, Keara Dixon. Do you feel sick?'

'No. Just thirsty.'

'Try another sip or two.'

A shadow fell across them and with a further effort Keara turned her head to find a buxom, stern-faced woman dressed in severe navy blue frowning at her from a doorway.

'So you've come to at last, Dixon!' she said.

Dixon? What did she mean? Keara wondered, but it was too much trouble to contradict her about the name.

'I want it to be understood from the start that there's to be no drinking on board ship. I've searched your bags and there are no bottles there, but I'll search your trunk as well later in the voyage, when they bring it up.'

Keara gaped at her. '*Ship?* What do you mean, ship?'

'I mean your friends carried you on board just before we sailed so you're now on your way to Australia, my girl. And you can think yourself lucky your friends got you here on time, because they were nearly as drunk as you.'

So Nancy had been telling her the truth. Keara didn't know whether to be glad or sad that she was on her way to find her sisters. But she hadn't had a chance to say goodbye to Theo. That realisation hurt so much she closed her eyes, trying hard not to weep. When she opened them again, the woman was still there.

'I'm Matron Kirby, in charge of the single women's quarters, and I'll be keeping my eye on you from now on. I don't know what the agent is thinking of, sending drunkards like you out to Australia as maids.'

Keara closed her eyes and let the voice rant on. When she opened them, Matron had gone and a woman of about her own age was sitting on the lower bunk opposite, grinning at her.

'You won't be able to breathe without her looking over your shoulder from now on,' Maggie said with a chuckle. 'You should have had your farewell party earlier and come on board sober.'

Keara was certain of one thing at least, though the rest puzzled her. 'I don't drink and there wasn't a party. Someone wanted to get rid of me and they forced laudanum down my throat. I don't remember anything after that. And I certainly didn't book this passage.'

Maggie looked at her quizzically. 'Look, if you start telling tall stories like that, Keara, people will take against you whether they're true or not. Just keep quiet and behave yourself for a while, eh? Let the fuss die down.'

'I'm not telling lies. And what's more, my name isn't Dixon. It's Michaels. Keara Michaels.'

Maggie stared at her thoughtfully. 'And you're Irish by the sound of you. Matron's going to hate that as well. The Irish girls have all been moved near her cabin so that she can keep a close eye on them. She thinks the Irish are scum. You don't speak like them, though. It's more of a lilt in your voice.'

'I've been living mostly in Lancashire since I first went into service.'

'And since you married.' She gestured to the ring on Keara's finger.

'Married? I –' Keara broke off, suddenly remembering the queasiness she'd been experiencing. The old woman had said she was going to have a baby. 'Yes, till I married. Only I'm a widow now. I – um – lost my husband three weeks ago.'

Maggie reached across to clasp her hand for a moment. 'I'm sorry. I'm a widow too, but it's over a year now and anyway, I hated him.' She scowled at some memory.

'Am I really on my way to Australia?'

'Yes.'

'I've got two sisters there, so I do want to go, but not like this.'

'You've an honest face and you look like you're telling the truth, only – well, it all sounds a bit far-fetched.'

'It feels it to me, too.' Keara sighed and closed her eyes again, improvising a story. 'I only met Theo six months ago, and now he's dead and I'm on my way to

Australia. His, um, mother is probably the one who got rid of me. She always hated me.'

'How did your husband die?'

'He caught a cold and it went to his chest.' She remembered a neighbour dying like that in Ballymullan. 'He couldn't breathe and his chest was rattling and he was gasping for air. It was awful to watch him. Then suddenly it went quiet and – and they told me he was dead.' She willed tears into her eyes, and by thinking of her mother managed to squeeze a few out, though she hated lying to this pleasant-faced woman who was being kind to her.

'You poor thing.'

A hand rested briefly on hers again, then there was silence. When Keara opened her eyes she was alone. Had she really told all those lies? Was she really on her way to Australia?

And could she be carrying Theo's child?

As drowsiness overtook her once more, she didn't fight against it. It was all too much to take in when your head felt thick and stupid and all you wanted to do was sleep.

When Keara awoke, it was night and the cabin was dark. She levered herself out of the bunk, wondering where you went to relieve yourself on a ship.

'What's the matter?' someone whispered.

'I need to find a privy, or whatever we use here.'

Maggie got out of the lower bunk opposite. 'Well, we'll have to ask Matron to let you out, then. They lock us in at nights to keep us from throwing ourselves at the sailors. Ha! You should see 'em. I wouldn't touch 'em with a clothes prop. Come on. I'll help you.'

When Keara staggered, Maggie put an arm round her and helped her into the main cabin, which had a table and benches in the middle. It was dimly lit by one small lamp hanging on the far wall.

Matron roused herself quickly, a massive figure in a flannel nightdress. She scowled at Keara. 'If this is an excuse to try to get near the sailors, Dixon, you'll soon learn that I don't allow my girls to associate with the crew. Maggie, you can show her where to go and are to stay near her every minute and bring her straight back afterwards. Is that clear?'

'Yes, Matron.'

Keara found the sanitary arrangements far better than in the houses where she'd grown up, with a seat built over a hole so that the filth could go straight into the sea. Maggie showed her how to use the hand pump, which brought fresh sea water up to swill everything clean again after you'd used what she called 'the necessary'.

When Maggie helped her back to the cabin they found Matron waiting near the door, this time with a shawl over her nightdress. She locked it immediately they were inside.

'Can I have a drink of water, please?' Keara asked.

'Wait there and I'll get you some.' Maggie left her sitting at the long, narrow table and Matron retired to her own cabin.

When Maggie brought the water she watched

Keara gulp it down and said, 'If you'll take my advice, you'll stay Keara Dixon and behave like an absolute angel. Tell Matron someone must have put something in your drink and you're sorry to have been such a nuisance. Don't spin her any tales about people trying to get rid of you.' She hesitated then said, 'I do believe you, though. I could smell the laudanum myself.'

Keara nodded. This advice made sense. Who would believe it when she hardly believed what had happened herself?

'Are you hungry?'

'No.'

'Then let's get back to bed. I'm tired even if you're not.'

In the morning Keara felt almost normal again. Two other young women were sharing the tiny cabin, occupying the upper bunks. One gave her a distinctly unfriendly look and said, 'I'm telling Matron if you try to bring any drink in here.'

'I'm *not* a boozer. Someone must have put something in my drink. I don't remember anything after that.'

They looked at her cynically, but Maggie winked from the other lower bunk and nodded approval of this lie as she swung out of bed and began to dress. 'We get up one at a time,' she said as she made a sketchy wash and put her clothes on. 'There isn't really enough room for two people to move around at the same time.' She jerked her head in the direction of the upper bunks as she finished. 'These are Alice and Brenda, by the way.'

'And I agree with what Brenda said. If I see you

drinking gin or anything else, I'll go straight to Matron.' Alice wrinkled her nose in disapproval.

'And as for saying someone put something in her drink,' Brenda added with a sniff of disgust, 'well, I could *smell* the gin from across the room, couldn't you, Alice?'

'I certainly could.'

'They must have spilled it on her clothes, then, mustn't they?' Maggie said.

Alice and Brenda left the cabin as soon as they were ready, but Maggie sat on her bunk and waited for Keara. 'You look like you need a friend and those two stick together like glue, so I'm offering my services. I'm feeling a bit lonely, too.'

'I do need a friend,' Keara admitted. 'You've been very kind and I'm grateful.'

'Well, it's going to be a long voyage. Seventy days, they say – if we're lucky. Did you bring any books with you?'

'I don't know. Someone else packed my things.'

Maggie shook her head but didn't comment. Keara was certainly sticking to her story. If she was a liar, she was a good one. Only she didn't seem like a liar to Maggie.

And anyway, hadn't they all got things to hide?

The next morning Keara was sick as soon as she stood up, retching and bringing up nothing but a froth of yellow bile.

Maggie, who was again waiting for her, stared. 'What's up, love?'

'I think I'm pregnant.'

'Your husband's?'

There was only one thing Keara could say. 'Of course it's his. Only he'll never know, will he? He'll never know!'

She began to weep because although Theo wasn't her husband he would definitely have wanted to know about the child. She could not stop weeping. Maggie made her lie down on her bunk, clearing the mess up, fussing over her and eventually fetching Matron when she continued to weep.

'Stop that at once, do you hear!'

The sharp voice at last penetrated Keara's misery and she managed to choke back the sobs, though her breath was still shaky with grief.

'Did you know about this child when you booked your passage?'

Keara shook her head.

Maggie tugged at the older woman's arm. 'Her husband only died three weeks ago. She's going out to live with her sisters in Australia.'

'Well, she can't lie there and weep all the way, can she?' Matron looked over her shoulder into the living area where women were gathering quietly in their messes to eat breakfast, some of them watching what was going on with open curiosity. 'Go and get your breakfast now, Maggie, but save Keara something to eat later.' She turned back to the young woman in the bunk, her voice softening just a little. 'It's very sad when the father doesn't live to see his child.'

Keara nodded and could not prevent more tears

from welling in her eyes. All the years Theo Mullane had longed for a child and how easily she'd been able to give him one. Only, if she told him about it, he'd come and drag her back to be his mistress, she was sure of that, and then she might never find her sisters.

She was torn two ways and that was what was upsetting her most.

But at least Theo already had a son. She laid a hand on her still-flat belly as she waited for the nausea to pass. This child would be hers and hers alone. What's more, she'd make sure it was brought up with love and never, ever went hungry. No father at all would be better than one like she'd had.

But she wished she could tell Theo. She wished it so much!

Two days later Keara found out that the ship was going to Western Australia, not the colony of Victoria. Someone had a map of Australia and showed her where Perth was. Someone else knew the distance to Melbourne and it shocked her rigid that she would still be 1,700 miles from her sisters, which was farther than the whole length of England from north to south, the woman informed her smugly. That brought home to Keara how big the world really was and she could only sit and stare at the map in shock and dismay.

Matron overheard the conversation and added a further piece of information: the only way to get from Perth to Melbourne was by ship.

Keara sat trying to take it all in, feeling as if the

world had turned upside down – again. 'How much will that cost?' she asked in a voice rendered hoarse by agitation.

'About twelve pounds, I think,' Matron said. 'Maybe a little more.'

Keara escaped to the semi-privacy of her cabin where she sat on her bunk with her head in her hands, too numb to weep. Nancy had done this on purpose. She must have.

But she remembered Nancy's face. The old woman hadn't seemed malicious, just determined to get rid of Keara for the sake of her nursling. She seemed to hear again that creaky voice saying, 'I don't set out to harm people. And one day you'll be glad I did this, I promise you.' The voice rang with sincerity even as it echoed in Keara's mind.

Perhaps Nancy hadn't meant to harm her, perhaps she simply hadn't known how far away the city of Melbourne was from Perth – but she had harmed her, nonetheless. Keara understood only too well how difficult it was to save even a pound on a maid's wages. To save twelve for the fare to Melbourne from Perth, not to mention setting money aside for expenses on arrival – well, that would be nearly impossible. She had a baby growing inside her and not only would it also have its needs, but it'd be hard to find work in the meantime with a bulging belly.

She could write to the nuns as Theo had done, for she had memorised their address, but would they write back, let alone tell her where her sisters were? Would they even know? People changed jobs, moved on.

Though surely they hadn't sent Mara out to work as a maid at eleven years old?

Overcome by this additional blow, she lay staring blindly at the bunk above her. Maggie had to shake her to get her attention.

'You really didn't know you were coming, did you?'

'No.'

'And if your sisters are in Melbourne, you're in a right old pickle, my girl.'

'Yes.'

Maggie leaned over to give Keara a quick hug. 'I never could abide people being tricked. When we get there, how about we stick together?' She hesitated, then admitted, 'I'm running away from someone.' After a quick glance over her shoulder, she added in a low voice, 'My husband, actually. He isn't dead – though I wish he was, the sod – but he used to beat me and he hit our little girl so hard she died. I'll never forgive him for that, never. That's when I decided to leave him.'

'Oh, Maggie, no!'

She nodded. 'I stole his savings and used them to get away. I'm not sorry for what I've done and I don't intend to tell anyone in Australia that I'm still married.' She gave a shaky laugh. 'Brett isn't my name any more than Dixon is yours, but I'm never using *his* name again as long as I live. Eh, we make a right old pair, don't we?'

Keara clasped her hand. 'It'll be good to stick together.'

'And we'll find some way to get to Melbourne, I promise you. Both of us. If you'll have me as a friend?'

'Of course I'll have you. It seems very drastic, though, running away to Australia. Couldn't your family have helped you?'

'They're all dead, all the ones who count anyway. I just wanted to get as far away from him as I could. Hey, maybe you could adopt me as a cousin instead of just a friend?' Maggie spread her hands wide as if offering herself, grinning as she did so.

Something hard and unhappy began to melt inside Keara at her words. 'I always wanted a cousin Maggie,' she said trying to smile through a mist of emotion. The two women hugged one another again, then went out to face their shipmates – together.

Two weeks later Theo went into the nursery, worried about Richard who had seemed very listless that morning. He had been visiting his son at times when he knew Nancy was busy with his wife, but this evening she was sitting beside the cot with Richard in her arms, rocking him gently.

She looked up as Theo came in, a wary expression on her face. 'I can leave if you wish, sir.'

'No. I may not have forgiven you for what you did to Keara, but I know you've helped Richard.' He stood there, feeling restless and uncertain.

She looked down at the child. 'Why don't you sit here and hold him? He's a bit uneasy today, but he always responds to you.'

So Theo sat and rocked his son, glad when Nancy slipped quietly out of the nursery.

If only he was free, he'd have followed Keara and married her. But he wasn't. He had this estate to sell, a foolish wife to provide for, workers depending on him for their livelihoods till someone took the estate off his hands.

And most important of all, a son to care for. He looked down at Richard and was struck again by how frail the infant looked. Dear God, was he to lose everything? His son as well as the woman he loved?

From that night, the baby's health went from bad to worse and for all the care and attention lavished on him, no one could doubt that little Richard Mullane was failing. Theo abandoned everything to spend as much time with his son as he could, though Lavinia did no more than come to stand in the nursery doorway in the morning and stare at the child who spent most of his time in his nursemaid's or father's arms.

It was in his father's arms that Richard breathed his last one evening, just a sigh and he was gone. Theo looked down at him and when he realised what had happened sat very still, unwilling to put his son's body down, reluctant to bring others running.

When Nancy appeared in the doorway, as if she had sensed what had happened, he looked up at her in numb misery. 'I think – he's just died.'

She sat down beside him, touching the child's pale cheek in a farewell gesture. 'Yes. He had a heart problem like his mother's, but worse.'

'Like his mother's?'

She nodded. 'Haven't you noticed the blue shadow on Lavinia's lips? She isn't aware of it because as we both know she sees only what she wants to. Her mother was just the same and her grandmother. It's better that they don't have any descendants.' She leaned forward to take the child from his arms. 'I'll lay him out. He'll look beautiful. Now, go and weep.'

So Theo went down to the stream because he remembered how Keara had comforted him there. That seemed a long time ago now.

But he didn't weep, couldn't. The grief and pain went too deep for that.

When he went back to the house, all the servants were speaking in hushed tones and someone had tied black crêpe to the doorknocker.

As if that made any difference!

Dick was the only one who spoke to him. 'I'm so sorry.'

Theo stared at him, then gave a helpless shake of the head. 'I can't talk about it.'

So Dick gave him a big hug.

And even then he couldn't cry.

Dick attended the funeral, watching from the rear of the church as Lavinia wept beneath her heavy veil and Nancy comforted her. But it was Theo's face he kept seeing for a long time afterwards. Never had he seen a man so ravaged by grief. It had also upset Dick to see how small the baby's coffin was, carried out from the church by his father who had moved forward and pushed away the two men assigned to this task with a brusque, 'I'll take him.'

Dick wished there were something he could do to help his half-brother, but there wasn't. He remembered how desolate he had felt when his own mother had died, because there had always been just the two of them. But at least she'd enjoyed her life and lived to be fifty. Enjoyed it too much, some would say, but Dick had loved her dearly nonetheless.

After the funeral collation the guests left and Nancy settled Lavinia for a rest before going in search of Theo. She found him sitting in the library with an untouched glass of cognac in his hands.

'Go away!' he said, without so much as turning his head to see who it was.

She ignored his order and moved quietly forward to stand behind him, putting one hand on his shoulder, feeling the tension radiating from him. She couldn't have left him in such unpurged pain.

He tried to shake off her hand and as he turned his head, caught a glimpse of her face. It had completely lost its stern expression and was full of compassion. 'Just leave me alone,' he muttered, turning away again.

But instead she walked round to sit beside him, putting her hand on his arm. 'You haven't wept. You must weep for him.'

'Damn you, let me be!' He pushed her away, stood up and went to stare out of the window, but she followed him and raised one hand to stroke his cheek.

'*I've* wept for him,' she said. 'He was so little and there was nothing I could do to help him. I've wept

several times because he was my Lavinia's child as well
as yours. He was such a pretty baby.'

Theo tried to stem the great tide of grief that swept
through him at her words and the memories of his son's
face they conjured up, but the grief wouldn't be held in
any longer. With a cry of anguish he dropped the glass
and turned towards her, and when she put her arms
round him, he buried his head on her shoulder. Hoarse,
racking sobs shook him and as he began to weep, she
did too.

He didn't even notice that she guided him back to
the sofa and held him, patting his back and making low,
soothing sounds, letting him weep out some of the pain
at least.

Born of a long line of healers, Nancy could never
pass by when someone was in distress. Witch, they had
called her in the village where she'd grown up. It had
made no difference to them that she used her power for
good. It frightened them. It frightened most people. But
she'd been born with an instinct to respond to need,
which was why she'd cared for Lavinia for as long as
they'd let her. Poor Lavinia. Unloved the whole of her
life except by Nancy.

She had not hesitated to send Keara to Australia
because some instinct told her that was where the young
woman's future lay. And she had not hesitated to
approach Theo Mullane either and offer him comfort,
though she was the only person in the house who would
have dared go near him tonight. Even Dick had not
attempted to intrude.

When Theo's first outpouring of sorrow was spent,

he leaned his head back against the sofa, staring unseeingly up at the ceiling.

'No shame to weep for a child,' Nancy said quietly. 'The shame would be in not weeping.'

'I wanted a son so much,' he muttered.

'I've already told you that you'll have a child yet.'

He stared at her. 'How can you be so sure of that?'

'I have the gift of second sight.' Nancy smiled at his cynical expression. 'Whether you believe me or not, it's true. You *will* have a child one day.'

'Not from Lavinia. I could never touch her again.'

'Lavinia won't always be with you. There will be another wife.' Then she got up and left as quietly as she'd entered.

He sat on for a long time, staring into the fire, not setting much store by her foretelling, which was probably just a way of offering him comfort. His thoughts turned instead to Keara. Where was she now and how was she feeling? Had she discovered yet that she was going to the wrong part of Australia?

Would he ever see her again?

Alex Jenner turned up again in Rossall Springs one hot February day, demanding to see his granddaughter as if he had not tried to kidnap her the last time.

Mark refused quietly and when his father-in-law had gone, ran out of the rear door and across to the Johnsons' to make sure they were all right. Since Kalaya looked apprehensive, he took his daughter home with him while Mr Jenner was in town and asked Kalaya to come there to feed Amy. He returned to the eating house by the back way.

The old man returned in the evening, making the same demand just as loudly, so Mark brought Amy out to show him, though he refused to allow the old man to hold her. Alex began praying loudly and the baby jerked in shock at the sudden harsh noise, then began to wail.

Mark shushed her and waited till Alex had finished praying. 'Please leave now.' To his relief, his father-in-law went away, turning once at the door to stare at the child and shake his head reproachfully at Mark.

The following day Kalaya's eldest son, who had been keeping watch, came to tell Mark that the old man had left on the coach for Melbourne. He sighed with relief and took Amy back to Kalaya. He was getting better at looking after her, but she wasn't used to him, so had been fretting.

However, a month later Alex appeared again and Mark's heart sank at the mere sight of his red, angry face.

'I've come to see my granddaughter.'

'Will you stop doing this, Mr Jenner?' Mark said. 'You frightened her last time with your loud voice.'

'I shall be coming here every month until you take that child away from that filthy heathen and let her grandmother look after her.'

'Mrs Johnson is as clean as you or I, and she attends church regularly, too. She looks after Amy as well as anyone could wish and I'm certainly not sending my daughter away to Melbourne.'

'How you can let your child drink a native's milk, I

don't know. We can find someone far more suitable – a white woman – to act as wet nurse.'

'No. My daughter is staying with me. And I'd be grateful if you'd leave my premises and not return to Rossall again.' When the other man didn't move, Mark took a step towards him.

Alex walked slowly outside to stand in the middle of the street and yell, 'I have a right to see my granddaughter.' Then he fell to his knees and began to pray, still at the top of his voice.

By this time people had come out of their houses and shops to watch.

Mark looked round, gave an exaggerated shrug and went back inside, keeping watch through the front window.

'He's a determined man,' one of the customers said. 'And why don't you let him spend time with the child? He is her grandfather, after all.'

'He upsets her. What's more, he made his own children very unhappy. My wife was terrified of him and her brother ran away from home.'

'Aw, this one's only a baby,' said another. 'What harm can he do? And I agree with him about one thing. I wouldn't like my child being fed by a native woman. They're not like us and you won't convince me otherwise.'

Mark didn't intend to get into an argument. 'Mrs Johnson takes excellent care of Amy. I know because I go to see her every day.'

The man scowled, muttered something and applied himself to his meal.

It seemed a long time to Mark until the constable came striding along the street and even longer before Alex would be persuaded to move on, by which time Kalaya had slipped in the back way, bringing Amy to her father for safety.

The following day Mark went to consult Samuel Grove, with whom he'd formed a vague friendship. 'Is there nothing I can do about my father-in-law? The man's deliberately damaging my business.'

Samuel hesitated, then said, 'There is some sympathy with him in the town. You could have found a white nursemaid if you'd made the effort and just used the native woman until then.'

Mark hadn't realised that even Samuel shared the general prejudice. 'Kalaya has been wonderful with Amy. I couldn't have asked for a better nursemaid.' As his friend threw him a cynical look, he added with a sigh, 'Well, we clearly won't agree about that, but I have a business matter I'd like to discuss with you. I want to sell my eating house and move away.'

'Because of the old man?'

Mark nodded.

Samuel's face grew thoughtful. 'I might just be interested in buying it myself. I'd have to see the accounts first, though. Check the profits, so that we can fix a fair price. My wife could run it. She's a good cook.'

'Come round tonight, but don't mention this to anyone or the deal is off. I want to leave without anyone knowing where Amy and I have gone.' He didn't tell Samuel that it was one thing to be a good cook, quite another to cook for a lot of people, day after day.

Disapproval clearly coloured his voice. 'That's running away.'

'Yes. And I want your promise that you'll not tell anyone where I've gone.'

Samuel nodded. 'You have it. It's your life and your decision.'

'Even if my father-in-law asks you?'

'We might not agree on some things, but you've been a good neighbour.'

Mark nodded and returned to work. It seemed to have become the pattern of his life, running away. He felt sad. He'd hoped to stay in Rossall Springs.

Two days later the larger possessions which Mark wished to take with him were carried by night to the rear of the general store and hidden on the big wagon. They were shipped to Melbourne when Samuel went up the following day on his weekly trip to purchase more goods. He put them in storage in a warehouse near the docks.

Mark told only Kalaya what was to happen and asked her to teach him as much as she could about caring for his little daughter.

She looked at him in surprise. 'A man doing such things?'

'There is only me, man or not. You've been wonderful with her and I'm deeply grateful, so if you're ever in need of help tell Mr Grove and he'll see you right. I'll make arrangements with him.'

'We're all right. Billy has a good job, this is our home now. But thank you.'

Mark didn't find caring for a baby demeaning in the slightest. The love he felt for Amy had grown over the months and she was now a plump and happy child of five months, the light of his life. It probably took him longer to do things for her because he could never resist playing with her and making her give the fat chuckle that always brought a smile to his face.

Sometimes he would wonder how his other daughter was getting on in England. He would look at the photo of Faith and her grandparents nearly every night, trying to imagine how she would have grown and changed. He was sure she would be loved and happy because his father and Kathy adored children. He could not help comparing Alex Jenner with John Gibson, who was also deeply religious but in a loving, kindly way. Alex had driven his own children away with his harsh faith, but John was deeply loved by all his family and all except Mark lived nearby.

He wrote to his father to say he'd be moving to Western Australia and would let them know his address there once he was settled. He also told him that he had another daughter but his wife had died bearing her, and asked if he could have another photograph of Faith and if possible of the whole family. He wished he could have a photograph taken of himself and Amy to send to them, because photographs were a great comfort, but that would require a special trip into Melbourne and he didn't dare risk that. Later, perhaps.

★

The following week Mark pretended to be so ill that Ginny and her sister had to run the eating house unsupervised. Samuel's wife would take over in two days' time, only then revealing that Mark had sold it to her and her husband. She would tell everyone he had gone to live in Sydney. He had timed his departure to fit in with the sailing date of the steamship for Western Australia and hoped that Alex Jenner would never find them again. Surely the man wouldn't even try? What good would it do him?

On the final evening Mark finished his packing and got everything ready for feeding Amy quickly in the morning, as well as putting together food for the journey which would be much slower in the cart than by coach. He then wandered round the house, not as sorry as he'd expected to be leaving it. He had done quite well here and Samuel had given him a fair price, but the place held sad memories for him. He would still turn occasionally to say something to Patience, or look up when someone came into the kitchen and expect it to be her.

He knew he had made her happy in the short time they'd spent together, which was a consolation to him, but he had only been fond of her, had not loved her deeply. And sometimes her docility had irritated him. He could admit that to himself, at least, though he hoped he hadn't let her see it. That was one of the reasons he didn't want Amy brought up by Alex and his wife. He wanted his daughter to be as lively as his nieces and nephews in Bilsden had been, not cowed and fearful.

Before dawn the next day he and his sleepy child were hidden on Samuel's wagon, together with the rest of their possessions. It left as soon as it was light for its weekly run to Melbourne and not until they were well out of town did Samuel rein in the horses and call, 'You can come out now.'

The young assistant driver goggled as Mark and Amy emerged from behind some boxes and were found a more comfortable place to sit.

Samuel fixed Zeke with the basilisk stare for which he was famous. 'If you tell anyone we brought Mark and his daughter with us today, I'll see you never work in Rossall Springs again.' He relaxed into a genial smile. 'But I know you wouldn't do that, Zeke, would you?'

'Certainly not, Mr Grove.' He looked at Mark. 'Getting away from that father-in-law of yours, are you?'

'Yes. Wouldn't you?'

'I should say! The old fellow's raving mad.'

In Melbourne they dropped Zeke at the lodging house Samuel always used, so that he wouldn't know any more than that Mark had come to Melbourne. Then they went straight to the docks, where they confirmed the passage Samuel had booked the week previously to Western Australia for Mark and his daughter.

'One day they say there'll be roads all the way across Australia,' Samuel said thoughtfully as they came out of the shipping office, 'a railway even. There's a great future for this country of ours, Mark, and I hope you'll still be part of it over there in the west.'

Mark clasped the hand that was offered. 'I shall. And thank you for all your help, Samuel. I'm truly grateful.'

The other man shrugged. 'You've been a good neighbour and friend. And besides,' he grinned, 'I'm going to make a nice lot of money from that eating house you started.'

'Remember, we've agreed that if Kalaya and her family are ever in need, they can come to you for help and I'll pay you back. I've told them, too. You can always contact me through the Parkers.'

Samuel sighed. He'd been reluctant to agree to this, given his own prejudices against natives, but when Mark offered to pay any expenses involved plus ten per cent, he had accepted the commission as he would any commercial transaction. 'You'll never make a fortune if you go round giving people money.'

'I don't want to make a fortune, just a decent living for both my daughters.' Only after he had said that did Mark realise that his ambitions had changed since he'd first started up in business. He wasn't his sister Annie, who seemed to have a hunger for money, and his life wasn't going to be like hers. He wasn't sure what it would be like, but his prime objective would be to bring up his daughter and make her happy.

'Daughters? You've got another child?'

'Yes. She's living in England with my father at the moment.'

'You're young to have been married twice.'

'I wasn't married to the other one's mother. My father and stepmother are bringing Faith up for the moment, but one day I hope to fetch her here to live with me.'

Mark had to wait in lodgings for two days while the ship was loaded and his things were brought out of storage and added to its cargo.

He intended to disappear absolutely for the second time in his life, but at least he wasn't on his own this time. Amy was a great comfort to him. What's more, he might not be the most skilled nursemaid, but she didn't seem to be suffering from his attentions. She was eating mashed foods quite well now and drinking cow's milk.

His landlady was amazed to see a man looking after a child and when she found out that his wife had died (he didn't say when) she fussed over the two of them and didn't seem to mind doing the piles of washing from keeping Amy clean. She even went out and helped him buy some more napkins and clothes for the child, because it was clear that he'd need extra during the voyage.

Once or twice he wondered if he should have stayed to outface Alex Jenner, but he didn't want always to be watching over his shoulder as he brought up his daughter, didn't want her to be nervous in case her grandparents turned up.

He wanted so much more for Amy than her poor mother had had.

CHAPTER SIXTEEN

May–June 1864

———◆◆———

Theo was lucky enough to sell his Lancashire estate quite quickly. He made arrangements to move to Ballymullan, feeling nothing but a sense of relief at the thought of leaving Lavinia behind.

She and Nancy were already settled in a snug modern villa in the centre of town. Out of courtesy, he paid them a visit before he left.

They received him in the parlour. His wife was looking puffy in the face, though she had lost weight on the body.

'You had no need to come here,' she said at once. 'I wouldn't have cared if I'd never seen you again.'

'Lavinia!' Nancy warned.

She flounced one shoulder and went to sit in a large armchair upholstered in blue velvet, stroking the pile absent-mindedly and avoiding looking at him.

'You can get in touch with me if you need anything,' he said, wondering why he had bothered to do this.

Nancy waited for Lavinia to say something and

when she didn't, said it for her. 'We'll remember that, sir. I hope you have a pleasant journey.'

Lavinia was now fiddling with the braid on her armchair.

With a short, exasperated sigh, he stood up. 'I'll take my leave of you then.'

Nancy went to the door with him. 'It was kind of you to come. And don't worry, I'll look after her for you.'

'I'm sure you will.' He hesitated, then asked the question that had always puzzled him, 'What has she done to deserve such devotion from you?'

She smiled. 'Needed me. Had no one else to love her.'

It made no sense to him.

'It's how I'm made – a healer by nature. Have a safe trip, sir.'

She watched him stride away, then went back to find Lavinia watching him from the window.

'He's good-looking, isn't he, Nancy?'

'Yes, chickie.'

'But I didn't like living with him. Shall I have to see him again?'

'Not if you don't want to.'

'I don't.' She turned round suddenly and hugged her maid. 'I'm much happier with you.'

Nancy held her close for a minute, knowing this was as close as she'd get to being appreciated, then she pushed Lavinia to arm's length and said briskly, 'Well then, let's go for a stroll into town.'

*

Theo moved to Ballymullan, but it seemed to have lost its charm for him and he could not settle to anything. He was short-tempered with the staff, even with Dick, and spent a lot of time simply riding aimlessly across the countryside, often not noticing that someone had greeted him, so lost was he in his thoughts – and regrets.

When a letter arrived from Caley and Noreen, he stared at it for a long time before he opened it. He almost wished they weren't happy in Australia, which was silly. Of course he didn't wish that. He ripped open the envelope and read the three pages Noreen had written because Caley wasn't good at letter writing.

They sounded to be enjoying life greatly in Western Australia but then, he thought wistfully, Noreen would enjoy life anywhere. His cousin was lucky to have met her. He envied them their closeness.

When he wrote back he'd send some money for Keara. Surely they'd be able to find her, give him news of her? But he couldn't bring himself to put pen to paper, though he read the letter several times. He couldn't seem to settle to anything.

And, oh, how he envied them the weather in Australia! So much sunshine. He looked out at the grey skies and scudding clouds. What was it Keara used to say? 'Bring me back a pennyworth of sunshine.'

How much was a pennyworth? Enough to warm your hands and face?

Not enough to warm your heart. For that you needed someone you loved.

★

Towards the end of May, Mark arrived in Perth. He hadn't realised how small it was, more like a country town than a state capital. But he felt more comfortable in small towns than in big cities. He found lodgings, though it was not easy as there seemed to be a shortage of accommodation.

Unfortunately this landlady seemed to regard a baby as a nuisance and was at first reluctant even to take a man and a child who didn't have a woman to care for them. Eventually she shrugged and said, 'All right. As long as the baby doesn't cry a lot. I'm not having my other lodgers disturbed. And you'll have to make your own arrangements for the washing. The woman next door might do it for you.'

Mark at once set about exploring and investigating the possibilities for opening an eating house in Perth. It seemed as if there would be enough custom, but somehow the thought of starting such a business for the third time did not appeal to him. Perhaps there was something else he could do instead?

It was by sheer chance that another lodger turned up who ran a country inn. The two got into conversation. Jim Porting was an older man, and was growing tired of the life he led. From what he said, there wasn't as much scope for making money in a country inn as there would be in Perth, but Mark was still drawn to the idea and agreed to go and inspect the place. Apart from anything else, the trip would allow him to see something of the countryside, even if Jim's inn did prove unsuitable, and he would definitely look for other lodgings when he came back. This landlady was not only surly, but couldn't cook a decent meal.

They set off from Perth the next day, driving at a leisurely pace in Jim's cart, drawn by two sturdy horses which, he said proudly, were mostly Welsh cob in breed. Mark had no experience of horses, but set himself to observe how to handle them and Jim proved an enthusiastic teacher.

'I were a groom once,' he said regretfully, 'thought to better myself by coming out here, an' I suppose I have, but it's a lonely life.' He looked at Mark. 'You make sure it's what you want, lad, living in the country. I don't want to take advantage of you.'

'I'll think it through carefully, don't you worry.'

It was winter now and Mark had expected it to be dull and cold, but when he commented on this, Jim laughed. 'We still get plenty of sunny days in winter, though when it rains, the heavens open.'

That was demonstrated the very next day. Mark had never seen such a deluge and after a short time, Jim pulled off the road under some overhanging trees to wait for the downpour to end and dragged out a small tarpaulin under which they could shelter.

Amy entertained them both by kicking and crowing.

'That's what it's all for,' Jim said as he watched her. 'The children. And the grandchildren.'

Mark quickly grew to love the quiet rustling forests with their stands of huge trees through which they sometimes passed. He had seen nothing quite like this in Victoria where the land near a diggings had had a ravaged look to it. Around Rossall Springs the forests had been mostly cleared for farming, so there had been nothing to compare with these soaring giants.

Sometimes when they stopped to rest the horses the air was so still you could hear all the tiny sounds of nature and he felt he could sit there for hours, just listening. To a man who'd grown up in a smoky industrial town in Lancashire this seemed truly wonderful, but Jim, who seemed determined that he should understand what he would be taking on, spoke gloomily about bushfires and mud up to the axles in winter.

They were delayed by the muddy roads and had to spend that night in a farmer's barn, arriving at the inn around noon the following day. It was situated on the Bunbury road, which they'd followed down from Perth, and was halfway between the tiny town of Pinjarra (Mark learned that no one called such places villages here, even though they were smaller than most English villages) and the much larger settlement of Bunbury. They had seen other vehicles regularly during their journey, which ought to provide opportunities for offering hot food and accommodation to passing travellers, Mark felt.

Jim said that beyond the inn, half a mile into the bush, was the small settlement of Meriniup, not big enough even to have its own store but with several farms and smallholdings in the neighbourhood. Mark wondered why Jim hadn't thought to run a general store as well as the inn, then smiled at his own reaction. He might say he wasn't out to make a lot of money but he couldn't help seeing the opportunities. Maybe there was more of his sister Annie in him than he had realised.

The inn itself was bigger than Mark had expected, a sprawling set of rather ramshackle buildings to which bits had been added at different times.

There were three bedrooms for travellers in a separate block to the right, with space in front of them to stand wagons, and a shelter for the travellers' horses to the rear with two walls only to fend off the prevailing winds. There was a small stable and tack room for the owner's horses, and the living quarters were to the left of the public part of the inn, angled slightly so the occupants could keep an eye on the comings and goings of customers.

It surprised Mark that the inn kitchen was completely separate at the rear and when Jim got talking about bushfires, he looked round and wondered why the man hadn't cleared the ground near the house of shrubs and trees and woodland litter if that was such a danger. He would have done. Even a newcomer could see it would be a wise precaution.

Mrs Porting was thin and stooped, with ill health written all over her face. She said little, leaving her husband to show Mark round, but she asked at once to hold Amy and cooed over the child in quite a different tone.

Jim watched her with a fond smile and confided, 'She loves babies, the wife does. Wants to live near our daughter and help with hers.'

'That'll be nice. What liquor do you sell here?'

'Beer when I can get some down from Perth, but

rum mostly. I sell it at a shilling the glass to travellers, and by the gallon to the settlers round here when they run out. Of course you'll have to get a licence if you want to sell booze,' Jim said gloomily, 'and they'll charge you for that. This new governor – Hampton's his name – is no different from t'other officials and wants his pound of flesh from everyone. But how you'll manage here without a wife, I don't know.'

'Surely there are women nearby who'd come and work in the inn?'

Jim shrugged. 'Never tried. Don't trust outsiders, only family.'

Mark knew he should look round, see other places, but somehow this one appealed to him. 'Can we walk round Meriniup? Meet some of the locals?'

Jim shrugged. 'Why not? Won't take long.'

'I'll look after your Amy,' Mrs Porting offered at once.

The settlement consisted of half a dozen houses, one of which stood empty, having been built to house the convicts who had laboured to make and maintain the roads, and still being used occasionally to house the surveyor and his staff when they travelled south.

The people living in the central settlement mostly worked on the farms or at a nearby homestead, and all had enough land to keep a cow or a few sheep and grow a lot of their own food. The women Mark met seemed pleasant enough and there were usually one or two young children running around, so he could see that Amy would have playmates as she grew older.

'Mr Dangerfield is the main landowner,' Jim said.

'He lives at the big homestead with his young wife. She's his second. The first one died a few years ago and his children are all growed up. He's got plenty of money, but *she's* the daughter of a convict. You'd think he could have done better for himself, eh?'

Mark had heard that tone before. In Australia, even the poorest person seemed to consider himself superior to anyone with the taint of convict blood.

'They employ a couple o' women in the house and two men outside at the homestead, but no gentry ever visit 'em, not even his children don't come, and the women don't live in. He likes to keep his pretty young wife to himself, I reckon.' Jim tittered. 'Well, she's a real looker, so you can't blame him.'

He led the way back to the inn at the shuffling pace he favoured, a pace which made Mark twitch to stride out properly.

After a plain and not particularly appetising meal that evening, Jim looked at him. 'You interested in buying or not?'

'I might be. But we'll have to agree on a price. Can I see the account books?'

Jim could only produce a tattered notebook in which a few figures were written down, and seemed to think that was more than adequate. 'The inn pays for our own living costs and a bit more. But there's all the buildings to take account of when you're doing your sums about price, remember.'

Mark tried to estimate how much income was brought in and went on to demonstrate with figures how much profit the place would need to make if it was worth the price they were asking. But from his companion's puzzled expression, he realised Jim didn't really understand such calculations and Mrs Porting was not even pretending to listen, more interested in rocking Amy and gazing dreamily into the fire.

Cutting short his discussion Mark said abruptly, 'I'm prepared to offer you half of what you're asking and no more, and that's to include all the fittings except for your personal possessions and furnishings.'

Jim frowned. 'I'll meet you halfway Three-quarters of my asking price.'

Mark shook his head. 'No. That's my only offer, based on what profits can be expected, and if it's not suitable, you can take me back to Perth tomorrow and start looking for another buyer.'

'Would that be cash?' Mrs Porting asked suddenly.

'Yes. Payable in Perth.' Mark had already lodged his money with a bank there.

'Then we accept.' She looked down at the infant sleeping peacefully on her lap. 'I want to go, Jim, and the sooner the better. This'll save us a lot of trouble and waiting around.'

'But—'

'Jim, I want to leave as soon as possible!'

So it was settled.

When the Portings had gone to bed, Mark wandered outside, staying within earshot of his daughter. Peace and quiet surrounded him. The hens had gone to sleep and there was no sound from the stables. Even the two scruffy dogs had not bothered to come out to investigate him. He breathed in deeply, feeling good about this. He was young and strong, and intended to make this place into a thriving wayside inn and general store.

But it would have been easier with a wife, he knew. Well, he definitely wasn't looking to remarry and such problems could be solved if you set your mind to it.

Two weeks later, having pushed through the formalities with a speed that seemed to amaze everyone, and having put in a successful bid to act as a sub-Post Office for the expanding district, Mark drove down to Meriniup for a final time with Jim to take over the inn. He now felt quite comfortable driving the cart which he'd bought together with the horses. It was loaded with his possessions and carried a considerable amount of food supplies which Mark had chosen carefully, not to mention a cask of good beer.

'You'll not need that much food, you know,' Jim said as he helped load the cart.

'We'll see. Better too much than too little when you have to come all the way up to Perth for more. And most of it's stuff that'll keep. Besides, I'm going to sell groceries as well as run the inn.'

'Too much trouble,' Jim said gloomily.

Mark didn't reply, just enjoyed the scenery and the fresh air, looking forward to this new life. The Portings had spoken of a young woman from the settlement willing to help out with the baby and the house, so all seemed set fair for him to make a new start.

Two days later Jim and his wife left with one of the

neighbours who was driving up to Perth and Mark turned to the woman who had agreed to act as house-keeper-cum-nursemaid. 'Well, Edith, let's get started on cleaning the house. I've been dealing in food and eating places for years and if there's one thing I'm sure of, it's that you need to keep things clean.'

At the end of the second week, during which they'd had only intermittent travellers staying or stopping for a meal, Edith said bluntly, 'My dad said I should give this a try, Mr Gibson, because he wants me to stay at home but it's too lonely a life for me and I'm not fussed about babies, even though your Amy's a good child. I'll stay on till you find someone else but after that I'm moving up to Perth and nothing Dad says will stop me because I'm twenty-two now.'

He was not surprised by this. Although Edith looked after Amy adequately, she made no extra efforts unless he told her what to do and never seemed to play with or talk to the child. He wanted better care than that.

'If you'll stay till I get other help, Edith, I'll give you double wages for the last week.'

He watched her face brighten and knew he'd hit the right note, but that night he sat staring into the fire for a long time. What sort of woman would want to live and work in such an isolated place? And where did he start looking? Not in Meriniup, that was sure. And yet he'd been told that in Perth there was a 'servant problem' with ladies often having to do their own housework.

Still, Perth was the only place he stood any chance of finding the help he needed, so he left Edith and her young brother to deal with any travellers and drove up there in the cart with his daughter securely fastened in a wooden box beside him.

Alex Jenner arrived in Rossall Springs in mid-June and went confidently into the eating house. In the doorway he stopped and looked round him, frowning. It seemed different somehow. A woman came across to greet him. He couldn't quite remember where he'd seen her, but not here. The one who worked in the kitchen was older and plumper.

'Can I help you, sir? Would you like a meal?'

'I'd like to see my son-in-law, Mark.'

A nervous expression replaced the impersonal smile on her face. 'He isn't here, I'm afraid.'

'I'm not leaving till I've seen him! So wherever he's hiding, send someone to tell him I'm here.'

She left the room and he remained by the door, arms folded, determined not to be fobbed off. When he'd questioned her about weaning times, his wife had said a child could easily be weaned at seven months. He wasn't giving up. He had been too hasty in his efforts to seize Amy, he realised that now – and hadn't even planned the escape properly, either, relying on the stage coach. Stupid, that had been. Next time he'd work things out better and have his own transport.

The woman returned, accompanied by a man whom Alex recognised as the owner of the store next door.

'Your son-in-law left Rossall last month, Mr

Jenner,' he said. 'I'm the new owner of this eating house.'

Alex stood very still while anger throbbed through him, making his brain feel as if it were full of screaming noise. The room seemed to swirl around him and when he managed to compose himself he found he was sitting down and the woman was holding out a glass of water.

'Are you all right?'

'Yes. Just a – dizzy turn. The news shocked me.' He looked at them and lowered his eyes to hide the anger that was still there. 'I haven't always behaved wisely, I admit, but my wife and I are desperate to see our grand-daughter. We've lost both our children and the little one is all we have left.'

A quick glance showed him that the woman's eyes had filled with sympathetic tears. The man was showing no signs of emotion, so Alex looked at her. 'I'm sorry, Mrs—?'

The man answered for her. 'Grove.'

'Do you know where my son-in-law has gone?'

She shook her head.

'When did he leave?'

It was Mr Grove who answered. 'A few weeks ago. No one saw him go.'

Alex frowned at him. 'That's not possible. Someone must know where he's gone.'

'I'm afraid not. It caused quite a lot of talk in the town.' Samuel pulled out a pocket watch. 'And now, Mr Jenner, we have to get about our business. Do you want a meal or shall I direct you to the hotel? Or there's a new daily stage coach running now and you can go back to Melbourne. It leaves at three o'clock.'

'I'll have a meal first, I think.' Alex looked at the woman. 'Is that all right?'

She glanced quickly towards her husband, who nodded. 'Would you like the ordinary or the special, Mr Jenner?'

'The ordinary.' He ate the food slowly, watching as other customers entered. When she came across to take his plate, he said very quietly, 'If you have any idea where I can start looking for my granddaughter, I'd be more grateful than I can say. My dear wife is fretting, longing to see the child.'

She shook her head and after a quick glance round, whispered, 'He's left the state, I'm afraid. I do hope your wife will reconcile herself to that. He'll not be coming back.'

Alex paid for his meal and then took a stroll round town. At the rear of the general store, he found a man loading a cart. 'That looks hard work,' he said.

The man shrugged. 'Not to me. Do it every week, regular, before we go to Melbourne.'

Samuel Grove came out of the back door and yelled, 'Zeke! I need you in here.'

Alex wandered on. Two pieces of information. He doubted he'd get more. He booked a seat on the coach to Melbourne and was amused to see Samuel Grove walk past and go into the booking office as it prepared to set off. He was sure the man knew something. But maybe that didn't matter. If the cart went up to Melbourne at the same time every week, there might be more to be found there. Like which steamships had left about a month ago to go to other states.

He was in an almost genial mood when he arrived home, but his wife burst into tears when he told her Mark had taken their granddaughter out of the state.

'See what you've done, Alex Jenner, with your demands and ranting! Now I shall never see my only grandchild again.' And she fell into such a fit of weeping he could get no sense out of her that day. Nor would she prepare him an evening meal, which made him angry. It was a wife's place to obey her husband in all things and to serve him meekly. No wonder his daughter had been disobedient.

But his wife was mistaken. She would definitely see Amy again because he was simply not going to allow his granddaughter to be brought up by a man who employed godless heathens to look after her.

He'd find them, if it took him years, and then he'd save Amy's soul.

As the ship neared the West Australian coast, the stormy weather abated a little and everyone on board got very excited about being so close to the end of their long journey.

At first Keara stayed in her bunk instead of joining Maggie on deck to look out at the distant smudge of coastline. She had proved an indifferent sailor, not suffering as much as some but never feeling quite right unless the sea was very calm. She couldn't think what she would have done without Maggie's help since she hadn't had a ship's kit and Maggie had shared some of her own things with her.

She did get up to look at Rottnest Island as they waited for a pilot, but wondered why she had bothered. It was very low-lying and the vegetation wasn't particularly beautiful. What did please her, however, was the sunshine and the blueness of the sea, which looked quite different from the northern waters. She lifted her face to the warmth of the sun. If this was winter, what was summer like?

Before they went ashore, Matron came up to Keara and said quietly, 'I've put in a good report on you and your friend. I don't know how you came to be in that deplorable condition when you were brought on board, but I speak as I find and have no complaints about your behaviour. This report may help you to obtain a temporary position, but I doubt anyone will employ you permanently, given your condition.' Her eyes went to Keara's belly, whose swelling was now beginning to show.

They were taken up the river to Perth by paddle steamer and when they disembarked, the single women who were looking for work and had no families to meet them stood in a group while Matron handed over a list to the official who would be in charge of housing them. Keara would have preferred to make her own way and not go to this Poorhouse-Home, but with only a few coins in her purse couldn't afford to refuse help. Their cabin luggage was put on a cart and they followed it in a straggling line.

'I can't believe this!' Maggie muttered.

'What?'

'This sand. I don't call it a proper street.' She looked down in disgust at the fine white sand, not even firm enough to be walked on easily.

When they arrived, they found themselves in a group of eight who were to be housed temporarily in a lean-to built on to one side of the building. They inspected their new living quarters in dismay, then Maggie said loudly, 'Cheer up, girls! At least we're out of the rain and the floor isn't heaving beneath us.'

A grey-haired woman with an unsmiling face came to the door and clapped her hands to gain their attention. 'I'm the supervisor in charge of the women. Because we're short of space, your trunks will have to be stored elsewhere until you find employment. If you need something from them, you must apply to me for access.'

'I hope there's somewhere for us to do some washing, then,' Maggie said at once. 'I've used up all my clean clothes.'

'Silence, please! Your clothes can be washed with everyone else's laundry.'

'Not likely,' muttered Maggie. 'They ruin things when they do everyone's at once.'

The supervisor directed a quelling glance in her direction then continued, 'Meals are served at six in the morning, noon and six in the evening. We're hoping most of you will soon find work as servants and not be a charge upon the government for too long. You did, after all, come out here to work. But in the meantime you will be required to contribute towards your keep here by working either in the laundry or in the kitchens and by sewing when you are not otherwise occupied. Has anyone experience in cooking?'

Maggie immediately put her hand up and dragged Keara's with it.

'I haven't!' Keara whispered.

'Well, I've experience of working in a laundry and I hate it. Anyway, you helped look after our mess on board ship and I had my own home for a while. So we're not exactly ignorant of what a potato looks like.' Maggie smiled at her triumphantly as they were assigned to the kitchens.

They found themselves spending most of their time peeling potatoes, chopping up poor quality meat or preparing vegetables, all of which were cooked under the direction of a dour woman with muscular arms. The result was edible, but not appetising.

At the end of the first day the cook beckoned them over and said, 'I can tell you've had no experience of kitchen work, so don't bother to deny it.'

Keara and Maggie exchanged worried glances.

'Still, you're clean and willing, I'll give you that, so you can stay on.'

To their further dismay, they found that the single women awaiting employment were treated like school-girls, their comings and goings monitored and regulated.

'If they treat us like this,' Maggie complained, 'I wouldn't like to be in with the paupers on the top floor.'

Keara shivered. If she didn't find some way of earning a living that was where she'd end up to have the baby.

Even in their spare time they had little chance to explore Perth and weren't allowed the pleasure of strolls in the sunshine because they were confined to the grounds of the Home. This was all the more galling because although June was early winter here, the rain was only intermittent and in between there was more of that wonderful clear weather.

'My mother would have loved this,' Keara said one day. 'She often asked me to bring back a pennyworth of sunshine from the shops. There are thousands of pennyworths here, though, aren't there?' Her voice broke and she couldn't continue. She would never, ever forgive Lavinia Mullane for not allowing her to go to her dying mother and pangs of grief still took her by surprise sometimes. And there wasn't a single night when she didn't think about her sisters as she settled into sleep, wondering where they were and what they were doing.

Potential employers began to turn up the very first afternoon to inspect the newcomers and make offers of employment. Alice and Brenda, the two young women who had shared the cabin with Maggie and Keara, went off the next day, each throwing a triumphant look over her shoulder towards her former cabin mates as she walked away.

As soon as the ladies seeking maids were told by the supervisor of Keara's condition, however, they moved on to the other women. Maggie received a couple of offers of employment but refused point-blank to be parted from 'my cousin Keara' and wept loudly (and falsely) when the female supervisor tried to insist on her accepting the second offer.

On the Sunday Keara was allowed to attend Mass at the Catholic Cathedral with a few inmates of the Home who shared her beliefs, and was allowed out a few days later to attend Confession.

'And this is only because there's a good report on you from the matron of the ship,' she was told by the supervisor, who seemed to grudge them even the smallest outing.

On their way back one of the older residents of the Home took them to look at the new Government House, to which alterations were being done because this governor had not felt it to be suitable.

'Well, I wouldn't mind living there,' the woman next to Keara said. 'I can't see what's wrong with it.'

'It looks like a palace to me. I'd be happy with one room as long as it was my own.' Keara sighed and looked down at her stomach. She couldn't think of looking for her sisters until after the baby was born and even then it'd be hard to find employment which would allow her to keep her baby with her and save for the fare across to Melbourne. But as soon as she had a permanent address, she'd write to the nuns. That was all she could do for the present.

By the time a man drove up in a cart looking for a maid there were only two old women from the new arrivals left unemployed besides Keara and Maggie. As he got down from the cart he reached into it to extract a bundle of what looked like clothing. When the bundle waved a chubby pink fist, Maggie nudged Keara. 'It's a baby. He'll be wanting a nursemaid, I should think. Must have lost his wife or she'd be doing the choosing.'

As he went to speak to the supervisor, Maggie winked at Keara. 'Good-looking, isn't he? Well, he would be if he'd smile.'

'I suppose so.' What did she care about how he looked? Keara thought. All she wanted was a job.

A few minutes later the supervisor brought the newcomer towards the room where the four women were sitting waiting. 'Come and line up over here, please!' she called in a sharp voice, then spoke more gently to her companion. 'These are the ones I told you about, Mr Gibson.' She fixed Maggie with a stern gaze. 'And this time, Brett, I'm not having you refuse employment just because you want to be with your cousin.'

A woman came running up to whisper to her and she clicked her tongue in annoyance. 'Please excuse me for a moment, Mr Gibson. There's a small domestic crisis.' She hurried away with the woman.

'My cousin and I are staying together,' Maggie informed the man before he'd even spoken. 'We're good workers and we'll work for lower wages if you'll take us both.'

He blinked at her in surprise. 'You don't even know what sort of work I'm offering.'

'It can't be worse than working in the kitchens here. We're not even cooking decent food most of the time.'

'Ah, you've got kitchen experience.'

'Yes. And my cousin was a housemaid before she got married.'

The bundle heaved and wriggled. 'Can I see the baby?' Keara asked, remembering how she'd loved holding Mara as a baby. She moved across to stare down at its rosy face and the infant gurgled up at her. Smiling, she poked a finger gently into the soft little tummy and murmured some nonsense, which set the baby off chuckling, for some reason.

'What are your names?' Mark asked.

'You don't want them to work for you. That one's expecting.' One of the old women pushed forward, pointing at Keara. 'She *says* she's a widow, but who knows if she's telling the truth?'

He took an immediate step away from them. 'I'm sorry. The job wouldn't be suitable for you. I live in a fairly isolated place and there'd be no one to help you when your time came. Besides, I only need one person.' He turned back to Maggie. 'Are you sure you wouldn't consider taking the job?'

'Go on, take it!' Keara whispered. She felt her eyes filling with tears and hurriedly looked away, but Maggie put an arm round her.

'Sorry, Mr Gibson. I'm not leaving my cousin on her own, not when she's so recently lost her husband. We're only taking work that keeps us together.'

Mark turned to study the two old women, both of whom looked at him hopefully, but they didn't even look clean, let alone strong, so he shook his head. As the supervisor came back just then, he turned to her and said, 'I don't think any of them would be suitable. I believe Mrs – um –' he jerked his head in Keara's direction, 'is expecting a child and her cousin wants to stay with her.'

She shot a furious glance at Maggie. 'This won't do, Brett! I told you before you'd have to take the next job offered to you. You're not staying here unless you abide by the rules.'

With a sigh Mark turned and walked away, leaving them to it. He didn't want an unwilling employee. Surely he'd be able to find some help elsewhere in Perth?

Maggie set her hands on her hips and glared at the supervisor. 'I'm *not* leaving Keara.'

'Then you'd both better leave the Home. You don't qualify for assistance if you refuse offers of employment.'

Keara gasped.

Maggie stared at the woman, furious that she was trying to separate them. 'That's not fair. You know there's a shortage of lodgings in Perth or they'd not be housing us here.' And anyway, they didn't have enough money to keep themselves, as the supervisor was well aware.

'The government isn't here to pander to your whims. Unless you promise to accept the next job offered, you have one hour to remove yourselves from the Home. You can leave your trunks here for a week, then if you've not collected them, the contents will be used for the paupers.'

'We're not going to be separated,' Maggie insisted.

'Then you'd better leave.' She folded her arms, her

expression implacable, but as she watched them go inside, she smiled confidently. They'd be back in a day or two. They weren't the sort to turn to selling their bodies. She could always tell those. But sleeping rough would be a salutary lesson and these women would be easier to deal with afterwards.

Maggie led the way inside the lean-to and began to throw her possessions into her bag, muttering to herself, colour flaring in her cheeks.

'I'm sorry you're in trouble because of me,' Keara said, following her inside. 'Perhaps you'd better try to find Mr Gibson, after all, and accept his offer of employment?'

'And what are *you* going to do if I go off to the country?'

'Miss you very much. But I'm sure something will turn up for me, even if it's only temporary.' She tried to smile, but failed.

'Well, I'm *not* leaving you.' Maggie looked at Keara and for once let her bravado drop. 'Let alone you need me, I've never had a friend like you, someone I trust and care about, and I'm not giving that up. I'd rather die.'

Keara went across and hugged her. 'That'll mean you coming to Melbourne with me after the baby's born.'

Maggie sniffed away a tear. 'Well, I allus did want to see the world. Now, let's get out of here.'

They finished packing and left the Home, carrying their bags. As they walked towards the town centre, Maggie said, 'At least no one can stop us having a good look round now.'

'But where are we going to sleep? They said it'd be hard to find lodgings. Do you have any money?'

'A pound or two. There wasn't much left over from the fare. What about you?'

'Only a few shillings, I'm afraid. The people who drugged me stole my savings.' Which she'd mostly stolen from Theo, so she supposed she shouldn't complain.

'We'll have to sleep rough then.'

They walked round town, but although they went into shops and a couple of boarding houses, no one needed a maid, let alone two of them.

As night fell, they bought some bread and took it down to the river to eat, walking further upstream till they came to a tangle of vegetation.

'We can sleep here,' Maggie said. 'If it rains we'll have to find some shelter, but there aren't any clouds, so I think we'll be all right.'

They slept badly because it grew quite chilly. As soon as it was light, they got up and tried to straighten their clothes, washing their hands and faces in the river.

'Come on,' Keara said as Maggie sat down on a rock and stared glumly into the water. 'Let's try again. But if we can't find anything, we're going to have to return to the Home and do as they want, you know we are.'

Maggie's expression was bleak. 'I'm not going back there, whatever. If we can't find work in Perth, we'll walk out into the country. We're bound to find some-thing eventually.'

'And what if we can't? This place isn't like England.

You've heard people saying that the settlements are few and far between.'

'But there *are* settlements.'

'We'll discuss it again in a day or two.' But Keara didn't think it'd make much difference. And she wasn't going to let her condition blight Maggie's chances of getting employment. If necessary she would go back to the Home on her own. She was sure Maggie wouldn't go wandering off without her.

CHAPTER SEVENTEEN

June 1864

The day soon turned chilly and damp, with rain threatening. Keara and Maggie walked all over the centre of Perth, knocking on doors and asking for work. But although one kind woman gave them some bread and butter, most people were too busy to do more than tell them curtly that they didn't want to employ two people, thank you.

They were standing on a side street, wondering what to try next, when they saw a cart trundling towards them, drawn by two sturdy chestnuts. As they stopped to watch it, Maggie whispered, 'Hey, it's him!'

Keara turned and saw Mr Gibson.

He noticed them at once and reined in the horses, staring at their dishevelled appearance and the travelling bags they were carrying.

As he opened his mouth to speak, Maggie glared at him and called, 'Did you find yourself a maid yet?'

'No.'

'You should have taken us, then, instead of getting us thrown out of the Home!'

'They threw you out?'

'Yes. Because I wouldn't leave Keara. And I still won't.'

Mark looked beyond her to the pregnant woman, who was tugging at her friend's arm and looking embarrassed. 'Perhaps we can—' But the baby interrupted before he could gather his thoughts together. Amy sounded angry and he realised she was hungry and needed to be fed and changed now. He fished his watch out of his pocket, surprised to find it was nearly one o'clock, then looked at the two women. 'I have to feed my daughter. Would you come and join us for a meal, then we can talk in comfort? I know a place where we can eat just round the corner.'

'We haven't any money to spare for eating houses,' Maggie said at once. 'We don't even have enough money to get lodgings. We had to sleep rough last night.'

'Since I invited you, I'll be paying.' Mark looked down at Amy, who was now red in the face from crying. 'Come on. Madam is insisting on her food.' He didn't wait for their agreement but beckoned an urchin across. 'A shilling to mind the cart for an hour.'

The lad brightened and nodded.

The two women exchanged surprised glances, then picked up their bags and trudged across the street after Mr Gibson.

He ordered three meals and a glass of milk. When the food arrived, he began to mash up his potatoes and gravy for Amy, but she was still sobbing and wriggling and nearly knocked his plate off the table.

'Here, let me hold her while you do that.' Keara

took the child who looked at her doubtfully, bottom lip quivering. 'Sure, he'll be feeding you in a minute, little one,' she crooned softly, jiggling the child about and continuing to talk to her.

Amy quietened and reached out for the dark hair that was as usual falling out of its pins, tangling her fingers in it and crowing with triumph, which made Keara laugh as well.

Mark watched in wonder as his daughter nestled against this stranger. 'You've a way with children, it seems.'

'I've had a fair bit of practice with my sisters, me being the eldest.'

Her expression was so sad he didn't ask her for details, but tucked a handkerchief under Amy's neck and concentrated on getting food into her mouth, instead of all over her clothes.

By the time the meal was over he had come to a decision, partly from watching the warmth of the two women's friendship and partly from watching Keara deal with his daughter. 'Look, I'm sorry I caused you such trouble. I'll employ you both, all found, but I can only afford to pay one wage between the two of you until my inn is better established. If you want to take the risk – and there may not be anyone in Meriniup to help birth the baby – well, you can. But you'll have to decide what to do about the baby. Maybe you'll want to move back to Perth for that?'

Maggie clapped her hands together and let out a crow of laughter. 'I knew something would turn up! I knew we wouldn't have to go back to that place! And there's bound to be someone to help with the birthing, there always is.'

'We'll have to hope so. As long as you realise there may not be.' He turned to Keara again. 'You're a very recent widow, I believe. I'm sorry about that.'

She hesitated, then shook her head, not wanting to base her new life on lies. 'I'm not a widow. I've never been married.'

He looked at her in shock.

Maggie gasped. 'You fool! Why did you tell him that?'

'I don't like lying. It's a bad way to start.' Keara looked at him. 'The child I'm carrying is my employer's. I loved him greatly, but his wife sent me to Australia to get rid of me.'

'They didn't *send* her; they drugged her and put her on the ship. I saw them bring her on board and she didn't wake up till after it'd sailed.' Maggie was determined to see justice done. 'I could smell the laudanum.'

Keara nudged her. 'Shhh. That doesn't matter now.'

Mark's eldest sister had once been pregnant and thrown out of employment, but they hadn't sent Annie halfway across the world to get rid of her. And he still felt guilty for abandoning a pregnant woman himself.

Keara waited, wondering if he'd just walk away and leave them.

Instead he looked across at her and said quietly, 'That must have been very difficult for you. Thank you for telling me the truth, but it makes no difference to my offer of employment.'

Keara swallowed hard, her eyes over-bright. 'Thank you, Mr Gibson. We'll be making sure you don't regret your generosity.'

He took his now drowsy daughter back and cuddled her against him, smiling at them. 'That's settled, then.'

It was strange to see a man looking after such a small child, but he seemed quite used to that and clearly loved his baby. Keara's own father had never picked up or cuddled any of them. But Theo loved his little son, you could hear it in his voice when he spoke of Richard. She wished – oh, it was stupid to wish for anything. She should just be thankful that she'd found herself work and somewhere to live for a while.

Mark pushed his chair back. 'Right, then. How quickly can you be ready to leave?'

Maggie followed suit, grinning broadly. 'The minute we get our trunks back from the Home. I'm really looking forward to telling that supervisor we've found jobs.'

An hour later they were sitting on either side of him on the bench seat at the front of the cart, with the baby sleeping peacefully in her wooden box behind Keara.

Mark didn't speak for a while, then said, 'It's nearly full moon tonight. We can get to the inn by late tomorrow if we press on for as long as possible today. We'll have to rest the horses at regular intervals, of course, but if we don't try to go too fast, they'll keep going. They're a sturdy pair. We'll have to sleep on the cart, though. Is that all right?'

'As long as you don't try anything on,' Maggie said at once.

Keara rolled her eyes to heaven at her friend's blunt speech.

He scowled at her, his voice suddenly sharp. 'I'd *never* force myself on a woman.'

As the baby began making whimpering noises, Keara leaned back and picked her up from the box-like cradle. 'Ah, you're a little darlin',' she said softly. 'Did you want to see a bit of the world, then?'

Amy settled in her arms, beaming up at her and waving one chubby fist, which Keara kissed without thinking.

'You're good with children,' Mark said. 'Perhaps we could make looking after Amy part of your duties?'

'Suits me,' Maggie said at once.

'I'd love to.' Keara kissed the child's pink velvet cheek still not realising she was doing it. 'I used to look after my little sister Mara when she was a baby. She's in Melbourne now, so I have to save my money for the fare across to the other side of the country. Only I can't do anything till after my baby's born.'

'Can you not write to them? Bring them across here?'

'I don't know exactly where they are. I was working in England when my parents died and the nuns sent them away to Australia without telling me. They do that sort of thing to Irish orphans.' Her voice was bitter suddenly. 'But I'm going to find them again if it takes me the rest of my life. They can't just have vanished. The Sisters of St Martha and St Zita will surely have records and know where they've gone.'

He was only too well aware that people could easily

vanish in Australia, where the distances were enormous and communication difficult. Some got lost on purpose, others died far from their loved ones, with no one to send word about what had happened. He'd seen these anonymous deaths a few times on the goldfields. But he didn't tell her that, just changed the subject, telling them more about his new home and business, even mentioning his hopes and plans for the future.

They bought some food and fresh milk for Amy from a farm they passed, but Mark refused an offer of a night's accommodation there. As soon as the horses were rested and fed, he harnessed them again.

As they travelled on, he fell silent, wondering what he had got himself into. A rundown inn in the middle of nowhere, two employees, one of them pregnant, a tiny daughter dependent on him for everything. And not a lot of money in reserve now. Well, it'd all work out somehow. He had to believe that.

As the moon came out, Keara looked up at the sky. 'Did you ever see anything as beautiful as those stars?'

He liked the sound of her voice, with its hint of an Irish lilt as well as the trace of a Lancashire accent. The other one's voice was flatter and sounded more like those he had grown up with. She seemed ready to fight the world to stay with her friend. Well, he valued loyalty. 'The stars always seem brighter here to me than they did in England,' he agreed. 'I've grown to love living in Australia. If you're prepared to work hard and you don't expect things to be like they were back home, I think you'll like it, too.'

His words seemed to linger in the air and the two

women exchanged thoughtful glances as they considered them. Maggie laughed suddenly. 'Eh, I've done nowt but work hard all my life. I'm not afraid of that. And I didn't come here to be miserable, either.'

'Why did you come here, then?' he asked. 'Looking for a husband? A lot of women do.'

'No, thank you. I've had one of those and I don't want another. I came to start a new life for myself.'

'You're a widow?'

'Yes.' She avoided looking at Keara as she replied. 'You don't need to worry about us, Mr Gibson. We'll earn our keep and we'll neither of us be rushing off with new husbands.'

He smiled wryly. 'That's good.' But he knew that they would both be sought after, even the pregnant one. Decent women were in short supply in the colony and Keara was pretty, while Maggie had a liveliness about her that was also attractive, though her thin features and bony nose suffered by comparison with her friend.

'I hadn't expected the countryside to be quite so – so empty,' Maggie said suddenly. 'It's miles since we've seen a house. Is your inn like that, all on its own in the middle of nowhere?'

'Well, there's a small settlement nearby, about thirty or forty people. It's hard to tell how many exactly.'

'Blimey,' said the irrepressible Maggie. 'Nearly a city.' She grinned at him. 'I hope there are plenty of people going past, then, because you'll never get rich otherwise.'

'It's the main road south, so there's fairly regular traffic and more settlers will come as the colony grows.'

He gestured around. 'Look how beautiful it is. Who wouldn't want to live here?'

Maggie pulled a face at Keara, but didn't contradict him. She'd rather live in a town any old day. Still, this would do to be going on with. It was a godsend, really. And she'd loved telling the women's supervisor at the Home that they'd found themselves jobs.

They arrived at Meriniup long after dark, following an exhausting second day's travel, to find lights still burning in the inn and a small wagon standing outside the guests' quarters, its load covered by a tarpaulin.

'What's going on?' Mark asked. 'We never stay open this late. Here, hold the reins, Maggie. Keep an eye on Amy for me, will you, Keara?'

He strode inside to find a scared-seeming Edith pouring out some rum for a rough-looking fellow with a beard who took it without making any attempt to pay her. 'Has he paid for that? And why are you open so late?'

The man swung round and stared at Mark. 'What's it got to do with you? Go and find your own company.'

Edith suddenly screamed, 'Look out!' pointing to one side of him. Mark jumped sideways just in time to avoid a chair being smashed down on his head. He seized his opportunity while the attacker was off balance to crash his fist into the fellow's jaw, sending him to measure his length on the floor, groaning.

Edith screamed again as another man rose from where he had been sleeping under the side table and lunged towards Mark.

Outside, Maggie and Keara heard the rumpus and looked at one another in dismay.

'Something's wrong. We've got to help him,' Keara said, then froze as there was a crashing sound from inside.

Maggie shivered. 'Sounds like they're fighting. I'm not going in till I'm sure it's safe.'

Keara thrust the baby at her. 'Well, I am. Mr Gibson may need help.' She leaped nimbly down from the wagon and ran towards the door where she paused to find out what was happening.

Her new employer was struggling with two men while a young woman, presumably Edith, was standing behind them weeping instead of going to his aid, and a scrawny lad was standing near her with an expression of sheer terror on his face. Keara looked round and grabbed the nearest heavy object, which was a wooden stool. A man was sitting up on the floor, rubbing his jaw. 'If you don't stay where you are, I'll clout you with this, so I will.' She brandished the stool close to his face.

As he spread his arms wide in a gesture of surrender she hurried forward, hovering for a minute on the edge of the struggle, moving back when the men suddenly surged her way, looking for an opportunity to hit one of the two strangers and even the odds for Mr Gibson.

Ah! She saw an opportunity and pounced, crashing the stool down on the nearest man's head and shoulders. He fell and didn't rise. She risked a quick glance to see if the other man had moved, but he was still sitting there, cradling his jaw, so she turned to see if Mr Gibson needed any more help. He didn't. He landed a punch squarely in his opponent's guts and, as the man doubled up, swung another blow to his temple that sent the fellow crashing to the ground.

He waited a few seconds to make sure his opponent was in no state to continue fighting, then ran behind the bar and came back holding a revolver in a way that said he knew how to use it. He was panting, but his hand was steady as he watched the three men. As none of them made any move to continue the fight, he looked across at Keara, threw back his head and laughed. 'You're an amazing woman.'

She smiled. 'Sure, I learned to defend myself and my sisters when I was a child. I hadn't any brothers to help, you see. And besides, Maggie and I need this job. We don't want anything happening to you.'

As the man Keara had hit started to get up Mark said loudly, 'Any more trouble and I use this.'

The man stared at the revolver and Mark's face. 'Aw, it just got a bit out of hand. We didn't mean no harm.'

'Well, so that it doesn't get out of hand again, take your friends, harness up your horses and find somewhere else to stay tonight.'

The young woman was still sobbing so Keara went over and shook her, saying sharply, 'Enough of that, now! Have they hurt you?'

Edith shook her head. 'No, but they were going to.'

Keara didn't dare be too sympathetic. 'Well, they didn't.' She looked at the lad, who seemed to be about twelve. 'Are you all right?'

He nodded, but stayed close to his sister.

'Better stay where you are.' Keara turned to look at her employer questioningly.

'Go and fetch Maggie and the baby in,' he said quietly. 'But don't get between me and them.' He gestured at the men.

She nodded and slipped outside again. 'Just some rough types causing trouble, Maggie. Mr Gibson's got a revolver pointed at them, so don't get between them and him.' She held out her arms for the baby and waited till Maggie had got down.

Even as they turned towards the inn a man stumbled out of the door. He noticed them and scowled but said nothing, lurching along to the other cart. As the two others followed him, Mark came to stand on the veranda, revolver at the ready. 'There's enough moon-light for me to be sure of hitting my target,' he said in a conversational tone. 'You learn to shoot first and ask questions later on the goldfields.'

But the fight had gone out of the men and they harnessed their horses quickly, bringing out their gear from the room Edith had allotted them. Mark went across to check that they'd not stolen anything, then allowed them to drive off into the night.

When the sound of their horse and cart had faded into the distance, he let out his breath in a long whoosh and looked down at the revolver. 'I didn't think I'd be able to use it again. But when you're defending your home and child, you feel a bit different.'

'Use it again?' Maggie asked.

He hesitated, then said, 'I killed a man with it once, a bushranger who held up the wagon I was on. If I hadn't, he'd have killed me, but the thought of what I did still gives me nightmares.' He shrugged and gestured to the door. 'Sorry it's been such a poor welcome to Meriniup. Won't you come inside?'

Maggie was uncharacteristically quiet as she stared round the big public room where everything seemed to be made of dark, reddish wood – walls, floor, furniture, even the ceiling. She looked across at the young woman who was sniffling as she put more fuel on the fire and swung a kettle over it. The lad was standing doing nothing. 'Does this sort of thing often happen?' Maggie wondered aloud.

'Heavens, no.' Mark shuddered visibly at the thought.

Edith came over, wiping her eyes with a corner of her apron. 'They had trouble once before, my dad told us about it. When they first built the inn.' She let out a sudden wail. 'I want to go home! I'm not sleeping here. They might come back.'

'I doubt it,' said Mark, but she wouldn't be persuaded to stay until he asked her if she and her brother really fancied walking home in the dark.

'Won't you take us?' she begged. 'You've got a gun. We'd be safe with you.'

'And leave my baby and these two women on their own?'

'Well, me and our Johnny aren't sleeping over in them guest quarters.'

Maggie sighed. 'You can sleep here with us, love. We'll take the rolling pin to bed with us, just in case.'

'I think we should all sleep in here – just for tonight,'

Keara said. 'In case they come back. We can bring the mattresses in.'

Mark nodded. 'I'll drive the wagon round the back and unharness the horses.' He looked from one to the other. 'One of you should keep the revolver while I'm gone.'

Keara jiggled little Amy. 'I can't. I'll be changing this young lady.' And anyway, she was reluctant to hold the thing.

Maggie surprised herself. 'I'll take it. But you'll have to show me how to use it.'

Within an hour they were all lying on makeshift beds in front of the fire with the doors locked. It felt cosy and safe to Keara and she lay watching the flames until she drifted into sleep.

In the morning it was hard to believe they'd had such an eventful arrival and they all pitched in to help unload the cart and put away the provisions. It seemed like an omen that the sun was shining once more.

'Will you be all right if I take Edith and her brother back now?' Mark asked. 'She's not going to be much use.'

'She's no use at all,' said Maggie. 'Jumps at every sound. I'll be glad to see the back of the silly creature.' She went out to watch him and the others stride away along a track that led through the forest, then returned to Keara. 'Well, how do you like Meriniup?'

Keara grinned. 'It's all right, as long as we don't have fights every night.'

'You must have been mad to join in – especially in your condition.'

'Mr Gibson needed some help. And *we* need him.' Keara chuckled suddenly. 'Besides, I forgot about the baby.'

From the time he got back to Melbourne, Alex Jenner spent every half-day off work prowling round the docks. He got into conversation with several people, but it was not until his third visit that he met a man who seemed to know about ships to other states. Even though it went against the grain to indulge in alcoholic beverages, Alex bought him a drink of beer and continued to question him.

His son-in-law could have gone by ship to either Western Australia or Brisbane, it seemed, at that time of the month.

'How would I find out which?' he pondered aloud.

'If you were to slip me a bit of money, I might introduce you to the stewards from each ship. But they'll want paying for their time, too.'

'I'll bring some more money next time, but I'm not a rich man. I'm a grandfather saddened by losing his grandchild to a wicked fellow who will bring her up in his own evil ways.' He saw the man frowning and moderated his language. 'Here. This is for your trouble today.' He slipped five shillings into the man's hand and saw his face brighten. 'When shall I come back?'

He had to pretend to be ill in order to take time off work to meet the first of the stewards, but the man could tell him nothing except that he hadn't seen anyone of Mark's description board the ship to Brisbane.

The following week, Alex took another day off to meet a second steward. This time, when he described his son-in-law, the man remembered Mark Gibson perfectly, even giving his name.

'Not often you see a fellow looking after a little baby, is it? But he didn't seem to mind and she was a happy little soul.'

'Ah. You've set my mind at rest. I don't know how to thank you.' Alex slipped some coins into the hand that was held out to him and put others into his guide's hand. 'The Lord bless you both.'

He went home and sat lost in thought that evening while his wife tiptoed around him, trying not to disturb him.

'I've found out where they went,' he announced abruptly.

Nan brightened and came to sit next to him. 'Where?'

'To Western Australia.'

Her face fell. 'That's so far away. We'll never be able to see them again.'

'Leave it to me. The other members of our congregation may be persuaded to help us.'

She stared at him in shock. 'What do you mean, Alex?'

'I intend to follow him to Western Australia and bring my granddaughter back here, to raise her properly.'

'But, Alex, you can't! He's her father. We have no right to—'

He slapped her face and sent her sprawling. 'Woman, hold your tongue!'

She crawled away from him, weeping, and took refuge in the bedroom.

He forgot about her as soon as he sat down again. He didn't have enough money saved to pay their fares, but he might be able to persuade his fellow worshippers to open their purses in the cause of rescuing a young soul from peril.

Mark Gibson was *not* going to raise Alex's grandchild. He might have failed with his own son and daughter, but he would know how to be more strict with Amy – as he was learning to be stricter with his wife. Chastisement for the good of the soul, that's what it was.

He sat on until the fire died in the grate, not noticing that he had not had an evening meal.

Nan lay on the bed and wept, not knowing what to do to stop him. He had gone beyond reason now, and was treating her more like a servant than a wife. But she had no family except him in Australia and without him she would have no way of living, so she could see no way out.

What had got into him lately?

CHAPTER EIGHTEEN

August 1864

———◆———

Caley came home one day triumphantly brandishing a
letter from Ireland. 'He's written at last!'

'About time too! What does he say?'

He began to read Theo's letter aloud:

My dear cousins
I was delighted to receive your latest letter and hear
that you'd found somewhere to settle at last.
Bunbury sounds to be a pleasant little town, but
best of all you're happy with the conditions on your
homestead for rearing horses. And, yes, I'll send out
the two mares and stallion which you left in my
charge by the next ship, which will be the Golden
Empress. *They tell me it'll arrive in Perth about a*
month after you receive this letter.

'I'll have to go up and meet the ship,' Caley said at
once. 'Will you be able to manage on your own, me
love?'

'Of course I shall. I've got the children, and Jack and

his wife living in the servants' quarters nearby, haven't
I? Now finish reading the letter.'

*To my great sadness my son Richard never thrived
and only lived a few weeks, which is why I haven't
written before. I can't face trying again with
Lavinia so we've agreed to live separately, she in
Lancashire and I here at Ballymullan. I don't
really know what I'll do with the rest of my life. It's
too soon to see my way clearly.*

'Ah, no! Not again. That poor man!' Noreen forced
back her tears. 'Your uncle should have been hanged
for pushing him into that marriage.'

'I wouldn't have bred my children from a woman
like that,' Caley murmured. 'I don't think people are so
different from horses. Bad stock gives sickly offspring.'
For a moment or two they both stopped speaking to
smile at one another, thinking of their own healthy children, then he continued reading:

*What I have to tell you now fills me with shame
and you're the only people to know apart from
Diarmid and, of course, Dick. (Did you know he
was a half-brother of mine, by the way?)*

Noreen gasped at this news. 'Well, did you ever?
Your uncle having a child out of wedlock . . . the old
hypocrite! After all he said to us when he found out we'd
been a bit previous.' She caught her husband's eye and
let out a gurgle of laughter. 'Sorry, darlin'! I'm interrupting you again, aren't I?'

He smiled at her fondly. 'You always do, but I wouldn't have you any other way. Now, be quiet, woman, and listen.'

She pulled a face at him and clasped both hands across her mouth.

During my wife's pregnancy, Keara's parents died and Lavinia had her sisters sent out to Australia forcibly so that she wouldn't lose Keara's services.

'Oh, no! What a cruel thing to do.' Noreen looked at her husband, her eyes brimming now with tears. 'I remember talking to that girl and her telling me about her family. Sure, her love for them showed even to a stranger like me. Oh, that dreadful woman should be locked away!'

Although they went in the care of some nuns, who apparently make a habit of sending young Irishwomen out to the colonies as servants, and so can be presumed safe, I can never forgive Lavinia for that. When Keara found out, she left my wife's service and came under my protection for a time.

To my further shame, while I was away from home, Lavinia's maid had Keara kidnapped, drugged, and put on a ship bound for Australia. I was too late to prevent this, still find it hard to believe anyone would get away with such a thing in this day and age, but they did.

To make matters worse, the two sisters were sent to Melbourne, but Keara went to Perth. The reason I'm telling you is that I want to beg you to find her and make sure she's all right. Could you give her the fare to get to Melbourne, together with enough money to pursue her search for her sisters once she arrives there?

I need quite desperately to know that she's safe, my dear cousins. I hope and pray that she can be reunited with her sisters as quickly as possible. Enclosed is a bank draft, which should cover all your own and Keara's expenses.

Thinking of you fondly,
Theo

Noreen took out a handkerchief and wiped her eyes. 'He sounds so sad and hopeless!'

Caley thumped his clenched right fist into the palm of his left hand, repeating the action several times as was his wont when upset. In the end, Noreen gently took hold of his hand and raised it to her lips.

'We'll find the girl, for him,' she said quietly. 'Perth isn't a big town. She might disappear in a city like Liverpool or London, but in Perth someone is bound to know where she's gone. When you go up there for the horses, you'll be able to make enquiries.'

'That's not for another month.'

'She won't fade away in a month and a strong girl like that will easily find work. You're always so impatient, Caley Gallagher.'

He gave her a knowing smile. 'You're not always particularly patient yourself.'

Hands clasped, they sat on for a while, then Noreen

jumped to her feet. 'What I'm doing sitting here when there's a meal to be cooked, I don't know.'

But as she worked she couldn't stop thinking about that poor young woman, cut off from everyone she knew and loved, alone in a strange land, no doubt worrying about her sisters.

Diarmid looked at Theo, who was sitting studying the accounts but who hadn't done more than stare into space for several minutes. 'Someone has to say it, so I will: you can't go on like this.'

Theo started and looked up. 'What?'

'I said: you can't go on like this. Since you came back from England you've been moping around like a dog that's lost its tail.'

'I can't settle, don't know what to do with myself.'

Diarmid didn't pretend not to understand. He and Dick had got drunk together one night and Dick had let out why Theo was so low in spirits. 'Because of Keara Michaels?'

Theo nodded. 'I can't stop thinking about how frightened she must have been when she woke up on that ship. I saw for myself how hurt she was that her sisters had been sent so far away. I'll never forgive Lavinia for that – or myself for not looking after Keara properly.'

'She's a sensible young woman, not a child. She'll cope better than most.'

Theo nodded, but seemed only half-convinced.

Footsteps sounded outside and there was the

familiar triple rap on the door that heralded the approach of Father Cornelius.

'Come in, Father, and sit yourself down.' Diarmid vacated his own chair and waved the priest into it.

'It was Theo I came to see.' He pulled out a letter. 'I've heard from the Sisters.'

Theo sat up, suddenly very alert.

'The girls arrived safely and gave no trouble during the journey. A place was found for the older one, Ismay, and the younger one was taken into the convent's orphanage. She was lucky. A couple wanted to adopt her and they took her away a month later.'

'Do the Sisters say where?'

Father Cornelius looked up in puzzlement. 'Where?'

'Where Ismay went and Mara, too.'

'No. No, they don't. But they would check any employers very carefully, I'm sure, as they would any-one wanting to adopt a child. The family would have to be Catholics and in good standing in their parish, I'm sure.'

Theo was still frowning. 'You don't know that for certain, though, you're just trusting them blindly.'

'I think one can trust nuns to look after their charges.'

Father Cornelius was looking huffy, so Theo asked for the letter.

'Why should you need it?'

He looked from the priest to Diarmid, a wry smile on his face. 'Because I'm going out to Australia. If I have that letter, the nuns will know I'm not a trickster, especially if you could write me a few words, introducing me . . .'

'Are you sure about this?'

'Very sure. My wife sent the girls away, so it's my responsibility to bring them back. I shan't rest till I've righted that wrong.'

'Very well.'

Theo settled the old priest at his desk and paced up and down the room as Father Cornelius wrote and then passed him the letter. It was short and to the point, but it would do. He wasn't at all satisfied that he knew enough about what had happened to Ismay and Mara, or how to put Keara in touch with them, but this would give him a start, surely?

When the priest had left, Diarmid looked at Theo. 'Are you sure this is the right thing to do?'

'Yes. It's not good enough, you see.'

'What's not?'

'Not knowing exactly what's happened to those two girls – or to Keara. Not being certain they're happy. I'll not rest easy until I've found out for myself.' For the first time in weeks Theo gave Diarmid a genuine smile. 'You know, it feels like the right thing to do.'

He strode out of the agent's office and up to the house, sending the bell pealing for Dick. He didn't even wait for his half-brother to close the door of the bedroom. 'I'm going to Australia. I can't do anything till I know she's all right – and then I'll help her find her sisters.'

Dick was so shocked he couldn't speak for a moment or two. 'Have you run mad, man?'

Theo nodded. 'In one sense, yes. In another, I think I've come to my senses for the first time in months. Will you come with me?'

His half-brother stood there for so long looking rigid and shocked that he repeated his question.

Dick bowed his head, then looked up and said, 'I – don't think so.'

Theo pressed his lips together to hold back a sharp response, then spoke quietly, 'May I ask why not?'

Dick waved towards the window. 'This. I miss Ireland more every time we go away. I'd have gone for you, if there was no other way, but if you're going yourself, there's no need for me. I couldn't bear to leave home for ever, you see. And what if you decided to stay? You used to speak about emigrating, making a new life in the colonies.' He shook his head. 'That's not for me.'

Theo turned round and moved across to the window to stare across the mist and rain-filled landscape. 'It seems as if I'm losing everyone I care about.'

'Will you still be going?'

'Oh, yes. I must.'

Dick went across to lay one hand on his half-brother's shoulder. 'It's the right decision for you, I think. You look more like your old self already, even though I've disappointed you.'

Theo turned round. 'I was asking too much. You have a right to your own life.' A slow smile dawned on his face. 'Besides, I need someone to help Diarmid run the place. Who better than family? Will you do it?'

'Of course.'

'I'll travel out with the horses. I'll be able to keep an

eye on them during the journey. And I'll take a couple of my own with me.' Theo was fairly crackling with energy and excitement now.

Strangely enough he slept well that night, better than he had for a long time.

It was definitely the right decision.

He wrote a curt letter to his wife to tell her that he was going to Australia to right the two wrongs she had committed, and that she should apply to Diarmid if she had any problems, but he reminded her there would be no more money available if she overspent her allowance. After that, he went into a whirl of preparations that didn't give him a minute's leisure until he set off for England with the horses to board his ship.

Which was the way he wanted it.

After Mark had taken Edith and her brother home he hurried back to the inn, where Keara and Maggie had already prepared breakfast.

'We'll need to make some damper bread,' he said, working out which tasks needed doing first. 'Which one of you wants to do that?'

They both spoke at once, then laughed, and Keara waved one hand at Maggie, inviting her to speak first.

'I don't know how, because we always bought our bread already baked back home, but I like cooking,' Maggie said.

'It's the same with me,' Keara admitted. 'You'd better teach us both how to do it, Mr Gibson.'

It felt wrong them speaking to him so formally when

they were going to be living together for the next few months at least. 'You may as well call me Mark. People aren't so formal about names in Australia.' Wondering how useful they were going to be if they were so ignorant about cooking, he got out the baking equipment and showed them how to make damper. 'I'll show you how to make real bread another time.'

While the loaves were cooking in the kitchen oven outside, he picked up his daughter, whom Keara had just changed, and soon had her chuckling as he played with her. Afterwards, still carrying her, he took his new employees on a tour of the rambling outbuildings of the inn, opening every cupboard, unearthing piles of equipment of all sorts.

'They weren't very tidy people,' Keara said disapprovingly. 'It's not much better inside the house.' She stopped to look back at the sprawl of buildings. 'I hadn't expected it to be so big.' There were lean-tos and sheds and outhouses scattered haphazardly round the rear of the inn.

'It might be big, but they didn't plan things properly,' he said. 'Look how far away the main store-room is from the kitchen. That's plain stupid.'

'And are we really expected to cook out here, with one side of the kitchen open to the weather?' Maggie asked, scowling round in disapproval.

'It's what the settlers usually do,' Mark said. 'But it feels strange to me, too. Which reminds me, I must get you both leather aprons to guard your skirts against sparks. I keep a kettle over the fire in the public room and I've been doing some simple cooking there, but when we get going, we'll need better facilities. I think I'm going to build a proper kitchen on the back of the inn. There are enough rocks lying around to build a chimney.' He kicked the ramshackle kitchen structure that sheltered the old iron range. 'Look at this. I could pull it down with my bare hands.'

'Will we need a carpenter, then?' Keara wondered.

He smiled. 'I can do it myself. My father was a handy sort of fellow and taught me a lot. I used to work in my sister's junkyard, which wasn't all that different from this place. We often mended furniture or made things from scrap wood.'

He led the way into the owner's house. 'I think you two had better sleep in here. If I'm away in Perth buying provisions, you'll need to be with Amy. You could share the bedroom at the back, or even have a room each.'

Keara grimaced and stared down at her belly. 'I think I'm going to be needing a room of my own.'

He looked at her and closed his eyes briefly.

'Did I say something wrong?' she asked.

'No. It's just – my wife died in childbirth so the thought of it makes me a bit nervous. But she was always rather delicate, not a sturdy woman like you, Keara.'

'Living here will suit us fine.' Maggie didn't want them to keep talking about dying in childbirth. 'I wouldn't want to be sleeping near the guests if there are many like those last night.'

They spent the rest of the morning setting the public room in order and Mark watched with approval as they worked together, their standards of cleanliness every bit as high as his own. He went out to tend the horses, fed the hens and made a simple stew for themselves and any stray travellers. He was beginning to feel at home here and that was partly due to the two women he'd tried not to hire. Strange how quickly they'd all grown comfortable together.

The first customers arrived in the middle of the day, two young fellows riding up to Perth. Their eyes brightened at the sight of young women, one of them so pretty, and Mark suddenly realised this might be a common reaction. He watched as both Keara and Maggie dealt with them easily enough, since they were polite young fellows, but he knew other travellers might be more difficult to handle. When men had been without women for a long time, they were usually polite but a few could become troublesome.

In fact, the very next evening, three young fellows from the settlement came in and sat huddled over glasses of rum and water, since the beer hadn't yet settled down after its journey from Perth. It was clear that it was the women who'd drawn them. They were perfectly polite, but they hardly even looked at Mark.

'Are they that short of women in the country?' Maggie demanded after they'd left. 'One of them lot asked me to start walking out with him. The cheek of it! He must be five years younger than me, too.'

'I didn't enjoy the way they looked at me, either,' Keara confessed. 'Even with the baby.' She was quite sure that no other man would erase her memories of Theo. He'd been in her thoughts ever since she'd left England and was there still. She was surprised at how much she missed him, considering they'd been together such a short time. Though they'd lived in the same house since she was sixteen.

Mark looked at her in concern. She had that sad expression again, a look that sometimes appeared when she thought no one was paying attention to her. Had she loved this employer of hers, then? he wondered. She didn't talk about him at all. He didn't even know the man's name.

His eyes slid inevitably down to her stomach. She didn't seem worried about the baby, was carrying it easily and seemed to have undiminished energy, unlike Patience. He was the one worrying about the birth. That gently rounded stomach seemed a constant reminder that two women had died because of bearing his babies. He didn't think he could go through that again. Not that this was his baby, but he did feel some responsibility for her safety.

But there were still three months to go before the birth so he said nothing, just kept a careful watch on her state of health, determined that if she looked to be getting into difficulties he'd take her back to Perth and get medical help for her.

'He's a bit stiff, isn't he?' Maggie said one night as they were sitting in front of the fire, too lazy to stand up and go to bed.

'Who?'

'Mark, of course.'

Keara thought about this, head on one side, lips pursed. 'He's just a bit shy, I think. Some men are and I prefer them that way.'

'No, it's more than that. He watches you all the time. You don't suppose he's fallen in love with you, do you?'

'No, I don't. I don't even want to think of love and that sort of thing. I'm never going to marry. Never! And anyway, I can't be settling down. I have to look for my sisters as soon as we can get the money together. Unless you've changed your mind about coming with me? I shan't blame you if you want to stay here.'

Maggie reached out to squeeze her hand. 'Of course I haven't changed my mind.' She sighed blissfully. 'Eh, I've never been so happy in all my life, Keara love, as these past few weeks. Enough to eat, nobody thumping me, people to talk to – it isn't half as lonely here as I'd expected – and you treating me like a real cousin.' Her voice was choked with tears. 'I keep thinking something will go wrong.'

'Why on earth should it?'

A month later a traveller rode up on horseback. Keara watched through the window as he tied up the animal. When he strode into the inn she moved forward to serve him, then stopped, gasping in shock as she recognised the man who had once visited Theo at Ballymullan and whose wife had been so kind and understanding about the difficulties of dealing with her former mistress.

Caley Gallagher stopped dead in his tracks and stared at her, equally shocked, because he recognised her instantly. He recovered first and moved across to join her. 'Keara Michaels! It *is* you, isn't it?'

'Yes, Mr Gallagher. I – um – hope you and Mrs Gallagher are happily settled here now.' She fumbled for words, trying not to let her unease show. He was sure to write to Theo and say where she was. How could he not? And what if Theo came looking for her? She didn't think she could bear to see him again because it would mean she would have to part from him sooner or later when he went back to England.

And what if he tried to take the baby away from her?

'My wife and I are living just down the road in Bunbury. Amazing, isn't it?' Caley turned to glance through the window. 'Is there someone who can look after my horse? He'd welcome a drink of water and a good feed, I'm sure. And I'd like something to eat if you have it.' It was a cool day and the roughly painted sign outside the inn saying *HOT MEALS* had tempted him to stop and sample their wares otherwise he'd have ridden past. But he had heard that there was a new owner who offered better service and hoped this would be a good place to stop for refreshments on the trip to and from Perth henceforth. Other men might ride their horses hard, but he didn't. Or himself, he admitted wryly.

He hadn't realised when he came to Western Australia that they had no railways or even decent roads in the country districts, and although he loved their new home and relished having his own acres, he wasn't best pleased at how long it took to get up to Perth and back, a journey you had to make from time to time.

'I'll call Mark.' She hurried out to the back before

he could say anything else, stopping just outside the door to lay one hand on her chest because her heart seemed to be beating too fast.

'Are you all right?'

She looked up to see Mark standing next to her. 'Sorry. I've just had a bit of a shock, that's all. A man I met in Ireland – he's a cousin of my former employer – has just come in. He wants someone to look after his horse while he gets a meal.'

Mark frowned. 'He'll have to look after it himself, I'm afraid. Tell him to bring it round the back. There's water here and I can sell him some feed, but I can't afford to employ a stable lad yet.' When she didn't move, he asked again, 'Are you sure you're all right? He's not upsetting you?'

'I'm fine. I was just surprised to see him.'

Mr Gallagher nodded when she told him what to do. 'You and I need to talk privately before I leave, Keara. I have a message for you from my cousin.'

She closed her eyes and when she opened them, he'd gone out again.

He came back through the rear door a quarter of an hour later, by which time she had regained enough control over her emotions to say crisply, 'We only have stew, but it's a good one. And we've got damper still warm from the oven.'

'A bowl of stew will suit me just fine. And fresh damper's as good as any bread I've eaten.'

'We've got apple pie and cream as well.'

His face brightened. 'I'd love some. I stopped at this inn once before but the food was unappetising. I didn't expect to see *you* here. I was going to look for you in Perth.'

'You were? How did you . . . ?' Even before he spoke she had guessed.

'Theo sent me a letter soon after you left England. He'd traced you to the ship, but was too late to help you. He's deeply ashamed of what his wife did and worried sick about you, so he asked me to find out if you were all right.' When she didn't speak, he looked at her and saw that she was fighting against tears. 'You're not all right, are you?'

She gulped and tried to speak normally. 'I'm just – a bit upset – hearing you talk about Theo.'

He thought her love for his cousin showed clearly in her eyes and felt sorry for her.

'What did he say?'

Caley started to speak, then as Maggie came in, said in a low voice, 'Can we go somewhere private to talk after I've eaten? I've other things to tell you as well.'

She served him a bowl of stew and a big chunk of crusty new damper bread, then went to stand at the rear of the room where Maggie was waiting for her.

'What's going on? Are you all right, love? That man hasn't been annoying you, has he?'

'Mm. Oh, no. No, of course not. It's just – I know him. Well, I've met him before. He's Theo's cousin and has a message for me. Can you keep an eye on things after he's eaten? I'll take him along to sit on the guests' veranda. We can talk privately there.'

'You look proper flummoxed,' Maggie said in concern.

'I feel it. I never expected to meet someone from home, not here. Does the baby show?' Without realising what she was doing, she laid one hand on her stomach in that age-old protective gesture women have towards their unborn children.

'Not if you're careful.'

But Caley had two children and another on the way, had seen his own wife making that same gesture many a time. He forgot to eat the spoonful of stew as the implications of her condition sank in, then realised his meal was going cold and concentrated on eating the excellent food she had provided.

Half an hour later he stood up and paid. 'Can you come and talk now, Keara?'

She nodded, exchanged glances with Maggie, then led the way outside.

When Mark came in for his own meal, Maggie told him what she knew and they both went to peer out towards the guests' veranda. But all they could see were two figures sitting in the winter sun in the sheltered corner.

Caley couldn't think how to say it tactfully, so as soon as Keara had sat down on the wooden bench he asked straight out, 'Is that Theo's child you're carrying?'

She nodded.

'Does he know about it?'

She shook her head.

'For heaven's sake, you know how he longs for a child. How could you keep this from him?'

'He has a son. This one is mine.'

'His son died. We got a letter from Theo a month ago, sent not long after you'd left. He sounded very sad.'

'What? Richard's dead? Oh, no! No, not again!'

Her face had lost all its colour and she pressed the back of her hand against her lips but could not hold back the tears. Caley watched her in concern.

'He must have been so upset. And *she* would be no comfort to him.'

'I doubt she'd even care,' Caley agreed. 'She's a dreadful woman. He's sold Eastwood House and they're living separately. She's staying in Lancashire and he's back in Ballymullan. He's worried sick about you. Said you had no money, no way of going to Victoria after your sisters. He wrote to ask me to look for you in Perth. See!' He pulled out the letter. 'You can read it for yourself.'

But when she looked at the piece of paper the words all ran together and she shook her head. 'You'll have to read it to me. I'm not very good at reading, and today I can't even see it for the tears.' A sob escaped her and she bowed her head.

So Caley read the letter aloud to her in his soft Irish voice, and that in itself made her long quite desperately to be back in Ballymullan. When he had finished she was silent, then took a deep breath that hitched into a sob in the middle. 'Could you read it again, please, so that I'll remember it properly?'

He did so.

After another long silence, she said, 'He's right, you know.'

'What do you mean?'

'I won't live with him in sin again. We should never have – I didn't mean to –' Then she began to sob in earnest.

Mark appeared at the edge of the veranda. 'What's the matter, Keara?' The look he threw Caley was filled with animosity and mistrust.

She tried to stop weeping long enough to explain, 'He's not – it's not him. He's Theo's cousin.'

Maggie had followed Mark across and pushed past the men to take Keara in her arms and say fiercely, 'Go away and leave her to me.'

They did.

'You'd better come back inside, Mr Gallagher,' Mark said curtly. 'You're not leaving till I've found out why she's so upset.'

After some hesitation, Caley explained what he knew.

Mark heard him out, sighed and made a pot of tea. 'Keara *was* kidnapped and shipped out there, then?'

'Yes. And the baby's father is my cousin Theo.' Caley stared into the fire. 'What's more, he's desperate to have a child and has just lost his only son, so it would be cruel to keep this child from him.'

'What happened to Keara was cruel, too.' It made Mark feel furious to think of anyone kidnapping a pregnant woman and sending her so far away from all she knew.

'That wasn't Theo's fault!'

'No, but the baby is and he still can't marry her since he already has a wife. She's a decent lass and deserves better than he can offer her.'

'He knows that. He's sent me some money to give to her. They even stole her savings, apparently. He knows she'll have to go to Melbourne to find her sisters. He feels very guilty about what his wife did.'

'So he should.'

Caley sighed. 'Can I have a rum? I need something stronger than tea. And let me buy one for you, as well.'

When Keara and Maggie came across to join them, Caley got up so hurriedly he knocked his chair over. 'Are you all right now, Keara?'

She nodded.

'You can give me the money,' Maggie said. 'She doesn't want to see you again – or him. Especially him. She just wants to have the baby and find her sisters.'

'Is that right, Keara? Is that really what you want? You know how Theo will feel about this.'

'What else can I do? It was all my mother had, her respectability. All I had too, for most of my life. Bad enough that I'm carrying his bastard, unthinkable that I should become his mistress again.' She was feeling unaccountably weary and sank down on the nearest stool, putting one elbow on the table and leaning her aching forehead against her hand.

Caley fumbled in his pocket and spilled a few coins on the table. 'I'll have to bring you the rest of the money on my way back from Perth. Theo sent a bank draft and I have to cash it before I can pay you.'

When her friend didn't move, Maggie scooped up the coins. 'I'll look after these for you, love.' She turned a suspicious glance on Caley. 'Where do you live, Mr Gallagher?'

Keara tugged at her friend's sleeve. 'It doesn't matter.'

Maggie shook her hand off. 'Oh, yes, it does. We have to be practical, Keara. This is the answer to our prayers. If he gives us the rest of the money, then after the baby's born we can afford to go and look for your sisters.'

Caley fumbled in his pockets, found a scrap of paper and wrote down his address, together with directions for getting there.

Maggie took it from him, her suspicious expression not relaxing in the slightest. 'Right, then. I'm taking Keara to lie down. I hope you'll be gone when we come back, Mr Gallagher. She's had enough upsets for today.'

He watched her go, admiring her loyalty to her friend. As for Keara, in spite of her sadness and tears, she was prettier than he'd remembered, or was it the baby which was giving her that luminous glow? He turned to find Mark watching him. 'I will leave now, but I'll be back in a week or two. I have to meet a ship – Theo's sending me out some horses – so I can't give you an exact date for my return. But I *will* come back with the money.'

Mark nodded. But as he watched Caley Gallagher leave, a new worry crept into his mind, a purely selfish one. If Keara had the money to go hunting for her sisters, she'd be leaving Meriniup soon after the baby was born. You only had to hear her talking about Ismay and Mara to know how deeply she loved them.

And then what would he and Amy do?

Was it time to start thinking of remarrying? He'd decided not to but maybe that was wrong, given that he had a child to raise. A girl needed a mother as she grew older and Keara was wonderful with Amy. Only— if he ever changed his mind, he'd want it to be because he truly loved someone. He didn't feel attracted to Keara in that way, though he liked her and admired her courage.

CHAPTER NINETEEN

August–September 1864

———◆◆◆———

Theo expected to find the voyage tedious, but it was actually interesting. The ship was carrying quite a lot of livestock, and the captain was an experienced sailor intent on making good progress and happy to share information with his passengers about where they were and what speed they were making. He ran his ship efficiently, too, catching fresh rainwater whenever he could, providing hearty, well-cooked food, keeping order among the rougher element in steerage and setting up regular entertainments for all the passengers. The steerage passengers especially loved dancing and Theo enjoyed watching them, joining in sometimes.

He kept himself busy in the daytime helping care for the horses. Sometimes he simply kept them company, for the poor creatures were penned up most of the time in large wooden crate-like stalls on deck, or led below into the darkness in rough weather or when they were at their furthest point south ploughing through the icy seas that kept the passengers similarly confined below decks.

Theo didn't suffer from seasickness at all and in fact, revelled in the surging motion of the ship when the water was rougher. He found the passengers an interesting crowd, whether steerage or cabin class, and learned a great deal about his destination from those returning to Australia, for he had the gift of getting people to talk to him. From what they said, he guessed – hoped, prayed! – that it would be very difficult for Keara to vanish completely in Perth, which was by far the smallest of the capital cities. In fact, he'd have called it a very small town, from the sounds of it, and the others spoke openly of Western Australia as 'the Cinderella Colony'.

He pushed the thought of Lavinia to the back of his mind, because she was now his wife in name only and what did a piece of paper matter? But he couldn't forget Richard and dreamed often of his baby's face, the delicate features and fleeting smiles.

By the time they arrived off Western Australia in early September, however, he was more than ready to leave the ship and was looking forward to fresh food and real exercise – not to mention releasing the poor horses from their confinement.

When he disembarked at Fremantle he was told to come back the following day to help unload the horses. He had been hoping that Caley would be there to greet him, but smiled wryly at himself. His cousin would presumably know the procedures and wouldn't turn up to collect the horses until the following day, so he would just have to contain his own impatience.

He laughed with the others at their rolling gait as

they tried to get used to walking on a surface which didn't move beneath them, then accepted the help of a man he'd spent a lot of time with on board to find lodgings in Fremantle. By evening Theo was exhausted and wanted only to have something to eat and then sleep in a bed which wasn't moving.

The following morning he was down at the jetty early, but was told the horses wouldn't be disembarked until nearly noon. He stayed there, except for a couple of short walks, because he wanted to catch Caley as soon as possible. When he saw his cousin walking towards him in the clear spring sunshine, he felt a surge of affection flood through him. Caley looked fit and strong, tanned by the sun, smiling confidently at the world.

When he saw Theo he stopped dead in his tracks to gape, then ran across the short distance that still separated them. The two cousins embraced and made the usual jokes about how the other had grown uglier during the time they'd been apart, but they hugged several times.

'It's so good to see family,' Caley said in a voice grown husky with emotion. 'That's something you miss greatly when you go to live in another country – not having any family nearby, no one you can turn to with confidence if you're in trouble. Though we've made one or two good friends near our home.' Then he gave an embarrassed laugh. 'Listen to me going on about my feelings. Tell me what brought you out here.'

'Keara.'

'Ah.'

Theo didn't miss the undertone to his cousin's voice. 'You haven't – found her already?'

'Yes.'

'She's all right?'

'Of course.'

Theo closed his eyes as a wave of relief threatened his self-control. 'Thank God for that! Oh, thank God!' When Caley didn't say anything else, he burst out, 'Well? Where is she? Can we go and see her?'

'She's living a couple of days' ride south of Perth, working at an inn, and we have to pass the very door to get home. But, Theo, I'm not sure it's wise and –' He saw the determination on his cousin's face and added awkwardly, 'Actually, she said it was best that you were so far away and – well, she's clearly not the sort to be happy as anyone's mistress, which is all you can offer her. Unless anything has happened to Lavinia?'

'No. For all that Nancy says she has a weak heart, she was looking happy and well when I last saw her. She'll probably outlive us all.' He paused for a moment, fighting to keep his voice and emotions under control. To be so near to Keara! To ride past the very place she was living. No, he couldn't do that, he simply couldn't. 'I have to see her and make sure she's happy – and I *owe* it to her to help find her sisters. That at least I can do for her.'

Caley sighed. 'And nothing I say will make you change your mind?'

'Nothing.'

'Then I'd better tell you the rest.'

Theo grabbed his arm. 'What do you mean? She hasn't got married, has she?'

'No. Given the circumstances, that's the last thing she'd do.' Caley hesitated, wondering how best to put this, then decided there was no way to soften the shock. 'She's carrying your child, Theo. Your wife's old nurse realised that and it's probably the main reason she got rid of Keara. So I . . .' He stopped talking as he saw the anguish on his cousin's face and put an arm round his shoulders. 'Come on. Let's get out of this crowd.' He guided him away from the jetty and found a wall where they could sit down with their backs to the world.

For a long time Theo didn't speak, then he gave Caley one agonised, accusatory glance before turning again to stare into the distance. 'And you wanted me to ignore that?'

'To tell you the truth, I don't know what the best thing to do is. Look, we'd better go and see about the horses. They'll need a few days to recover from the voyage before we set off, so we can't do anything immediately. I've found someone who'll let me keep them in his paddock as they find their land legs again, but we'll have to take things gently, feed them up and travel in easy stages. And maybe that's best. You've a lot of thinking to do.'

Theo nodded, his expression still inward-looking. But he followed Caley back to the jetty and waited with him until the horses had been unloaded. That roused him a little from his preoccupation. He hated to see how thin and nervous they were and it seemed a miracle that none had died on the way. Looking at them, he knew it'd be at least a week before they dared set off, and even then they'd have to travel slowly.

Caley breathed a sigh of relief as Theo pulled himself together and began talking to the animals, gentling them, letting them find their land legs, then tethering them one by one. Three of Caley's, three of his own, in each case a stallion and two mares.

'Sure, we'll be set up with these beauties,' Caley said, viewing them with an expert eye, estimating what they would be like when they'd put on flesh and muscle again. 'I suppose you'll be bringing them to my place till you find somewhere of your own?' He looked at his cousin as he realised what he had just said. 'You have come out here to settle, haven't you? You used to talk about doing that.'

Theo nodded indifferently. 'Perhaps.'

'Will you give us a loan of your stallion, to cover my mares?'

'Mmm.'

Caley stopped trying to distract his cousin and concentrated on the business in hand. Surely by the time they reached Meriniup, Theo would have come to terms with the news and worked out what to do about it?

Surely he wasn't going to try to force Keara to live with him again?

But there was the child to consider. That might make a big difference.

Ah, what did he know about anything? Noreen always said he was hopeless at understanding other people.

★

Alex came home from the chapel radiating triumph, with his wife trailing unhappily behind him. 'You heard them, didn't you?'

She nodded.

'They saw the justice of my case. They gave me money. They are in truth my brethren.'

She didn't try to argue with him about that. It might be disloyal, but she had wondered if the other members of the congregation were seizing this opportunity to be rid of Alex because he'd had sharp disagreements with some of them lately.

'We'll leave on the very next steamer,' he said.

'Shouldn't we try to find out where Mark's living first?'

'No, we shouldn't. We can do that sort of thing far more easily once we're in Western Australia than we can from here. Besides, we don't want to give him any warning that we're coming, do we? He might move on somewhere else, even go back to England. People do.'

She shook her head in despair at what Alex was planning, but he took her silence for agreement.

'You'd better start sorting out our things. We'll sell what we don't need and travel as light as possible. I'll give notice at work first thing tomorrow, then go down to the shipping agents and find out when the next steamer leaves.'

When they got inside their cottage, he pulled out the collection money which had been donated to his cause and counted it out again, gloating over it. This would more than cover his expenses, he was sure. He lost himself in dreams of how he would return in triumph with his granddaughter one day.

His wife began sorting through their things, weeping as she caressed her ornaments and mementoes. She was sure he would not allow her to take them with her.

She was right.

'Fruits of Mammon!' he said scornfully, smashing a vase that had once belonged to her grandmother.

That was, she thought bitterly, the last straw. What sort of a husband was he? A bad one, that's what. And if she could find a way to leave him, she would.

Mark waited a day or two, till Keara had stopped staring into space, then suggested they go for a walk in the forest together, something that made her stare at him.

'Why would we do that, then?'

'I want to talk to you and I don't want anyone to interrupt.'

'Will we take Amy with us?'

He hesitated, then shook his head. 'No. She'd be a distraction. This is – well, it's important.'

As they strolled along the path she breathed in deeply, enjoying the faint tangy scent of gum leaves in the air and admiring the wildflowers that seemed to be blooming everywhere in this fine early spring weather, a carpet of beauty which she loved to see.

She knew some of the flowers' names now. The strange red and green blooms were called kangaroo paws and did indeed resemble them, and there were orchids of all kinds, from tiny delicate flowers to larger, more brightly coloured ones, as well as the papery ever-lasting flowers, some of which she'd picked and put in a jar in the public room. And there were red and blue creepers, which sometimes climbed the trees to a height of twenty or thirty feet. The blue ones in particular took her breath away, such a splendid display of her favourite shade of blue, one verging on violet.

There were strange, tree-like plants which the settlers called 'blackboys'. They had sooty trunks, dark-ened by bushfires perhaps, made from the stumps of hundreds of roots of the long, coarse, grass-like leaves that grew in twisting layers, round and round. These were so brittle they'd snap off in your hand and yet could build up into a trunk. Some of the blackboys had a flower, a gigantic spike like a native's spear, which was how they'd got their name.

Flying among the trees were all sorts of birds, including parrots and cockatoos, which she'd never even seen before, tiny honey eaters and her personal favourite, the willy wagtail, which did indeed wag its tail to and fro just like a dog and was cheekier than the other birds.

She realised Mark was speaking and tried to give him her full attention.

'I saw how upset you were when Mr Gallagher turned up,' he began. 'Are you afraid of this man, the one who's sent you some money?'

She stopped walking to consider this, then shook her head. 'No. I'd never be afraid of Theo.' It was her own feelings that frightened her, because she had not forgotten him, not stopped longing to see him again. Couldn't.

'He's the father of your child but he's married, am I right?'

'Yes.' She nodded, continuing to walk, staring down at her feet as if choosing her path with care.

'What are you going to do after the baby's born?'

'Now that I have some money, I'm going to travel across to Melbourne to look for my sisters.' She looked up at him, suddenly guessing where this was leading. 'Oh – you're worried about getting help here. I promise we won't leave you in the lurch. We'll wait until you find someone else.' They owed him that.

'I'm more worried about you, Keara,' he said gently. 'It's very different over there. Melbourne's a big city now and growing fast. People in cities are not always – kind – or helpful. And you're not used to big cities, from what you've said.'

'Maggie's coming with me, so I shan't be on my own.'

'Is she any more experienced than you at living in big cities?'

Keara stopped walking to look at him in puzzlement. 'Why are you saying this? You surely don't think I should stop looking for my sisters? I'll *never* do that!'

They began moving again and after a few paces he said quietly, 'I'm worried about Amy too. You're the only mother she's known and you're wonderful with her.'

'I love her,' she said simply. 'It'll tear me apart to

leave her. But she'll have you and I know how deeply you care for her.'

He abandoned any attempt to approach the subject delicately. 'Well, I'm not sure that will be enough. So I wondered – might it not help us both if we got married? You'd be safe then from this man who's given you two sleepless nights.' He reached out to touch the dark circles under her eyes with the tip of his forefinger. 'And I'd have a mother for Amy, not to mention a wife to work beside me.'

'And what about my sisters?'

'I'd be prepared to sell the inn and travel back to Melbourne with you to help you look for them. I can buy another over there. You'll not find it easy if you try to do this on your own. You need a man to protect you.' He was even prepared to brave his father-in-law again, though he would try to avoid the Jenners, if he could.

Keara stopped to look at him. He was tall and good-looking by any standards. He was kind, too, a caring father, an honest, hardworking man. So why did he not make her pulse beat any faster, as Theo could do simply by entering a room? She liked Mark very much, but in a sisterly way, and the thought of lying in a bed with him made her take a step backwards, her face flushed at the sudden memory of making love with Theo. 'But you don't love me, Mark. And I don't love you.'

'No. We get on well, though. I enjoy your company and you seem to enjoy mine. Surely that would make a good basis for a happy life together?'

'You didn't love your wife either, did you?' she asked, guessing the answer even before he spoke.

'I – cared about her, was fond of her.'

'That's not the same thing.' She broke off, not knowing what to tell him. What he had said made sense. Only *she* had experienced real love and the passion it generated. She was not sure she could marry without it now.

He laughed, a dry, bitter sound. 'My older sister found that sort of love. I haven't been so fortunate. I don't think many people are. Do you expect to meet it again?'

She shook her head. 'No. Theo was special. Even before we became lovers, there was always something between us.' She'd held him while he wept, he'd done the same for her. It was far more than passion. 'But I couldn't have stayed with him as his mistress. That never felt right.' She wrapped her arms around her body and looked at him. 'You're a kind man, Mark, but you've taken me by surprise. I don't know what to say.'

'Don't say anything, then. Think about it. Take your time. I shan't change my mind.'

'All right.' She turned round and began walking back to the inn, moving briskly in spite of her heavy body.

He followed her, not even trying to catch up. He hoped she'd say yes. You couldn't live with Keara Michaels for long without realising her worth and growing to like her.

She didn't even see the snake coiled up in a patch of sunlight and by the time he'd opened his mouth to warn her of it, she had passed it. So he said nothing, just took care how he went past the creature. He would, he decided, give the two women a lesson that very night on how to deal with snakes, something he'd learned early on at the diggings.

But as he lay in bed thinking over what she had said, he knew he didn't believe he'd ever experience the sort of love she had felt for this Theo. He'd run away twice now. What sort of man did that make him? Not the sort to win a woman's undying devotion, that was sure.

And in a few weeks, Keara would give birth. The thought of that made him shiver. She didn't seem afraid of anything, though. She was in blooming health, a magnificent creature. She even talked about how quickly her own mother had always given birth and expressed a conviction that she'd be the same.

He definitely hoped she'd say yes to his offer, and was disappointed when the following day she told him she couldn't decide anything until after the baby was born.

When two weeks had passed without a sign of Caley Gallagher returning, Maggie said firmly, 'If he doesn't bring you the rest of the money soon, we'll go to this address and ask for it.'

Keara smiled. 'He'll come.'

'How can you be so sure?'

'I just am.'

Maggie gave a sniff of disdain. 'You're too trusting by far, my girl.'

Two days later they heard the sound of several horses and when Maggie went to the window to look out, she called excitedly, 'It's him! He's got another fellow with him, and they're leading some horses. They're going round the back, so they must be intending to stay the night. Come and look, quick!'

But Keara was holding Amy on her knee, letting the baby bounce up and down, and was feeling lazy today. 'They'll come inside when they're ready. You'd better go out to the kitchen and get that meat pie finished and into the oven. It should be hot enough now. I think we'll be needing the pie and something else as well. Good thing Mark shot a kangaroo, isn't it?'

Maggie pulled a face at her and flounced out.

In the yard at the back of the inn, Caley greeted Mark with a cheerful, 'Can you put us up for the night?'

'Of course. You'll have to see to your own horses, though. There's a small enclosure over there with plenty of grass still. We've oats and feed in the bins, as well, which I can sell you by the bucket.' He'd have to go up to Perth soon to replenish his stocks. Word seemed to have got out and more travellers were stopping, either for a rest and a meal or an overnight stay, and people from Meriniup were coming in to buy supplies as well.

'Is Keara around?' Caley asked.

'Yes, of course. She's inside and—' Mark looked enquiringly at the other man, waiting for an introduction, but Theo had gone striding towards the inn without a word, leaving the horses to mill around.

Mark took a step after him, wondering what he wanted.

Caley laid one hand on his arm. 'Let him speak to

Keara in private. He's my cousin, the father of her child.'

Shock held Mark motionless for a moment, then he scowled at Caley. 'You should have broken the news to her gently, told us what to expect last time. A shock like that isn't good for a woman in her condition.'

'I didn't even know he was coming to Australia.' As Mark took another step towards the back door, Caley said more sharply, 'Leave it, I said. Those two need to talk.'

Mark didn't want the fellow anywhere near Keara. What if he persuaded her to go away with him? How would he manage with Amy then? But Keara wasn't stupid, wouldn't be taken in by promises that could lead nowhere. Surely she wouldn't?

Maggie came round the corner of the house, humming, and broke off to say cheerfully, 'So you came back, Mr Gallagher.'

'I did. And I've brought Keara the rest of the money.'

'He's also brought the father of Keara's child with him,' Mark said grimly. 'The fellow's inside talking to her now.'

She looked at Caley. 'Has he still got a wife in England?'

He nodded.

'Then he should have stayed away.' She turned towards the house and Caley stepped forward to prevent her, looking at them both and repeating, 'Let them talk. It's up to them to settle their differences, not us.'

★

Inside the house, Keara was still playing with Amy, singing a little song to her and jiggling her up and down. She did not at first realise who had come in, so didn't turn her head.

Theo was able to watch her, to study the swell of her belly with a nervous lurch of his heart. But she wasn't Lavinia. Her face had that glow that comes from good health. He'd seen paintings of the Madonna and child, but had never in real life seen a scene as beautiful as Keara and this child. The breath caught in his throat and he couldn't move or speak.

She turned round, smiling, 'Maggie, did you –' then gasped. The smile faded and all the colour left her face.

For a moment Theo thought she was going to faint and took a hasty step towards her, stopping as she shrank back.

'*Why did you come?*' she asked at last in a voice ringing with anguish. 'Why didn't you leave me alone, Theo?'

'Because I was worried sick about you.' He broke off and admitted, 'No. That's not the main reason. I *was* worried, but I simply couldn't live without you, Keara. I love you too much.'

She swallowed hard and closed her eyes, but his face stayed in her mind and she opened them again. He was tanned now, looking even more attractive than before. And she believed him when he said he loved her because his eyes showed that even more clearly than the words he'd spoken. Did her own eyes betray her feelings to him as clearly? She supposed they did. She opened her mouth to speak then closed it again, not knowing what to say or do, so conscious of his presence that there seemed to be nothing and no one else in the room.

Amy broke the spell by suddenly crowing and reaching out towards the newcomer, trampling up and down on Keara's knee in great excitement.

He knelt down in front of them. 'She's a beautiful child. Whose is she and what is she called?'

'Amy's my employer's child. Her mother died soon after she was born. I've been looking after her for a few months now.'

'Will she come to me?'

In answer Amy reached out towards him and he picked her up, speaking softly, trying to give Keara a moment or two to recover from the shock of seeing him – trying to keep himself calm as well.

After a minute or two she managed to speak in a more normal tone of voice. 'It's no good, Theo. I can't – *won't* be your mistress.'

'I know. Believe me, I understand that. But I can't live without you, my darling.'

Keara wanted so badly to touch him that she ached with the pain of it. She closed her eyes and stared down at the floor, but was no less conscious of the lean, strong body next to hers.

Amy suddenly began to wriggle and make protesting noises and Keara had to look up again. Theo was holding the child too tightly, so she moved to take her back. But this brought her closer to him and she froze, just a handspan away from him. Time seemed to stand still as they stared at one another. Their love was there in the very air that separated them, a current of awareness, the recognition of the other's body, reactions that could not be prevented, only denied.

But when he reached out one hand towards her, she twisted away from it. 'No. No, Theo. Not again.' She jumped to her feet.

He drew his hand back and sat very still. 'Don't leave! We must speak.'

But Amy was tired now, grizzling to be put down and rubbing her eyes with her plump little hands.

'She needs a sleep. I have to put her down.' Keara went across to the door that led into their quarters. 'I'll be back in a minute.'

'You won't run away?'

She looked over her shoulder at him. 'No. I won't do that, Theo.'

But when she had put Amy down, she stood and pressed both hands to her cheeks, wishing desperately that she didn't need to go and talk to him yet.

When she went back into the public room, she tried to ignore her emotions and behave normally. 'Would you like a glass of beer? Or a cup of tea, maybe?'

'I don't want anything but time to talk to you, my darling.'

'We have nothing to say to each other that hasn't already been said. I know you care about me, but you have a wife. That hasn't changed.'

'How can you say nothing has changed when you're carrying my baby?'

Automatically she put one hand on her belly and looked down at its swell.

'If I promise not even to try and touch you, will you sit down again and talk to me, Keara? We must work out what we're going to do.'

'Do? *We* are going to do nothing.' And then it came to her: the one thing that would drive him away. 'Anyway I've had a proposal of marriage. I don't need anything more from you.'

He stared at her in shock. 'You can't have! You're still carrying my child.'

'He doesn't mind that. He needs a wife and I need a home.'

'Who is he?'

'The man who owns this inn, of course.'

Theo's face was suddenly filled with harsh lines each graven by pain. 'You can't marry him, Keara.'

'Why can't I?'

'Because you don't love him.'

'I like and respect him.'

He shook his head. 'That's not enough. You still love me and that'll come between you. Believe me, my darling, it's hell on earth to have to live with one person while you love another.'

She stood up and began to pace the room, avoiding passing too close to him.

'Besides,' he said from behind her, 'I'm damned if I'll let anyone else bring up my child.'

She swung round. 'My child, too!'

His voice softened. 'Ah, Keara, you of all people know what it's been like for me. If that child lives, you couldn't be so cruel as to take it from me, give it another man's name. You *couldn't*!'

She stopped near the front door, looking out into the sunlight, feeling lost. Richard had died. Who had comforted Theo then? The pain in his voice made her want to run to him. She took hold of the door frame instead as she admitted, 'No. I'd not take your child away from you, Theo.'

He took a step towards her. 'Ah, Keara, Keara.'

She spun round. 'But I'm *not* going to fall into your bed again. I'm not!' She backed away. 'Don't come any nearer. Just – leave me to think.' Then she ran into the living quarters and slid the bolt on her bedroom door.

He sank down by the table and buried his head in his hands.

Outside Maggie had tried to eavesdrop on what Theo and Keara were saying and this time it was Mark who took her arm and pulled her away from the door.

'Leave them their privacy,' he said quietly.

'But what if he hurts her?'

Caley came over to join them. 'Do you think he's going to hit her or something?' he asked scornfully.

'Men do.'

'Not Theo.'

'Their friends always say that.'

Mark put one arm round her thin shoulders. 'Was your husband like that, Maggie lass?'

She scowled at him, then shrugged off his arm

before turning back to the cooking. 'Most of them are like that.'

'No, they're not.'

His voice was so certain she paused and frowned. 'How can you say that for sure?'

He smiled. 'Because I have eight brothers and sisters, most of whom are happily married, and a father who's married for the third time.'

'You're lucky, then.'

His expression grew sad. 'No, I'm not. I ran away to Australia and haven't seen my family since. I miss them very much.'

Her eyes met his. 'I've no one to miss. I'd rather be you.'

Caley finished tending the horses and came back to chat to Maggie and watch her cooking. But like her, he kept looking towards the back door, wondering what Theo and Keara were saying.

Mark pottered around, trying to take his mind off Keara by feeding the hens and changing their water, bringing up a bucketful from the narrow stream which locals called a river and which they thought wonderful because it ran all year and didn't dry up in the summer. It was that small stream which had drawn people to settle at Meriniup. This side of Australia was very different from Victoria, so short of good water courses.

It was a full half-hour before Theo came out. Watching him, Caley knew that things hadn't gone well for his cousin. He could only hope Keara would let Theo into her life again and take that bleak look from his eyes.

Mark and Maggie exchanged glances then, as the minutes passed and there was no sign of Keara, she said abruptly, 'I'd better go and check that she's all right.'

Mark nodded. To his dismay, Theo Mullane was as personable as his cousin and it was very clear he loved Keara deeply. And she him.

Did he want a wife who loved another man so deeply?

Hell, he didn't even know what he wanted!

CHAPTER TWENTY

September–October 1864

Theo and Caley stayed overnight at the inn and Keara avoided them as much as possible. She knew her behaviour was hurting Theo, but the problem of what they were to do seemed so insoluble she thought again about marrying Mark. Could she do that? She didn't know. Her emotions were in such a turmoil she couldn't seem to think straight.

Besides, she wasn't sure Mark was ready for another marriage. He seemed to her to be living behind a mental barrier: polite, friendly, hard-working and keeping his deepest feelings to himself. Theo wasn't like that. His emotions showed in his face, whether it was passion or anger – or the pain they were both feeling at present.

She couldn't deprive him of his child. Just couldn't.

Theo came across to her after breakfast the following morning and she stopped what she was doing to look at him warily. He wasn't as tall as Mark, but he had a presence and vitality that made him stand out among other men.

'We're leaving soon. Could you spare me a minute or two before we go?'

She hesitated. 'What else is there to say?'

'A lot.'

She spread her hands in a helpless gesture. 'Very well. There's a path behind the inn. We could walk along it a little way.' She loved the feel of the forest around her, the dry whispering of the gum trees, with their leathery leaves that crunched underfoot at all times of the year, so different from the soft green leaves of Ireland in summer and the bare branches of trees in winter. Regret flooded through her when she thought of her home. She would never stop missing it, but she didn't think she'd ever return to Ireland now because there was nothing for her there. All the people she loved were here in Australia. Even Theo now.

She decided to show him the wildflowers, knowing he'd enjoy their beauty, hoping they would distract him a little.

'Will you promise me not to leave without telling me where you're going?' he asked abruptly as they walked along the path. 'I won't leave here if you don't.'

She didn't want to promise anything, but then she saw his eyes rest on her thickening figure, saw the raw longing in them. 'Very well. I promise.'

His breath came out in a whoosh that betrayed the intensity of his relief. 'Thank you.'

She tried to change the subject to something less charged with emotion. 'The wildflowers are very beautiful at this time of year.'

'Hang the wildflowers! It's you and me we need to

talk about, the baby, our future.' He walked for a few paces, holding back a branch for her to pass more easily, and as she did so their eyes met and she paused, breath catching in her throat at the memory of what it was like to walk into his arms, nestle against him. It was an effort to start moving again.

'After the baby's born, once we're sure it'll live, I want to help you find your sisters. Will you let me do that?'

'I sometimes wonder if I'll ever see them again.'

'You will because we won't stop searching until we do find them.'

She stopped walking to close her eyes for a minute. 'I try to tell myself that, but this is a big country and Mark said once that people can easily disappear. I've never forgotten that.' She opened her eyes again to see him stretch out one hand towards her. She didn't dare take it, didn't dare touch him, and started walking again.

'Your sisters are as pretty as you are,' he said as he moved on after her. 'People won't forget them. And the nuns will have kept records.'

'I wrote to them as soon as we were settled here, but they haven't written back to me.'

'Damn them! How dare they take young Irish girls and force them to leave the country? But damn Lavinia most of all! She not only stands between us and happiness, she's also hurt you and your family.' His voice was hoarse. 'I can never forgive her for that, never.'

'She was very unhappy herself.'

'She deserved to be!'

'I thought so when I found out what she'd done, but

since then I keep remembering how like a child she was, a very selfish child too, as if she had never really grown up. And she hated sharing your bed, yet you forced her.'

'I was married to her, for heaven's sake! What else was I to do? Besides, some women are like that. They're brought up to think bed a duty and they never enjoy it.' He saw that she was unconvinced and tried to explain. 'In my class, especially for an impoverished landowner, marriage is a business arrangement, not a means of finding pleasure in bed. One has one's duty to one's family, as my father did not fail to point out. And hers did the same, I've no doubt. So I married at their urging and I tried, Keara, I promise you I tried heavens hard to make it pleasant for Lavinia. But she wouldn't, couldn't respond. I would happily have left her alone if she'd been able to give me even one living child.'

She considered what he had said and then found herself confiding in him. 'My parents were unhappy too. They had to get married because my mother was expecting a child – me. Only *he* didn't want to marry at all, and if he had to have a child, he wanted a son. She was so unhappy with him, but she was a loving mother to us three girls.' She looked up at the dappled light, watching the patterns made by the sunbeams play across the forest floor and glow on the skin of her hands. 'I sometimes think how she'd have loved it here.' She made a sweeping gesture with one hand. 'She always hankered after sunshine and warmth, and instead she had a harsh life in a draughty one-room cottage with an earth floor and never enough to eat. All she had was her children and her respectability. She said as long as she had those, she could hold her head up.'

'That's why you won't live with me.'

She nodded.

'Would you live with me if I promised not to touch you?'

She stopped walking to look at him as she said, 'And how long do you think that would last? We didn't intend to go to bed the first time. It just happened. And would do again. So no, I won't live with you, Theo.'

'But you'll let me help you find your sisters? Ah, Keara love, I shan't rest easy till we do that.'

She hadn't intended to let him stay near her, but how could she deny him that – or herself? It would be so much easier if they had a gentleman to deal with the nuns. Or was she fooling herself, finding excuses to keep him near her? 'Maggie will be coming too,' she warned him.

'Very well.' With that he would have to be content, but he knew he would never let her go willingly. The child would hold them together. If it lived. Oh, God, if it lived! None of his other children had. Was Nancy right and the fault for that lay with Lavinia? Or was he flawed as well?

That worry had kept him awake many a night.

'We'd better turn back now,' he said with a sigh, knowing he had won as many concessions from her as he could possibly expect at this stage. 'I'll go and settle the horses in at Caley's and I'll come back to see you regularly. When the baby's due, I'm coming to stay with you.' He saw her open her mouth to protest and held up his hand. 'Nothing you say or do will change my mind about that, Keara. Nothing! I'm going to be with you for the birth.'

They began walking back.

'You might at least notice the wildflowers,' she said softly. 'It's very beautiful here, you know.'

So he stopped and looked round, his breath catching in his throat at the glorious wealth of flowers he had been too upset to notice before. 'I must have been blind to walk through all this and not notice a thing.' He looked sideways at her. 'That's what you do to me, Keara.'

He did it to her, too. To break the spell she moved across to her favourite creeper. 'Isn't this the most beautiful shade of blue?'

'Very beautiful, but not as glorious as your eyes. I hope our child will inherit those.'

'Oh, Theo!' For a moment she touched his hand, then she jerked away, turned and hurried on. Already she was forgetting her resolve, touching him. She would never be able to live with him without wanting to love him, and wanting him to love her. She had to keep him at a distance. If she could.

When they got back to the inn she left him without a word, going to find Amy and keeping herself busy.

She had too much pride to go out and watch them leave and he didn't come to find her again. But she peeped through the window, shushing Amy when she grew restless – and stood there long after he and Caley, with their strings of horses, had disappeared southwards. She tried hard not to cry, but failed.

From the rear of the big public room Maggie watched her, sad to see her friend's shoulders drooping, not knowing what to say or do.

Even Amy stopped fretting for a minute or two.

Then Keara turned round and said brightly to the child she was holding, 'Right, young lady, let's get you something to eat.'

She smiled just as brightly at Maggie and refused to discuss Theo Mullane with either her or Mark.

Alex Jenner purchased passages for himself and his wife on the coastal steamer. During the voyage to Western Australia he spent many hours standing by the rail, staring out across the sea, ignoring attempts by other passengers to get into conversation with him. This gave Nan a welcome chance to chat to the other women, or even just sit and rest.

It had been years since she'd been so idle, and as she was a good sailor and Alex wasn't she enjoyed the voyage greatly, wishing it need never end.

'Fine-looking fellow, your husband,' one woman said to her. 'For his age.'

The words burst out before Nan could hold them back. 'Handsome is as handsome does!'

'Oh. Gives you a hard time, does he?'

In answer, Nan rolled back her sleeve to show the bruise he'd given her the day before when she'd dared to interrupt his prayers to suggest he come and eat before the food got cold.

The woman sucked in her breath then looked at

Nan's bowed head. 'You should hit him back. I can
never understand why women put up with that sort of
treatment. I wouldn't.' She looked across at her
husband, who had a lumpy face but a kind smile. 'Not
that I've ever had to complain about my Josh. Kindest
man I ever met, he is, and a good provider, too. I'm very
lucky.'

Nan sat on considering what the woman had said.
It had never even occurred to her to fight back, but the
urge to do so had been growing inside her for a while,
she realised suddenly. She had had enough of Alex's
bad temper and unreasonable demands. He had driven
both their children away and was intent now on stealing
their granddaughter from her father.

That was so wrong.

Gradually an idea crept into her mind and grew
there, so that by the end of the voyage she knew that if
she could stop him, she would. And the next time he hit
her, she lashed back at him, catching him on the arm.
He raised his hand again so she raised hers.

'How dare you?' he roared.

Someone nearby yelled at him to be quiet.

Nan stared at him defiantly. 'I'll fight back from
now on every time you try to hit me, Alex Jenner. I don't
deserve to be treated like that and I won't let you do it.'

He could not have looked more dumbfounded. His
hand fell and he turned his back on her.

She was surprised at herself. But rebellion felt good
after years of meekness and suppressing her own
wishes, even trying to suppress her own thoughts, God
help her. It was as if she had suddenly woken up.

She dreamed of her daughter smiling at her and took it as a sign that she was doing the right thing.

When they disembarked in Perth the Jenners found lodgings, a tiny room of the poorest sort, not particularly clean. Nan bided her time, speaking quietly to her husband, waiting until she saw her way more clearly. Then she would act.

Alex went off to ask about Mark Gibson and came back scowling because he had found nothing out and the government clerk had refused to see him without an appointment. When the meal their landlady supplied was poorly cooked, his scowl grew blacker and Nan guessed he would try to take his temper out on her later.

Could she . . . dare she?

As they were getting ready for bed, she said something that displeased him and he raised his hand to her. She slapped it out of the way.

'I meant what I said,' she told him in a low, angry voice. 'I won't put up with it any more.'

'Woman—' he began.

'Don't you "woman" me, Alex Jenner! I have a name and that's what I answer to.' She went on in a low voice, 'I've had enough of your bad temper. I've been a good wife to you, better by far than you deserve, and you should treat me with more respect.'

She stood ready to fight, even though she knew he was stronger, but instead he swung round and opened the Bible he carried everywhere and began reading it aloud in a droning undertone that you could not quite make out – another of his annoying habits. He ignored her completely, so she got ready for bed, turned her back to the room and pretended to be asleep.

In the morning he refused to speak to her.

She made a hearty breakfast and exchanged several remarks with the landlady instead.

She was glad when he went out, though, because it was a strain trying to appear cheerful when she felt miserable and worried. Wondering how to spend her day, it occurred to her to ask their landlady about ways of finding their son-in-law.

Alex came home that evening in another foul mood.

'Did you find any sign of where Mark went?' Nan asked.

He ignored her, except to say as they were getting ready for bed, 'I have an appointment with the government clerk tomorrow. Is it possible for you to iron a shirt?'

'I'll ask the landlady in the morning. I dare say she'll let me. She's a kindly soul.'

This time he came home from his appointment radiating triumph, but refused to tell her what he had found out. And nothing she said or did would change his mind. He looked so triumphant that she stopped trying. She might have known he would find some other way to get at her.

The following morning when he went out Nan hesitated for a moment then followed him. He never looked at other people when he walked nowadays, just forged ahead, barely missing collisions, always in a hurry to do something. He was getting worse, not better. Where would this end? she wondered with a little leap of fear in her breast.

He went from one carrier or livery stables to another and she guessed he was trying to hire a vehicle to go somewhere. She couldn't help wondering if he intended to take her with him – and whether she'd even care if he left her behind. She certainly wouldn't miss him, but she was sure he was bent on mischief again and still intended to stop him if she could.

He went home so suddenly she couldn't get back before him so continued walking for a while. The river was very beautiful, wide and slow-flowing near the city. But this was another strange place to her. How long was it since she'd been able to call anywhere home? Not since before they left England. Home had been with her daughter and, to a lesser degree, her son – and now they were both gone.

When she got back to the lodgings Alex was packing furiously, with their possessions pulled out of the drawers and scattered across the bed.

'Where have you been?' he shouted. 'We have to be ready to leave early tomorrow, you stupid woman! Come and pack our things.'

She moved into the room, taking the things out of the bags again and repacking them carefully. So few possessions now. But he hadn't found her favourite ornament because he had avoided her bag of 'women's rubbish'.

'What time are we leaving?' she asked when she had finished.

'We must have the bags down at the carrier's by six

o'clock this evening so that they can be fitted on to the cart. How long will you be with that packing?'

'Five minutes.'

'I'll go and borrow the landlady's handcart.'

He puffed in and out with their bags, but Nan kept the smallest one with her, reminding him that they'd need their nightclothes.

When he had gone she sat down and wept. She hated him. He had torn their lives apart and for what? Nothing. Now all they had left was a trunk and two bags.

An hour later he still hadn't come back, so she decided to go to bed and took the opportunity to have a good wash. He sometimes went out walking at dusk. It was always a relief to have the room to herself.

She woke a couple of hours later to find herself alone in the darkness. What time was it? No way of knowing. They only had his pocket watch now to tell the time by, because he'd sold her little clock.

She got up and peered out of the window. The street was very still and quiet, so it must be the middle of the night.

She was too worried to sleep again and by the time dawn silvered the sky, she had guessed that he'd abandoned her.

She went to wake the landlady and explained her problem. The woman gaped at her. 'I don't know what you expect me to do, but if you haven't the money for a room, then you can't stay here. He only paid up to today.' Some remnant of pity made her add, 'He paid for breakfast for two, though, so I'll give you something to take with you to eat later. You'd better go and see the police, ask if anyone's found a body.'

Nan knew they wouldn't have because she could guess what Alex was doing. He was going to see Mark and the baby. What she didn't understand was why he hadn't taken her with him. If he did manage to kidnap Amy, how would he look after her? The child must be getting on for a year old now. They were quite lively by that age, crawling about.

What made her most anxious of all was that he'd bought a revolver before they left Melbourne, insisting the colony of Western Australia was a backward and dangerous place where a man needed to be able to protect himself.

What was he planning to do with it? Surely he didn't intend to kill Mark?

She began sobbing. She had failed in her plan to foil him, failed before she had even started.

When Theo next returned to Meriniup, he rode in alone and went straight round the back with his horse. Maggie saw him and rushed to warn Keara, who was taking a short rest. She was only a week or two away from her time now, as far as they could work out, and although she was still feeling well, she was beginning to tire more easily.

She hauled herself off the bed, feeling grumpy, and picked up Amy who had been lying kicking beside her. 'Thanks for warning me, Maggie. You should get back to work now.'

'Don't you want me to stay with you?'

'No. I can tell him to go away without anyone else's help, thank you very much.'

When Theo walked in through the back door, she greeted him with a scowl and snapped, 'What do *you* want?'

'To see you, of course.'

Amy looked up at Keara, her soft little mouth wobbling at the sharp tone of voice.

'Sorry, darling. I didn't mean to frighten you.' Keara dropped a kiss on the child's head and turned her back on Theo.

But he came up behind her and seized the opportunity to put his arms round both her and Amy. 'I'm not going to stop coming, so you may as well get used to it.'

His breath was warm in her ear and for a moment she closed her eyes and leaned against him, then made herself move away. 'Can I serve you with something?'

He had felt her response but knew better than to say so. 'Yes. I'd like a meal, if that's not too much trouble – and a room for the night.'

'That's what we're here for. And that's *all* we're here for.' She tied Amy into the chair that Mark had modified for her. 'There you are, sweetheart.' She found a hard crust and gave it to the child to chew on since Amy was teething again.

Theo went to sit at the big central table. 'I wish you'd let me take you away from this, even if you won't come and live with me. You shouldn't be working so hard in your condition.'

'Don't be silly. I'm not ill. What would I be doing

with myself all day, do you think, if I had no work?'

'Resting.'

'I'm not made to rest. I'd go mad in a week if I just had to sit around, so I would. Now, I'll be back in a few minutes with the food. Would you watch Amy for me?' Not waiting for an answer, she slipped out of the rear door and stood for a moment, trying to stop her pulse racing as it always did when Theo was near.

Mark came round the corner and stopped to eye her. 'Are you all right? He's not – bothering you?'

'Of course I'm all right and of course he's bothering me. I wish he'd leave me alone, but he won't.'

'He cares about you.'

'He's married.' She reminded herself of that often. Had to.

Mark watched her frying some ham and expertly breaking an egg into the pan. 'We really should do something about this open kitchen.'

'I like it, especially now the weather's getting a bit warmer.' She glanced round, smiling. 'In fact, I like Australia.'

'So do I.'

When she brought his meal, Theo said, 'Won't you come and sit with me while I eat?'

She wanted to but was afraid to give in to the temptation. 'I've work to do.'

He grasped her wrist before she realised what he intended and pulled her down on the chair beside him. 'It can wait. Besides, I can't keep an eye on Amy as well as eat.' He waited till she was seated, then said, 'I should have told you last time, but I wasn't thinking straight.

Father Cornelius heard from the Mother Superior of the convent here in Australia and he gave me the letter. I found it in my things and brought it for you.'

Her breath caught in her throat and everything seemed to whirl around her.

'Keara! Sweetheart, are you all right?' He shoved his plate away and put his arms round her.

She leaned against him, trembling. 'They're all right? Tell me they're all right, Theo. I can't bear it if anything's happened to them.'

'They arrived safely in Australia.' He chewed one corner of his lip. 'But the Mother Superior feels no good would come of upsetting things. She said Ismay was found employment soon after her arrival and Mara was adopted by a good Catholic family a week or two later. She declined to give further details.'

'Not even an address for me to write to?' Keara pressed one hand to her mouth. 'Not even that?'

'No, my darling. I'm afraid not.'

She astounded them both by bursting into tears and sobbing against his chest. 'It's cruel, so it is. Cruel.'

'I agree.' He dropped a light kiss on her forehead. 'So we'll have to go across to Melbourne, beard this ferocious woman in her den and insist she tell us more.'

She realised she was in his arms and pulled away from him. 'I'm not your darling,' she said crossly, then sniffed and wiped away her tears with the back of one hand.

'Do you never have a handkerchief?' he teased, pulling out his own. 'And of course you're my darling. Why else would I have followed you to Australia?'

She looked at it, remembering another occasion when he had found her weeping. Only this handkerchief was not immaculately ironed and she was no longer an ignorant young girl. Nor was he quite the same man. He was sadder – and yet seemed kinder and more at peace within himself, too. She moved away from him, sighing as she eased her back, taking her time as she wiped her eyes, feeling reluctant to go back to work. 'Show me the letter,' she said at last, 'then get on with your meal. I hate to see good food going to waste.'

He took a piece of paper out of his pocket and passed it to her.

She read it carefully, her finger moving slowly along each line of writing. 'This Mother Superior sounds very severe. Why will she not tell us where they are?'

'I don't know.' That worried him more than he would admit.

'We'll have to wait till the baby's old enough to travel,' she said at last.

He dropped the knife and fork again. 'Thank God you haven't changed your mind, Keara. I was so worried you wouldn't let me help you.'

She looked at him and admitted, 'I need you. A woman who writes a cold letter like this,' she flicked the piece of paper scornfully, 'won't pay any attention to an ignorant Irish peasant like me, will she now? It'll need a fine gentleman like you to deal with *her*!'

He smiled and looked down at himself. 'I can't promise to work miracles. And I may be a gentleman, but there's nothing fine about me, Keara. I like being outdoors more than doing the pretty over teacups. I always have done.'

She knew that already. 'So Maggie and I will go with you. But Theo . . .'

'What?'

She had to force the words out. 'After we find them, I'm not staying with you.'

'We'll see about that. Even if you won't live with me, I'm not going to be shut out of my only child's life. Nor would I believe it if you said you intended to do that. You're not cruel, Keara.'

She sagged against the hard wooden back of the chair, remembering when she'd held him while he wept for a dead child. 'We'll discuss that later.' She pushed herself off the chair, hesitated, then said, 'I'm sorry Richard died.'

He looked at her through his tears with his soul in his eyes. 'He died in my arms.'

'Was there anyone to comfort you?'

'Only Nancy.'

She looked at him in surprise. 'Lavinia's maid?'

'Yes. I wept all over her after the funeral. She was – kind.'

Keara took his hand for a minute, feeling its warmth, feeling his love, then let go and stepped back. 'I'd better go and wash my face. Eat your food now, will you?' She picked up Amy and left the room.

He cleared the plate but tasted nothing. He'd won another small victory. Well, maybe not so small. But he still had to win the war. He wasn't letting her go again.

And they still had to see whether this new baby

would survive. That was his biggest worry of all at the moment. Not only the child's safety, but Keara's. Childbirth was so dangerous a time for women.

He hadn't realised he had it in him to love anyone like this. Had often lain awake during the night since he got here, in a cold sweat of fear that he would mismanage things and hurt her again.

Nan went first to the place whose address she had seen on a scrap of paper her husband had left on the table for a few minutes. She asked if they could tell her where Mark Gibson lived. If it were not too far, she would walk there. But the clerk told her it was two days away by cart, so she left again, feeling alone and afraid, not knowing what to do with herself.

All day she wandered the streets, worrying, carrying her one bag, so small that it made her want to weep to think it contained all she now owned. When night fell she slept round the back of some houses, sitting upright in a doorway, waking at regular intervals, grateful it wasn't raining and the late spring weather was quite warm. She didn't feel hungry, just worried sick about what Alex intended to do.

The following morning she felt a bit dizzy and distant as she set off walking, so went to sit by the river where she fell asleep in the sunshine. Later, she went back into town and as she passed a church turned into it, not caring what denomination it was. She sat near the front, waiting for she knew not what.

She must have been there for a long time because

when a hand on her shoulder roused her from her abstraction, she was so stiff she could not at first move. She stared blindly up at a man silhouetted against the setting sun shining through the window.

'Are you all right?' he asked gently.

'No. No, I'm not.' She began to weep. 'My husband's left me and I've nowhere to live and I don't know what to do!'

Voices spoke above her head, but she couldn't seem to understand what they were saying. When someone urged her to stand up, she did so, not moving further until someone tugged her arm.

'Have you eaten today, dear?' a woman's voice asked.

Nan frowned, trying to remember, then shook her head. It was all too much trouble.

They gave her a cup of tea and a piece of bread and butter and when she said she wasn't hungry, they insisted she eat it. Afterwards they asked if she was able to walk. She nodded and followed the speaker, relieved when they found her a bed for the night, a real bed.

It wasn't until the following morning that she realised where she was: in the poorhouse. This brought on a fit of weeping but when someone with a very sharp voice told her to be quiet, she tried hard to stop.

'I'm – sorry,' she managed.

'You were too tired to talk last night. Tell us your name now, then explain what's happened to your husband,' the stern-faced woman said.

So Nan told them how Alex had made her pack the

bags, then gone out with them and left her, taking nearly everything she owned.

'I think we'd better take you in until we see whether we can find you employment.'

'It's the poorhouse, isn't it?' she asked fearfully.

'Yes.'

Nan gave a long shuddering sigh, too numb to weep any more. She had never expected to sink so low, felt so desperately ashamed she couldn't look any of them in the face.

'We'll put you to work in the infirmary, I think. You can help look after the sick.'

She did as they asked, alternating between shame and anger, weeping when she thought no one was looking.

How was she to get out of here? Would Alex come back for her? Did she even want him to?

CHAPTER TWENTY-ONE

Theo was away only for a few days, then in late October he came back and marched into the inn with a determined expression, even before he'd cared for his horse. 'I'm staying until you've had the baby,' he announced.

Keara couldn't find it in her heart to be angry with him.

'How are you?' he asked when she didn't speak.

'Tired of this.' She indicated her swollen belly.

He moved across to her and she looked at him warily, then glanced down with a gasp as the baby moved vigorously. 'It's very lively today.'

'Would you – let me feel it moving?'

She took his hand and guided it to her belly. They stood there while the child kicked again and again. When Keara looked at his face, it was full of joy. And love. She felt a treacherous warmth flow through her in response and could do nothing but smile at him.

'It feels strong,' he said at last. 'Poor Richard never kicked like that, even after he was born.'

'It keeps me awake sometimes at night.' Then,

because she was afraid of how close they were standing, she twisted away. 'Now, can I get you some food?'

'Only if you'll sit with me while I eat.'

She gave in to temptation. 'I will. They won't let me do much now.'

Maggie came in just then and looked at him with some hostility. 'You're back, then? I wondered whose horse that was.'

He risked teasing her. 'Nice to be made welcome.'

But she was not to be won over and only scowled at him.

He turned to Keara. 'I'll go and unsaddle the poor creature, then come back and eat.'

After he'd left Maggie said sharply, 'You're heading for trouble, my girl!'

'I know. But he *is* the father.'

That evening, Mark looked across the table as they were finishing their meal. 'Theo, you said you were intending to stay for a while?'

'Yes. Until after the child's born,' he threw a wry smile at Keara, 'even if I have to camp outside in the road to do so.'

'No need for that.' She had been feeling very placid for the past day or two, too placid to argue with him. And anyway, she wanted him with her when the baby was born, even though Maggie was horrified at the mere idea. He had been so wonderful with Lavinia. Keara didn't want to face the birth alone. She knew what had to be done and felt well enough to hope for a happy outcome, but she still wanted him beside her.

Mark smiled at them. No mistaking the way they

were looking at one another. 'Then would you mind keeping an eye on things here while I make a quick trip up to Perth, Theo? I need to buy some more supplies and I'm a bit worried about leaving Keara and Maggie alone, especially now.'

'There's no need to worry. We can look after ourselves,' Maggie said quickly.

Mark looked at her. 'There is a need and you know it.'

She scowled down at her plate, feeling left out, and when she looked up Theo was smiling at Keara and her friend was smiling back at him. What if Keara didn't want her any more? What if she went off to be *his* mistress? Maggie felt angry at the mere thought of that. 'He's a fine one to talk of protecting us. Where was he when they kidnapped Keara and sent her to Australia?'

Keara frowned at her and gave a quick shake of her head, so Maggie shut up. You couldn't protect someone who didn't want to be protected.

'I'd be happy to stay,' Theo said quickly. 'More than happy.' He gave Keara a wry smile, then looked beyond her to Maggie. 'I'm ashamed that I looked after Keara so badly, believe me.' He turned back to Mark. 'I'll do what I can to help out here, but I'm no cook.'

'Maggie's turning into a good cook. She'll see to that side of things.' He pushed his chair back and stood up. 'I'll leave straight away then.' He smiled down at his daughter, then looked at Keara. 'I'll make much better time without madam here. Are you sure you'll be all right looking after her?'

'Of course I will. I keep telling everyone I'm not ill!'

He bent to kiss Amy. 'She's lucky to have you.' He looked across at the other man. 'Theo, if you have a few minutes, I'd like to show you round and explain what needs doing.'

When they got outside, Theo said gruffly, 'Thanks for helping me stay here.'

Mark didn't pretend to misunderstand this. He looked into the distance, feeling at ease enough with this man to say, 'I've been dreading the birth. I've killed two women now, by giving them my babies.'

Theo looked at him in astonishment. 'That's not your fault. It's sheer chance whether a woman survives or not. Or a man. We all take risks in everything we do.'

'See how you feel about that if anything happens to Keara,' Mark said grimly.

He was gone within the hour.

When Theo came back into the public room, he grinned. 'Well then, looks like you're stuck with me for a few days.'

'I have a lot to do, so don't think I'll be sitting around chatting. You'll have to keep yourself occupied,' Keara told him.

But he must have been keeping an eye on her, because when Maggie took Amy and told her brusquely to go and rest, he came to join her.

'We've not had much time for sitting and chatting, have we?' he said, leaning his head back against the hard wood of his chair. 'What shall we talk about?'

'Tell me about your voyage,' she said in desperation, wanting to find a safe topic of conversation.

So he chatted about the voyage and she listened to

his deep voice, wishing she need never send him away again. When he questioned her about her own journey, she tried to turn the talk back to him, but he would have none of it.

'I want to know what happened, all the details, Keara: how they managed to kidnap you, how you felt when you realised what had happened. And I shan't stop asking until I know.'

So she decided to tell him a few things about the trip and found herself responding more fully than she had intended to his genuine interest, and even giving a sketchy description of how Nancy and the two men had kidnapped her.

'She's a strange woman. She told me the kidnapping wouldn't do you any harm because your future lay in Australia.'

'I think she was right. If Ismay and Mara are here, why should I want to go back?'

'And if you and our child are here, why should I want to go back, either?'

But this was going too far too fast, so she said lightly, 'Sure, you could charm the birds off the trees, Theo Mullane. And here's me sitting chatting when I've Amy to feed.' She pushed herself up awkwardly, wishing her belly were not so huge because it made her clumsy. Did he think her ugly now?

He came to steady her, his eyes warm and loving. 'I've enjoyed the past hour more than I can say.'

'It's asking for trouble, you coming here,' she blurted out.

He pulled her into his arms, leaning over the

bulging stomach to kiss her very gently on the cheek. 'Then I'll continue asking for trouble. May I touch it again?' He laid one hand on her belly, his expression so reverent she could not refuse him.

The baby kicked and he looked at her, his eyes bright with tears. 'It's wonderful to feel the new life, the hope and . . .' His voice broke on the words.

She couldn't resist raising one hand to caress his cheek. 'Ah, Theo, if only things were different. But you're still a married man.'

'We'll find a way to be together.'

But she shook her head and pulled back.

He let her go, vowing yet again to stay with her, whatever she said or did.

When Mark got to Perth, he took some letters to the Post Office from the people of Meriniup and asked if there was any mail for his sub-Post Office, because if so, he could take it back with him the next day. He was now taking care of the mail for his district for the princely payment of five guineas a year. Well, every bit of income helped, but more important than the money was the fact that it brought people to the inn to collect or send letters and parcels.

'You're the third person who's been asking about that place this week,' the clerk told him, 'though of course I didn't give the others the mail, them not being officially appointed to the service.'

'Oh? Have we got other settlers intending to take up land nearby, then?'

'No. First of all there was an old fellow asking about you – Mark Gibson, he says, asking for you by name, saying he was a relative. Well, there's a list of the sub-Post Offices on the wall over there, with names of officers in charge, so I couldn't very well refuse to tell him, could I?'

'What sort of an old fellow?'

'A bit strange, if you ask me.' The clerk tapped his forehead and rolled his eyes.

Mark felt a sinking feeling in his stomach. It couldn't be . . . surely it couldn't? 'Did the old man give you his name?'

'No. I sent him across to look at the list.' He looked at Mark suspiciously. 'Why shouldn't I? Not in trouble with the law, are you? If so, you've no right to be running a Post Office.'

'No, of course I'm not in trouble with the law.' He was turning to leave when he suddenly remembered that there had been a second person. 'Who else asked for me?'

'An old lady. She'd been crying, I think. She looked at the list as well, then came to ask me where Meriniup was. But she cried even harder when I told her. She said she had no money and I felt sorry for her, if you must know. I don't like to see old ladies weeping.'

'Did *she* give you her name?'

'Yes. I have it written down. Not that I thought I'd ever need it, but you can never tell, and it seemed to comfort her that I took it down.' He searched through the drawer of his desk. 'Where is it? I know I put it – ah, here it is! A Mrs Jenner.'

Mark sagged against the counter. It was definitely them. Only why had they gone to so much trouble to plague him? And why had they come separately to ask after him? 'Where is she? Is there an address?'

'I heard she'd been put in the poorhouse. Destitute, poor soul. My cousin's wife works there, said she felt sorry for the poor old lady because you could see that she was respectable. Her husband up and left her, apparently, and she had no money, nowhere to go.'

Which gave Mark a great deal to think about.

He nearly didn't go to the poorhouse to see Mrs Jenner, but in the end had to find out what was happening. Patience had been fond of her mother, though the woman had been so much under her husband's thumb she had seemed to have almost no personality or thoughts of her own. But why had Mr Jenner abandoned his wife like that? It didn't make sense.

At the poorhouse he had to answer a lot of questions before they would let him see an 'inmate' and he was horrified to find Nan Jenner clad in pauper garb. She stared at him as if she didn't know whether to be happy or afraid to see him and her mouth formed his name, though no sound came out.

'I'm sorry to see you here, Mrs Jenner. What's happened to your husband?'

'He's gone looking for you. He didn't tell me he was going, just left.' She began to weep. 'And I had no money, no one to turn to. Look what he's brought me to!'

He took her hand and patted it. Gradually she

calmed down and he asked, 'Do you know what he wants?'

'Yes. Your daughter. He's grown obsessed by the thought of bringing Amy up himself in the ways of his sect.' She hesitated, then added in a low voice, 'He's been behaving so oddly lately. I think you ought to go home at once. How long does it take to get there?'

Her words had set fear trickling into his belly like ice water. 'Two days. I may even have passed him on the road.'

'Can't you get there any faster?'

'No. It's not like England, not even as advanced as Melbourne. It's a rough country road and the horses can only go so fast.'

'Who's looking after Amy?'

'Some friends.'

She was wringing her hands, twisting them to and fro, her expression anguished. 'They won't be expecting him. He'll take them by surprise and steal Amy. He won't know how to look after her. He never even touched ours when they were children.' She began to weep again. 'And what about me? What am I to do if he doesn't come back for me? I don't want to go back to him, but if I don't, I'll end my days in the poorhouse.'

He couldn't bear to see her in such distress. She was very like Patience, only older and faded, beaten down by life. And he would not allow a man who had made his daughter and wife so unhappy to interfere in Amy's life. Surely Mr Jenner wouldn't manage to steal her? Theo was at the inn and Keara was never far from the child.

Mark heard Nan sob again and laid his hand on hers. He couldn't leave this poor woman weeping. 'Will you trust yourself to me?'

She stared at him as if she didn't dare hope, then clapped a hand to her mouth as more tears welled in her eyes. 'Are you going to take me out of this place?'

'Yes. Only we have to hurry.' He went to see the supervisor and had his mother-in-law out within the hour. They were so delighted at getting rid of one of their charges that they even found the clothes and bag she had brought with her.

It made Mark very sad to see how little she owned, but he didn't comment, just settled her in his cart and set off for the food wholesaler's. He could not possibly get home in time to prevent Alex Jenner getting near his daughter, so another hour buying supplies would make little difference. At least, so he told himself. But he spent that hour fretting. He had been wrong to trust in Theo, who wasn't expecting anyone to come after the baby. He should have set off at once, only by the time he came to that conclusion he was in the middle of various trans-actions and they were loading his cart, so he finished as quickly as he could and told his team to 'Walk on'.

Nan Jenner sat in silence as they drove south, turning once to look back at Perth. 'It's a pretty site for a city, but I've been so unhappy here. But then, I've been unhappy for a long time.' She turned to Mark. 'I can't thank you enough for getting me out of that place, but I'm not going back to live with Alex again if I can help it. I know I promised to take him "for better, for worse" but he's the one who abandoned me.'

He looked sideways at her. 'What shall you do instead?'

'I thought . . .' She started twisting the material of her skirt, avoiding his eyes as she said, 'I could look after Amy for you, if you'd have me. I promise you, I'd care for her as you wish. I'm not like him. I tried to be the sort of person *he* wanted because I thought it was my duty. But I was wrong, and my children suffered for that. I'm not letting my granddaughter suffer as well. Children should be allowed to laugh and play and enjoy themselves. It isn't a sin to be happy!'

'We'll have to see how things turn out,' was all he could think of to say. First he had to make sure Amy was safe, then he had to find out what Keara intended to do about finding her sisters, if she really was going off with Theo Mullane.

Nan fell silent again, sighing from time to time.

That night as they camped beneath the stars, he said, 'What if your husband *insists* on your returning to him?'

'I shall refuse. I'd kill myself before I'd go back to him.'

'I'm making no promises about Amy. We'll have to see how you get on with her. But I will make sure you're all right, even if you don't stay with us. There are plenty of opportunities for employment in service. They can't get enough maids here.'

'That's good enough for me.' But as they drove slowly southwards, Nan vowed to prove to him that she could do what he wanted. She was longing to see the baby again. Though Amy wouldn't really be a baby now, because it was almost a year since Patience had died. A dreadful year it had been, too. The worst of Nan's whole life.

Keara was relieved when some travellers stopped at the inn on the second afternoon and asked to stay overnight. She was not only spared a tête-à-tête with Theo but kept busy helping look after the Wallers and their three sturdy children. She enjoyed chatting to Mrs Waller, who was a comfortable, motherly person, happy to be able to spend the night in comfort on the way up to Perth. Clearly this family had made a success as settlers and had money to spend.

Keara tried to help Maggie with the cooking, but her friend was very capable now and kept telling her to sit down and rest.

Theo also did what he could to help look after the guests. He took charge of Mr Waller and the son Bert, who at fourteen considered himself a man, while the two daughters, twelve and nine years old, stayed with their mother. He showed Mr Waller where to stable their horses and stood chatting with him about a settler's life, something which interested him more and more.

But though they were not alone, that evening Keara was conscious all the time of Theo watching her. How could she not be when she found her own eyes straying back to him, however hard she tried to ignore him?

CHAPTER TWENTY-TWO

October 1864

The following morning Keara woke very early, for some reason, and as Amy was already stirring, she changed the child's dirty napkin and got her some food. She loved to be the first person up and greatly enjoyed this cool dawn stillness before the heat of the day. There was no sign of Theo or the Wallers, just her and the child, who, though she had not yet taken her first steps, was pulling herself up regularly on wobbly legs. Today she stood holding a stool and brandishing her crust.

When Keara heard footsteps behind her, she continued stirring a pan of porridge, assuming it was Theo until a strange voice said, 'Keep very quiet or I shall be obliged to shoot you.'

With a gasp she turned to find an elderly man pointing a revolver at her. 'What do you want?'

'My grandchild.'

'You're Patience's father?' Mark had told them about the problems that had driven him and his daughter from Victoria and she couldn't believe that Mr Jenner had found them again.

'Yes, I am. And that's enough talking. I mean exactly what I say.'

When he waggled the revolver again, so carelessly that she was terrified it'd go off accidentally, she froze where she stood.

'Come with me and bring the child.'

She picked Amy up as slowly as she could, listening carefully, hoping someone would get up and see what was happening. But the rest of the inn remained still.

'Hurry up!' he snapped, when she had delayed as much as she could. 'And don't make a sound!'

She left the pan over the flames. It would soon start burning and perhaps the smell would bring someone out. It was the only thing she could do. He didn't even seem to notice it.

He gestured with the gun, his eyes so staring and fixed she felt a shiver run down her spine. What did he intend to do with Amy? And her?

He pointed towards the path that led through the forest. 'We'll go back that way.'

'But—'

He jabbed the revolver hard into her side. 'I told you to keep quiet, woman!'

So she held back the questions and worries, walking along the path in front of him, conscious all the time of him following her. It was hard to see the ground because of the swell of her belly and the child she was carrying. Once she tripped and bumped into a tree, narrowly preventing Amy from being hurt. Several times she stumbled and nearly fell.

The child seemed to grow heavier by the minute.

Keara stopped walking to lean against a tree, panting with the effort of carrying her. As he growled something and gestured, she pushed herself into movement again, clutching a branch and managing to snap off a smaller shoot from partway along it that would show clearly from the path, leaving it hanging by a shred of bark. Maybe no one would notice this small sign, but she had to try to leave traces of her passing.

'Watch where you're walking!' snapped that rusty voice from behind her. 'I don't want my granddaughter hurt.'

'Where *are* we going?'

He gave her a push that sent her stumbling forward again. 'Shut up and keep walking.'

The path meandered through the forest. She'd strolled along it several times, never reaching the end, and couldn't think where the man was taking her. Unless he was just going somewhere to kill her? That thought made fear settle in her stomach like a heavy stone.

She was genuinely panting now with the effort of carrying Amy.

'Stop!' he said suddenly. 'We'll take a short rest here.'

Keara had a stitch in her side now. As she bent to set Amy down and give her aching arms a rest, she felt a pulling feeling in her belly, then it went very stiff. Surely she couldn't be having her child now? She waited for another pain, but it didn't come. It must just be the strain of carrying Amy for so long.

When she stole a glance in her captor's direction she

saw that he was staring round, frowning as if puzzled. Was it possible that he was lost? Surely, if he was trying to kidnap the child again, he'd have a vehicle waiting near the road to take him back to Perth? It didn't make sense to penetrate deeper and deeper into the forest. None of this made sense.

As they set off again, with him leading the way this time, she dropped her handkerchief, her heart thumping in fear that he'd notice till they had rounded the next bend and the tell-tale piece of white was hidden.

Maggie got up, yawning and stretching, seeing the world through her usual morning blur until she'd had a cup of tea. When she went out to the kitchen, however, there was no sign of Keara and she wrinkled her nose at the smell. There was a pan of porridge burning on top of the stove and with an exclamation of dismay she rushed to pull it off the heat, then looked round anxiously. It wasn't like her friend to forget a pan for so long that its contents burned black.

She couldn't see her anywhere, so went inside again. Keara's bedroom was empty. Methodically Maggie searched the living quarters, then went outside to check the storeroom. There was no sign anywhere of either her friend or Amy.

Feeling really worried now, she went along the front veranda of the guests' quarters, but there was no sign of life from the Wallers, though Keara had agreed to waken them as soon as she got up herself.

She knocked on the end door, Theo's room. He

opened it a couple of minutes later, blinking at her in surprise. 'Is something wrong?'

'I hope not. Only I can't find Keara or Amy and I've looked everywhere.'

'I'll be with you in a minute.' He slammed the door and Maggie walked slowly back to the inn, going to peer round the back again, even glancing into the stables, though Keara rarely went there.

By the time Maggie got back to the big public room, Theo was there, fully dressed, though he hadn't bothered to shave and his chin was dark with stubble. 'Tell me,' he said at once.

'Well, Keara always gets up first. She wakes at dawn and so does Amy. I get up a short time later. This morning there's no sign of either of them and I've looked everywhere. I can't help worrying with her so near her time. Anyway, where could they be? There isn't anywhere for them to go, let alone Keara wouldn't just vanish without telling anyone. And there was a pan of porridge on the stove. It must have been there for a while because it was burnt black. She wouldn't have willingly left that. *What's happened to them?*'

He felt worried too, but controlled his anxiety. 'Keep calm. You won't help her by getting hysterical. Has anything like this ever happened before?'

'She hasn't disappeared. The only trouble we had was when we first arrived and there were some hooligans making free of the place. She helped Mark drive them away. But we haven't seen a sign of them since.'

'Did you upset anyone in Perth?'

She gave a short laugh. 'We were only there for a

few days and they kept us shut up inside the poorhouse most of the time.'

'What about Mark, then? His daughter is also missing. Does anyone have any reason to wish him ill?'

She stared at him, frowned, then shook her head. 'No. No, it can't be . . .'

'Can't be what?'

'His father-in-law once tried to kidnap Amy. But Mark left Melbourne secretly and didn't tell anyone where he was going. No, it can't possibly be them.'

'You'd think not, but it's not too hard to trace people. We traced Keara to the ship quite easily.'

'Mark says Mr Jenner is a dreadful man, half-crazed with religion.'

'If he had come here, surely someone would have seen him?' After a pause, he asked, 'Perhaps Keara's gone to visit someone in Meriniup?'

'Everyone round here is too busy to waste time visiting, especially first thing in the morning. Keara likes to walk into the forest a little way, but not usually at this hour. She does that in the afternoons.'

The Wallers came into the public room just then, clearly expecting their breakfast.

'I'm sorry,' Theo said curtly. 'Keara and the baby have disappeared and we're worried about them, so we haven't had time to get anything ready for you. Perhaps you could get your own food?'

The lad brightened. 'Are they lost in the forest?'

Theo looked at him in surprise. 'Why do you say that?'

Bert shuffled his feet. 'I woke up early this morning

and went out to the privy. I saw Keara in the distance walking towards the forest – with a man. She was carrying the baby.'

Theo stiffened. 'What was he like?' Surely she wasn't trying to escape from him?

'Old. White hair, balding, 'bout the same height as her. I only caught a glimpse of them. Thought it must be a neighbour.'

'There's no one like that in Meriniup,' Maggie said at once. 'The ones who've settled round here are mostly younger folk.'

'Show me where they were going,' Theo said to young Bert, who led him eagerly outside.

'I could come with you, help you. I'm friendly with some of the natives at home and they've been showing me how to track.'

His parents looked at one another, clearly uneasy with this suggestion.

'You need a native,' Mr Waller said. 'They're the ones who know how to track properly.'

'We don't have time to bring anyone in,' said Theo. 'Will you let your son try? I know so little of this country. I've only been here a few weeks.'

'Aye, then. But I'll come with you as well, if you don't mind. And I'll bring my revolver.'

Theo looked at Mr Waller in surprise. 'You think a gun necessary?'

'Won't hurt.' He gave Theo a steady look. 'This isn't England and you'd do well to remember that. Those forests can hide a lot of secrets. We found a body when we were clearing our land, didn't we, Jane?'

His wife nodded. 'Dressed in European clothes, too, so it wasn't one of the natives. He'd been shot. My Len's taught me and the girls to handle a gun. You can't be too careful.'

This made Theo even more anxious about Keara. He turned to Maggie. 'You stay here, but be on your guard. We don't want you vanishing as well.'

'I'll keep the carving knife handy,' Maggie said at once.

'We'll stay together. There's safety in numbers.' Mrs Waller put one arm round each of her daughters' shoulders, looking watchful but not afraid.

Bert led the way to the beginning of a narrow path that meandered into the forest, holding up one hand to stop them. 'They went along here. See the footprints? Let me go first, so that I can look for signs.'

'All right, but move as quickly as you can,' Theo said. 'We don't know what the old man wants.' If the fellow harmed Keara or the unborn child, Theo would kill him.

Bert held him back. 'Slow down. If we go too fast, we'll miss things.'

Theo sighed. 'Then go slowly, but for heaven's sake, go!'

Keara stopped and clutched her belly, gasping as another pain jabbed through her, much stronger this time.

'What's the matter? Why have you stopped moving?'

'I'm having the child now. Oh!'

'You're lying!' The old man's eyes were chilly as he looked at her. 'You either keep moving or . . .'

He waved the revolver, holding it so carelessly she bit back a protest and tried to put her own body between the gun and Amy. Gritting her teeth she moved on, but after two or three minutes another pain ripped down her belly and she cried out, stopping again. The pains were coming more quickly now, one following soon after the other. Her mother had usually had babies very quickly. All the other women in the village had envied her that. Was she going to be the same?

And if she had to stop to bear her child, would this man really shoot her? She moaned and managed to start walking again, but could move only slowly.

A minute or so later, Amy began to howl and thrash around in Keara's arms. It was the sound she always made when she was hungry.

'What's wrong with the child?' he demanded.

'She's finished the crust and wants her breakfast.' Keara risked stopping to try to soothe Amy, but the child continued wailing, demanding the food that had always been promptly available before. 'How far do we – ouch! – have to go?'

He looked round, rubbing his forehead with one hand. 'Not far, I think. The turning must be round here.'

As far as Keara knew, this path led only through the bush and any turnings were mere animal tracks. How had he got to the inn? He must have left a vehicle somewhere near the road and they were moving into the forest instead. She didn't say that, however, hoping he was lost, because she could easily find her way back from here.

'The baby will just have to cry,' he said curtly. 'In this Vale of Tears, we must all learn to be patient.'

'She's too young to understand that. And she's wet, needs changing. Do you have some clean baby clothes?'

'We can get some in Perth.'

Perth? Surely he didn't think Amy would be able to wait two days until they got to Perth? But Keara could see no sign of understanding in his face, only annoyance at the child's continuing sobbing. She gasped and bent forward as another pain took her by surprise.

Before it had even finished, he moved forward and prodded her with the revolver. 'Move along, but slowly so that I can look for the turning. It's around here somewhere.'

She tried to obey, but a groan escaped her and she bent over, moaning as the pain urged her to co-operate with it. When it slackened, she felt moisture trickle down her legs and knew the waters had broken. She stumbled forward a few steps and as they came to a clearing where a tree had fallen, she stopped again and put Amy down, clutching her stomach and screaming at him, 'I *can't* go on! The baby's coming now!'

He looked at her with disgust. ' "In pain shall they bring them forth". Women are uncleanly creatures.'

Keara tried to keep watch on Amy as she succumbed to the urge to push, crouching with her back against a tree and lifting her skirts to free her legs. She didn't care whether he saw her body. Her only concern was to do as it demanded now and birth her baby.

He moved backwards, shuddering and averting his eyes.

The pains were very close together, but after a few of them, Keara turned to check that Amy was all right. What she saw filled her with terror. A large snake must have been basking in the sunlight of the clearing and it was slithering slowly towards the child, who was weeping and waving her arms about. It was the sort Mark called a tiger snake and he'd said its bite was deadly. Keara tried to push herself forward, but couldn't move. 'Quick!' she called to her captor, pointing. 'Do something. Shoot it.'

He turned and his mouth fell open in shock as he saw the reptile.

'You can't let your granddaughter die!' Keara looked round for something, anything, to hit the snake with, but although the ground was littered with small branches, leaves and pieces of bark, there was nothing large enough to act as a weapon.

A moment longer he hesitated, trying to aim the revolver at the snake. But the creature was between him and his granddaughter, so he lowered the gun again. 'I can't shoot,' he muttered hoarsely. 'It might kill her and she's not yet been brought to grace.'

As another wave of pain racked Keara and made her groan and pay attention to her body, he flung the revolver aside and leaped forward.

As the pain receded she saw him pounce on the snake, grabbing it in the wrong place, for Mark had told them how to deal with snakes, which were quite common in the bush. 'No!' she yelled. 'Grab the end of its tail and swing it against a tree!'

But even as he turned to look at her, the snake twisted its head round, angered at being disturbed, and sank its fangs into his wrist. With a yell he hurled it away from him and clutched his arm, yelling hoarsely, panic on his face.

Without even trying to see where the snake fell he turned and started running back the way they had come, yelling for someone to help him. As she watched, he fell over, bumping his head hard against a tree root and lying winded for a moment. Then he dragged himself to his feet, blood streaming down his face, and ran off out of sight.

Keara looked round, searching for signs of the snake, but couldn't see anything. Amy was still sitting there, showing no signs of discomfort or agitation now, but sucking her thumb. Then the pain swept Keara away again and she could only heed its demands and push.

Bert found a broken branch where there were signs of someone stopping. 'Look, that can't have been broken accidentally and it's a fresh break, too. I bet she did it on purpose. Clever.'

Further along he spotted the handkerchief and picked it up, handing it to Theo.

'I saw her using this very one last night.' He recognised the ragged corner that the baby had been chewing on.

'You're doing well, son,' the father said encouragingly.

Just then they heard someone yelling in the distance and footsteps crashing through the bush towards them. Theo pushed past the lad and began to run along the path.

If Keara was in trouble . . .

CHAPTER TWENTY-THREE

But it wasn't Keara. An old man appeared, staggering drunkenly towards them, clutching his arm. He had blood running down his right temple and grazes on his face. 'Help!' he yelled. 'A snake's bitten me. Help me!'

They had to hold him to stop him running past them, because he was jerking about and groaning as well as continuing to shout hoarsely for help, as if he didn't quite realise they were there.

' "That old Serpent, which is the devil!" ' he muttered. ' "Yea, the devil shall tempt thee." '

'What was the snake like?' Mr Waller asked and slapped him across the face when he didn't answer.

He jerked in shock and stared wildly around him. 'Big. Striped.' Then he began muttering again.

'Hell! That sounds like a tiger snake.' Mr Waller and his son exchanged glances.

'Is that bad?' Theo asked.

'Yes. Very. The bite kills 'em often as not.'

Terror made Theo's breath catch in his throat. 'You

look after him and I'll go and search for Keara. She can't be too far away.' He grabbed the old man's arm and shook it to make him pay attention. 'Where are the woman and child? Have they been bitten too?'

'Back – there. With the serpent!'

Theo's blood ran cold and he threw the old man aside.

Mr Waller said, 'Look, I'll take this fellow back to the inn. You go and—'

But Theo had already set off running along the path.

When he burst into the clearing he saw Amy first, sitting playing by herself. Where was Keara? He spun round as a groan alerted him and saw her lying on the ground behind a large tree, groaning and writhing. He flung himself towards her. 'Did the snake bite you?'

'No. The baby — it's coming.'

Relief shuddered through him. Even as he held her, she began to push down, groaning with the effort. He had shared this experience with Lavinia more than once, but unlike his wife Keara needed no urging to work with her body. As the spasm passed he murmured, 'Can you walk back if I help you? We need to get you to a bed, my darling.'

She gave a shaky laugh. 'I'm sorry, Theo. There isn't time. You know what to do, don't you? If not, I can tell you.'

'I know what to do.' He kept his voice calm and soothing as he helped her raise her skirts, praising her bravery and holding her hand as she pushed and heaved. He wondered vaguely where the others were, then forgot about them as he saw the baby's head appear. He could not believe it was happening so quickly. Tears welled up in his eyes. His child. Oh, dear God, let it be alive! He realised they would need something to wrap it in and hastily pulled off his shirt, smoothing the ground beside her and pushing away the twigs and forest litter.

After a few more minutes of grunting effort, Keara pushed the baby out and Theo laid it gently on the shirt, grateful that everything was going so well. 'It's a girl – and she's breathing. *Keara, she's breathing*. She looks pink and . . .' He couldn't speak and tears were streaming down his cheeks as he looked at the woman he loved and saw her smiling at him. When the afterbirth appeared, he did what was necessary with his usual efficiency, pulling the lace from one of his shoes to tie off the cord. Then he cradled his daughter for one precious minute, the first person ever to hold her. Pressing a kiss on her soft little cheek, he laid her reverently in her mother's arms.

'Our daughter,' Keara whispered. 'Oh, Theo, she's so beautiful.'

The child blinked out at the world, waving one tiny arm and nestling instinctively against the warmth of her mother.

He wiped his cheeks. 'I'm a fool. This is not something to weep over.'

'They're tears of joy,' she said tenderly, closing her eyes for a minute, knowing that her own cheeks were wet. She had never realised what an overwhelming surge of love you felt towards your new-born baby.

'Are you all right, my dearest love?'

Though her lids felt heavy, she opened her eyes again because she knew how anxious he must be. 'Just tired, Theo. Let me rest – just for a minute or two – then we'll start back.'

'You're not walking back in that condition!'

She let out a soft gurgle of laughter. 'Well, I can't fly so I'll have to walk.' Her lids fluttered closed then flew open again as anxiety replaced the softness on her face. 'Amy! Where is she? There was a big snake.'

'She was all right when I got here.' But he'd been so engrossed in the birth he'd forgotten to check the child again after that first quick glance, so he jumped to his feet and went back across the clearing. He found her sleeping peacefully on the ground, thumb in mouth, her face tear-stained and dirty. Picking her up gently, he carried her to Keara and laid her down on the edge of her skirt. 'She's fine, my darling. Just sleepy like you.'

She reached out one hand to lay it on the older baby's head, then sighed and dozed off, her own baby cradled against her breast.

He crouched beside them, keeping watch for snakes or spiders, sure that the others would come back to help them as soon as they could, not even wanting them at present, treasuring this moment, the happiest of his entire life. At one point he bent his head to listen to his daughter's snuffling little breaths and closed his eyes in sheer ecstasy. She was plump and rosy, with a cap of dark fuzz on her head. He had never seen anything as beautiful as her lying there in her mother's arms.

He was sorry when he heard the sound of people approaching from the direction of the inn.

As Maggie and Mr Waller came into sight, she called out, 'There they are!'

Theo put one finger to his lips, but it was too late. He looked down to see Keara stir and open her eyes, her first glance going to check at once that her daughter was all right. He knelt beside her and helped her sit up. 'Time to get you back, my darling,' he said. 'Maggie, will you carry Amy? Keara, Mr Waller and I can make a chair with our hands and—'

She laughed. 'I can walk on my own two feet, Theo Mullane. Just help me up and lend me your arm.'

And so she did, with his arm round her waist for support, and Maggie and the stranger walking behind them, each carrying a baby.

When they reached the inn, Keara was tired and glad to get to bed. She allowed Maggie to help her clean herself up, but in no way would she let them treat her like an invalid.

Theo lingered in the doorway watching until Maggie clicked her tongue and made shooing movements with her hands.

So then he stood staring at the closed door, unable to stop himself smiling, not caring if he looked stupid. He could not believe how strong Keara was. She had been quite magnificent, birthing a child without fuss in such extreme circumstances. And what a fine, healthy daughter she had given him! His throat tightened with emotion every time he thought of the baby.

Bert poked his head into the public room and sighed

with relief when he saw him. 'Mam says to come quickly. She thinks the old man's dying.'

Reluctantly Theo followed him and found Alex Jenner lying on a bed in one of the guest rooms. Even as they watched, he had a fit, gasping and jerking, his eyes rolling. Afterwards his breathing sounded odd, almost like snoring.

Mrs Waller stood at the foot of the bed, looking extremely worried.

'He was thrashing around for a while,' she whispered, 'complaining about the pain in his head. His arm's swollen to twice its size. Look. Then he said he couldn't breathe. There isn't really anything I can do to help him, I'm afraid.'

'Tiger snake bites usually kill you,' Mr Waller said calmly.

Theo moved forward to stare down at the man who had endangered his child and was horrified to see the staring, uncomprehending eyes and congested face. His wheezing attempts to breathe seemed to fill the whole room.

'No. I doubt anyone could help him now.' And you could not stay angry with a dying man, Theo found.

He went away to check that Keara was all right then went out to the horses, leaning his head against his mare's neck, needing a minute or two of peace.

An hour later he returned to the old man's bedside and stayed there as the laboured breathing continued, growing fainter and less desperate until suddenly there was silence.

'He's gone,' Mrs Waller said in a more normal voice. 'He was lucky. It all happened quickly. Some of them take nearly a day to die.' She covered his face and looked at Theo. 'Do you know who he is?'

'I've never seen him before, but I think he's the owner's father-in-law. He's not been acting very rationally for some time, apparently.'

'Me and Len will lay him out, if you like. We've done it before. We'd better keep the contents of his pockets. He's got quite a bit of money. Is there somewhere you can bury him?'

'I don't know. I only arrived here a few weeks ago myself. I'll go and ask Maggie.'

He went back to the public room, where the two Waller girls were sitting in one corner, and found Maggie just coming out of Keara's room. She put a finger to her lips, which he took to mean Keara was sleeping. He longed to go and sit with her, wanted to watch his daughter again, simply for the pleasure of seeing her breathing so steadily, but there were things to be done.

'The old man's dead,' he said. 'Is there somewhere round here to bury people?'

'Heavens, I don't know! I think I'd better go into the settlement and ask. Someone's bound to know. Will you listen for Keara waking? She'll want plenty to drink to make the milk come. I'll nip along to the settlement now, while it's quiet. Do you two girls want to come with me?' They jumped up with alacrity. She picked up a shawl, then as she got to the door, turned and brought it back with a shamefaced smile. 'Eh, I keep forgetting I don't need a shawl. Isn't that sunshine lovely? And it isn't even summer yet.'

Theo followed her to the door, standing with his face turned up to the sun. Life went on, whatever happened to an individual. And the sunshine was indeed lovely, its warmth almost like a caress. He heard Mr Waller come into the public room and turned to join him.

'I've been thinking, the old man must have had some sort of a vehicle. Did you hear any passing?'

Theo frowned and tried to remember. 'There was one went by late yesterday, heading south, a cart with one horse. But it didn't stop and we thought nothing of it.'

'He'll have left it somewhere. Me and Bert had better go and look for it while it's still light. Best we go on foot, I think. It won't be far away if he walked back to the inn today. My wife says she'll look after Amy for you. Loves a baby, my Jane does.'

The inn grew quiet again. When he heard Keara stirring Theo tiptoed into the bedroom and found her staring towards the door. 'Thirsty?'

She nodded.

'I'll brew you a pot of tea.'

'I'm hungry, too. Ravenous.' She grinned at him.

'You're amazing. You're supposed to lie there languidly, exhausted by your ordeal.'

'No, I'm not. Poor women have babies all the time and carry on looking after their families. My mother never lay abed for long.'

'I still think you're amazing.' He tiptoed across to smile tenderly down at his daughter and kiss Keara's cheek. They exchanged smiles, then he went to brew some tea, thankful to find a full kettle on the hob in the outside kitchen. He refilled it again afterwards and set it back on the heat before carrying the teapot inside.

He didn't want to tell Keara, but she demanded to know what had happened to Mr Jenner and would not be fobbed off. 'He's dead.'

She was silent for a minute or two. 'Well, it may sound heartless, but I think that's for the best. He seemed more than half-crazy to me.' For the first time that day he heard her voice falter. 'Oh, Theo, I thought he was going to kill me and my unborn baby.'

So he had to hold her close – very close.

And she couldn't bring herself to push him away until the baby woke and began to search for the breast.

He watched her start to feed their daughter and helped her take sips of tea, laughing softly as they manoeuvred round the tiny warm body nestled against her.

'What shall we call her?' she asked.

'Do you want to call her after your mother?'

'No. My mother's name was Betsy and I think there are prettier names. Besides, I'd rather give our baby her own name.'

'Nell?' he suggested. 'I've always liked that name. Short for Helen.'

She considered this, repeating it once or twice, then nodded. 'Yes. Nell.' Her smile was glorious.

'Oh, Keara, I love you with all my heart.' He had

not thought it possible to care so much for anyone.

She couldn't deny her own feelings. 'I love you too, Theo.'

'If it's ever possible, I *will* marry you one day. But nothing on this earth will persuade me to leave you and Nell now. Nothing.'

Her face clouded over, then she gave him a sad smile. 'Ignorant Irish lasses like me don't marry gentlemen like you, Theo.'

'Maybe they don't back home, but I think in Australia it might be easier.'

'And what about Lavinia?'

'I don't know. Nancy said she wasn't well, hinted that she wouldn't make old bones.'

'I'd hate to base my happiness on another woman's death,' she said sombrely, wiping the infant's soft, milky mouth.

'I want to be with you and Nell, married or not, sleeping together or not.'

Silence fell and once he raised his hand as if to reach out to her, then let it drop again. He knew what he was asking. What would she decide?

At last she looked up at him and her eyes were shimmering with both tears and love. 'Theo, it's wrong, it's against everything I was taught, but I'll live with you as your wife. I love you as well as need you. We both need you.'

Then they were sobbing and kissing until the faint wailing protest of the baby caught between them made them pull apart.

Theo looked down to red-faced indignation, a

vitality that had never been there in Richard, then up again at the beautiful blue eyes of the woman he loved. 'I am the luckiest man alive,' he said huskily.

Mr Waller and his son returned over two hours later, leading a thin, weary-looking horse which was pulling a ramshackle two-wheeled cart.

'Poor creature was tethered to a tree just off the road,' Mr Waller called out to Theo. 'No feed. No water, either. Bert here noticed the wheel tracks going off the road, though the fellow had tried to hide them. We found a stream and gave the horse a drink before we harnessed it, but it didn't look strong enough to pull two stout fellows like us, so we walked back.'

He clapped his son on the shoulder as he spoke, the sort of easy affection Theo hoped to develop with his own children one day. His heart lifted as he realised that now he really was likely to have a proper family.

As well as the woman he loved.

What the hell did it matter if they were married or not?

But if Nancy had been right about Lavinia, if he was ever in a position to marry Keara, then he would do so without the slightest hesitation.

The following morning a man rode up the track from Meriniup on a fine, thoroughbred horse. He stopped at the inn and tied his horse to the rail at the front, hesitated a moment, then walked inside.

Maggie looked up. 'Can I help you, sir?'

'Who's in charge here, girl?'

She didn't like his tone, but something about him made her bite back a sharp answer. 'Mr Mullane. I'll fetch him.'

He waited, slapping his gloves idly against the palm of one hand and when Theo came in, eyed him searchingly.

Theo stared back, waiting for him to speak.

'Charles Dangerfield.' He stuck out one hand.

'Theo Mullane.'

They shook hands.

'Irish?'

'Yes.'

'M'mother was Irish. I – um – believe there's been a death here.'

'Yes. Snake bite.'

'I have some ground that's been blessed by a priest. My first wife's buried there and other folk from hereabouts have started to bury their dead there as well. I prefer it. Don't like Margaret to lie there alone. You can have a space, if you like.'

'That's very kind of you. Let me offer you some refreshments. Maggie?'

She might have guessed the two of them would get on well. The gentry always did stick together. 'There are some griddle scones and tea or beer or rum.'

'Tea and scones would be fine.' Theo gestured. 'Sit down, please, Mr Dangerfield. I'm not the owner. Mark Gibson's gone up to Perth, but he'll be back in a day or two.'

'Haven't met the chappie, but they tell me he's a hard worker. There's another woman here, isn't there? His wife?'

'No, she's my wife.'

The other man looked at him as if he rather doubted that, but did not challenge Theo's statement. Perhaps he had secrets of his own to hide. After all, you didn't expect to find someone like him in such a tiny settlement.

The door to the living quarters opened and Keara came out, dressed and carrying her baby.

Theo abandoned everything to hurry across to her. 'Should you be up?'

She smiled. 'I told you: I'm not ill. And Nell wants to see the world.'

'Let me introduce you to Mr Dangerfield, who lives in Meriniup. My wife, Keara.'

She gave him a quick, startled glance, then turned to nod to the stranger whom she hadn't met before because he rarely left his homestead. 'People said you'd been ill, Mr Dangerfield. I hope you're feeling better now.'

'Yes, thank you.' His gaze was shrewd, but his manner perfectly courteous. 'Congratulations on a happy outcome to your *accouchement*. May I see your daughter, ma'am?'

She walked across to show him the sleeping infant, wondering what *accouchement* meant.

'Fine child,' he said. 'Looks healthy.'

He consumed several scones with great relish, then took his leave of them.

'I felt embarrassed being introduced as your wife,' Keara said as the sound of horse's hooves faded into the distance. 'He must know I'm not when I've been living here for months with no sign of you.'

'He might guess but he won't say anything. And when we leave here, no one apart from our friends will know it isn't true. In fact, we can hint that it's why we came to Australia: because my family wouldn't accept you. But as far as I'm concerned, you *are* my wife, darling.' His tone changed to teasing, 'Now, sit down or I'll tie you to a chair. You may have escaped the confines of the bedchamber, but you're not lifting a finger. Maggie and I can manage perfectly well without you, and Mrs Waller is enjoying looking after Amy.'

So Keara sat down and enjoyed the simple pleasure of spending time with him and their daughter. She could not ask much more of life.

They buried Alex Jenner that afternoon. The Wallers had stayed on to help, Mr Waller saying cheerfully that he was his own master these days and could come and go as he pleased. His elder son was not only perfectly capable of looking after the family homestead but would enjoy being in charge.

He and Bert walked to the bush cemetery with Theo, who led the poor old horse drawing the cart with the simple, home-made coffin on it. They passed through some big gates and turned to the right as they had been directed, moving along an overgrown track that led to a patch of cleared ground. A hole had already been dug and a spade was standing upright like a sentinel nearby.

The two Wallers helped Theo lower the crude coffin into the grave, then stood in respectful silence as he said a short prayer. Then they took it in turns to fill in the hole and stamp the soft earth down. There were four wooden markers in the small graveyard and one marble headstone inscribed to *Margaret Dangerfield, beloved wife of Charles*.

'Not often you see real marble round here,' Len Waller commented as they walked back together. 'He must have loved her very much to have brought that all the way from Perth.'

Or maybe, Theo thought more cynically, he had felt guilty. Maggie said his second wife was much younger than he was and very pretty, but that his children from his first marriage never came to visit them.

They were all thoughtful as they walked back.

To Mark's surprise, Nan Jenner not only coped well with the journey but seemed revived by it, lifting her face often to the sun and commenting on all they passed. Her first remarks were made in such a hesitant way it made him realise yet again how dominated she had been by her husband. When he encouraged her to speak, Mark found her sensible and caring. Setting aside his worries about Amy, he told her about his life with Patience.

Though that made her weep, she said earnestly, 'I'm glad she had that happy time, at least. We led a very quiet life the rest of the time. Alex wasn't always as bad as he has been the past year or two, but he was very strict with the children. When we arrived here, he was so disappointed to find that his brother had died, I think it soured him. I never did understand why he wanted to come out to Australia anyway. He seemed to hate it here from the very beginning.'

A little later, she sighed and reiterated, 'No, whatever happens, I won't live with him again.'

Mark didn't comment. He pulled out his pocket watch and glanced at it. The miles seemed to be crawling past, but there was no way of travelling more quickly. He tried to forget his worries about Amy and pay attention to what Nan was saying.

'I'm just – afraid he'll try to *force* me to go back to him.' She cast a quick pleading glance sideways.

'I won't let him do that if it's against your wishes.'

'He can be very loud and angry – and I *am* his wife.'

'He abandoned you and has ill-treated you. I think that changes things.'

As they got near Meriniup he pointed out the landmarks, desperate now to get there. Alex Jenner had had two days' lead on them. What had he done with that time? Mark wished he could whip the horses up and gallop down the road, but the poor creatures were tired and had done their best. Why had he bought an inn in such an isolated place? Rossall Springs had suited him much better. There were so few people in Western Australia and he couldn't see more coming. People had poured into the colony of Victoria in search of gold so that its capital Melbourne had grown bigger with every year, but over here in the west there didn't seem to be any talk of gold, only of land and timber, sheep and crops.

As they rounded the final bend, he called, 'Ah! There it is!'

The horses clopped round to the back of the inn, tossing their heads in pleasure at getting home and coming to a halt next to their stables. Mark abandoned the reins and jumped down just as Theo came out of the back door.

'Is everything all right?' Mark called, seeing the other man's sombre expression.

'Your daughter is fine, but there's been some trouble.'

Nan Jenner moaned. 'It's Alex, I know it is.'

Keara appeared behind Theo, carrying Amy in her arms. Mark sighed with relief and went to take his daughter from her, holding the child close for one shuddering moment of relief.

He turned to see Theo helping Nan climb down, sorry to see how apprehensive she was looking.

'This is my mother-in-law, Mrs Jenner,' he said. 'Theo Mullane and Keara, who works for me, and—'

'Worked for you,' Theo corrected.

Mark realised suddenly what had changed. 'You've had the baby, Keara!'

'Yes. I'll introduce you to our little Nell in a minute.' She watched with a smile as he cuddled his daughter then lifted her high above his head, something the child loved. Then he turned to Nan, who was still hanging back. 'Come and meet your granddaughter.'

She moved forward, tears welling in her eyes, and
held her arms out. Amy considered her, head on one
side, then smiled and waved her arms as if wanting to
be held.

As Nan cuddled her granddaughter, with tears of
joy streaming down her cheeks, Mark looked at Theo
and Keara and asked quietly, 'What trouble?'

They both looked at Nan uncertainly.

'She knows her husband was coming here and why.
He abandoned her in Perth. I found her in the poorhouse.'

'That's terrible!' Keara moved forward to the older
woman. 'Won't you come inside, Mrs Jenner? I'll make
you a nice cup of tea and if you're hungry . . .' She put
an arm round her and led her inside.

Rapidly, Theo explained what had happened and
Mark whistled in surprise.

'How do we tell his wife?'

'I'll do it. I think she'll be relieved more than anything else. He's given her a dreadful time during the past
year or two. She didn't intend to go back to him, whatever happened.' He gave a wry smile. 'Actually, this
simplifies matters for me. If she and Amy get on, she's
going to stay and look after her for me. I know you and
Keara want to go and search for her sisters.'

Theo nodded. 'We do. And we've decided to live
together as man and wife.' He looked at Mark chal-
lengingly as he said that.

'I think that's an excellent idea. She loves you very
much.'

'Thank you. I love her, and please understand that

I'd marry her tomorrow if I could. Living together is not the solution of my choice and she considers it a sin – but we don't intend to be parted again. And there is the child to consider now.' A smile crept over his face. 'Come and meet her. Come and meet our little Nell!'

Mark followed, but paused at the top of the three wooden steps that led up into the house. It didn't feel like home. He didn't think it ever would now. He wanted – more. He wanted what Theo and Keara had. What his sister Annie had had with Frederick. And he wouldn't find that by hiding away here, in the middle of the bush. As he watched Theo and Keara, saw the loving glances they exchanged, envy speared through him, although he pushed the feeling aside.

Would he ever find a love like that? He hoped so.

When they had all admired Nell, Mark took Nan aside and told her what had happened.

She looked at him, neither weeping nor showing relief, then said quietly, 'It's for the best. He wasn't rational towards the end. But there must have been some remnant of good in him if he died saving Amy and that will always comfort me.'

'Do you want to be alone? You can use my bedroom.'

She shook her head. 'No. I want to be with people. I've been alone too much. Most of all I want to be with my granddaughter. Eh, she's a lovely little lass, Mark. You must be so proud of her.'

He smiled. 'I am. And I can see already that you two get on well, so I hope you'll stay with us.'

That did make her weep, but they were tears of joy and soon over.

The Wallers came in to be introduced to the newcomers and join everyone for the evening meal. They seemed quite at home and not at all in a hurry to continue their journey.

'I envy you, Mr Gibson,' Jane Waller said frankly as she finished her meal. 'We've worked hard but it's been lonely. We're looking to start a new life ourselves, actually, and want to find something easier than farming. Our elder son wants to get married and take over the homestead and I want something different before it's too late for me and my daughters, though Bert's going back to live with Peter.' She looked round and sighed. 'I'd like to live somewhere like this, somewhere you can meet new people, see folk passing every day.'

He stared at her in amazement. 'Do you mean that?'

'Yes, of course.'

Her husband put his arm round her shoulders. 'Jane gets a bit down in the dumps sometimes at home, not seeing another soul from one week to the next. She's a fine woman and if she wants to change our lives, then change we shall.' He chuckled. 'We can well afford it.'

Mark took a deep breath. 'Mr Waller, I'm thinking of selling this place and going back to Victoria. Perhaps you'd like to consider buying it?'

Mrs Waller brightened and turned to her husband. 'Oh, Len, it'd be just right. Close enough that we could visit our Peter sometimes, but not too close that his wife will think we're peering over their shoulders all the time.'

'We'll have a good look round tomorrow,' he said. 'I couldn't think of buying anywhere till I'd seen every corner and thought it over.'

She smiled as if she'd expected him to say that, but began to look round with an almost proprietorial air.

Keara found herself sitting next to Mark as Maggie cleared up after the meal and Theo went out to see to the horses. 'What shall you do afterwards?' she asked him.

'Go back to Victoria, run another eating house or inn – but somewhere more lively.' He looked across at Nan, who was jiggling little Amy on her knee, playing games with her and clearly enjoying herself enormously.

'We can all travel together, then. We're going to look for my sisters as soon as I'm fully recovered.' She saw Maggie standing by the door, watching them all with a sad expression on her face, then her friend slipped outside.

As Keara stood up, Theo came back inside. 'Where are you going? You need to rest till you've recovered.'

She flapped one hand at him. 'Ah, stop trying to coddle me, will you? I'll not be playing the invalid for you or anyone. I feel fine and so does Nell. In fact, it's about time I fed that young woman again.'

'I'll come with you,' Theo said at once, moving towards the makeshift cradle at one side of the room. He loved watching his daughter suckle so vigorously.

'You take her into the bedroom, then,' Keara said. 'I just need to have a word with Maggie.'

She went outside and found her friend standing silently in the kitchen area, fists clenched by her sides, her face in shadow. Keara didn't hesitate, but went and gave her a hug.

Maggie swung round. 'What's that for?'

'To stop you being so miserable. Did you think I'd leave you behind?'

'I don't fit in now.'

'You do, and you always will. Aren't you my cousin?'

'You know I'm not.'

'I know nothing of the sort,' Keara said firmly. 'Unless *you* don't want to be related to me any more?'

Maggie's voice wobbled as she said, 'Do you mean that?'

'Of course I do.'

'Oh, Keara, you've all got someone, and I was w-worried that I had no one.'

'Aren't you the eejit then? Don't you know me better than that?' She chuckled. 'Though you'll have to get used to looking after Nell sometimes.'

Maggie burst into tears and it took a while to comfort her.

'Come on, then,' Keara said at last. 'That's enough weeping. I have a child to feed. And we have a journey to plan.'

She went inside just as Theo opened the door of their bedroom to look for her. At the mere sight of him she forgot everyone else and went straight into his arms.

As the door closed behind them, Nan gave a sentimental sigh. 'Isn't it wonderful to see such love? Mr Mullane's lucky in his wife, very lucky indeed. Come and sit by me, Maggie lass. I've hardly had a chance to talk to you. Tell me about yourself . . .'

And suddenly Maggie felt as if she was part of a loving family, which made tears of joy come into her eyes. She would never, she vowed, let them down in any way.

As the coastal steamer chugged on across the Great Australian Bight on its way to Melbourne, Keara and Theo stood by the rail, his arm round her shoulders.

'We shall find your sisters,' he said softly. 'I promise you, we'll find them. We shan't stop looking until we do.'

She turned sideways to smile at him. He always seemed to sense it when she was feeling sad. 'I wonder where Mara and Ismay are now.'

'Wherever they are, if they're anything like you, they'll be coping. I'm quite certain of that.'

There was a wail from behind them and when no one paid any attention to it, the wail turned into a loud roar of anger.

Keara turned round with a chuckle. 'Is no one paying attention to you, then?'

Four-month-old Nell waved her fists in the air and let out another roar, before blowing a few bubbles to emphasise her need for food.

'Come on,' said Theo, picking up the carrying

cradle he and Mark had made. 'Let's go down to the cabin and deal with Madam.'

Keara turned to laugh at him as she went carefully down the companionway. 'She's got you twisted round her little finger already.'

'You both have. And I mean to keep it that way.'

The story of Keara's sisters is continued in Twopenny Rainbows, *now available from Hodder.*

Anna Jacobs is always delighted to hear from readers and can be contacted:
BY MAIL:

PO Box 628
Mandurah
W. Australia 6210

If you'd like a reply, please enclose a self-addressed envelope, stamped (from inside Australia) or an international reply coupon (from outside Australia).

VIA THE INTERNET

Anna now has her own web domain, with details of her books and excerpts, and invites you to visit it at: http://www.annajacobs.com

Anna can be contacted by email at anna@annajacobs.com

If you'd like to receive the latest news about Anna and her books by email newsletter every month or two, you are cordially invited to join her readers' list. Just email her and ask to be added to it.